ETUDE

A NOVELLA

by

DONOVAN HAMILTON

Order this book online at www.trafford.com
or email orders@trafford.com

Most Trafford titles are also available at major online book retailers.

Printed in the United States of America.

ISBN: 978-1-4907-2488-1 (sc)
ISBN: 978-1-4907-2489-8 (e)

Trafford rev.   02/25/2014

www.trafford.com

North America & international
toll-free: 1 888 232 4444 (USA & Canada)
fax: 812 355 4082

Acknowledgments

Alliance Francaise of Tulsa
Edward Dumit
Robert Scott, Ph. D.
William Shambaugh

"If I wouldn't be in love with my music, what could I do? People who have nothing in their insight, in their souls, are fools. But a man or a woman who has a conviction that something is beautiful, something is profound, it helps him to overcome his dreams."

Wanda Landowska
(1879?—August, 1959)

To Rascal

Chapter One

July 1968

MAYME WAS THE BEST waitress in Sterling and Marvin's Café was proud of that fact. His cafe was not a huge one as other eateries were in town but it had a reputation of having great hamburgers and, of course, good coffee. The old menu said so and everyone who was any kind of a wise judge of food, and hungry, said so. Marvin, now past forty and wearing a dirty apron, noticed someone had parked a nineteen-sixty-six Studebaker directly in front of his large front window. That was all right with him so long as the driver would come inside his establishment and eat. The driver was a woman, a rather nice looking one, with a small kid in the front seat with her. She was a stranger in Sterling. That, too was all right because the town saw a great many of them from time to time.

From the first moment that Marvin saw her he stopped what he was doing merely to determine if she was coming inside or not. She looked in the rear-view mirror, removed the scarf from her head, smooth her hair, said something to her little boy in the seat beside her. Marvin would never forget that sweltering day in July. He stood there wiping his wet hands and watched her open her door, call to her child, and amble through the screen door to his establishment.

Betty Hannah, the only waitress at the time, had noticed Mayme too. She appeared suddenly out of nowhere, knowing no one but with a positive gait, still with a smile on her face, disheveled, with a dark scarf over her blonde hair, wearing a cotton blouse and loose slacks on this hot day with a six-year-old boy in the front seat. She grabbed a kleenex, wiped the sweat from her face, adjusted her blouse, and mentally counted the number of cars parked. Betty finished clearing a table when Mayme entered holding a Now Hiring sign from the front window.

She spotted a middle aged man wearing a stained apron. He was standing between the food shelf to the kitchen and the narrow counter with three customers. She placed the sign next to one of them and inquired politely. "You must be Marvin?" He eyed her as he answered with a soft *yes*.

Called her into a stock room where he proceeded to hear what she had to say. But now, a week later, after she cleaned herself up with a shower, took care to see that her son was asleep in the back seat of her car, she proved that she was a good worker. "I'd had a lot of time slinging hash and making coffee and I needed to get out of Nebraska. It's cold where I came from, and no, I don't know where the boy's father went." She was used to anticipating any question that Marvin would ask. And Betty winked at him to offer her affirmation. He took a chance with her and she was fairly well known all across town in a short amount of time. More than one customer commented on the pretty woman who was his new waitress. Marvin liked her, too, right away. The cooks were happy.

Betty Hanna commented to Marvin from time to time that Mayme knew exactly how to handle the food. She herself embroidered *Mayme* on a new apron and counted the blessings that she had another waitress to help especially in the busy lunch hours. Word got around as it usually does in Sterling, in the back alley during cigarette breaks and among calloused workers while they ate breakfasts.

Mayme came from the middle of Nebraska with hardly any knowledge of where she wanted to go. But she did decide that she should be careful what she would say to almost everyone about her background. She was a lost soul, a product of one of those small towns not as popular as those of the eastern part of her state. She realized that an early infatuation with a man who turned out to be a nobody, that she was pregnant without the blessing of God—as her own mother would tell her—that she would think of something. She became a waitress for a few years until her child was old enough to travel. Those few years became six. She got in her car with her kid and stop somewhere. Anywhere with just enough gas took her to Sterling, Colorado. A lot of people left that part of the state where she was born, and she was one of them. It had a lot to do with the weather, she told herself. She saw a road sign for Marvin's Café so when she decided to stop, that was just as good a place as any. "It gets cold here, too, Mayme," Marvin chided her. Back in Nebraska, she had learned long ago how to determine the traits of many people by the expressions on their faces or in their eyes, especially their eyes, what they said, and by the clothes they wear when they came into the Eatery, the place where she first learned the noble trade. Marvin liked to talk to her when he could. "I bet they came in for coffee just like they do here. Wheat farmers, all of them, mostly," When it was slow, in mid-afternoon, they used to sit down, themselves, and have a bite to eat. "We used to have a movie theater here, over on Main. Not any more, TV, you know. We got three churches and a good school system and a principal who seems to want to improve things. Mr. Carpenter, his name is. He comes in and you'll get to meet him. Tell him about your kid. You say his name is Bobby? Mr. Carpenter is principal at the junior high and has been there for about ten years or so. Your kid can start this fall, being six years old." Marvin was not able to understand just how she needed to leave Nebraska but he was the kind of man who did not ask too many questions. Mayme was young and a lot of those citizens of that fair city began to like her. Standing back to look at her, Marvin decided she should be about twenty-three or four. Mayme had a kind of sparkle about her, that nice smile of hers, that eagerness she manifested to every hungry customer, despite the sad story she had told Marvin and the two cooks in order to get the job. Not everyone deserved to know about her case.

Some seven years ago now she thought she did find a man with whom she could fall in love. That seemed a long time ago. Back in Nebraska, as part of the tale she told. While he was yet one of many to drink coffee and chat, they managed to date heavily. "I'm pregnant," was more of a surprise to him than to her. "Hey Mayme," he finally spilled the beans, "I've got to go, just like I told you. I can't find nothing here in this stinkin' town, you can see that. I've got to go look for a better job for myself." He waited while she swallowed the shock because he had never mentioned this idea to her. "I'm doing this for you, too, of course." She had seen many a doubt in his handsome face but she refused to believe his lies. Mayme at first said, "Sure, go ahead. Just leave me with my baby but you better come back." It sounded bitter, whether she meant all of that or not. He could leave and never come back. And he did. Standing forlornly by the side of the Greyhound Bus, she saw him step aboard, wave carelessly to her from his window seat, and disappear down the road toward Denver. She lost her boyfriend.

This was a must: she still had her career to consider. So now with Marvin, at his café, the music box played every current piece of music on the Hit Parade and truckers soon found a new waitress in an old Greasy Spoon.

One day, Mayme thought, about the time when Bobby began to grow, she did find a man whom she called 'Mr. Colorado.' He made a habit of ordering from her. She liked that idea. He was a local who came in every morning wearing a nice blue serge suit and a bright tie, with immaculate clean hands But one day when she just happened to notice that he took a wedding ring out of his suit pocket and put it on his third finger left hand, she dismissed him right away. She stood transfixed and watched him get into his new Ford. She remembered *Once, burned, twice shy. Maybe* Maybe he did not care for her kid who was by her side at the moment. Mayme took a deep breath and learned to smile at her new customers. Betty Hanna took Mayme's hand in hers and patted her on the back. "I could have told you he was no good," Betty soothed the hurt in her green eyes, "I'm sorry, kid."

One new face came into the café one afternoon. Marvin introduced the old gentleman who ordered coffee and said he was Mr. Wright. Away from the counter, Marvin whispered to her. "Maybe this could be Mr. Right." He did not have sufficient time to warn her that he was the town clown. Betty Hanna tried to intervene but Marvin shook his head with his index finger against his lips. After Mayme brought him a steaming cup, she smiled, and noticed the teasing grin on her boss's face. Shortly thereafter, Mr. Wright, stirring his coffee, called to her. "Oh, Miss," he said, "Come look what this hot coffee did to the spoon." When she slowly returned with a question on her face, he extracted the spoon and half of it was *eaten away*. Mayme looked directly at the wrinkled face which instantly broke out in loud laughter. "I'm glad to meet you, Mayme," the old man said. "It's just an old trick spoon of mine." He pulled it out of his coffee to show her how the bottom half had been cut away.

Herschel Kaplan was yet another regular among the many customers. He came in one cool Saturday morning on his way to the grocery store. He was a wheat farmer whose fields were east of town and he knew everyone. Herschel, still young at thirty-eight despite the calluses on his hands and the rigors of his chosen work, had learned to be conscious of the life he led with Julia, a frumpy little wife and a daughter who preferred to remain in the truck to watch for boys. He and Julia began to call her 'Sis" now that their son was old enough to gather the eggs and learn to milk their three cows.

The sky was cloudy with rain that morning so he stopped to chat with Mayme. She learned about corn and alfalfa and even sorghum from the busy hungry men who worked that business, but Herschel Kaplan was the first farmer who introduced her to wheat and answered her questions. While still busy with everyone, she was pleased to make his acquaintance. "I learned just yesterday," she smiled at Herschel as she leaned against her side of the counter, "that your little Billy is going to start taking piano lessons." She put the full cup in front of him. She could not understand how a five-year-old kid would be smart enough to do something like that. Her own six-year-old never professed any interest much in anything. "You sure he can learn to play the piano? I've got a kid, you know. I think you saw him once when you and your Missus came in about a week ago. What makes you think a five-year-old can learn to play something as complicated as a piano?" She wanted this wheat farmer to think she knew everything about music. She was careful not to declare too much about the art because she was never musical. With Herschel she wanted to be helpful and not to appear insolent. Her music appreciation never went beyond the record player that was prominent just inside the front door. Much of it was western swing with Johnny Cash and a few others who had made a quiet success for themselves. Mayme had no artistic impulse except to hear all the tunes. One Ella Fitzgerald number was her favorite. She always said "thank you" to whoever played it.

Actually, Herschel was caught between a rock and a hard place. This very question, coming from this waitress, was much on his mind and a continuing sore that festered even now with Julia. They were always in contention with each other about music, an art which was very much on Julia's mind these days and agriculture which was the source of income for all the family. This did not set well with Herschel. Before he could answer he removed his work hat and wiped his forehead with a dirty handkerchief. "Oh, Mayme, I don't know." He took a sip. "Julia already decided that is what she wants for our kid." He did not carry the argument any further, if it were going to be one. Ever since Billy was born, Herschel was happy to realize that this son would grow up to help him bale hay and milk. Later, when he would assimilate all the chores that his father would expect from a growing boy, Herschel's dreams would come true. That was the dream Herschel dreamed every time he looked at his son.

Julia was the stronger of the two. Her kitchen was her castle, always full of plenty of left-overs, bread she herself had learned to cook when she was old was her daughter. She had long ago promised both Billy and this nice looking young daughter that they would have pancakes every Saturday morning after milking. Julia maintained her own side of the family as well as possible, as well as her avid love of church and her prayers she would deliver in her kitchen after her husband would go to the barn, and also when she was alone with her cup of coffee and toast after their breakfasts every morning. Sterling, Colorado was predominantly a rural community where many wheat farmers in and around this area were just that, wheat farmers. That was as much a part of this stalwart woman as anything. Her one side issue, as she always announced to Herschel was what the Rotary Club announced often to the State Chamber of Commerce. One of the bank tellers was always trying to entice Herschel into joining the Rotary Club. And Julia was always seconding that motion.

"This is what I get for marrying a girl who wanted to be a musician, herself. We even got an upright piano in the house that's been there for a long time. I don't even remember where she got it. Some music store in Denver, I guess." He reached in his pocket and pulled out his grocery list for the week. He stood from the counter stool and reached in his jeans' front pocket for some money. "What do you do, Mayme," he joked, "eat to live or live to eat?"

Between customers and chatting with Herschel, Mayme did not accept Julia's story about taking Billy to see a piano teacher. She thought she had heard from another customer of this Miss Shriner, that one lady who teaches piano, right here in Sterling. But she had enough troubles herself to try and understand how it all began. No music was in her own meager background. The Shriner Family was just another family in this part of the road that led eastward to Nebraska, where she never looked, and to Denver on the west, which by now was still a mystery. Mayme did not care for large cities. The people were usually rude and the traffic was too heavy, all the time. "Julia heard one day that Miss Shriner was advertising for pupils." This was the last bit of conversation Herschel was reluctant to bear. The waitress had no artistic impulse except to hear all the tunes that the customers played. One Ella Fitzgerald number was her favorite and when a customer dropped a quarter and punched that number, she would comment and say a big 'thank you' to whomever played it. That, Bobby, and Marvin's Café were her own little world.

Herschel Kaplan drove his old Dodge pick up around town more on the weekends than during the week. He would wave to all he knew and sometimes all he didn't know. That was out of habit he had learned from his wife who explained once over coffee in their kitchen, "I always like to say hello to people or at least wave to them because I never know, one might be an angel."

On this trip, Sis was with him. "When's your birthday, Mary Louise?" He was busy loading the bags of food into the bed of his truck and she helped him. "Oh, Daddy, you know!" was all the thirteen-year-old could manage. "It's already past for this year. April twenty-eighth." They hurried to occupy the cab and Herschel started the engine.

"What do you know about this Shriner woman teaching music?" He asked cautiously. "Is she any good?" He really wanted to know and the best person to ask was his daughter. It was a fair question because he was never in a position to inquire secretly from anyone about this ol' maid whom everyone in town knew. Sis felt suddenly out of place. Her father had hardly ever asked her of anything, especially her opinion of an art of which she did not know how to respond. Music to her was at church where the congregation sang all the old hymns again and again and she sat in her regular pew directly behind three brothers who were slightly older thant she. She heard one of them mention current songs by the Rolling Stones, raucous noise that permeated the eardrums of her fellow classmates. She lowered the window and allowed the breeze to run through her brown hair. "I don't know too much about her,

Daddy. She used to teach a lot of kids and she usually started them out at the age Billy is. Frances Wilson took from her. She plays for church and you could ask her. Frances once let Billy sit beside her on the bench at church one Sunday not so long ago. I don't think she still takes lessons but she is in high school now and plays for the glee club when she has time in her schedules. She plays this year. Frances plays pretty well. She quit taking lessons, though." Secretly she reminded herself that Frances was in love with Harry Morris. But she also reminded herself that Harry was in love with basketball.

Herschel did not know what to expect. His mind was on his wheat and he was certain, more than certain that he would have to need a helper in the fields when Billy would be quite a bit older. He was depending on that, to have someone drive the bailer or the tractor, when he needed it. Billy was to be that someone. Billy would start school in the fall. Julia already talked to the superintendent about enrolling the boy earlier than he should. Billy was bright. He was musical. He pounded on the keys of the old upright and that gave his mother the idea that he was going to be a musician.

"Herschel," Julia said one morning at breakfast, continuing the gentle debate, "that's what I've decided to do. He is musically inclined, all right." His wife would mention it from time to time since spring. I've decided to take Billy over to the Shriner house and talk to Patty Allen Shriner herself, yes, that's what I want to do." The whole family lived just down the road and Herschel's wheat fields lay between their house and the Shriners' handsome homestead.

One evening after supper, when Julia and Sis were washing dishes and Billy was in the back yard with his Collie dog, Angus, Julia and Herschel argued about the cost, the trouble they may have in getting him to and from lessons, the clothes the boy would have to have since he's growing up right before our eyes. "What am I going to do for some help, Julia?" Herschel would throw at her. "Not very many men, I don't care how old they are, can suddenly appear out of nowhere to help with what I've got before me!" And then he added as if this bit of information was not applicable to the problem, "Billy will be seven on July thirteenth."

Little William came bouncing through the back door and that halted the discussion. He headed toward the hallway where the piano had stood for a very long time. He sat on the bench and his feet dangled in front of him. He stared at the keyboard and slowly lifted his left hand to remember what his teacher said to him in his first lesson. His right hand rested beside his left, thumbs practically touching each other. He struck a few white keys, a few black ones, and smiled, not at his father who marched silently behind him on his way to the front room, but at the keyboard.

Chapter Two

October 1975

"BILL KAPLAN!?" MR. CARPENTER screeched, "The Bill Kaplan that plays for assemblies? The piano player?" Totally astonished, the principal tried to listen to what the math teacher said, most assuredly. He still could not understand it. This situation raced through Mr. Carpenter's mind. Something like this just does not happen anymore, not in my junior high school. Oh, maybe once every other year or so but not that he could recall. But in other schools, not mine! "My God," Mr. Carpenter muttered, "I can't believe it. To do a thing like that!" Together, the teachers raced down the tile hallway and turned the corner to his small office. Joe Dowd was more concerned about his math class. He had three or four rowdy youngsters who could easily wreak havoc when he himself was out of the classroom. Mr. Carpenter, so proud of his improvement in the last ten years, looked directly at Mr. Dowd. "You say they're in my office?" Mr. Dowd, out of breath, nodded yes. Miss Salyer, one secretary, was standing by the doorway into his office. She still had a pencil in her hand and a look of shock on her inquiring face. "Wait!" Mr. Carpenter cautioned. He stopped to think. "As principal . . ." and he interjected a minor point, "and I do know the Kaplan family . . . oh," and he pursed his lips and tried to surmise before he continued. He turned to the secretary. "Miss Salyer, please stand outside this door and don't let anyone in here." He turned to the math teacher as they passed inside the room. "Joe," he began, but Estelle, the office student help, looked from the principal to the math teacher. "Wait a minute," and then to the student, he confided, "Estelle, dear, step out into the hall for now, if you will, please. Despite her presence, Mr. Carpenter whispered to Joe Dowd, "Who was the other boy?"

Slightly embarrassed, Joe Dowd looked toward Miss Salyer and confided. "Harold told me it was Bobby Martin. It was Bobby, Mr. Carpenter, not Harold. Harold was the one who found them. Harold had a pass and went into the boys' restroom and when he pushed the hall door to enter he found both the boys standing together. Billy standing there with Bobby . . ." and he stopped to catch his breath, "and Bobby was . . . getting ready to . . . to urinate into the . . . the stool with his pants down and . . ." Joe Dowd could not continue.

"My math room is right next to the Boys' Rest Room. Harold Morgan burst into my room when I was in the middle of a problem. I looked up to see Harold and the kid suddenly signaled for me to come with him. It all happened so fast. He told the math teacher what he saw. Their classmates knew that Harold Morgan was not a bright kid. But he was honest. "He said he reversed, fled past Billy, slammed the hall door, and fled to my classroom just twenty feet down the hall. I was on my chalk board and I was surprised to see Harold anyway." Joe Dowd paused with chalk in hand and the class looked at the intruder. Having encountered a similar interruption at least three or four times by Harold, Joe Dowd continued writing his equation and asked without looking directly at the student. "What do you want, Harold?"

All he could do was motion to the teacher to come in the hall. "Mr. Dowd," the child began, breathlessly, "I saw two guys in the boys' room, Mr. Dowd, and one was . . ." and he hesitated. He pantomimed an obvious gesture of sexual movement. "That's what Harold told me, Mr, Carpenter, I swear it was." Joe Dowd, being a well organized teacher that he was bit his lower lip and pulled is tie down away from his shirt collar. "Then I proceeded to take matters on my own."

Mr. Carpenter tried to remain calm. "I'll want to talk to Harold too, but not first." Mr. Dowd interrupted. "Both of the boys are waiting in there, in your office. I made them sit down and wait. Harold is with the nurse and she said he did not want to talk about it." Mr. Carpenter could see how nervous his math teacher was with Estelle, present. "Mr. Carpenter, I have my Algebra class beginning now. May I go?"

He did not answer him. To the student helper, he murmured, "Estelle, dear, please . . ." and he paused to think of what to tell her, "please leave us, if you will. Go . . . to the study hall and tell whoever is the monitor at this hour that I have excused you from your duty in my office. Please." And to Miss Salyer, "I will need you for one witness since Mr. Dowd has to return to his class." To him, he spoke softly, "Joe, listen . . . just . . . don't say a thing. It's probably all over school by this afternoon." Mr Carpenter appeared calm but deep inside his heart was beating wildly.

The principal tried to remain quiet, at least to project an image in control when Joe Dowd left. He glanced quickly to his secretary with a frown on his anguished face. "Miss Salyer, call the counselor in here. I'll need a second witness. All you have to do is stand in the corner and listen to all that happens. Bring your pad and pencil. Now I'm going in." Rubbing his mouth and chin in a gesture of confusion, he closed his eyes and took a deep breath. His experience in this sort of thing was minimal, very minimal. He wished he still had his reference notes from his adolescence psychology studies during the time when he was successful in earning his position as principal. That was ten years ago. Boys will be boys.

He was not surprised by what he heard from Joe Dowd. He grew up, himself, with three brothers and two sisters in Pueblo, enough to startle anyone who was ever curious enough to learn what was transpiring in the maturing bodies of anxious kids. He must try to recover the notes. Incidents of this kind are few and far between yet are worthy of additional study. He tried to tell himself that this was necessary.

Mr. Carpenter tried to breathe calmly. He opened the door with his name on it and entered. Miss Salyer meekly followed him, nervously holding her pencil and note pad. Bill Kaplan, who was seated in a chair facing his desk, politely stood. The boy's face was in turmoil. Bill had grown in the last eight years into a fine boy who helped his father whenever his dad called him to milk cows at eventide when he so wanted to run his scales according to the latest lesson with Miss Shriner. Somehow, just in those past four years, he had also found time to get acquainted with Bobby Martin who successfully engineered their own private rendezvous. Now Bill was embarrassed. He knew he was not *doing anything*.

Bobby Martin, with his head bowed, stood in the opposite corner from where Miss Salyer positioned herself. She noticed how insolent he appeared, with his hands in his pockets. Turning his back to her, he looked out the window when he saw who entered and zipped up his pants. Miss Salyer already had maintained her own opinion of this strange and aloof ninth-grader. Bobby hardly ever talked to anyone between classes, in the halls or on the campus grounds. Mr Carpenter cleared his throat, looked at both boys, turned on the lamp on his cluttered desk top and sat in his own chair. He motioned for Bobby to close the window.

A hundred or so remembrances raced through the principal's mind that afternoon. This was not the first time he had encountered sexual behavior in the boys' room at his school. Every teacher was warned to expect such clandestine action, and to expect it at the age when boys were brave enough to investigate and take their own steps to learn. It was absolutely so natural for anything like this to occur. This sort of lesson, if he should label this as lessons, happened usually once every school year if not at school, then most assuredly in other areas where curiosity could be satisfied. Yes. That is how he would look at this again since it was not a new occurrence for any of the three of them. "Sit down, boys," he tried to remember his calm image. "I . . . I've been told that you two were discovered in the boys' room . . . sexual abuse." Bobby Martin snickered softly as he slouched in the nearest chair. Bill Kaplan squirmed and sat quickly. "I don't need to tell you that such an act is pretty common for kids your age." He glanced quickly at his secretary who put her pencil in her dress pocket. "But to commit this sort of thing on campus . . . and to do it . . . together . . ." Bill Kaplan stole an instant glance at Bobby. Mr. Carpenter was flustered. He cleared his throat and moved more comfortably in his leather chair. He silently remembered another such incident, but in high school, ten years ago. He was the history teacher there and was shocked, as all the faculty was, to learn that within two weeks, one of those boys committed suicide.

He could not imagine Bill Kaplan to be that desperate, nor the Martin boy, too, for that matter. The principal had learned long ago that this young boy seated opposite him was destined to have a very good future with his music. The Carpenter family knew the Shriners. Mary Louise Kaplan was a student in his American History class. That, also, was in the back of his mind when he looked at him. Mr.

Smith, the boys' glee club director had used Bill as accompanist for the previous school year, and so far, for this one. Bill interrupted," It wasn't together all the time!" Bill was obviously nervous. "Well," the principal shot a disapproving look at both of them, "the report is that you were together, doing what, I don't know." Mr. Carpenter rubbed his face with both his hands.

Bobby Martin spoke hurriedly in an arrogant tone. "Harold Morgan is a little liar if you got it from him. Harold Morgan is a damn tattletail anyway". Miss Salyer uttered a guttural cry. "Who'd believe that little piece of scum? Harold is a nobody."

"All right, Bobby, that's enough." Mr. Carpenter stood and moved his chair. "I don't much believe any of it, in the first place," he said and then sat down again opposite Bill Kaplan. He waited before he said anything, looking directly into the painful face. Bill returned his gaze and then looked at the ceiling. "Bill." He glanced at Miss Salyer. "Billy, I'll want to talk to Bobby first, individually, so if you please step into the outer office and wait, I'll talk to you afterward. Please, Bill. Miss Salyer, go with him and see that he's all right."

Within twenty minutes, Mr. Carpenter opened his door and motioned for Bobby Martin to leave. "Miss Salyer, write him a pass to his next class, please." The counselor finally arrived and apologized. "That's all right, I don't need you now. Come in, Billy." And he closed the door. "No need to sit again, Billy, I really don't know what to say to you now, other than just . . ." but he could not continue. Specifically, the principal could not choose words to satisfy this moment that both of them shared. The adult thought it too embarrassing to try. He thought, but no words adequately came to mind. Bill was far more comfortable now. When Carpenter did not say a word, Bill looked at him, more in reference to curiosity of this man rather than any word of reprimand. Undoubtedly, both of the boys were satisfying a logical type of curiosity. But the principal did elect to phrase it in that way. Of course it was out of curiosity, to allow Bobby Martin to perform while just inside the booth. To the recipient, it was natural for a kid his age to desire an answer for the question of what was happening to him. It could resemble a piece of music, for him to desire to know what the notes would give him, what the composer wrote, what he wanted to imagine from the staff before him.

Mr. Carpenter was a kind man. With no other advice, of any kind, he simply smiled at Bill. "Do you understand? I won't take any more of your time." He cleared his throat and stood opposite him by the windows. "I'm in a tight situation here, for I'll have to report this as an . . . incident at school. I'll try and keep names out of the paper work. I have to say that I would not have expected this from a fine kid like you, from a talented pianist. I'm referring to the incident, not the curiosity. And everyone here at school and at church will agree with me. Do you still play at church?" Bill Kaplan nodded. "Well that's fine. Mr. Smith, the glee club director, will never hear of this. If he does, I'll speak to him. He'll still want you for a pianist for the chorus, I'll see to that. I understand the glee clubs are planning on a nice spring concert next April." He waited while he took another deep breath. "I suggest that you stay clear of Bobby. He's just not good for you, in more ways than one. He comes from a broken home, I just learned that, just now." Such examples of this are becoming more prevalent, it seems, examples that no one can ignore. "His father left him and his mother and one other child about nine or ten years ago and I think she worked as a waitress somewhere, in one of Sterling's cafes. Please give my regards to your parents, will you, and just remember, this incident does not go beyond this school, you hear? It'll disappear anyway. Don't worry about it. You'll be just fine. A great piano player that you are, I can expect great things from you. Believe me."

Chapter Three

1978 and After

BILLY KAPLAN WANTED TO change his name. After all, he would turn twenty years of age on his next birthday. Why change? He did not exactly know why. It was, more than likely, one of those ideas that grew out of the empty space between his school locker and the door to the glee club room. But by now, high school was indeed a thing of the past. Two years ago, as a matter of fact. The memory of his class hopping on a bus and high-tailing it to Denver for a nice dinner and a choice of entertainment was one to remember, all right. Such memories, for him, began to disappear. At one time he even wanted to forget how to milk a cow. But for them, He chose a concert somewhere in an old nineteenth-century building with some orchestra from the east coast. He thought he would have to go alone. It was only when two other students decided to accompany him on this venture that he was pleased to find that his life-long companion, the awesome Miss Vivian Anderson, was one of those two others. In Junior High School she was a pest. In those more grown-up days of yesteryear, when she became a stalwart friend did he discover that something most profound was this young lady's *savoir faire*.

For the next six years at a time when he continued to wonder at his misgivings and to forget all the little inconsistencies that happened along the way, when he had met Vivian Anderson, a charming blonde, blue eyes and charming breasts, when he lived with his piano in the home out in the country, Sterling Colorado became the home away from home. Vivian lived in Sterling, too. He was able to perceive the many times when his father refused to accept the young son and his ability to charm everyone with intricate passages from Chopin,

Schumann, and Liszt. Especially Liszt. Now, quite the young man with a dynamic character that everyone in eastern Colorado adored, he had nothing to worry about, but everything to make him the man-about-town. Dressed in his tux when he played for a variety of venues, when he offered spectacular programs often on a moment's notice, he was essayed by many who were always astounded by this pianist's amazing talent. Once, upon an invitation from the choir director at the church, he provided a concert on their new organ, a gift from a wealthy couple in Sterling. He was glad to do so, even though the handsome gift was somewhat foreign to him. After a twenty minute lesson from the director, *The Stars and Stripes Forever* sounded swell, according to a neighbor kid.

And then one day, eons ago, he sat on the top step of the front porch with Angus, his collie, and looked out at the July sky and counted clouds and waited for rain. He took a deep breath and questioned the whys and wherefores of his unusual existence. It was not a case of his never questioning the mysteries of the universe. The pastor at church tried to solve those with him. Such a question of that kind was the beginning of his history class at Sterling High School. History was his history, yet, for him, it overshadowed dates, incidents, personalities, and obvious happenings that the teacher taught, things that made up his ordinary life. But his life was not ordinary, by any means. In their places, his whole world took on a new reality. His personal explanation of it all was just that: his own relevant satisfaction which kept his heart beating, his motivation for existence, and the reason for living in the first place. Music became the strength for which he was seeking. And when he and his dog were together, out of the house, on the front porch, often he would grasp Angus' face in both his hands, would look into eyes that reflected nothing but love. "I'm glad God brought you into my life—if that is what He did," is what he would whisper to the Collie. Angus, slobbering in the July heat, continued wagging his tail.

He met a lot of fascinating people along this journey, people, like Bobby Martin, who shocked this boy from the farm, others, who made Bill laugh when he forgot how to laugh, especially when he hit a wrong note. "Life is a comedy," his speech teacher said, for she had this delightful statement printed on a nice colorful poster on her classroom wall. Sometime between graduation and his first year at Denver's private university, his life took on a new direction. He decided to think about the direction he was going. This *new* direction that seemed to infiltrate his thinking had a lot to do with growing up.

Then, one day he became aware of one hilarious female. It was not exactly an awareness for she had been around for as long as both of them lived in this small town. Oh yes, Vivian Anderson, a name that had been with him all the previous years. Her hair had always been a natural blonde and her figure had grown into a gorgeous "Mae West" shape, even though both of them did not know Mae West. He was certain she was a part of his own history. She did not, actually, merely appear out of nowhere. He kept thinking that he had seen her, surely, as far back as the fifth grade. Yes, of course, that was it! Together, they questioned the mystery of the Universe, the pros and cons of algebra, arguments on politics, and how to make Mexican tortillas. She was a lot of fun, a bit odd at times, but the very essence of laughter when she wanted to laugh, the very essence of tragedy when they read *Romeo and* Juliet in Miss Gregory's English class. Why had he not met her in Junior High School? Where had she been? She was probably a bean pole wearing ugly dresses that did not compliment her in the least.

Of all the people who came and went with him in the months that became years, she was the one to remain strongest in his adventures. "I was born in Sterling, too, or hadn't I told you?" was her question. "I saw you almost every day but you were glued to your piano bench in the glee club room and didn't have a word to say to me. I stood on the outside in the hall because I can't carry a tune, as you musicians say. Anyway. We're twenty now and here you are at Denver U. and there I am way up in Boulder. We'll never see each other again. That sounds so dramatic. Life's like that. Two ships that pass in the night, if you've never heard of that phrase." Vivian was energetic, a joyful sprite when she wanted to be and a sardonic complainant when things did not go well. "My God, Billy, I don't know how we do it. I've heard you play a thousand times and you're getting better. You're getting so you can play almost anything you set your mind to. Don't you think of anything else except that damn piano?" Of course, by now, William was used to this wonderful crazy nincompoop. He would retort with "Don't you do anything else except read? I bet you've read every book in the Sterling High School Library or the library down town. I bet you can tell me what the price of eggs in China is."

One day in early July of that same year, they were together in Marvin's Café on a cloudy noon, drinking cokes and eating hamburgers. William surprised her by commenting on her new car. "I see you got a new nineteen-eighty-eight Ford whatever-it's-called. Your daddy gave it to you?" She was pleased that he finally mentioned it. Maybe he'll grow out of his piano thing and become a tycoon in the automobile industry and buy her a Mercedes Benz. "Yes, he finally gave me a car. It's because I'm a Chi Omega now. My mother is a Chi Omega. The next time you're in Boulder, if you ever are, I'll invite you upstairs."

He teased her with a sly grin. "Let's go on a date. Remember my birthday is the thirteenth."

"Write that down on this napkin for me, will you?" She feigned disappointment. "Oh, darling, I'm going to Boulder. I'm seeing a football player." She was in the mood to perform her "sophisticated lady" scene. She could be one at the drop of a hat.

"You don't love me anymore!" He too knew how to show disappointment. Her report was swift in her back-to-normal voice. "It's more than that. He asked me to marry him! Imagine, sweet girl from Sterling, dating a hero on the football team. I don't know a thing about the theory of football. Well, it's his first year on the team. His name is Kevin something, I think. You'll have to meet him if you're ever up Boulder way." She giggled. "That is, if you ever get off your piano stool!" Suddenly, Vivian's mother appeared, coming through the front entrance to the café. She was with two other women, all dressed in summer frocks and big smiles. "Vivian, darling," she purred as she saw her daughter, "I bet this is Bill Kaplan." He rose as she extended her hand. "I saw you play at church when you presented your concert. That was nice, Billy." William cleared his throat in objection to being called what many home town people called him, now. She smiled and followed her two friends to their own table.

On their way out, Marvin said thanks. And so it went, a quick and easy summer, but William had plans for himself in Denver and Vivian, girl-about-town, went to be with her sweetheart. It was just that way. Sterling, Colorado was that kind of town, often a lackadaisical carefree and rural wheat center with hardly any care at all, no movie house anymore, and two fast-food palaces which did not worry Marvin in the least. The Rotary Club met every Wednesday noon at Holiday Inn because Marvin's Café just was not big enough to seat twelve farmers. They somehow managed to leave their wheat fields and come in and sit around and drink coffee and listen to a speaker or two each month in a special room added on by Marvin, complete with an upright. One time, Rotary entertained William Kaplan who entertained them with an amazing rendition of a Schumann sonata. "Do you ever play with the Denver orchestra?" one matron asked and not necessarily out of curiosity. He decided that she just wanted to gaze into his deep brown eyes. But he did answer her. "No, and it's called the Colorado Symphony Orchestra."

Miss Patty Allen Shriner did manage to see and talk to her ex-student of piano. It was on his birthday that year, and she had jotted that date and made a large half note design on her kitchen calendar. On this year, William Kaplan completed twenty-three years and eighteen of them were with her, he, on a piano stool and she sitting on her tall kitchen stool next to him so she could follow him and his progression. "Very good, William," she would comment from time to time but with a sincerity that actually was part of her demeanor. "I'm glad to hear of your work with M. DuPres at the university. He's young but he is French and he knows what he is doing." When she first mentioned that, William turned his head and peered directly at her as if not to believe that she would make a point to meet this Frenchman when he first enrolled in his lessons. "Oh, yes, William, I do know him. And by the way, I am very happy you got to meet Mrs. Amelia Tomassi. She's quite a character, you know. She and I have known each other a long time, before her husband died. Do you know what she said to me?" Here, again, William was used to her humor, for he smiled when she patted him on the shoulder. "Since this is close to your senior year, she asked me for my opinion. Would you care to move into her condominium?" She waited for an answer before she explained.

Mrs. Tomassi was a wealthy lady who lost her husband but not his cash. He was in the lumber business and she had become a notable and lovely patron of the arts. She and Miss Shriner had become close friends. A woman now of about sixty-three years, Mrs. Tomassi made it known to her friend that this young musician, this William Kaplan, could have his own suite of rooms and could play on her baby grand. Her condominium on the twelfth floor was the only one occupied, so he could play all he wanted and no one would object. When she approached this idea with the music teacher, Mrs. Tomassi began to realize that this plan appeared to be strongly resembling Mrs. Robinson from a movie some years ago. "Most assuredly, it is not what it seems, Patty. Please, if you will, make certain that he should have no fear—if that is the word I should use here—at all in this situation. But I do—and I will tell him myself—yes, I do believe that Bill Kaplan is on the road to success in becoming a vibrant concert pianist. You'd be surprised by the amount of compliments I hear often, from Dr. Graham and Maestro Young about this young protégé. Two years or so before Gilberto died, I mentioned Bill to him. I'm sure you can approach this young man with this invitation with a better foundation than I can do. Please."

William Kaplan looked at his teacher in awe. At church, William remembered meeting this lady. For such an extraordinary invitation to come from out of nowhere, he remembered also the term, 'divine appointment.' "I . . . I hardly know her. She is a nice lady, that, I know. This is sort of an unusual offer. I do have my senior year, and with M. DuPres. Why don't you go with me while I give her my thanks for this . . . opportunity, this gift." He was genuinely grateful; he exhausted his words. But in his few meaningful adventures with gracious ladies at tea or at church or even at one or two cocktail parties where he sipped clear ginger ale, he was learning how to congregate. All this was nice for a young piano player.

"It is a gift, all right," Patty Allen Shriner conceded. "We'll plan to do that. In another month you go back to the university, and I'll call her and explain and we'll go together and see her." It was a most unusual gift in that the city was so large, now, that locating a living quarter for himself could have become a large challenge. She rose from her kitchen stool as he stepped over to the cabinet where he returned a sheet of the complete Liszt prelude. He wanted to ask her opinion. Her smile was genuine. "I may have some other ideas for you for your future. You deserve the best. By the way, give my regards to Vivian. She asked me about you recently at the grocery store." She paused before she added, "She thinks you're fabulous."

Chapter Four

1983 and later

GERALD CHAMPION WAS A wild kid who lived in Monticello, New York and had never heard of William Kaplan. But he did know a bit, here and there of classical music, including the piano. By the time he calmed down he managed to survive high school fairly well. Monticello was not especially alive with high school sports, somewhat aware of football, according to the local coach . . . Gerald did not care for football. He wanted to play basketball but he elected to accept the tennis team. He told himself that he was especially good at it.

By the time he was nineteen years old, his father and mother both noted an improvement in his behavior and personality. His eyes and hair attracted almost everyone when the wind blew the long brown tresses across his handsome face. So he frequented the tennis courts of a fashionable resort hotel in Monticello mainly because the fashionable crowd sat around at the restaurant tables under the wide eaves and drank Coca Colas doused with a bit of rum when no one was looking. But often he kept himself aloof from that crowd by reading as many books as he could, one right after another. He was a *reader*, but he still cared for his own physical strength. He played Bridge well but tennis became his favorite pastime. He supposed. Monticello was not especially a large city but it did have two large resort hotels, this one, always full of the twenties to thirties generation. The other one nestled south of the Catskill Mountains. That one attracted the older crowds, those whose standards were foreign to Gerald. *That* crowd was en route from New York City who enjoyed the mountains as much as he and his own family did. Many of them were descended from Italy as was his mother. She always reminded him and his brother that they both had "terrific grandparents."

His father was altogether pleased about how Jerry was absorbed with a growing interest in the oil industry and chemistry. "Things like that were my cup of tea," he would announce often. The older of his two sons, Jerry had deep blue eyes, a notable trait and the first thing which everyone noticed. An uncle joked about how this nephew suddenly realized that there are more undertakings to his life than eating and sleeping. He was one year out of high school and very much the thinker of the clan.

He came from a healthy family, a father who enjoyed classical music, a brother, Geoffrey, who was more of a pest than a sibling one who professed already knew a horde of people from upper Manhattan, and a dear mother who had been born a fabulous Italian lady who loved to cook. Monticello was the only town Jerry knew. Maybe he was certain of others in that immediate part of the state. His high school senior class decided long ago to save money for the jaunt they all took in March. It was the first time for many of them. They caroused, they told dirty jokes in their hotel room, they bought a bottle of wine without the chaperon's knowledge, and when it came to attending a musical, Jerry and two others walked out because they did not care for the music or plot.

One day just after graduation, his curious father, one to ask questions because this was the time to do so, began to wonder just what in the world his two boys were going to do with themselves. After all, their father was of an older generation even if his two sons were not aware of that fact. He came from the "old school" of thinking, a scholastic habit of planning, of mapping out a future. This father merely presumed that such a feat remained unknown to his sons. So the only thing to do, at this point for them and for himself, was to bring them together to discuss the preeminent question which he had put to his sons. They were good sons, inquisitive, intelligent, bright, and all the other "boy scout" traits, even though they were never boy scouts. So the moment arrived when it was necessary to bring them to the front porch of their modest two-story dwelling. After all, their father's father did the same for *his* sons back when *he* was nineteen years old only *their* front porch was in a house that no longer existed.

Even so, it was not the first time their father brought them to this porch. He sat them down on the top step, one of three, that led to a sidewalk and to the wide residential street which made its way through the old neighborhood. While Geoffrey leaned against a pillar that separated the railing from the open space, Jerry sat facing forward with his elbows on his knees. This was a time, a most unusual time in all three of their lives, when decisions had to be made. It was best that way. The mother remained in the kitchen and cooked their favorite lasagna. Their father took his usual place in the porch swing and gently rocked to and fro while planning his strategy.

Geoffrey spoke first. He wanted to invade New York City, or possibly Boston, with all kinds of exciting plans for himself. He did not particularly include college for the time. He wanted to investigate the bohemian life and byways of Christopher Street, based on the delicious and exciting rumors. He had heard, from other sources, that this is what he really, actually, most assuredly desired. Mr. Champion, slightly exasperated, did not comment for he elected to give it some more consideration. Geoffrey was only a junior this fall in high school. His father asked him to remain while they heard from Gerald.

Jerry Champion was altogether a separate entity than his brother. He was a tall man with a wistful way about him, one that attracted the eyes of many a girl and the appreciation of many a male friend. At an earlier age he started asking his mother if she could tell him what went into the pie he liked and how to make it, himself. His grandparents on his mother's side were pure Italian and of course the cooking was always a part of his growing up. When Geoffrey asked to be dismissed, their father was able to concentrate on Jerry. He moved from the porch swing and sat down beside him. "What's on your mind, son?"

One to be specific about many topics, Jerry looked at his dad and then down at his own hands. "I want to go to M.I.T." This astounded his father because Jerry had not previously mentioned this interest to the family. "Yes, I know," he noticed the frown on his father's face, "but I wrote a letter to the administration for some information and that is what I really want." His father breathed heavily, raised his eyebrows to show that he essayed this plan, and concluded that if this is what he desires, then so be it. His mother was pleased, his father was pleased, his brother was surprised and had only one comment, "If you live in Cambridge, let me know what you think of everything." Then he grabbed his skateboard and fled.

That was just the way it was. He moved to Boston, he enrolled, he studied, he succeeded, he read, he was pleased, he was elated. His B.Sc. In geology was just the thing for him. With this behind him, he remained on campus and plunged into his M.Sc. By May of 1993, at a time when his father had died suddenly, he sat down on the front steps of the porch and held his mother's hand for a while and cried with her. "Mother," he began, "if you don't mind, I found a doctorate program at the University of California at Berkeley. Aunt Ursula lives in San Francisco and I'm applying, if it's all right with you." She gave him a strong bear hug and smiled. "I asked her when she was here for Dad's funeral and she said that U.C. is a good school." After blood, sweat, and tears, after hours, days, and weeks in the M.I.T. library, after a time when he first encountered this idea, the librarian at the library, that dear Miss Hooper, the oldest librarian on the East Coast, was surprised and tried to change his mind. Complete with her 'granny glasses' perched on her nose, and a smile a mile wide, she took his hands and stated bluntly, after she learned of his imminent departure, "Oh, Jerry, you'll come back. The West Coast just may not suit you at all. You're an East Coast man, my boy!" Maybe he would meet another librarian who would sweep him off his feet.

Once there, established in his rugged ritual from which he hardly ever escaped, after many discussions with a variety of faculty, he discovered at the last minute of a possibility of a job along with his application for Ph. D. To do all this so suddenly reflected his spontaneity of almost everything he did, unplanned as it appeared to be. But that was the way Jerry Champion committed himself to a variety of choices. His was spur-of-the-moment personality. He was just that way. But he matriculated. He even fooled his mother, his Aunt Ella, even Geoffrey. He even studied diligently and told himself that he was very pleased by it all. After all, he was five years older. Nothing would ever intervene and alter his course.

It was more or less a quiet beginning for him, in the lab as a teacher for all the freshmen scientists. So he became Mister U.C.Berkeley in the summer of 1993. He thought perhaps he should slow down. He never did, even when he became enthused about his new career and his new advisor who directed his research. His committee of five faculty members was the catharsis to warn him. "You are a fine student, my boy," the head of his committee told him. "But we five must tell you that you seem too rambunctious. In a word, slow down. Keep in mind that we've given you your assignments through the second semester and that is the one coming up this fall. You have a lot to do and we want to be ready to work with you on your commitment. It's very evident that you do have a total commitment. Your GPA must be at least 3.3. We're certain you understand."

He understood. He slowed down. He was happy in his studies. He kept telling himself this.

By the summer of 1994, he had passed a qualifying exam of two parts, written and oral. The committee was pleased. He was pleased also. He had even had time on a few weekends to visit his aunt in her house on Green Street. He was now a forthright outright West Coast student. And a promising and vibrant candidate for a Ph. D.

One evening, a year later, one of the loveliest of ladies, purported to be an O.R. nurse, actually, invited Jerry to a concert. "I'm just amazed at your progress, Jerry," she announced for the first time. They had a few *coke dates* on campus. To find a lovely lady as she was actually a fine moment that both of them soon realized. He was somewhat pleased even though he was not totally acquainted with her. She was on of those students whom he had seen often in the union cafeteria with another girl. The invitation to this concert was a total surprise, for it was to be a classical pianist. He was especially alert to that kind of music. Often, when he could, his father invited botth brothers to listen on the radio on Sunday afternoons. So he went along with her. And he did remember his father enjoyed that kind, with his old seventy-eight recordings of a few symphonies. He remembered seeing a poster on a wall in the union. With no other plan in mind he locked the door to the lab, took a quick shower, and met her not far from the performance hall. "You'll like the music, I'm sure you will," she confirmed as they walked across campus. Then she invaded a trait Jerry did not know she learned. "You spend a lot of time by yourself . . . yes, I know you have to do that, but tonight, well, get ready for something else besides the chemistry lab. A nice man like yourself. Time to broaden your horizons." She had previously explained to him that she possessed a *mother* instinct. They spied another poster. "An evening of Mozart and Bach. And if you don't know those guys, I'll tell you before the music starts." He felt that she was far too young to relate to motherhood.

Then, very quickly, a friend of hers interrupted them. "Gwen," he announced, "you're wanted in surgery. Sorry. It's lucky I found you." And she excused herself and gave Jerry his ticket. "Sorry, Jerry," and she fled. "I got to go!" It was oh so quick.

Jerry had actually no specific knowledge of these two composers, but he did want to walk in the part of the campus he did not know. The young pianist for this concert was William Kaplan, so yet another poster announced, booked on a concert tour that took him to St. Louis, Tulsa, Albuquerque, and now, U.C. Berkeley, to perform in as many colleges and universities that would have him. In small letters at the bottom of that poster—and Jerry noticed another one in the Science Building—was a promising reference that RCA was to become his "official" Recording Company. Also, in a small paragraph noting Mr. Kaplan's home was a slight notation that he was a native Coloradoan. Jerry was glad he had a ticket. It would help pass the evening until tomorrow's classes . . . His seat was center row three. A good location, he thought, to see his hands. He had once heard from the librarian that above all, one must observe the pianist's hands if one is to grasp the beauty of the music. Okay. He'll go along with that. He accepted a one-page program from an usher and excused himself as he found his seat. Shortly the house lights dimmed. Just as the pianist appeared from stage right, a round of applause welcomed the young Mr. Kaplan who bowed gracefully and sat at the keyboard.

As if suddenly hypnotized, Jerry was uniquely thrilled at something intangible he felt within himself. It was, evidently, the first occasion for him to realize this new moment for him. He had heard this Mozart played over the radio in his room, music that filled his study area without being offensive or disturbing his concentration on the papers he wrote for his classes on a good typewriter that his brother ignored. Even Bach was not new to him. Jerry even had learned a lot from the Bach family, through his father's instruction. The audience was more than receptive, eagerly applauding and gracious. He felt himself in some kind of new mode. Geology, for the while, was hidden somewhere. What was it? He searched for this answer to the question of his being captivated.

He decided, then and there, without hesitation, that it was not the music, although he did realize his new appreciation of this art, but that it was the pianist himself who gave the selections this new existence. Jerry could not totally define it. The pianist, whoever he was, apparently was the crucible. Or perhaps it was the lessons his father related to him about the music which were obviously stowed away in the back of his mind. They were now coming full front.

William did play very well. At one quick split second, Jerry thought, William looked directly at him when he acknowledged the joy of his audience as he took his bow. He did, Jerry said to himself, he looked right at me. William then proceeded to offer an encore. The number was by DeBussy, *Clare de Lune*, and while Jerry was not familiar with the French composer nor the number, he sat enchanted. Amid gracious applause, William bowed, and left the stage. The house lights awakened Jerry from the new sensations he had discovered. Not very many new geologists could be treated so well. Jerry remained in the trance all the way to the front steps where he casually saw the patrons exiting. He would not forget this evening. He glanced again at the program, Tuesday night, April 30, 1995. He laughed at himself: his M.Sc. a year ago, his decision to apply to U.C. Berkeley for a doctorate, his job possibility and now, the charm, the vivid feeling he hardly could decipher which he experienced in that auditorium. Something happened to him.

When he turned, he heard laughter from the side of the building and saw a small crowd surrounding the pianist himself at the rear stage door. For no reason whatsoever, he waited. He did not know exactly why to wait. Jerry noticed this pianist who was busy shaking hands. One lady was some kind of hostess who had a nice smile. Jerry heard her over the noise. "Good bye" she muttered, "and thank you on behalf of the committee that brought you to us." Then she departed.

Jerry saw her go quickly but he also noticed that the pianist turned to the stage manager who patted him on the back. He looked at his watch. The fans dispersed. With no one else to offer kudos or rush to want an autograph, Jerry walked slowly toward him. What he had in mind, he did not quite know, but he felt the urge to say hello and to see, up close, just what he would say to him. With no one else there, the artist turned to him. Without knowing what exactly should be protocol,

Jerry stated, "I heard you play tonight," merely a weak greeting. He stopped and William grinned. "I thought . . ." William looked directly at him and waited. "I thought you did really a nice job." He stammered, a bit nervous.

William was used to this sort of greeting. He had, in his lifetime, discerned many an embarrassing moment when a fan had no immediate word. "Do you play the piano?"

Jerry was surprised. "No," he answered before he thought of a better reply. "I'm a geologist," and then he quickly added, "I'm . . . a candidate for my doctorate." William blinked his eyes and stuffed two programs into his suit coat pocket. "Rocks and stones, I guess. But . . ." Before Jerry could proceed, he laughed, "I'm William Kaplan," he offered offered his hand, "and I'm glad to see my program in your other hand. I hope you like what you heard." He too was at a loss for words, likely for the first time. Bill was used to a flock of girls but never a geologist.

Jerry shook his hand after slipping the program in his coat pocket. "Well, yes, I did." They stared at each other. "Yes, I . . . enjoyed it. I had a father who liked your kind of music. I heard some of it, growing up." Jerry surmised that this dialogue was not what he wanted to say, after all. William began walking toward the street where few people were still waiting for vehicles. Jerry followed. "Are you from California?"

William laughed softly. "No. From a little town you never heard of, Sterling. I guess you are from California?" Their eyes met and both of them smiled. "No, from Monticello, New York. You probably never heard of it, either. I've been here, for about a year, now. I'm working on a doctorate in science if I can afford one." For a short moment, they did not speak. William found himself pausing in the conversation as well. He glanced at a few pedestrians. Then, on the spur of this moment, he suddenly announced. "I have an idea." He hoped this would not sound too presumptive. "Let me invite you to get some supper with me." Without waiting for an affirmation, William continued, "I ate a steak about three o'clock before I played and then I grab a sandwich or a glass of red wine afterward." Jerry was too surprised to say anything. "There's a nice little all night place just a block from here. I don't like to eat by myself."

Chapter Five

THE PIANIST DID NOT give too much concern to the unusual encounter. But he did, in short and precise seconds, glance at the man's features. The blue eyes were staring back at him and his nose was narrow, but that was all he could manage while in route. Once when their eyes met, he found a smile on his lips. All too often while on tour, especially this one, he met several young girls—all college students—who were overly curious and asked him if they could write to him. His own agent warned him from time to time to anticipate such requests, so the word was stowed in the back of his mind. This particular occasion was, however, the first for a young man, likely his own age, who quickly gave his name. William and he had small talk on their short walk down the side street to the cafe. This was a legitimate student, nice looking, with short brown hair and was one who glanced his way as they crossed the street. Traffic was noticeably heavy for the campus.

Once inside the small bar and grill, their conversation over sandwiches and cabernet was stilted slightly since they did not know each other well enough to make it sensible. William laughed at the idea that this was a 'first' for him. Being with this fellow was an adventure and a compatible bearing was obvious to each. Further comment still remained unidentifiable in such an awkward situation, the first of its kind apparently for both. A few other patrons were in the place. William and Jerry simply sat, ate, and drank until midnight and laughed at this brief encounter. At best, this whole scene was enjoyable for both of them. They merely decided that they were eating and drinking together and that was all that is necessary. Jerry gave it no more concern than did William. In fact, they laughed at each other.

But after a short moment when neither said anything, after the waitress presented the check, Jerry asked, just as awkwardly, anyway, for his address. Something about this encounter made the inquiry logical; "Just in case I may want to send you a Christmas card." That was not how he wanted to put it. He had never, in his entire Monticello life or in his entire MIT life, in his entire existence ever wanted to ask for something as personal as an address, immediately, unless, of course, it was to be freely given. If so, then his embarrassment would disappear and this moment would be all worthwhile. He added hesitantly, "I'm here in Berkeley and I don't have an address, myself. He did think of his aunt but he had not been over to see her sufficiently enough to ask her to keep mail for him. "But I do have a box number." He looked immediately at William to discern any reticence on his part. "I just have my post office box." He looked at William's hands, and then, into his eyes. "I don't know much more than that." He slid the concert program over to him. "I just know that . . ." and he paused, "that maybe I could write to you sometime." It sounded so forward for him to say it, just that way. He claimed the check and put it in his pocket.

William took the last bite of his roast beef sandwich and finished with another sip of the wine. "It's a nice campus. I've played here just a year ago." Then, slowly, he opened his coat pocket and produced a pen. "I usually think of my New York agent's address but he is so forgettable when it comes to correspondence to me. Let me . . ." and he stopped, looked at the quiet face opposite him. Then, he gazed at Jerry after a sly smile, "Let me give you this one. It belongs to my crazy wonderful friend, Vivian Cole, and she passes on to me bills, junk mail, and what-have-you. Sometimes she asks questions, oftentimes, she doesn't. It's Denver." Under his name on the program, he provided his signature. "Do you know Denver? I mean, have you ever been there?" By now he felt comfortable at the table. He took the last sip of wine and waited.

"No, I haven't," and with another strange feeling, he relaxed. He asked, "You flying back to Colorado tomorrow?" And then, he thought to himself that he may be asking too much information from him. This pianist did not seem to mind all the chatting that they enjoyed over food. This whole situation was really a nice one, just the kind to brighten up relaxing after performing. But he was tired. To Jerry's surprise, William rose and softly explained, "If you'll excuse me, now, I have to go." He perceived a sudden look of disappointment on the face of this stranger. Oddly enough, he was not like all the other hangers-on after a concert. A girl and her date stopped at their table to say they enjoyed the music. They thanked him and then departed.

He was not at all like the teens who crowded around him at the stage door, or back stage as an orchestra would pack up and depart. This Jerry Champion was by no means an excited autograph hound. He was quiet. He was strangely aloof, standing when he did. Jerry folded the program and shoved it quickly into his pants pocket. He said softly, "I've got the check and he stumbled away from his chair. William explained after noting a slight disappointment. "My plane is early tomorrow. I better get some sleep." More relaxed now, than before, Jerry decided to forego any attempt to talk. That would be impolite. The April evening was cool and they noticed a threat of rain.

At the noisy street corner they shook hands. "Thanks a lot, Mr. Kaplan." The moment was awkward again but when their eyes met, each one smiled. "I figured this has been a really nice night for me." Jerry wanted to add more but he could not choose adequate words. With a wave of his hand, he turned away and disappeared in the crowd.

William had had few such encounters in his journeys. But too many of them were with over-excited women, those on committees to see to it that he was comfortable, that the piano was tuned, that his steak would always be ready at 3:00 pm, that the programs were just the way he wanted them and in the order of presentation of the numbers. For just a short minute or so, he thought about this encounter. He looked again on a program where he had jotted the name. Gerald was crossed out and Jerry was put in its place before Champion. He did—for some reason—remember the blue eyes, the height, slightly taller than he, the serge suit he was wearing, even the shoes. Why was he remembering such trivia? Now, after saying goodbye, why did he remember the sincerity of that final hand shake?

Vivian Anderson Cole, the one who always met his arrivals, at the airport, the one who always wanted to know how he was and what he wanted for dinner that night, the one who always had a smile, a cheery welcome home, did not appear as friendly. Such a greeting was odd for his friend. But after he grabbed his bag and saw her standing waiting for him, he found no cheery welcome. She immediately informed him that she had a million things to report as they left the terminal and climbed into her Buick.

William was tired but he listened. "First, Mrs. Tomassi left for Chicago to see her new grandson. She told me the condo is yours and she's expected back in about five or six days." William peered at her from the passenger side and secretly hoped she could drive without getting any more upset. She was dressed in blouse and slacks and her hair was not exactly combed although he knew she was careful always to look her best, especially in public. When she spoke of their great friend with her full surname, Tomassi, rather than merely saying "Mrs. 'T'" as most everyone called her, he knew she was distraught. "The keys to the condo are in the glove box. She apologized for leaving before you got back from Berkeley but apparently little Josh arrived on time so everyone is happy." She waited with no further comment when they stopped at a traffic light. Then, peering over her dark glasses, she announced, "I wish I were happy." William let her talk as long as she wanted before he interjected any questions. "Now, I'm having trouble with Kevin. All the time you have been gone on your tour, he pulled a sly move and I don't mean on the football field. God, I wish he would get hired by the Buffalo Bills or the Dallas Cowboys or the Podunk Rascals because he's always been good at the sport." She kept telling herself that. "He sure would like to play professional."

William was beginning to put it all together, finally. While he had hardly ever known what her husband did, now that the Football Hero was graduated from Colorado U. perhaps, through the conversation they were having, he might learn some more clues about Kevin's shenanigans. At least he began to suspect something 'rotten in Denmark' as he once told her. She conceded. "He moved out two months ago, as you know," she said when they had stopped behind heavy traffic. William never did feel comfortable about asking why, because he was busy preparing for that tour. He stared at her and for a split second she saw the questions in his eyes for which he needed answers. She took a deep breath and sped through the intersection. "Well, now I know but I guess I never suspected. Kevin is gay." She said this bluntly, as if t he piano player already knew this situation. But he didn't. This was the first time she mentioned it to him. William accepted the information, blinking his eyes and then he took a deep breath, also. Vivian, brave and ready for almost anything, the one girl who was intelligent but exhausted, continued. "It was not altogether a genuine surprise to me. One of the other team members and I guess it had been going on for the two years they've been out of C.U."

William had never even thought of this situation. He was a pianist and not an ex-football star, if such a resolution were pertinent in this case. Being gay was a term which he had heard from time to time but it never did, really, actually, register with him. He thought of himself, now that he had heard the soap opera about Vivian's plight, as, perhaps, a mere bystander, listening as attentively as he could to her recitation as she pulled into the empty space at the curb. "Okay." She concluded, "you're home again. Forgive me for ranting and raving." *Gay* was never a suitable word for Kevin's condition. He had hardly heard enough of the word for it to be registered in his own vocabulary He heard it this time for it to be a surprise even for Vivian.

She got out of the car and opened the truck for his suitcase. "I'll bring your mail to you later on. You have a pile of it." She kissed him on the cheek and tried to smile. "Go on up and relax. And welcome home." She gave him a terrific bear hug and slipped back into the driver's seat. For just a second or two, he watched her speed away. A neighbor lady who passed him on the sidewalk waved. "How's my favorite music man?" she called a quick greeting. William had only a moment to nod his head as she rushed by him.

this Frenchman what he may do to accomplish a stronger impression with the concert community, a better rapport with the orchestras throughout the music world, including Ray Hicks, if Ray Hicks could ever calm down and take his medicine when he should do so. Maybe it was something that he said, innocently, that provoked concern from Dr. Graham.

Raymond Hicks was the best man for him, for this one agent some time ago began to develop William Kaplan as a splendid new talent on the keyboard. Dr. Graham, along with Steven Michael Young, the conductor of the Colorado Symphony Orchestra, provided this expert advice. "I'm happy to be of service," replied Dr. Graham. "I'm sure I speak for Steven, too." He dropped his napkin but retrieved it.

Gratefully, William listened to this scholar. "I'm glad to be back in Denver and yes, I'm going to relax and not fret about anything whatsoever. I'm glad to be home again. Mrs. Tomassi went to Chicago and she left me a list of things. I just don't want to go to Sterling, not now, anyway. I called and mother was okay. Sometimes I get the idea that my dad works too hard. Graham noticed that he did mention his father but he already knew Herschel Kaplan was hardly ever a subject that William mentioned often. Across those six years, both this confidante and William soon began to share intimate subjects, reasoning, incidents, and personal opinions, even gossip, that somehow colored their capacities for getting things accomplished. "I don't want to go to Sterling for some time, I guess. Mom said she and a friend will be driving into Denver next week, I think, so I'll wait and talk to her then. I don't . . ." He balked and Freddy Graham noticed the stoppage. If it had anything to do with music, then, yes, he would care to hear of it, but he would never openly ask for problems which were yet submerged in the pianist's psyche. Graham surmised that something existed anew. He knew this young man too well. Whatever it was, William would mention it, perhaps, if he would care to do so.

They ate in silence, more or less, until the teacher smiled and offered the reason for the correspondence he had placed on the third chair. This would bring a smile to Bill. "I have a piece of information for you which can be exactly what you're looking for. I like to spring surprises on people. It will bring a big smile to that face of yours." William took a deep breath and looked at him. "It's from your favorite agent in New York. He sent me a nice letter—and you are mentioned in it, of course—and he wants my own personal opinion on this matter." He took another bite of salad. A look of curiosity surrounded William which brought a smile. He waited for Freddy to finish his soft laughter before he asked any questions. Freddy flashed the letter in front of him in a wild theatrical gesture and laughed again as a villain would tease a heroine. This did bring a stronger smile to William's lips. "Are you ready for this?"

William smiled deeply this time, the beautiful smile he always had, complete with his dimple. "Yes, you crazy nincompoop," he laughed. "Yes, I guess I am. What can you be withholding from me that is so desperately important to schedule this Union cafeteria repast?"

"I shall read the letter, if I may." And he proceeded to do so. He ignored the usual first paragraph, full of questions about William's health, has he rested? Is he all right? After he glanced at William, he laughed again. "Ah, here it is: In late April of 1996, the Paris Conservatoire," he stopped; French was his other language but he purposely mispronounced words for this occasion, "is inviting the American pianist, William Kaplan, to attend and perform one of two concerti for the celebration of music by either Saint Saens or Ravel." Freddy put the letter down next to his cup of coffee and continued. "There you have it! The choice is yours, and I'm happy to reply immediately to Mr. Hicks that I heartily endorse this trip across the Pond for Colorado's Own. Hicks must know what I think and whether you accept or not. He has to know NOW, because, evidently, the invitation has been sent to you first—probably—and, secondly, you may choose either Saint Saens or Ravel—before any other invitation is sent to anybody else. I think that's great! That's good thinking. I wouldn't be surprised if the second artist were to be that famous Russian. I plan to call him on the phone because what I think cannot be put into any kind of letter. I want to telephone him this afternoon. You crazy nincompoop, what do you say?"

William remained quiet, completely spellbound, with all the excitement swelling up inside him. He drank the last of his coffee so he was thinking, and quickly. Paris! France, not Texas. An invitation from the most notable and worthwhile institution in Europe! "I've always wanted . . ." And Freddy interrupted with "Yes, go on, you always wanted to go to Paris, Texas!" Both of them laughed so loudly that other people laughed with them. "God, I'm jumping up right now and going to my phone and calling Hicks. Yes! Yes! I'm not giving you a chance to change your crazy mind. Oh!" And he stopped after standing and spilling his own coffee. "Which do you want to play? Saint Saens— you'll have a choice of five, or Ravel, either the Left Hand Concerto or his first one?" He waited, more excited than William. "Quick quick! Tell me!" So William stood also, unable to move. Immediately his answer was on his tongue. "I vote for Saint Saens' concerto number two. Put me down for that one. It's my favorite."

"Great! I agree. Do you have a score? I'll call Steven and have him get one for you. And away I go." Freddy picked up his briefcase and on the way out of the dining room, he yelled back so that everyone could hear him. "Nice to see you again, William Kaplan!" And he was gone.

So that was the quickest time for any decision that had to do with Paris France (not Texas) and something that would occur next Spring. Time for him to learn the thing. At least he had a copy of the piece stowed away somewhere upstairs in the house in Sterling. Several faculty members came over to say hello and to ask what that was all about!

He thought about this on his way to the city bus route. He thought about this on the bus, on his way to the front door, up the elevator to the twelfth floor where he could joyously play with no one to bother him. He would think about it all the time. He would think about calling Sterling again, tonight, if not sooner, to tell his mom. He would tell Vivian as soon as he calmed down, his sister, too, so she could tell the doctor this good news. Whom else in Denver could he call and tell? He sat at the piano and played and played and played, almost anything, anything he wanted. He wanted to play the famous Concerto, for he chose his favorite. Camille Saint Saens! Thank You, God! Thank You for this . . . whatever it is! For my talent, for giving me this music in me, for just about anything, right now, because I'm so happy that I'm crazy. You hear me, God? Thank You Merci. Merci mille fois which he said whether it was correct French or not.

And then later, exhausted, he found himself on the sofa in the main room with the view to the north over the other tall buildings. He found himself in tears, joyous tears because he had Freddy Graham who thought so much of him for accomplishing all that he did. He said, yes, that William Kaplan would accept and choose the Saint Saens number two, and go to Paris and play and thank the French People because he already thanked God.

And then the telephone rang and he answered it quickly. Vivian's voice was quiet and sincere, and also had a worried tone to it. This delightful friend whom he had known since well before they knew the difference between girls and boys, this enigmatic someone who cared about him ever so much, this person was hopeful that he was all right and that she had not heard from him in two days. She mentioned her husband again and couldn't figure out what he was doing or thinking or being, especially what he was being. She anticipated any kind of word from him. "And, oh, yes," she added before he could say anything. "You got a letter postmarked Berkeley from a . . ." and she paused to read the return address, "from a Mr. Gerald Champion."

Chapter Seven

May 1992

SINCE HE HAD BEEN a candidate for a doctorate at U.C.Berkeley Gerald Champion was, admittedly, a 'loner', with the exception of visiting his father's elegant sister whom he called Aunt Urs. He had always called her that since he learned who she was. With a name like Ursula Champion Griswold, he was able to remember the whole title. She reminded him of some kind of regal queen with her elegant ways of walking, talking, and grooming. She lived in her castle, her nice house on Green Street, San Francisco, just east of Columbus Avenue and two blocks south of Coit Tower. He now had a logical excuse for going across the bay. In those two years he found reasons. Her handsome face, dark gorgeous eyes, and elegant dresses reminded him of his father, especially the jaw line. She understood the pace he maintained, each day's routine, the often few hours he slept in his own little bed in a rented two-room apartment. His mind was that of a burgeoning scientist and that is the way he wanted it. In those last four years, since he and his father and brother sat alone on the front steps of their Monticello home, eons of years swept by and he suddenly realized there was more to his existence than merely coffee, bear claws, and books to read.

He was literally by himself in his own little world because he wanted it that way. It had to be that way. There was no other way to prove to himself that he could manage his courses, his studies, his thinking, his research, his attitude, and his commitment to his goal. He was no longer the wild kid with an expensive tennis racket with lovely would-be teammates. All this was, he realized, a prelude to what he was desiring. He had a goal and he was the person who wanted to accomplish that goal. When he was at M.I.T., even the geographical closeness of New York City, where his brother found his own future, or of Cape Cod, or of his parents' curious questions—all of these goings-on interrupted a study ritual he had to develop. One day he stood on the steps of one of his class buildings and looked upon the campus, the whole area of trees and sidewalks, even the town of Cambridge, his own paths from one class to another, the library in which he fell in love with Miss Hooper, the aged librarian, with her aura of learning. These all became a magical change from the front porch sermons of his father.

Now, much, much later, as he stood before his shaving mirror, on one of those first weekends when he felt he could close the books and take the BART under the Bay and spend sometime with his aunt and her housekeeper, he felt obliged to explain all this rigorous ritual to them. After all, Mrs. Ursula Griswold and her Chinese housekeeper were all he had in the way of relatives, either on the west coast, or on the east coast. He had of course his mother and another aunt in Monticello. He would call her long distance but not often. He might write a letter to her, but not often. When his father died only five years ago, all the advice of this gracious man became like bricks in his future's foundation. "I shall think of you often," his mother wrote him. "We Italians are that way. That's just the way it is. You run along to California and know that your papa would want you to succeed. All this judgment I seem to be giving you will boil over in a great way one of these days. My own papa gave me and my sister a good talk, especially when I married your dad, even if it was half in Italian complete with all his hand gestures." All this information seemed mundane and in the far distant past. He felt this was true because he was on the verge of beginning his third year., according to his advisor, is to be crucial and exceptionally important. He would be told about all this very soon.

But he was well known as a bright young man and a fairly good student, on the campus and among the designated faculty to counsel him in his multitude of schedules. It was his advisor whom he had since he began, Dr. Nelson, who was a Brit with a beautiful accent. But one event for certain at this urgent point in time, Jerry began to think of William Kaplan, not often, and certainly never to be distracted from the help the good Doctor Nelson would give. He was careful—he had learned to realize this one lesson—that from now on, not to allow the memory of that concert to interfere. This Britisher, complete with English formality in bearing and attitude, arranged for the required consultation with his five-member committee in June. Jerry was not nervous when he appeared in Dr. Nelson's office, complete with tie and coat; he was just ready.

Dr. Nelson began. "One of your assets, my boy, is that you are a good student and that your appearance reflects your confidence. In these two years that you have been here, your good work is obvious. Your persistence shows in your work." He stopped to scratch his nose. "Your devotion to your thinking reminds me of a friend I had in my early studies at Oxford. He was an artist of sorts but in the realm of music." Dr. Nelson instantly recognized a look of surprise; he interjected, "Do you like piano music?" Before Jerry had a chance to answer, or to try to provide an explanation of whom he encountered recently, the advisor continued. "Nothing kept him from his own devotion to music. He told me this." He took a deep breath. "Well. Forgive me for offering a side issue. So now your committee is waiting in the next room. At this moment, and first before you see them, I am required to review with you your splendid record you have achieved in the length of time your committee has been *on your side* as you Yanks enjoy saying. I had to explain that to my wife." He laughed. "If I may say so, this is like a review of your own life—this is your life, so to speak, since you've been here. Your GPA at MIT for your M.Sc., as you know, was 3.8. Here, you must retain at least 3.3. Of the ninety hours required for your Ph.D. you have completed your first two years' requirement, with at least twenty hours of thesis research. You are well on your way. During your previous two semesters, including the summer of 1993, your qualifying exams both written and oral were splendid, I'm happy to remind you. Just one more item before you speak to the five members. In the coming twelve months, you will have another advisor, Dr. Clark, and perhaps yet even another one. It's normal for the candidate to expect this. I'm bowing out and I do wish you all the success in the world. Dr. Clark is in the other room, also. He will talk to you personally after the committee has its say." He stood to shake Jerry's hand. With a pat on the candidate's back he said, "Come along, my boy."

Vivian Anderson Cole remained mystified despite the attempts to rely on William to help her understand exactly what in the world was going on with that football hero she married. She did admit, to herself and perhaps to one other female confidante that this nice person, this hero on the football field, was her choice for a life-long husband. She even arranged for a meeting with the Presbyterian minister whom she had known all her life. With Kevin himself, she listened attentively to what this pastor would say and how he would answer her own inquiry regarding life in the fast lane. The Andersons whose own instructions were nil, were still her parents. Even her standards were obviously different and strange and certainly not like *theirs* . . . She had heard her own father comment that he could never understand "rock and roll something" The question of being gay was simply a question among Vivian's high school adventures. It remained a silly question at first. Some of her sincere and worthwhile girlfriends, those who had no concept that it appeared something more than merely *sophisticated*, or *charming* or *pleasant*.

Since she was now grown and more knowledgeable so to speak, she wanted to depend on what the piano player's opinion was. She had previously depended upon him covering a great number of subjects that they had coined their phrase *knowing the price of eggs in China*. Or maybe, what did he know about this mysterious condition? It's true: little Billy, the famous pianist at that time, did not disclose everything that had happened to him outside the realm of breathing. She had only heard rumors concerning Bobby Martin and 'his gang'—if indeed he had one—and somehow she had missed that story about Harold Morgan and the boys' rest room. Poor Harold. That was so far in the past, eons ago, that she had completely dismissed the entire ridiculous story. Why had that bounced back in her brain after all these years? But now, she was confronted by this new specter, this 'something' that invaded her world. She loved Kevin Cole and he kept saying the he loved her. "*Love you*" became a telephone ritual.

Vivian decided that little Billy was now the grown and mature thirty-one year old William Kaplan who is to her delight a successfully brilliant concert pianist. If she could not comprehend the Theory of

Football, maybe she could learn the Theory of Music. To herself she repeated that part of being a brilliant concert pianist. Yes. This opinion stuck to her like wood to glue, even if she could not carry a tune. That is exactly how she had learned to think of him. Vivian had a husband whom she loved and a piano player whom she adored . . . That minister never did come to conclusions about divorce but anyway, she dismissed that option.

The free-wheeling Mrs. Cole became mystified about three months ago when she began to notice misplaced empty glasses on the kitchen counter. At other times, two glasses half empty of wine were on the table at the end of the old sofa with its gaudy twin pillows. She could not account for these wine glasses, even though both she and Kevin drank cabernet regularly. She always carried glasses to the sink because they were too delicate. Ever since she married the football star who had not been a football star since they both were graduated from Boulder, she decided she would be a great housekeeper in all things domestic. She did not remember when she first realized that she was, indeed, most efficient, careful, and specific about where the income went and that used glassware should be in the sink.

Kevin Cole, who knew William Kaplan about as long as his wife did, tried, for the first year of their togetherness, to join the Buffalo Bills. When he did not succeed in that venture, he flew to Dallas and inquired about the famous Cowboys. Something was probably wrong with both attempts, and it never had anything to do with salary. Was it something the college coach wrote in correspondence to both teams which, apparently, Kevin never read? When Kevin limped back to Denver three weeks after getting drunk in a little bar and waking up in a bed in some guy's apartment, then he had no idea what he was going to tell Vivian. His six feet three inches, two hundred twenty-four pounds, remained attractive to both the women who swooned over him and the few men who shook his hand at the bar and bought drinks for this football star. He slowly returned to Denver but he had no idea what his future would be. He begged a job from one of his close buddies who told him he could be a successful insurance salesman. He did not exactly like that idea but he slowlydid become an insurance salesman.

Vivian first sat alone on the right side of their bed and thought about what had changed this dynamo on the football field. For a long period of time she thought with no obvious answers. Kevin appeared the same casual, nice guy with whom she had fallen in love back when she was a junior and a new Chi Omega sister. That was back when William Kaplan was a junior at the private university and played everything for everybody on campus, giving recitals, playing for the Men's Glee Club, at church, and for Denver's one or two whorehouses. The latter, of course, had become the delightful joke of the Music Department. One of the music students who laughed with William had a black T shirt with the words, "I Can't Tonight. I'm playing at Maggie's." So now, only a few weeks ago, after his fling in Dallas to try to become a big star again, Kevin did not talk to Vivian for four days. In fact, he never was in their apartment, or if he ever was, it was when Vivian was working and had never, never realized that he was home taking showers, lots of them. She found two separate blue towels. Trivia. Didn't mean a thing. But one day she came home and noticed, just casually, that the bed was not made. And she knew that she made it that morning before she left for work. All this nonsense began to add up. She did not exactly know how to handle this, how to speak to the star whom she thought she still loved. She was miserable. She confronted her own emotions. She refused to mention this paradox to the piano playeror to her own brother and sister.

So one afternoon she sat alone on the sofa with a glass of cabernet sauvignon. And before she could begin to shed tears—if any tears could be shed—Kevin Cole walked in the front door followed by a guy who was as surprised at seeing Vivian waiting on the sofa as Kevin was. This meant that Kevin turned, whispered something, and excused the guy who immediately departed. Then, en route to the bedroom where he slowly removed his coat, he said "hello, Viv." He returned just as quickly and asked for a glass of wine for himself. She preceded him to the kitchen, poured a glass, and handed it to him because she did not actually know what she would say if she could utter anything. This was a new incident for her. She looked at him but he avoided her eyes.

While she stepped by him, he remained standing in the archway to the kitchen, looked at her for a moment, and then moved to a chair near the sofa. "I found out about two months ago why I didn't make the Bills or the Cowboys." For just a minute or so, Vivian was surprised that he would mention this news that had perplexed her all this time.

He was a born footballer, as she said, able to maintain an excellent Defense and his Offence was awesome. Kevin was once nominated for a Heisman. At least she knew what that could mean … It was a big question, more on her mind than on his. She stared at him until he finished his news. He relaxed in the chair but then sat forward and stared directly at her. "I'm *that way*, Vivian." This was quietly spoken as if he may be ashamed of what the coach and everyone on the university team, evidently, deduced. After all, the fellow player with whom he had shared his furtive rendezvous dropped out of Colorado University and tactfully disappeared. She had no time to determine how the coach reached this bit of information but when Kevin spoke of it, that seemed to be the most obvious reply. Kevin was a fine player, a great guy, a splendid student, a remarkable athlete. And to the best of her knowledge there had been no "hanky panky" in the showers. That is what he was confessing, sitting forlornly in that chair, facing her with tears mounting in his gray eyes. He had been a Heisman nominee and she was not surprised. All the Chi Omegas were equally proud of him. When he was on campus, he was not in the least conceited or affected in any way. So his blunt statements to her were a total shock. She had never, in the least, suspected this condition. She did not ever think along those lines. All the giggling girl friends back in Junior High School were long ago erased from her mind.

Again, the questions began to surmount. Again, memories reared their ugly heads. Once or twice, in high school, back then, she and the girls heard stories about three or four of the boys who, perhaps, in only the words she knew, were different from the other jocks. She remembered seeing the players swatting each other on the rear when they made an advantageous run. Frankly, she had not given it much thought. For a split second, she tried to remember how her best friend, William, was labeled and just how he fit in with the high school crowds. William was William and he somehow just did not fit into any such crowd, whatever the group was called. Vivian fell in love with Kevin and she began to think of him as the most important man in her life. If Kevin began to "change" early in their junior year at C.U. she either did not suspect it or she had never thought of anything like that at all. She did not even apply the information found in chapter nine in her Abnormal Psychology text that she still displayed on the one vertical bookcase in the hallway. She figured it was merely a passing emotion, a hangover from when Kevin, himself, was a young teenager and did whatever boys did.

"I don't know why, Vivian," Kevin concluded. She still did not know, exactly, how to handle this, or what to say to him. Then she patted the pillow on the sofa next to her and beckoned him to sit there. So this football hero put his head on her shoulder and wept profusely.

And that is when William came back from his tour and when she telephoned him to give him some news that she did not know how to explain. Except to quietly mention he had a letter from Berkeley, California. Vivian waited while William tried to answer. "Did you hear what I said?" "Yes, I heard you." He was at Mrs. T's condo where she had called him. "And yes, I know what it means. I'm a big boy, now."

"And I'm talking about the letter, big boy!" Her delightful tone when she said that caused a bit of genuine laughter. "I heard both of your remarks, the one about Kevin and the one about Jerry Somebody. What's his name, please?" He waited for her answer and sipped water from a paper cup. She did not say. Vivian took a deep breath and produced the letter from a stack of his correspondence. She read the return address. "Jerry Champion, P.O. Box 430 Berkeley CA 94039. I thought you played at Berkeley recently." She waited when a fire engine with its siren sped by the apartment building. "This letter came a couple of days ago but you never did come by for it. Do you want it?" Both Vivian and now William were distracted and only each knew why. With no time to think he said quickly, "I guess I do." He could not reach a definite reason why this letter came. Champion. Of course, he remembered him but he had not mentioned that episode to anyone for as long as he had been back home. He thought there was no reason to do so. Short meetings with a multitude of hangers-on happened at every stage door or anteroom, people who flooded the moment with best wishes and had a pen handy for his autograph. Champion. "Are you there?" He laughed at himself. "Yes, I'm still on the line." She paused while she thought. "Let me meet you at Starbuck's down the street from you." He was surprised. "You're working?" "No, I'm home and Kevin just left. I'd like to talk to you, sonny." He said yes, but did not know why. He still had a lot of practicing to keep up his rituals and discipline. "I guess you heard already about the Paris thing!" Before she hung up, she quickly said, "Yes, I'm proud of you. I'll bring your letter. Fifteen minutes. Goodbye."

Vivian and William both were not ignorant, by any means of the Gay Scene, either on the West Coast where the largest contingent thrived, nearest to them, or here in Denver. They had subtlely learned how this new culture—new, perhaps to those from the little rural burg of Sterling, Colorado—arrived some years ago. Vivian realized this more so than William even thought, she once told him, she is not a musician by any means and does not have any mysterious genes that musicians have. She kept telling him she could not carry a tune. Upon listening to her discussions relating to the variety of personality traits, he surprised himself in that he discovered she knew more about the subject than she really presumed. He did not want to add that she knew more than he did. He had no time to ponder this avenue of thought. Once Kevin confessed to Vivian, she then began to piece together all the "ifs, ands, and buts" of the situation that Vivian now faced. So this is why she did not go to work today. This is why she suddenly became a hermit and sat on the sofa and tried to find the pieces of her jigsaw puzzle. Her big hero somehow decided that he was that way, the way he now claimed, and that it merely occurred overnight, that night in Dallas when he woke up. He guessed that is what it was, to begin with. How crude! My God!

William listened. He listened to her as he would do, any time, any where, even at a table at Starbucks, to listen as his best friend exposed the innermost thoughts she hardly knew she was thinking, all as a result of Kevin's long monologue with genuine tears. And when he realized that he still had practicing and study, and that he now had that letter from Jerry Somebody—Champion—so he sat and stopped this conversation and rose and sweetly said goodbye to Vivian. He left her sitting with a big question mark hanging above her head. She knew what he had to do and she was grateful to him for sitting opposite her and listening. "Okay." She said. "I'm trying. I'm trying to understand."

Chapter Eight

June 7, 1992

FOR THE FIRST TIME in several days William realized that he could not ignore a vague but persistent response that was haunting him. It was formless, a reverie, possibly, or the result of a musical pattern that he found himself humming as he waited for a city bus, or very likely frankly a thought he did not possess prior to this moment. This odd sensation could have appeared out of nowhere as a result of a melody that remained with him across the years only now to reappear to enchant his psyche. He sat at the keyboard. Previously, he told himself, such a situation had pestered him, often reminding him of old tunes from the radio he enjoyed or portions of tone poems that delighted him at one time and then escaped him only to return later with this kind of peculiar feeling. He was unable to pinpoint what exactly this newest lesson was, if it was indeed a lesson of sorts. It was nothing akin to his discipline in the study of his music. It was nothing that he discovered in the score of the Saint Saens concerto which rested on the stand directly in front of him. And he knew that Mozart did not have anything to do with it because he had studied several of this composer's concerti.

Yes! It was a feeling from down deep inside him. Mrs Tomassi, the dear lady who had provided the comfort of her suite, was in Chicago. He was comfortable in his own bedroom. He had the run of her small all-electric kitchen. He promised himself not to fret over Vivian's problem. Frankly, he was unable to analyze just what brought on this crazy sensation he had. He sat on his piano bench which was currently the library of the many pounds of music he had brought from Sterling. He attempted the brisk arpeggio more than once but was unable to proceed.

He tried to remember just what 'discipline in music' signified. Maybe that could help with the dimensions of the question. He thought it had to do with talent of some kind, his talent, mostly. Perhaps it had been some kind of intangible breadth and height that made every other phase of his work congeal. Such a feeling had to be inherent and already within the mind and focus of the pianist, in this case. At least that is what first came to mind. He had felt it or learned it ages ago when he was traveling through the confrontations of early teens. Miss Shriner was always there at his side, seated on her tall kitchen stool as she commandeered the lessons that he did enjoy. So he sat at the piano and stared at the music in front of him. This odd entity was very much a part of him now.

On his mind was not necessarily anything resembling scales or intricate arpeggios from Liszt. Immediately he determined what may have been the cause of all this consternation. He was haunted by Vivian's deep concern for her husband. Yes: that was a beginning. Also, he even allowed his eyes to wander back to the coffee table where the letter from Jerry Champion rested, unopened. Beside it was a letter which just arrived from Mrs. T postmarked Chicago. The source of his struggle did not stem from this dear lady who was most kind to him. He immediately dismissed that. He still experienced a whirlwind of indefinable dimensions. He even allowed a thought of conversations with Freddy Graham or Dr Young, the conductor of the Colorado Symphony to pass through his moment of concern,. He took another deep breath, arose, and wandered to her letter and opened it, to read that she was returning on the eighth. The eighth was tomorrow. Then he noticed the afternoon sun pouring through the French window to the balcony. He looked over his shoulder to the keyboard and to the pencil resting by the thick score. No: his indecision, his agony did not come from Saint Saens. This composer was too much a favorite to constitute the situation. He had always been extremely conscious of discipline in his work, the necessary commitment to his practice, even to the joy of the completed work. Just one month ago, at the late supper with this Gerald Champion, he heard the student mention discipline in his own chosen field of endeavor He believed in that, even though he knew hardly anything about geology, other than the few rocks he collected in his back yard at Sterling. There were many, nice, flat, rounded rocks that sit just right, in the crook of your finger.

He picked up the letter from Jerrry and sat in the chair nearest to the sun's rays. It was postmarked Berkeley with a post office box number. Strangely he believed he was on the right track to solve his dilemma. He opened it and read. It appeared informal, on one-page of paper ripped from a spiral notebook. "Dear Mr. Kaplan." It was dated just recently, in black ink. William's first impression was that it was hurriedly written. One, maybe two words were scratched out. "I hope you don't think me too presumptuous. But this is my address. I want to say again that I enjoyed our time together late that night after your concert. I'm writing for two reasons. One I am well into this geology program and have already met my new advisor. He has prescribed much work but I'm happy. So far as I can determine, I can finish by May 1996. That is my goal, my joy of the completed work." William noticed that he stated, *my completed* work. which were the very words he himself used just now. He sensed that this new person was a bit poetic. "The second reason is that I have an aunt living in San Francisco and she is happy to say hello and that she has a baby grand piano. Write me at that box number please when you have a minute or two from your piano. Sincerely, Gerald (Jerry) Champion." It was, William thought, most definitely, not the usual fan letter. An ink smudge was in the upper right corner.

It was a simple letter, so unlike the several letters and notes that Mr. Hicks, his emotional agent, writes to him. Hicks would always include marginal references, similar to "this gal really wants your bod" or "forget about this one, she wrote before and she is a Mrs.'" It dawned on William that he had given Raymond Vivian's address, something he had never done at any other occasion. On other various tours, after concerts when he was exhausted with sweat pouring from his face, crowds wanted to know what his favorite colour was, his shirt size, what his hobby was and if he had a favorite movie star, with teenage girls screaming for his personal home address and their dates who stood to gawk at him in awe. Jerry's letter was different. For just a moment he did remember this tall man from New York State. He skimmed the page again, noticing the definite attempt to write well, to write neatly as if he were not taking notes hurriedly in class. It was worth noting. It was fairly well prepared, probably written when he was grabbing another roast beef sandwich somewhere. William thought he detected a stain on the corner of the page other than the ink smudge . . . He smiled because he did remember that small café on campus where they became acquainted. Then again, he chuckled because he could not ascertain why he smiled in the first place. He folded the letter and returned it to its envelope and dropped it on the coffee table on his way back to the piano. He went immediately into some delicate arpeggios from Liszt. Billy always thought he was good at Liszt. He sat there thinking. He decided to answer Jerry Champion later. Something rang true, some of that unidentifiable surge of force that he felt in his fingers as he played. For now, for the first time in several days, he identified one phase of his new emotion. He took a deep breath, again and again felt his fingers succeed with the intricate passages because he knew the cause—or thought he knew the cause—of what was haunting him.

Mrs Amelia Tomassi telephoned from Chicago. William thought he could have the entire morning, that next morning, just to himself. Progress with the Saint Saens was most assuredly existing in his mind and he was still excited about going to Paris, even though it was not until next June. "My dear William," she spoke carefully so as to explain everything. "It looks like I'm detained further. The birth went well. I am a grandmother and I'm doubly pleased. I hope you are well and happy and I miss hearing you play on my baby grand. But play you must. I called Dr. Graham and he told me of your great opportunity for Paris. Congratulations. I shall always be proud of you. Take care of yourself and give my regards to Mrs Cole. Bye bye, my boy." And she hung up before William could get a word in edgewise.

Later, when he decided that he must rob the Ice Box for food, the telephone rang again and he answered. It was Steven Michael Young. Immediately when William said hello, he was pleased that he was hearing from the conductor of the Colorado Symphony. Instantly, William was delighted to be interrupted by this paragon who, this man, was old enough so that everyone related to this fine orchestra was able to call him a variety of names from Grandpa to Uncle Steve. He had been careful never to divulge his actual age. As f it mattered to anyone with the exceptions of a poetic reference or in some delightful *repartee* at a recent party . . .

The symphony office was in the center of the Performing Arts Complex located downtown, miles from the campus of the university where Dr Graham and the tall lady ruled. There, at Fourteenth and Curtis Streets, Dr Young ruled the entire floor. He was surrounded by musicologists and violiins. The wide deep closet closest to his desk which housed the harp among the instruments too big to take home was always handy. And Dr Young had Mabel. He had Mabel.

Mabel was his secretary who knew everything. She professed to know more than anyone else about eighteenth century history of music. She was also mother-confessor and brewer of their morning coffee. She was the first person to call Dr Young a paragon. It was Dr Young who reserved Mondays for the purpose of doing what he wanted to do, outside the realm of music But today was not a Monday . . .

"William!" this conductor said the moment the pianist answered. "I am taking just a moment to speak so I shall make it quick." William decided to listen just as quickly. Food could wait. "I want to say Freddy has already mentioned to me the plan for France. Next June, I believe. You can do it, I already know. But in the meantime, Life goes on and on and on ad I too have a splendid invitation in store for you." In the sudden breath that this good doctor took, William was able to utter only one word, "Oh?"

"Yes, just listen." Again, William listened. "Please drop everything and come see me tomorrow morning. Mabel will have a cup of her delicious coffee for you." William tried to interrupt. "No, just be here as early as you can. Put down the music for our friend M. Saint Saens and take the next city bus to downtown I have something for you!

Chapter Nine

WILLIAM DID JUST THAT. He awoke early and prepared to obey the one man who had always been kind to him in so very many occasions throughout his studies, his pianistic temperament when it came to sincerely obeying his most serious introspection. The city bus which he boarded only a half block from Mrs Tomassi's home was the perfect area for thinking alone. The buildings, the city businesses, the trees, all the same views when he went to class were still there. His solitary bearing changed from time to time. Fourteenth Street appeared and he rose to lgreet the inner sanctum of this dynamo who wanted to see him.

Mabel greeted him with a cup of coffee as promised. She and William had often compared notes. In the canteen, Mabel was sitting with her own coffee. "He's not quite ready," she announced surreptitiously. But oncne he is ready, we'll know. He will come to get me because I told him to take his time with a telephone call from New York." William sat opposite her in a new chair for the canteen. "Yes," Mabel continued, "the whole canteen is new, frankly and I'm trying it out for the first time. From the taste of *this* coffee, I'll make a better cup full just for you."

"Do you have any idea what he wants?" William was more than curious.

"Well," she started, "he found himself engrossed in the multitude of adventures concerning the orchestra and the players. He has been its main conductor for for the last thirty or so years and he was thoroughly familiar with every score performed by the "band" as he called his group of devoted stars. Steven was the principal conductor because he knew everything, also, but he does have three other highly talented conductors on the staff who occupy their own offices next to his." She took one final sip of the coffee and decided she must stop this yakking and proceed to making a better brew in her own area. "In his office he has available a host of opinions on virtually every subject about which anyone would care to discuss. I know. I've discussed some of them with him. I learned a lot about his personal life. He was thirty-one at the beginning of W W II although he lost a younger brother somewhere in the Philippine Islands. Because of that indelible moment in the lives of both his parents and him, he tells everyone who asks, and who may not ask, that he abhorred the Vietnam War and any other war and anything relative to mental and physical coercion. On the wall next to that crowded closet of his is a small sign he had printed, *God does not care for mental or physical violence.* Steven always assumed he had other adventures besides shooting an M.1 rifle or any other form of destruction. TV's contribution to culture was never his cup of tea." She rose from her chair and looked directly at William. "When he was growing up, he became interested in piano although he uses this talent now only for instruction. He never did assume to have the professional classical artistry that a few of his friend attained. He would often stop whatever he was doing to stand and admire the many photos of celebrities encased in simple black frames and hanging on tthe four walls. There were many of them. The portrait of Van Cliburn, who played at the opening of our Boettcher Concert Hall, was one of his favorites. That picture included him standing beside this celebrity but he apparently cannot remember the location or the occasion. Somewhere in Ft. Worth, likely, just the great smiles on both faces." William stood as well because both of them saw the great conductor approaching. "I'll run and make him—and you—some good coffee."

"Come in, come in," he announced as he excused Miss Davis. "You're right on time. Is it raining yet?" He skirted two chairs that were still positioned at his previous conference with Gary Fuller, his new cello player, destined, he silently presumed, to become a cellist with his band. He smiled and motioned William to the wide sofa at the far end of his room. "I must say, and you'll hear more of this later from me, that I am thrilled to learn of the Paris opportunity. And I don't mean Paris, Texas." This Texas reference was always a joke passed around to nearly all the members of his band. "We must perform in Paris, Texas some time." William sat but only giggled. While Steven did notice how taciturn William appeared to be, how he was waiting for any remarks, he did not call attention to the moment. "Good grief, just a year from now. How happy your parents must be! And your sister too, already a mother of two kids William had learned long ago to appreciate any gestures from this grand conductor, but hardly ever to abide his remarks about his mother and father. He often thought that Steven took it for granted that all parents were as gracious and congenial as his own had been to him. "But forgive me, that is not totally why I invited you to my inner sanctum."

William managed with a simple thank you. "All this has come of a big shock but I'm used to the whole business now. I want to talk to you, too, but not necessarily about the trip." This from his friend caused the conductor to blink his eyes in question, raise his eyebrows and shift his body on the sofa next to him. William continued. "I know you want . . ." and then he stopped and immediately changed his statement. He realized he was rude to try to bring up a subject that was foreign to Steven, foreign to why he was here in the first place. "I'm sorry, sir," he muttered, "it can wait."

Now, Steven was indeed curious. He was used to the temperament of musicians and how often anyone of them can change subject in the middle of a heated *tete-a-tete*. "Well, anyway," he smiled again, "I think I have something that just may interest you, if you care to become interested." To this, William removed his jacket and waited. "The conductor of the San Francisco Symphony wrote me a letter just last Thursday. He's a man whom I don't completely know, well enough, anyway to have a drink with him. Steven softly laughed at this remark. Often those remarks of his are lost in translation.

Dr Young was quickly becoming factual. "He says that his committee is currently busy with preparing the 1995-1996 season. It begins in three more months, you realize. Ours, too, for that matter. And he knows you just got home from your tour. One of his scouts heard you play in Albuquerque. But apparently after a discussion over drinks at the Top of the Mark with two or three of his cronies the manager wanted me to talk to you about coming west, young man, to play with the kids in *their* band! They want you to play with the orchestra and they have suggested Mozart's Twenty-first." Steven tossed him the letter. This nice surprise brought William out of his mood, a time when he was caught thinking suddenly of Gerald Champion. Steven showed his enigmatic smile again and scratched his nose while he waited for an answer from this piano player opposite him. The lovely Seth Thomas clock resting on a Cherry table in a corner of the room chimed ten.

William sat overwhelmed. He blinked his eyes several times. That was his habit when he was confronted with too many—as he called them—"ifs, ands, and buts." He thought all of this at once. He did not know exactly how to categorize all of this series of events that has filled his hours and days.

"You can do it. It's short. Do you have a score?" William stood immediately and began to pace about the office. "If you don't, I'll dig one up for you." He walked to the door and opened it. "Mabel," he called, "please call Jimmy to see if we have a piano score to Mozart's Twenty-first Piano Concerto. Surely we have one around here some place." Then he closed the door and glanced at William who was, by now, standing by the window. He looked at Steven. "This is not what is on my mind, what mind I have left. And I don't mean Saint Saens. When is this performance scheduled? Not September first, by any chance?"

Steven smiled. "It's all there in the letter," to which, after finding his answer, exclaimed, "All this coming at once!" He glanced at it again and looked up from the letter. "November, just before Thanksgiving. Well!" "November!" William was even more surprised. "My God," he voiced suddenly, with a laugh that he did not have before all this news. "I won't have time to pee!" That answer delighted Steven and both of them uproariously laughed so loudly that Mabel opened the door to see what had happened. She was also the mail deliverer; she presented their coffee on the coffee table and several pieces of mail to him before she grinned and left. She forgot to close the door.

After a brief pause with the two of them staring at each other, Mable knocked on the door and waited. Steven opened it. "Yes, we have a piano score, the twenty-first, in C Major, k. 467. That one." She smiled and raised her eye brows. "Jimmy said he'd send it up to you as soon as possible." Then she closed the door.

"I am going to go ahead with this," William said slowly, "and play it, mainly because I'm aware of it. I even think I attempted the first movement at Miss Shriner's bidding." Steven could see that he was feeling much better. "This was back when I was foolish and youthful and stupid. Back then, when I didn't have much to do with myself."

"You are far more foolish and youthful and stupid now, my crazy friend!" Then Steven came over and grabbed him by his shoulders. He looked at him closely, peering deeply into his brown pupils. "I've always been jealous of you but I've grown up by now. Frankly, I wish I could play it so I could say, 'no, William can't, but I'll play it myself!'" He motioned for both of them to sit on the sofa again to drink Mabel's black coffee. "Now. I'll call, myself, this very afternoon and say 'yes'! Today is Tuesday and Mable knows this is my day to work. Please. I think you have something else on that mind of yours." He looked at William again and waited. Then, his phone rang and he raised his index finger to halt his answer.

With his coffee cup in hand, he returned to the window that opened to Sculpture Park. No. He decided then and there not to prolong his conversation with this friend. Kevin's confession—if it were a confession—was not exactly urgent. William came to a sudden realization about himself. He was who he was; God made him so. Music was his impetus. If he was anything at all other than a grateful "piano player" as Steven so beautifully put it, then if he possessed any other traits, any other forces inside him, then that is the way it must be. Music has always been his force now, nothing else was preeminent in his being at this moment. He remembered words he once had with Vivian, somewhere back in time, maybe fifteen years ago. "You do know what you want to be, surely, *by now*. don't you?" She had looked at him as if she were a nineteenth century school-marm holding a hickory stick. It sounded to her and her rowdy girl friends as if the talent was anathema. It was Vivian having had a secret conversation with three of them after school, and she was testing the piano player. "Of course I know, Vivian! I think there were a few, maybe five or six right there in the senior class." William was so matter-of-fact now. He told himself he knew everything. Vivian pulled him aside and cautioned. "I bet your bottom dollar Bobby Martin *is*! You look out! He's after you!" William frowned at this. "He's your friend, isn't he?" He felt his temper rise. "He's no friend and never will be. He's a big belligerent ass, if you ask me." For the first time in a long time, Vivian was suddenly amazed to feel the darkness come over his face, an otherwise pleasant and good looking one. He wished she had not mentioned Bobby Martin. "I gotta go."

Steven Michael Young brought him out of his reverie. "I said, what's on your mind? You must have been miles away somewhere."

"That's okay," and William skirted around him and walked to the door. "Tell the manager or conductor or whomever you call that I'd be happy to play Mozart. I'll come back tomorrow for that score. Thanks a million." On his way past Mable's desk, he noticed she was not there. But a small sign on her calendar politely informed everyone she was out to lunch and will be back by two o'clock. He walked casually down the hall and out of the complex onto fourteenth street where he was lucky to wait for a bus. A light sprinkle was the beginning of rain. He was happy. He was going to answer Gerald's short note.

Chapter Ten

July 1992

ANNA MARIA CERNA AND her sister, Ella, with their parents who were fortunate to come from the Old Country, moved from New York City all the way northwesterly to Monticello. This decision proved successful for it came just before the National Depression of the nineteen-thirties. Luckily, their father obtained a profitable position in one of the resort hotels near the Catskill Mountains, speaking Italian to the majority of patrons who frequented that entire area. Mr Cerna was able to continue his own study of English with the help of his two daughters and the myriad of immigrants from Firenze who departed Italy in 1927. Ella was born in 1935 and Anna Maria arrived in 1939. They gallantly flew the American Flag from the moment their parents were naturalized. That took some time but time they had. In the course of these events, Anna Maria Cerna picked up her share of Italian and was fluent. She also dated one of the brothers from the Champion clan. "Mama . . . Papa," Anna Maria announced on her twenty-fourth birthday, "This is Charles Champion. He and his brother and parents live down the street. He has something to ask of you."

The question, of course, dealt with Champion's request to marry their daughter. Perplexed by what was asked, because this was the first occasion to hear such a thing, Mr. Cerna, with his wife by his side, was overjoyed by the new American lesson he learned. Anna Maria had explained to Charles the necessity of attending to the Old Country Way of Doing Things. They all were in Monticello now. Despite the name of their town, they were all of the U.S.A. now. Gerald Champion was born July 9, 1964. Geoffrey arrived two years later. "I want American names for my boys," Anna Maria declared, and her parents went along with the plan.

"Happy Birthday, Jerry" was written on the card he received from his mother and Aunt Ella, postmarked Monticello. It was his third July away from the Catskills since becoming a Californian. His mother scribbled something in Italian. She had always wanted him to learn the language but somehow he never progressed beyond 'bon giorno.' Geoffrey managed phrases and "dirty slang" for he felt more related to the history of drug wars in New York. But that made Geoff more important to himself since he realized he was an American like Gerald. Geoffrey decided not to become a Godfather after all.

July nine that year fell on a Saturday and all those previous seven days he had planned well to accept the invitation of Aunt Urs to come and have Chinese with her and Li. A required meeting with his five-member committee was on Friday so he elected to study well before he departed for the City. He could afford three or four hours at leisure with this lovely lady and her Chinese housekeeper. Only a few times he had been able to skip his rituals and take the BART under the bay to Green Street.

At supper Friday night, he met a friend, Mark, in the cafeteria. This student, from Vermont, had only arrived recently and was finishing his first full year as a Freshman. "You look tired, Jerry," Mark was careful not to impose on matters that pertained to health. Yes, it was true. Jerry listened well to this fellow East Coast immigrant. It was only that this young man, Mark, was grateful that he had found a person so devoted to geology as he was, himself. While they had become acquainted, each was not totally adept to appreciating the worth of a close relationship. They were too busy; they really did not have much in common, other than their strong interest in science. This fact of a meager friendship—if one actually existed—became an obvious point of reference. It triggered Jerry's sudden realization that he was now aware of William Kaplan. Once, on an incidental moment when music was mentioned, Mark admitted that he did not know anything about a piano but that he did care for Rock and Roll. Jerry hoped, then and there, while Mark finished his supper, that he had taken more time to write that letter to make it better than it actually was, if he had just spent more time on it before he mailed it.

William probably never had given that whole incident in the café a second thought. Jerry wished that he had written a better one. Mark asked him again, "Hey, Jerry, are you off in left field?" The Freshman realized that Jerry was thinking alone, somewhere, in his own little world. An apology was forthcoming.

That morning he looked in the mirror while he was shaving and decided that he was too unsure about that first letter he wrote to a complete stranger, more or less, one who played the piano expertly, a talent he wished he could have. He even remembered that his father wanted him to study piano but his younger brother was far more adept at artistic impulses than he. But he was who he was. He told his reflection that he was a scientist instead of a musician. "I work differently than musicians no matter what Geoff had said." The water he splashed on his face muffled his further comment. "I have chemistry tables, beakers and Bunsen burners. I'm happy with my chemistry tables, beakers and Bunsen burners, items that I can pass on to Mark."

For two years he felt right at home in Berkeley. He had never felt more at ease with all the work ahead of him, according to the Brit. Apparently Dr. Nelson did like him right away, and Jerry was enchanted by this man's crisp accent. When they had time, over lunch one day, the New Yorker became acquainted with Oxford. Mrs. Nelson had sounded a bit different, having come from Yorkshire. Now, it was time for him to become acquainted with Dr. Clark, an American from Bakersfield, California, wherever that was. Jerry got out his map and there it was, the nice city just east of the bay. This Dr. Clark was just as helpful.

Mrs. Ursula Griswold had successfully become a Californian since moving to the Bay area right after WWII. She had always been pleased to know of her nephew's decision to study at Berkeley rather than anywhere else. The air and weather were somewhat of a change and surprise for him. The breezes off the bay brought a coolness he was not used to, for his birthday month, or for the summer, for that matter. "I want to have Li prepare for you whatever you want." He had mentioned that he wanted Chinese food more than once and Li, Chinese that she was, opened here thick recipe book and bought the ingredients. One time, prior to this anniversary, Jerry tried to explain that he wanted to cook it himself, but Li said "no." After two years Jerry became better acquainted with this Oriental and finally succeeded in his own attempt. By now, he knew how to hop on the BART and whisk himself over to Green Street by six-thirty or so. The ritual of study and schedules allowed him to do just that, to close up shop by four, turn out the lights in the lab, and be on his way.

Before he arrived at Berkeley's terminal, he made one stop at the post office. He was surprised, and he did not have many such surprises on campus or anywhere. He found a letter postmarked Denver from William Kaplan. He glanced at the address as he slowly retreated and found his way to the station just three more blocks. He discovered two pages of hand written greeting and while he dodged pedestrians, he began to read. He was surprised. He decided to sit on a bench while he did so. It was dated four days ago but the postmark that he read again was two days later. The writing was not necessarily neat but he was able to grasp every word. To think that a professional classical pianist took time to write him was somewhat of a joy which he felt, the emotion coming from deep inside him, something he was not used to experiencing. He always thought that he was a scientist; he was surprised by the emotion that surged from somewhere in his body. He read the letter the second time but his watch told him that he must go. Then, perhaps, if he wanted to, he could read it again. And that is exactly what he did. The ride to Market Street was uneventful save for the sway and tilt of the railroad cars as the train sped under the water. He was used to this transportation going to and from his visits. He did not realize the smile on his clean face nor did he see the commuters who sat with him. Once he laughed out loud and a small girl immediately to his right noticed that, and decided to laugh with him. To her, he quickly whispered, "Today is my birthday!" and the little girl replied with her delightful giggle and greeting. He was more satisfied and she was more gleeful.

When he got off the transfer bus to Green Street, the weather was more brisk and by the time he reached his aunt's house with the steep steps to her front porch, he was glad he brought his coat. He reached the door and knocked.

His aunt's housekeeper answered, with a winning smile when she saw who it was. "Ah, Mister Gerald, come in!" She stepped back as he entered and removed his cap. "I have everything you need to have when you wish to cook Chinese yourself. As they walked into the hallway, she continued, "I have even written the recipe for you to have whenever you wish to learn. I have a pan for you and the oven is ready." She stopped and gestured to the lady seated in the front parlor. Li was said to be fifty years of age but that was deceiving. Her smile, her small stature, her genuine loveliness were enhanced by the red garment she wore under her apron. His aunt rose from her chair to embrace him. She waited while Jerry returned the bear hug. She was used to bear hugs by now.

Mrs. Ursula Griswold, now seventy-five years old, a gracious and loving woman who had been a widow for ten years, had welcomed her nephew with open arms upon his first visit when he appeared to explain his enrollment across the bay. "Well, young man," she said softly, "you are now—what?—thirty-three or less, I cannot remember." He smiled and corrected her carefully with a soft "thirty-two, Aunt Urs." He had always called her that when the entire family was often together in Monticello when he was growing up and joyously content to entertain himself, his father, mother, and Geoff. This brother decided that he did not wish to study a science. He moved to New York City as if that in itself was a means of livelihood. "Sit down, please, and we can chat while Li finishes with the preparation of your dinner." Li nodded her head in agreement, "I will have it shortly. You sit and talk." This was said with a wide grin before she retired to her kitchen.

"You never did return to Monticello, did you, after Uncle Al died." The family was on his mind the moment he stepped into the front hall. A large photograph in an old gold frame was hanging on the cherry encasement just below the stairs. Another one, encased in a proper frame, hung above the hearth. "Mother never did come to see you." Only recently did he think that was odd.

"She did once, in August one year when it was cold." She smiled at him again. "I guess you're getting along fairly well with your studies. Oh, I'm so proud of you, Gerald. MIT and now U.C. I don't think I would ever understand geology, stones and rocks, except maybe the rocks that I have in the small garden in the back of the yard. You've seen them, of course. They've been there forever."

"Aunt Urs," Jerry interrupted. He stood and removed his jacket. "Remember I mentioned to you about a pianist name of William Kaplan?" She did remember. "Yes, I do."

"He wrote that he may be coming to The City on business." She noticed how his eyes glistened with an excitement not present when he arrived. "I received his letter just today. Here! Let me read a portion of it to you." He produced it from a pocket and unfolded it. He found the part. "You may want to know that I will be playing a concerto with the San Francisco Symphony in November, before Thanksgiving, I think it is." Already she was interested. "Possibly I can meet you somewhere if you are not too busy with your studies. I know what it is to be involved with studies. I'm fairly that way, myself, with my music, I mean." He paused because the rest of the letter would be foreign to her, not knowing how they met in the first place. He folded it and replaced it in the envelope. But she did realize that it was a very important piece of correspondence, evidently, by the way he looked down at his hands and the manner in which he glanced at her and grinned. It was a large smile, in his eyes, too.

She was remembering, in Monticello, how curious he was when a child, when he read stories from his books, how he wept on the spur of the moment, often without realizing what his tears meant. One time, when the two boys were preteens, Jerry was involved with a book. Aunt Urs noticed him by pure accident while he sat in the window seat. He was engrossed by its contents. Across the years he retained this love of reading. "Look at Gerald," she whispered to his mother, "He does like to read, doesn't he?" Now, so many months and books later, she was able to see how perceptive he became in writing, in correspondence, in books— be they about stones and rocks—that he showed when merely a child. Yes. It was something she noticed as he sat opposite her, waiting for dinner, to read the letter from this new friend. She noticed, too, that he had grown into a fine young man with a nice head of hair and those blue eyes that reminded her of her brother, a strong manner in which he held himself when he stood or walked. She noticed things like that. And polite, yes, polite, because his parents taught him and his brother the manners that young men must possess. Deportment was the word she remembered. Just in these last two months, she discovered a different nephew. She was rather pleased.

Li came in to announce dinner. They saw immediately how the sweet Chinese lady had set the table with fine china that manifested an intricate porch design with lovely Chinese ladies with their fans, all under a large tree in summer. Li joined them at the table for the food was served family style, just the way Aunt Urs wanted it. "Happy Birthday, Gerald. My, but it's grand having you in Berkeley where we can see each other often."

"Thank you, Aunt Urs. I'm happy." She smiled at him. "I'm happy to be with you and Li." And to that, the handsome lady graciously took his hand for a prayer which she had managed for every occasion at this table.

Jerry admired this old house for the months that he had been coming for short visits. A lovely two-storied Victorian design with a large gable for a roof which had its own small room, it was situated on an incline of the hill not two blocks from Coit Tower. He had learned of its gingerbread architecture from his mother to whom Ursula had mailed several pictures when she and Albert moved in 1945, right after he had been discharged from the war. He had remembered that his father was always complimentary of this sister. Ursula always seemed to possess a pleasant stature, a person who was careful of her own posture and bearing. She was elegant, he thought, yes, elegant. That was the word. Ursula nodded to Li, rose after dinner, and spoke to her nephew.

"Now, I want to show you a room you haven't seen since it's been redecorated." She preceded him into the hallway and turned to her right. "This is something your new friend . . . William, his name?" and Jerry nodded, "William will like, I'm sure."

They stopped at an archway whose two doors were enveloped by the wall. It was at one time a study of sorts but now contained a shiny black baby grand piano. "a notion of my husband," she began, "When we lived in Monticello. When you and your brother were little, Albert and I attended theatre. Also, when we found something we liked with the Philharmonic, we'd make a weekend of it. Your father did not especially care for such goings-on, but we didn't care." Jerry listened attentively and when they moved into the main room, he became more enchanted with stories he and his brother had never heard. "It's a wonder to me that as you grew up, you professed a genuine interest in science while Geoff was just the opposite, so to speak." Li entered with the suggestion of coffee. "Or maybe you'd like some wine?"

Jerry said no, that he would just as soon sit and listen to his aunt. He leaned forward, placing his elbows on his knees and folded his hands. Actually, he thought about that piano and, of course, of William. A thousand words passed through his brain and he discovered a new avenue of emotions, something he thought he did not possess or at least did not now realize that he had for a number of years. That was strange because scientists work without emotions. Somebody told him ages ago and he did not know whether to believe it or not. It was something that his ebullient brother would often throw at him when discussing the difference between any scientist—choose one—and, say, Jackson Pollack or Arthur Rubinstein. "I'm glad you do have it, that piano, I mean. I'll mention that to him." And then, in an after thought, for he could see how she was smiling, "I want William to meet you . . . sometime."

And then he rose and looked at his watch. "Aunt Urs, I have to go." He stumbled around with thank you words,. but he was sincere. He kissed her forehead and when Li returned to say goodbye, she had a paper bag full of goodies. "For you, Mr.Gerald." and she added, "from the cookie monster." He waved and smiled. In another moment, he was at the porch, closing the door, hastening down the street to watch for a bus to Market Street. The July night was cool and he shivered slightly, securing his cap and his jacket before he looked into the bag to see what oriental goodies Li had given him. He really wanted to hurry and get to his room to see, if by chance he could calm down and try to write a letter to William. What is happening to him? What, indeed, is going on in his scientific mind?

Chapter Eleven

DRESSED CASUALLY IN AN open-collar T shirt and slacks, William sat alone at the breakfast table. He was at his usual rested self before his day began, before he set his mind to categorize the music ahead of him that he must master. A cup of black coffee waited on a napkin in front of him which was part of this ritual. He made his toast and selected grape jelly from the fridge. He was, in a pure sense of the moment, quite pleasant and was assured that he had written exactly what he had wanted to say to Gerald Champion in that letter. While he had not yet firmly decided on whether to begin any specific correspondence with this U.C. Berkeley student, he was glad that he, at least, was thoughtful to respond with that first letter to him.

William was not in the habit of answering any sanguine notes, especially from idolatrous teenagers. He had received a variety of such letters and notes sent to him from Ray H. But in this Jerry Champion's letter something quite honest about the simple words glared at him from that piece of paper ripped from his spiral notebook. But Raymond Hicks had a habit of screening any letters that this agent received; very few fan letters ever got to William in the first place. His agent was a good agent. He could site an over-indulgent fan a mile away. William did give this some thought at this early hour of the morning. He reached a time in his life, this very week, that he could not dismiss the memory of that interlude after that last concert of the tour.

Mrs. Tomassi arrived late last evening from the Windy City. "I hate to startle you since you were so deep in thought." She appeared ready to meet the day. Resplendent in an attractive frock, she paused on her way out the door. "I don't want any coffee this morning," she murmured, "I'm joining your M. DuPres for breakfast at their faculty meeting. I think this is something new for Dr. Graham and his group of teachers." She looked at her wrist watch. "You want me to say anything about the day for you?" She had just returned from another trip to her daughter. "i've earned some more miles on my flying to Chicago and back," she laughed. "Well, the main thing, with a happy thought, is that I welcomed my new grandson into the world." The recounting of her trip was a joy to her. A photographer was present after a week to take the required memory shots. "I picked up the baby and he took our picture!" Then, reluctantly she boarded a plane and returned to reality. "I should own United Air Lines by now, by all the trips I've taken in the past two years alone."

William told her that all was well when she was gone although he did not go into detail about the conversations he had with Freddy Graham and Steven Michael Young until more evidence came his way. July was to be a busy month for her. When he did have a moment to discuss these invitations, "I'll tell you later." She was all excited.

But she did take a moment more and sat down opposite him. "Of course I'm happy for you, William," she had replied. "You certainly deserve the splendid future for yourself. I'm not quite used to the way you professional musicians operate. But I do know what Patty Allen thinks of your progress. She told me. I'm glad you are here in the condo with me so I can learn of this progress." Her remarks reflected the discipline and progression of thought that she managed when she was talking about her volunteering with the symphony. "I don't know too much about the Paris Conservatory. It certainly has a brilliant history. Maurice Ravel and Camille Saint Saens are good examples of French Musical history, whether they studied there or not. Once, about two months ago, I think, I was able to go to San Francisco on behalf of our symphony. Dr. Young was pleased to include me on three or four errands. They had just announced a complete overhaul on their entire workplace, including the auditorium." The lady was hardly ever so vociferous at that hour of the morning. But she was sincere. Before she departed, he felt grateful for this location in her condo. She had been such a delight that he was astounded at the generosity of this matron. Patty Allen Shriner had nothing but kind words for her. This was a mutual admiration society, Shriner and Tomassi.

"I know she is happy she invited you to live in the condo," the teacher told him once soon after he had occupied his bedroom. "She was so alone after Gilberto died. She certainly is not lonely now!" Miss Shriner commented on yet another phase of their lives. "I believe that people are overjoyed when they meet someone special, when a previous person is no longer with them. And I don't necessary mean through a death, although that is usually the case. I want to tell you another thing," and she grinned, "as long as I am on a 'soapbox.' I guess by now you realize I do believe in the way odd developments suddenly appear out of nowhere. Occasionally God will assign a human being to comfort another person—I mean, one who had indeed lost anyone significant in his life." William stopped for he did enjoy her manner in which she devised a small devotion—if that is what he would call it—for it came at the end of this lesson. He did not mind in the least her profound contribution. "No, no," she replied quickly, "don't look at me that way." Then it dawned on her to explain further. "I'm not saying that you took the place of Gilberto. No: that is not the case. Patty Allen Shriner is such a dynamic thinker.—I've know her a long time—that I want to pass that along to you for what it's worth." And then she departed.

A week later, William was waiting in line at the Union cafeteria where he went often to join others for lunch. This time, he was alone. A few people in passing waved a greeting. Directly behind him, speaking to someone else in line was Gary Fuller. William turned to look at him when the cellist called his name softly. It was an ordinary thing to do because many students and faculty knew of William by sight. He was congenial to everyone; that was part of his being well known at the university. There was one time when a stout woman invaded William's table and proceeded to outline her total appreciation for Sergei Vassilievich Rachmaninov. "Do you play Rachmaninov?" She presumed that it was a question to be answered as only the celebrity could, in twenty-five words or less. Luckily, she was called away to join her party.

"I'm glad to see you, William Kaplan." Gary's voice was soft and cordial and his eyes beckoned William to pay attention. "I'm Gary Fuller and we know who you are." He was taller than William remembered and persistent with his quick greeting. "I'm a student here, now, and with a new position with the symphony. I'm rather happy about that, you know! I saw you one morning some days ago when you came into Dr. Young's office downtown as I was leaving." His body was elastic; his eyes were dancing. "Isn't his office fabulous? All those pictures." His voice was quiet and full of an assortment of highs and lows as if he were practicing different pitches in vocal delivery. Gary immediately turned to his companion behind him and reported, "This is Bill Mason, a friend of mine." This was quite an honor for the youngster who did not appear old enough to be a freshman. He seemed delighted and his effervescence showed. Gary casually touched William's arm. "Do you mind if we sit with you?"

Often, when confronted with this type of encounter, William never negated such a request. The stout lady took him by surprise. Just as he was developing some kind of favorable answer, for it is not everyone who knows Sergei's middle name, a gentleman interrupted her and called her to join him. William was in the cafeteria almost every day. Students both in music and in other disciplines nodded to him or smiled when passing. But with this moment a multitude of questions invaded his psyche and he was perplexed. Both these people possessed a manner about them which, while not foreign to him, were slightly offensive. It was the way Gary moved his head when talking to him. This cellist reminded him of people who spoke in their own little worlds and cared not to elicit a reply. It was difficult even for this Bill Mason to interject a thought of his own. Once, when William managed an inquiry to this lad, "Are you a musician too?" but it was with a sudden noise of someone dropping a tray. He did not get an answer. Finally Mason appeared almost absent with nothing much to contribute to the conversation. He stood and announced with an air that he hated to interrupt Fuller's monologue, but that he had to leave. It was with an apology that he had a class and must go.

Gary Fuller ate and talked more slowly at the same time. "This Bill.Mason is a meek little boy." Gary rose once to get a napkin from the cashier but returned with more glib words, simple ideas not worth much in retrospect. He used his bow hand to gesture when he tried to make his points. The other hand hovered over his left shoulder with fingers pointing to his back which was, in itself, a normal position. But there was something a bit fey in this gesture for him. A cloud of doubtful remembrances haunted William. He was not able to define it with the clamor that was increasing in this noon hour. From time to time, William caught the same kind of atmosphere in Gary's dark eyes, the manner in which he refused to look at the pianist when speaking to him.

"I want some more coffee," Gary said quickly after he waved goodbye to Bill. He went to the coffee bar, poured, and returned immediately to make certain that William would not escape him. "I didn't get any desert because you didn't either." He sat not opposite him but to his left where, from time to time, he could verify the brown eyes and the dark beard that was growing. "Well now, William Kaplan, the famous pianist, we're alone at last." Gary looked directly at him for just a few seconds. At this close, the cellist was able to study his features, the clear clean complexion, the speck of food at his mouth which he signaled for William to remove, the stare which he himself returned to Gary. William did not say much during the lunch; he hardly had time. But now William was able not only to think about the musician who insisted on prolonging the lunch hour, but also to assimilate what this stranger possessed that plagued him from the beginning. "I read all about you recently in the paper, some column written by Stewart Parker. I remember that name because back home in "no place" Wyoming, we have some Parkers who think they are the answer to everything. One of those Parkers, however, did, actually make a name for himself. He played cello with the New York Symphony under Toscanini. He came back to "no place" Wyoming and is the one who got me interested in learning to play it. That was eons ago. The result turned out okay, if I may be so bold as to brag. Imagine, two cellists in the same little town. What you see is what Denver U. got!" He took a bite and continued. "Do you read this Mr. Parker's column in the *Post?*"

"I don't have much time to read the paper. Some times, I do."

"He is the Arts editor, I guess, or at least he has reviews on music. Already he heard about the Paris thing and I must say, it was well written. I hope to play a concerto with you some day." Gary took a sip from his coffee as William rose and started to move. "Oh, you're leaving?" Gary was instantly on his feet. "I enjoyed the lunch with you, Mr. Kaplan. "I heard a rumor that the symphony is to play the Saint Saens concerto with you upon your return next Spring. So you see, I'll get my wish, after all. Dr. Young has already asked that we include it at the very end of this season." Gary noticed that he was in a hurry. "Goodbye!" Gary offered his weak handshake.

Whether William realized it immediately or not, he was glad to walk from the Union Building and to the bus stop. He looked heavenward when he heard a peal of summer thunder. Ever since this morning rain was imminent. The one-sided conversation with this cellist was predominantly a display of characteristics closely akin to traits he had found in many other artists. They were not new to him. The weak handshake, the wavering eyes which were odd in themselves, the touch on his arm at the first encounter. The more he gave thought to this Gary Fuller the greater the consternation of this cellist became evident. He really did not know exactly why he was baffled by it all. Something was missing to give him a clue to solve the deportment of this youngest member of the Colorado *band*.

Under cover of the canopy where other people waited for the bus, his concern was interrupted by a greeting from two students whom he recognized. Then his hand rested on Jerry's second letter in his coat pocket which he forgot. He must have placed it there to read at another time. He leaned against the rear wall of the canopy to escape the sprinkles of rain. He re-read: "I'm glad to know that you are coming to The City on business, overjoyed to say the least. I introduced you to my Aunt Ursula at my birthday dinner last night and guess what? She told me again about her piano. It is her baby grand piano in her music room. Uncle Albert was evidently one who liked music and wanted to have one. It is there for you to play when you are here. I am very pleased you responded to my first letter. I like to read so I hope you will have time to let me know how you are and what you are doing. You are quite a good guy and I'm glad we met. I am fine and studying hard on my "stones and rocks" as you like to say. I hardly have been one to write letters but somehow all of a sudden I'm writing letters to you. Whatever that means." He added more in simple prose. Softly, aloud, William uttered "Words that could only come from a jubilant child instead of a college graduate with a Master's in science." No. After saying it, just like he thought, he did not mean it the way it sounded. Jerry was an enigma. He was a person who was so unlike any other person William had ever known. He told himself that he wanted to save these letters and to show them all to Jerry some day when they were old and ridiculously outdated. Perhaps when he and Jerry were old and outdated, too.

When he got to the condo, rain was falling. He waited a moment beside his piano while he thought of this new acquaintance of his. From what he did remember of the man seated on the other side of the table at the café, about his appearance, his posture, his mien, he was immensely glad that Jerry was so unlike Gary Fuller.

Chapter Twelve

August 1992

RECENTLY, ONE MORNING AT the kitchen table when he was pouring his coffee and Mrs. T sat opposite him, he was cordial enough but she realized he had a new thought penetrating his mind. She held the morning Denver *Post*. Her eyes glanced at him from time to time without his being aware of her curiosity. She was not psychic at all but she had a way of knowing. It may have been her female intuition. The quiet aura about him was not new. She had noticed it, even when she least expected it but his whole bearing was not as obvious as it was this morning. Perhaps it was his quiet movement about the room, the way he yawned or how he just was not himself. Whatever this attitude signified, she merely accepted it as one of many of his quirks, subterfuge though it may be. The radio played the classical station, at a low volume, melodies that filled the kitchen area but did not spill into the hallway or the piano room. Mrs. T eventually rose, excused herself and did not inquire about how taciturn he was. "I made plenty of Java for you so help yourself," and that was enough before she retired to her suite of rooms to finish her morning habit of correspondence. Her new grandson was on her mind. She closed her door and sat at her desk.

To him, at least, time often had a way of slipping by so rapidly that he did not know exactly what was happening nor how it colored his thoughts. He was startled by what was occurring between this man and him, Jerry, whom he had only met in Berkeley not more than three months ago. He mentioned that incident to no one and only to Vivian just casually. Nothing more was said about it. The house phone rang; he grabbed it. The guard downstairs was calling. It seemed that Vivian left a letter for him on her way to work. He went to get it, thanked the guard, and was glad to see that it was postmarked Berkeley. He was back in the kitchen before he was able to read it. The letter was a simple two line note telling him that Jerry had a telephone and its number. That was all. "Finally," William smiled. He agreed with himself that this one more bit of correspondence, something that nevertheless was what he wanted. He had not mentioned this attitude to Jerry; it was simply a mental wish of sorts.

Odd little things kept reoccurring. He had never been to Monticello, New York and he knew nothing of the Massachusetts Institute of Technology. The two or three letters that existed between them came via Vivian's apartment address. Those from Jerry to him were minimal in length and bordered on the simple attempt to be friendly and that appeared to be enough for the moment, it seemed. But Jerry once did explain that he was surprised—he had used the word elated—that even though this letter business was meager, at first, that William was able to find a drop or two of uniqueness that resembled sincerity. Those in answer were but the same. He could not understand, yet, how they mattered so much to either of them. Jerry had once explained that he was not the kind of letter writer that he wanted to be but that he did appreciate the worthwhile replies that William found time to return. "William," he said, early on, "your words are well chosen, more so than mine could ever be. I'm just glad that you did not think I was some kind of a fool for attempting to write you in the first place." Later, in the last letter that came, Jerry mused, "Frankly, I can't imagine just why I wrote you originally. After I mailed it, I felt a little silly that you might read it as just another fan letter. I needed to ask you if it was ok to write you and that you did not think I was too forward in this process My father really liked classical music and my brother, too. When you did write that first letter to me, all doubt just disappeared. After letter number two, I began to imagine that something valuable was happening to me. That was an unusual ending for a person who presumed he could not write well. Or maybe it was because Jerry presumed that the pianist was imagining that something valuable was happening to him as well. Maybe that is what Jerry wanted. The budding geologist had a different feeling. One that did not remain an integral part of his scientific thinking. Jerry decided to rise above any degree of sentimentality. He never did wish to be too maudlin. He did recall how he felt on that last nanosecond at U.C. as he stood on the curb after they shook hands just before he disappeared. He wanted his letters to be crisp and honest. This concert pianist was way out of his league. He was not a scientist. Jerry told himself he must remember that. This artist had no concept of what a geologist was, or what he was studying. This science was definitely not of his ilk. A part of the mysterious aura about this Mr. Kaplan had become the foundation for letters in the first place; at least that is part of what Jerry imagined. A scientist had to imagine and hope and perceive and desire. That thought was all well and good. It was part of being a scientist. Maybe concert pianists had to possess imagination, hope to a large degree, and as certain his own desires. For a strange moment,

Jerry agonized that he was forcing his own logic upon this artist. He was foreseeing possibly that this Kaplan would imply a close relationship which the pianist could not accept. He wrote to him, anyway. This was after he had rushed his new telephone number to William.

This last letter lay on William's bed table open for five days before he had a comfortable time to respond. M. DuPres demanded that he spend some time in lessons. The Frenchman had much to explain about Camille Saint Saens. William had learned long ago that this dynamic instructor maintained his own manner of instruction and that he should never object to the degree of persistence that only this man from Gaul could supply. William did find, after all, time to write concerning the Paris opportunity but did not go into detail more than likely until he received explicit instructions. He did, however, enlarge on a few more personal opinions but discovered how difficult his attempt was to talk about Vivian Cole and Kevin. As much as he wanted to be specific in a defining reference, he could not know just how Jerry would relate, since he was not acquainted with the two people involved. But yet he did feel compelled to write. That was what was so strange about it. Jerry welcomed the news. This latest letter from Denver was almost as delicious as the Union cafeteria chocolate cake. And coffee.

William did not practice any that morning in mid-August when he received a phone call from Maestro Young. It was Mrs T who answered. "Good morning, I'm glad to reach you." She sounded excited when she answered. When she called William to his phone, the conductor greeted him. "Can you come see me sometime this a.m.? Mable will put your name on the appointment book if I tell her when you'll be here! Drop everything. It's some more good news!" The pianist gave a time. "Okay. Eleven it is."

Mable was all smiles as William passed through her gate. She was holding her Wagnerian helmet in one hand and a dust rag in the other. "I'm getting it ready for a party at Maxine's Bar and Grill." She quickly handed him an invitation. "Here. For you in case you'd want to come. It's costume. Wear something dashing. Your swim suit!" Her phone rang and interrupted her gleeful comments.

Dr Young pulled him into his office. It seems that he received another epistle. "I think this is good news. At least it may develop something great for you and your future. Let's go sit down over there." They proceeded to the leather chairs away from his desk. "I got this just this morning from your friend and mine, Mr. Hicks, explaining that William should confirm to the management of the San Francisco Symphony that he is to report next week merely to converse and settle arrangements for their rehearsal times before the Thanksgiving concert. Yes, Mozart is fine, yes, the salary is okay, yes, the orchestra will have only so many hours to practice with the soloist, and those practice times will encompass a week at the most, yes, the hotel bill will be paid by the symphony budget. Raymond Hicks was at his usual vivacious self, full of excitement and glory for everyone. He finished this epistle full of instructions with the piece of news that his life was healthy and that he lost five pounds. The reference about loosing five pounds was on a scrap of paper with an added scribble that his doctor gave him another new pill to take.

"Okay, my boy," the maestro added, "let me tell you what is happening with the San Francisco Symphony. Very simply, it's this: the beautiful building in which they are located—among those of the plaza known as Civic Center—yes, yes, I know you've been there as well as I have. The building is fine but I gather from what Arthur Preston wrote," and Dr. Young flipped the letter to William, "Preston is the band's manager, that for some reason the management and work areas are in the process of being changed. You are to be aware that you will encounter these drastic new interior designs whatever they are.

"Dr. Young could see anticipation on William's face. "They want you there in the coming week. They have to practice with you now—in August—because this apparently is the only time they can arrange to get to see what you look like, how you play, et cetera et cetera. Their first concert requires a goodly amount of time and effort coming as it is in early October and your Mozart thing is far more readily creative than for a "last minute" get-together." William looked as if he had a heavy question mark hanging over his handsome head. "Okay . . . okay," the maestro took a moment to breathe, "I'll explain it over food further because I am hungry and you are always hungry. With all this in mind," Young joked, "I should be getting a cut in these expenses for being your Denver agent!" As a last bit of Chamber of Commerce he added, "August is cold in San Francisco. Mark Twain said so."

Chapter Thirteen

WILLIAM FOUND MORNING HOURS in which to concentrate on his practice. Miss Shriner's admonitions about laziness and sleeping late rebounded often. He learned long ago to drink his coffee early, walk around the block, and always say hello to the guard downstairs. Even though she came to the condo twice a month, this dear teacher was present with him every time he sat at the keyboard. First, the scales to warm those fingers and oil the brain. She was insistent on aiding her friend at times when he no longer remained the frequent student that he was. For some time now he progressed beyond the valued lessons that they once had together. In this sense, Claude DuPres attained the same level but this Frenchman still enjoyed the status of professor emeritus to the pianist. He was always there to guide him, especially through the avenues of French culture. "You must understand what goes on in the mind of Saint Saens," DuPres kept reminding him. "We French are very artistic." With the advent of Paris in the Spring of 1996, William felt more closely associated with this celebrity and his instruction. Miss Shriner was becoming less frequent now. That arrangement was most suitable to both the Frenchman and the student. Mrs. T remained pleased with his progress. She managed her volunteer work at her church then, so this allowed him to proceed with the two assignments, those of playing Mozart for the people of The City by the Bay and the French music lovers in The City of Light on the Seine.

All of this had no longer been "new" to him. He established a specific discipline in order to "learn and grow" as Miss Shriner's words echoed. She underscored her lessons and repeated them when he was but an eight-year-old learning exercises. He had forgotten *Kitten on the Keys*. That music was no longer in the piano bench. Today, in the condo, when he became bored with his artistic struggle he would shout angry epithets at the score, adult though he was, and go all the way to the ground floor, out the main double doors, and sit alone on the top step to stare at the sidewalk or watch his neighbors come and go. He presumed that reliving a habit of his when he sat on the front steps of the Sterling house and felt Angus's cold nose rub against his left cheek that he would begin to feel more confident, perhaps better. Now that he entered his thirties, eons later as he enjoyed tabulating his maturity, such an immature gesture was looked upon as one of his childish tantrums.

He looked at himself in the mirror every morning when he shaved and smiled, not especially at himself but he realized that he was about ready to embark on the next adventure. He was even excited that he would be able to see the hills of his favorite city again. It was his favorite city, long before Raymond Hicks obtained a booking in Berkeley for him. Today he would speak to Dr. Young and buy his air ticket for Oakland. Since April, he had developed his mind, his exercises, his curiosity considerably, enough to anticipate whatever was ahead for him, not only with the contingency of the symphony and seeing the two Bridges again, but with the adventure of this new acquaintance, whatever the latter could imply. He was used to business tactics with complete strangers although he would not assume that this Champion fellow was a complete stranger. And at best, Raymond Hicks had been a good agent, somewhat weird at times, with a wild imagination more than anyone he had ever known. But the New Yorker would guide him through this preparation for Mozart, for certain: Hicks, along with the beloved Steven Michael Young. William tried to determine which would be more hazardous.

Concertizing was "old hat." He was no longer apprehensive. Just in the last year he restudied the history of several enigmatic composers, those who professed an interesting life span full of highs and lows, pianos and fortes as he was able to deduce. Long ago he became aware of the lives and loves of the European masters, those nineteenth century brilliant artists many of whom cared to endorse the adage *Art for Art's Sake*. Even the American counterparts joined their lot. They composed because they wanted to promote emotions, to 'say' things as only their music could provide.

M. DuPres was guilty of introducing him to all of these masters. Time and again, despite how he endeavored religiously to say in English the specific word he wanted—and to make certain that William understood the emotional complication *behind* the lesson—this Frenchman often struggled too dramatically. The American instructor teaching Music History, for example, was never dramatic enough. This historian did not even play an instrument. But that was just the way it was. Practically everyone on campus, whether a musician or not, learned of Du Pres' fervor. After all, he was European. Du Pres worked, often struggled with his English, to say exactly what he wanted to tell William. A case in point was Tschaikowsky and that woman whom he never met. What was yet another matter was the manner in which Hicks had tried to explain to William once four or five years ago; this agent, always emotional, very much a *kook* as some people called him, had urged him more than once to move to New York. Hicks had always been one to ignore the pros and cons of Colorado. "This is *where it's all at*" became the salutation to letters he mailed to William. "I can't for the life of me understand why on this silly earth you insist on staying there," and he ended with "Good grief!"

Steven Michael Young soon became the Denver go-between. William had no concern whatsoever for protocol. He had no time for arguing or the consulting procedure. Long ago his concentration was his music, a fact which often mystified almost everyone but remained a significant trait of his personality. He wanted nothing more than to play his instrument. That is how many of his friends looked upon his unique talent. Even Vivian Cole, who was at this moment involved in trying to determine Kevin's convoluted mind, was at a loss to comprehend her beautiful husband's shenanigans with sex.

This concern alone made William put down the metronome one day to escape the confines of his keyboard. He did not go down to the main entrance, wave at the guard, or sit by himself on the front steps. During the few recent years, William ignored what many would argue that the artist should never pay attention to what anyone else would say about his personal life or how he could enjoy the beauty and depth of his work. Only Miss Shriner and the Frenchman had permission to chart that course for him. Those who were the artists, that is, the painters, the theatre actors, even the film celebrities and those devoted to the music world were off in their own little worlds alone and often by themselves. This was true, regardless of what the tabloids would print about Mr. and Mrs. Movie Star. Allowing Vivian's day to day comments about her husband should never interfere with what Mozart and/or Saint Saens was trying to tell him. He returned to the metronome and his keyboard regardless what people would think . . .

Maybe this was on his mind so much that he had no time to pursue this doctrine with Jerry Champion. At this point in time, when a few doubts began to sift through his mind, he did wonder, and often, how this theory of aloneness affected the young geologist, especially in his work to attain his doctorate. Jerry was beginning to mean a great deal to him in the long run. That was not too difficult to understand. Maybe what Jair—as he began to call him—had professed, what he subtly suggested between the lines of his quick notes, was the basis for all this opinion. In the last letter this Champion wrote, he intimated that his past was not altogether as good as he had wanted it to be. It was tinged with a closet full of skeletons, or the letter most certainly made that ingenious suggestion. Adventures at M.I.T. remained clandestine and mysterious and that perhaps someday . . . "I'll tell you all about them, because I want to tell you." That is what he wrote. This was directly from his last letter and William recovered it merely to read it again to make certain that is exactly what Jair had written.

It was raining again in Denver. He stepped to the window of the room in which Mrs. T's baby grand piano was placed. He was tired. He thought of Jerry and wondered what he was doing on this Saturday afternoon. By now, surely, he received the letter William mailed three days ago. It was the information Jerry needed. *The management there wants to see me in person because evidently that's the way they do things.* Without really knowing why, he sat down on the chair by the window and tried to visualize how Jerry would react to such a vital piece of ordinary news. Actually, William could not comprehend, himself, just how it was that he had begun to give more thought to him anyway. He was not a musician. He was not akin to the study of music in the first place. Jerry remained a scientist and usually scientists are never concerned with sharps and flats and treble staff and cadenzas and the power that only music can evoke.

For that matter, William was not a scientist. He was not akin to Bunsen burners, beakers, nor the study of stones and rocks, the three words which quickly had become a piece of poetry. Jerry had jokingly confronted William in a letter one day to ask for his primary knowledge of what geology is, essentially. William remembered how gleefully both had shared laughter over such a comparison. The rain had made him think of Jerry's bright blue eyes and the manner in which he once had touched his hands. He was glad he had already mailed that letter, for now he could see those same eyes become brighter and he could hear Jerry when he accepted the news.

After his ritual of practice the next morning, William consulted with Steven Michael Young. Mable was pleased to find him in great spirits so she ushered him into the inner sanctum. She did notice a kind of quick movement in his step that she missed in all the many weeks she had become better acquainted with this pianist. "You've been to San Francisco, haven't you?" She tried to make conversation as he passed her desk and aimed for the door into the office. "I mean, before this trip?" He smiled, not at the reason that he had indeed made a tourist venture at one time, but that he admired how buxom she really was, up close. "Oh, yes ma'am!" He knocked and entered.

Dr. Young was not alone. With him, standing as if he were about to exit, was Gary Fuller. "Excuse me!" The cellist spoke first as the conductor was still on the phone at his desk. "Well, now, Mr. Kaplan," he ventured to remark casually, "I see you are heading westward, even if it's just for a week." William noticed his summer shirt, cotton with a design of birds of some sort. He did not appreciate any information about this forth coming trip, even if Steven might have casually dropped the story about this opportunity. William replied quietly, "I'm playing Mozart in November." "Oh," Gary Fuller answered, as he made his way through the office door. "I wish I were going with you!"

Steven hung up the phone and stepped behind his desk to produce some papers and an airline ticket. "That was the manager in San Francisco and he will be seeing you first thing. I couldn't get you on Sunday night but the only seat that was available is Saturday morning. Weekend flights are less frequent than weekdays. Today is . . ." and he looked at his desk calendar, "Wednesday. Flight leaves 10:10 a.m. Can you find somebody to take you? That airport we have now, as you know, is miles and miles out in the country halfway to Sterling." He opened the envelope. "Here is the number the manager wants you to call when you arrive in case no one is there to meet you." He paused as William accepted all the information. "I got your air ticket from the symphony's rainy day fund. At least, that's what I'm calling it. Thank God for the few wealthy tycoons here in Denver who don't know what to do with their money. It is merely to help you and wish you good journey for a good cause." There was something about his statement that reflected a gratitude for being able to answer the request that he play with such a notable orchestra.

Perhaps Gary Fuller was here to accept good wishes, too. Maybe Steven was grooming this cellist to take over the chair number three. The current occupant, an elderly man, had given notice recently that he was retiring. William did not give it any more thought, but he did remember the remark from Gary at lunch some time ago that he just came to Denver from some place in Wyoming. "Come tell me goodbye on Friday," was the good doctor's word as he waved a quick hand.

When he had the opportunity once he was back in the condo, he telephoned the airline. "There's been a slight mistake," he began to explain, "I want to go to Oakland. Can you change my reservation, please?" In a moment he had the affirmation. And then he telephoned the number Jerry had given him. It was located, Jair had said, in his dorm room. On the second ring, he answered. He sounded tired. But the moment when William spoke, electricity shot through his veins. Arrival time, that Saturday morning, Oakland airport, United, flight number, please come for me, I have a lot to tell you. Jair sounded like he was ready to fight giants. There. That's done. Now he can get back to Mozart. And maybe Saint Saens.

Chapter Fourteen

WITH A HISTORY OF five letters in each direction which did not include the note with Jerry's telephone number, William was surprised that he had answered all of them. Ordinarily he was not much of a correspondent himself, with more time spent on the keyboard in Mrs T's large apartment. He made certain that whenever he practiced the piano room was muffled as best as he could arrange. Her own personal rooms were far to the opposite end of the hallway but she did comment once that when he played, she would often stop and listen.

He was bit apprehensive about this trip to the West Coast in the first place. Dr. Young was specific about the time element for this meeting with the orchestra, early as it was. The first concert required more rehearsal days to be performed first in October. it was the involved music and dance of *Carmina Burana*, a selection delayed from two seasons ago. The area for the orchestra and, in this case, space for the dancers of the Corps de Ballet, was considered by many to be too small for such an undertaking. That was the original contention. The Mozart concerto was to be the second performance and the only time their manager decided for *its* booking was the Saturday before Thanksgiving week. The entire personnel were to take a two-week break before the instrumentalists were to concentrate on the concerto. So now was the only time Kaplan was to be introduced to the orchestra. It was an odd situation but it had to be that way. The management and rehearsal rooms were under total redesign. An apology was already given to William. He thoroughly understood with the help of Dr. Young.

When his plane landed at Oakland, rain had been falling there for an hour. William remembered what Steven Michael Young had joked about August weather and how cool it was. The breezes that blew in from the bay, from under the Oakland Bay Bridge were not just for August's reputation. White Caps on the water were well known. To the natives, they were part of the history that deserved a paragraph in a pamphlet that the Chamber of Commerce mailed to tourists. He was glad he brought a zipper jacket with his cap. He did not appear in the least a classical pianist but the epitome of a tall casual thirty-year-old wayfarer and a simple cap with U.C. emblazoned on it which Jerry had mailed to him. He was glad the flight attendants had not recognized him.

William was the third to stand to watch the stewardess open the door. He held his briefcase as he proceeded. His eyes eagerly searched for the one person whose eyes were searching for him. He was doubtful that he would recognize Jerry after these days of just correspondence. "Hey, piano player!" was all that Jerry could manage. He grinned as William stood before him, swinging his briiefcase, heavy with music, over his shoulder. Yes, this was Jerry; yes, he remembered that wide grin, those blue eyes. The piano player's smile was as big as the scientist's. They were silent, totally quiet with each one trying to choose something to say. They blocked traffic at the gate. Finally Jerry offered three decent pats on William's back as they strolled through the departure lounge, finally uttering greetings but all at the same time. with all the hesitancy each could bear. That seemed suitable. Then they grinned again, this time, William, seeing for the first time, how large and wide Jerry's smile actually was when he laughed out loud as they turned and pushed through the crowd to the baggage carousel.

"You look like a student at U.C.," Jerry laughed, "with that cap I sent you!" They spoke together, laughed some more as Jerry took the small bag. William lifted his right arm to enclose Jerry's shoulders. They had no words for the while, very likely because each did not know what to anticipate. "I have a car. I mean," and he began to try to find words, "one of the students in the lab offered her car to come get you. She's waiting in a lot about a block away. She wants to meet you, celebrity that you are! She's been asking questions."

"What did you tell her, that I was a good looking movie star?" They laughed at that. "I'm . . . ." and William too was trying to find words which easily eluded him. "You look great! For one who is on the verge of a doctorate."

"I'll admit to that," Jerry laughed again, seeing how William's eyes lit up after the absence of three months and those letters. "I have a little 'saying' which I learned from my days spent in Mass. We're both good looking. I don't fuck around with unattractive people!" That remark was like a bombshell but it caused both of them to break out in uncontrolable laughter. That was the first time the pianist had heard Jerry improvise! "I didn't improvise, Billy," Jerry was quick to respond. "I learned a lot of life when I was at M.I.T. and I'm older now." He found himself staring at the musician. "What's happening to us, you rascal?" That was the first time he had used that moniker. William reached up to muss Jerry's hair.

They found the car and the student was waiting, leaning against the driver's side holding her umbrella. Another girl was with her, sitting in the front seat. After introductions, Jerry placed the larger bag in the trunk. William sat in the back seat and Jerry slid in beside him. The rain was decreasing. The traveler was nice to pretend he was listening to the chatter from the front seat, but he was not especially hearing what the girls said. He sat quietly to watch Jerry as he answered as well as he could. Too often, the geologist stole a look at William and professed an awkward moment when he apparently did not hear what was asked. "I'm sorry, what did you say?" William noticed a class ring on the left hand that rested beside him, something he missed when they were standing at the curb after that concert. Jerry noticed that he was curious. "MIT, my master's, Good grief! That was ages ago." They both were at a loss for words. It was apparent but only to them that a world of questions and answers about anything was waiting. "What's the price of eggs in China?" perplexed Jerry until, through laughter, William began to explain the meaning of that question which he had bantered between him and Vivian. He was surprised when William reached over to touch the ring.

William perceived a different kind of Jerry, one who was a great deal more relaxed and attentive than when they sat over sandwiches and wine. He had written those letters but to hear him speak now that they were there, the geologist was more talkative. He outlined for him a typical day in class, in the library, in his pint-sized apartment or with his instructors who anticipated Jerry's every question. Suddenly, Jerry grabbed both hands and softly commented how amazing they can play those numbers he heard last April. He reached over and patted William on the back. Softly he uttered, "Hey! I'm glad to see you again, Billy!"

And so later, after all the thanks to the driver, they found themselves in the lab to where Jerry had to return, to determine if any freshmen were working. They were in, and out, with the ceiling lights off, the door closed, locked after they stowed the two bags in a closet. In the dim hallway, on a Saturday, with no one on the appointment list to study, they stood together, like two nervous kids, staring at each other. As they walked slowly forward to reach the lobby again, they mumbled a few words. William could see that Jerry was attempting as good a conversation as he could manage, even when he was far more comfortable now than at the airport. "What's this eggs in China thing?"

Each was not alone, writing two-page letters with words that came easily because they had time to think about text. Now they sauntered along a sidewalk empty of pedestrians with the exception of a student or two, one with his dog. They laughed again, for no reason other than each was glad to see each other. William felt comfortable being here, seeing for the first time this person, this stranger. An acquaintance had to begin some time, some method, an attempt for both of them, first to comprehend how it all began last April. At least, this was their beginning, solidified with correspondence and cemented with this first moment or two to grab whatever they could make of it. Each discovered that both were staring at each other. *What is happening to us?* With no verbal question from the piano player, Jair repeated the question out loud.

For the whole last three months had been a weird compilation of words, reflections, efforts to tell what was on their minds. It was a good exercise in creative letter composition. They were writing to help solve the situation of how they met and why it was important for them to continue this charade of correspondence when, from the beginning they really could not discern why, exactly, they were writing long notes. They commented on this paradox, or at least each tried to do so. They could not provide an immediate and logical answer why they were here. But they were! It was August and William understood perfectly why he was to be in the Bay area. Suddenly they stopped and embraced each other for no reason whatsoever. They did not understand why, just that something was happening, because he agreed on this. By the time they realized they were hungry, after they found the small café near the auditorium, they laughed some more. It was all perplexing, a series of inexplicable events that were shrouded in a nice mystery. "We're not eating here," Jair confdied, "I have a surprise for you."

Two hours later, after having obtained the two bags from the lab closet, they stood before the desk at the hotel on Geary Street just west of Union Square. The clerk was a fastidious and organized one to receive guests. His uniform was a neat suit, with his blond hair in place, and his orange tie was the color that all employees wore. He looked at his reservation card and then at Jerry. "Oh, Mr. Kaplan," he gushed, and when he did, several other employees including the one bell hop turned their heads. "you're . . . the concert pianist we were expecting." He would have continued to deliver his well-intended greeting politely at Jerry, who giggled and replied softly while pointing, "No. *He* is Mr. Kaplan." The clerk was astonished. Embarrassed, he found words, "Oh, yes, of course. Well. We have you on the third floor as . . ." and he glanced at Jerry the second time, "a party of one." William confirmed and instantly the bell hop was at his side to claim the luggage. "I believe we have you for at least four days, if that is correct. I hope everything is satisfactory for your stay in San Francisco. May we say, welcome!" He then added furtively, "and, sir, my I have your autograph?"

Once in the room after a crowded elevator ride in which two ladies gawked at the two of them, Jerry waited patiently while William opened his big case, extracted his one suit, and hung it in a closet. Then, he put his carry-on bag on the dresser and took a deep breath. He stopped and looked at Jerry once again. As if the two of them were on cue, Jerry walked over to William and gazed into his eyes. "Please," he began, because he felt that this pianist might not necessarily know what he was thinking, for he slowly lifted his right arm and patted William on the back for the second time. It was four longer and stronger welcomes than when they were stranding on the sidewalk on the campus in front of the science building. "Excuse me," he mumbled, "but I had to do that. I promised myself that I needed to see what you thought." Jerry waited momentarily to learn how this new friend would react. He released him and stood, peering into his eyes again. After one split second during which a million thoughts raced through his mind, William returned his gaze and smiled. He returned the embrace and softly laughed in Jerry's left ear.

"And now, Mr. William Kaplan, superman at the piano," Jerry giggled, "wash up because my Aunt Urs is expecting us for dinner at her house."

Chapter Fifteen

THE SCIENTIST AND THE musician stepped down from the bus. From the curb they watched it proceed northward on Columbus Avenue and into the hills of the residential area to their left until it disappeared just south of the Embarcadero and Pier 39. They waited while traffic cleared so they could cross Green Street to proceed eastward. Jerry pointed to Coit Tower hovering stately before they spied Aunt Urs's house, along the north side of the damp street. They halted just a few feet from the stairs that led upward to her small narrow front porch.

Jerry wanted to show the view that he had always admired. Once at the top at porch level, they turned around, and beheld the panorama to the south, including the Pyramid Building. The Catholic Church where Aunt Ursula worshiped was to their far right at Washington Square. Immediately Jerry sat down on the top step and motioned for William to join him. That was quite a surprise because it reminded him of how he himself sat on his own front porch and leaned against the railing with his feet two steps below him. "I want to make sure you see this view first. Isn't it terrific! I learned to accept this place because the way the porch is designed, we're at the top of everything. Aunt Urs is waiting and I bet you anything she is in her favorite chair in the parlor." He waited a moment longer. "I'm glad you're here, Billy." The rain had stopped long ago. Traffic passed on the block.

Her house was a tall, thin one, the first of its kind that William entered. It rested on a high foundation with many steps to the front portico and a garage that was partially hidden to the right of the front area. It was 'Gingerbread' in design as were so many other such homes on Green Street. Like many of them, this home was constructed shortly before the famous earthquake. That disaster with the northern edge of the Fire did not reach this neighborhood but obviously became a logical cite of rebuilding for a great many families. Several of these houses were cataloged as priceless edifices. Aunt Ursula and her husband were pleased to find one.

Li was in the kitchen and did not hear them enter. This small delicate Chinese lady laughed her welcome and escorted them into the parlor. "Aunt Urs," Jerry began as he stood by her, "Coit Tower is still there." They both smiled because for a lengthy time when Jerry began to learn the history of the city from a book she had mailed to him and his brother, he presumed that the tall tower was destroyed by fire. "This is William Kaplan." He grinned, "My Aunt, Ursula Griswold. Now, I have some ideas for dinner," he continued, "I'll go help Li because I am going to teach her how to make Lasagna." He turned to William. "That's what we're having." Then, without waiting another moment, he removed his coat, hung it on the hall tree standing just inside the front door, grinned at the guest and disappeared into the kitchen.

Mrs. Griswold offered both her hands. "Sit down there, close by so I can be sure to hear you." William saw her as the beautiful woman she was, full of wonder with expressive eyes and a warm manner which flooded her room. She was a small delicate woman herself, wearing a red dinner dress just for this occasion. A pair of glasses dangled on a chain at her neck. Instantly her guest knew right away that he instantly fell in love with her. It was her hair, he decided, full white and coiffed elegantly. "Did Gerald speak to you at all about his family?" All William could do was shake his head, so enchanted by this lady's charm. "His father and I were brother and sister, along with another sister and brother. We're all from lower New York State, in that town that is closest to the Catskill Mountains." William understood how she could reminisce. "A happy family, William; do you want me to call you 'William'?" And to that he smiled. At her gesture he settled more comfortably into a large wing-back chair. "I do like to talk about my family, young man, so you'll have to forgive me!" She sat in her own chair, leaned back, and took another deep breath. "Gerald's mother comes from an Italian family." She smiled when she added, "he may have already told you that. It was she, I think, who taught him and his brother all about cooking. Geoffrey—that's his brother—didn't take to the lessons, I'm afraid. I am certain that is why we're eating Italian, tonight. He learned to cook in that style. Where he rooms now over in Berkeley, he doesn't have any kitchen privileges—perhaps no kitchen at all. So when the weekends come, I usually expect him to burst in on me with a bag of groceries and a bottle of chianti." She decided to add, "We had a lot of love in our family, William. And for a very long, long time, that was most apparent among us all." She turned her head toward the kitchen when she heard laughter from Li. "I'm sure Li appreciates his helping her with the menu. Her kitchen has become quite international." She stopped and applied her handkerchief to her nose. "Gerald tells me you are from Colorado."

To that, William took a leisure time to recite his history, telling her of his sister, now, wife of a doctor, and of Vivian Anderson Cole, who grew up, all three, together in a small town. "I lost an uncle in World War Two." With that he elected not to offer any further explanation, not about his family, perhaps, that could come later, but that he never wanted to discuss war at all. If that occasion would ever arrive, he did not have a clue how he wold exclaim that he is anti-war. He was tactful about that to her for he discerned her affirmation by the way she nodded her head and cleared her throat. With a gentle gesture, she pointed to a nice portrait of a gentleman in a narrow frame that rested on a table at the far end of the room. "My husband, William, was in the war. He is deceased, now."

She mentioned her piano. "Yes, my music," he continued. "Well, you see, I have a special opinion about that. I have a nice teacher back home who helped me realize that what I do have, if I have it at all, is a talent for playing." He promised Miss Shriner that when he would mention her that he would also underscore the statement that God provided the talent for him in the first place. Laughing gently, she stood and motioned for them to visit the baby grand. For a strange reason he was not reticent in his reference to his talent. In fact, he offered a slight giggle as confirmation. "At the university I have a Frenchman who expanded my appreciation. From time to time I still work with him."

He felt comfortable being there. "Jerry mentioned the piano to me in a letter." "Thank you. After dinner, I'd be happy to look at your library. I'll play for you, too, for that matter."

This kind lady rose and proceeded toward the room that was redecorated to accommodate her baby grand; she spoke of how difficult it was to manage to bear the instrument out of the delivery truck, with foour men to move itt up the few steps from the street and through the front door. She offered some music, stowed in a cupboard behind the piano seat. The piano was a Kimball and in tune as he struck a few chords. "I think you'll be surprised to know that you may have an audience tonight." She smiled. "If you don't mind, I've invited my neighbors. Just two people so you needn't be too surprised! I told them who you are and they know you, already, so to speak. Their daughter heard you play in Berkeley when you were there last April. They're neighbors. I took the liberty to bring them over. That comes from how Gerald's father and I used to act instantly on a moment's notice. That was some time ago when we were just kids, in Monticello. If we wanted to walk to the movie house by ourselves we'd do so, often without asking for permission. Before the war . . ." she paused to remember what William's opinion was, "people would walk alone to the park you will discover when you go to Coit Hill. I want you to include that since you're here. We had no need to be escorted." William saw that she was very perceptive from what Jerry had already told him of this lady. He was about to ask her a question when Li interrupted.

She and Jerry had just finished setting the table with wine glasses. "Excuse me, Mr. William, I hope you enjoy wine with dinner. Mr. Gerald drinks cabernet and what do you want?" William smiled to himself and answered, "Jerry knows! It's the same." He hoped that they would put plenty of onions in that dish. Inadvertently he said, "I like onions."

A part of being perceptive, Mrs. Griswold ventured another question but she presumed to know already her answer. She was able to see readily enough, that her nephew had spoken about this young pianist so often that she guessed they were old friends. "Is that the case, or am I wrong?" But there was no time for that answer. Maybe she knew. Maybe Gerald had already told her about the concert at Berkeley last spring. At any rate, she was able to see a definite camaraderie between the two men. Jerry poured their wine and everyone sat at the table. The hostess extended her hands as an invitation for prayer which she delivered most gratefully. Li smiled at both the men as she rose to bring on the dishes. The dinner was a success. From time to time, Jerry could know that it was. From time to time, He stole glances at William.

Rain in August can be a surprise but a blessing. The rain did come when the neighbors did, but all was well. William played and the people applauded. Then, as they left almost immediately, the two men stepped to the front porch to look into the sky and to say goodbye to the couple. An hour later, after the hostess explained about the third bedroom upstairs, William did not need to run to his hotel. "Tomorrow," Jerry suggested, "I'm taking you to a place on Polk Street. It's just an ordinary nice little café that I found one day. That is tomorrow, Sunday. It's the only time I have to show you Polk. This is before you begin your business on Monday morning. I have to get back to 7:00a.m. class because Summer School here has early classes. I'll explain." He looked into the sky where rain blurred everything between them and the Pyramid Tower. With no wind, the drops were gentle. Then he looked directly at William. "I'm glad you're here, or did I tell you?" He didn't wait for any answer. "Aunt Urs likes you. She told me. She whispered in my ear when you were playing tonight. But she always likes your kind of music. She always did, ever since my Dad wanted to learn to play. He did, you know! I don't think I told you that."

"Did you ever learn, when you were a kid?" It was a fair question because William was surprised to hear that music was a part of the Champion Family.

"I didn't. But my brother started to take lessons but somehow he just turned it off." I can remember when the teacher told Dad that Geoff just didn't have the talent that it takes." William accepted this, for he had encountered many children who could not learn. Long ago, Miss Shriner told him, herself, that she was pleased to work with young Billy because God had given him this great art form and she knew it. He had learned to accept this kind of gift in the form of a geologist, too, for that matter. At the start of their long distance communication, he wanted to comment on this but he did not have the time to put this into words. Coming to the West Coast was an answer to a prayer. In the beginning, in early May. He could not allow himself to become obsessed with this student; geology was too foreign to him. But Jerry persisted with letters and little by little, these letters forced William to commit to the gesture of providing answers.

Just how that came to be in the past three months was a baffling mystery. So if that is the case, if he does want to discuss talent, be it music or science, and talent is most apparent in both cases, then now is a good time. After all, he is to be here to talk business on Monday and Tuesday during the day. He can talk all the music he wishes with people for whom he is to play Mozart in November.

He chastised himself for being such a succinct disciplinarian. This man standing next to him on the front porch of this beautiful old house, this geologist come next May, this man means something to him which is relevant and extraordinary, and he must tell him so. He must tell him without writing him letters. He must tell him so because he feels more than merely a compelling urge to do so. He remembered what Mrs. Griswold told him, that Jerry came from a family that knew, most assuredly, what love can do in a family and what love can do for him, as well. He had seen it in Jerry's eyes, in the way he persistently mentioned "togetherness" in nearly all his letters. My God. This man next to him on the wet front porch is an enigma, but a special one, to say the least and very much so, now, to him. So tell him so. He's right here. Tell him now and you won't need to say it for the first time in a letter once you return to reality and your piano back home, in Reality.

So this is the strange change in himself that William began to suspect a week or so before he flew to Oakland. William stole glances at Jair. A million questions were now evident. He was attracted to this geologist and he does not know one smidgen bit about geology or stones and rocks, other than those that were chalk rocks from his back yard which he could use to draw pictures on the front sidewalk. He wants to stand beside him and listen to him talk, about anything, from the price of eggs in China, to the Pyramid Tower, to Coit Tower, to the Eifel Tower to the Tower of London, back to Green Street and the rain tonight and what happens when he puts his left arm around Jerry's neck and smiles at him and watches as Jerry giggles and reaches around William's shoulders and holds a bear hug longer than usual. He doesn't need to write Jerry any of these emotions. They are here. They are on the front porch, and rain is coming down more dramatically than ever and what-the-hell, it is August, 1995, and they both don't care about anything, except now.

Chapter Sixteen

SUNDAY MORNING WAS ONE of two days in which Jerry had to plan something, anything, to show a small portion of the downtown area. His "twenty-nine cent tour" as he called it was just enough space for the time he could spare. It was also amazing that this student learned to evaluate his own time and efforts to conform to a certain ritual by which he could succeed in his study-time and his short moments for his trips to Green Street. Shortly after he escorted his new friend to the hotel, he painfully realized that he did not have the full amount of time for touring. He did not mention any of this problem to William, merely to see that he was secure in the hotel. And so, Jerry had to change courses.

It was all worth the energy. Jerry stood before the counter at the Geary Street Hotel, early, very early, that Sunday morning. By his wrist watch it was eight a.m. The clerk recognized him. "Sir," he politely responded as they both saw William exit the elevator. "There he is now."

Wiliam was first to speak. "When you said eight a.m. you meant it."

Jerry motioned for them to sit near the entrance. "I slept at Aunt Urs' house last night." He proceeded with his explanation that this is the day in which he had schedled for himself, all to himself in the library. Only a few students had their own habits of being 'alone' as he put it. It was always quiet; on Sunday morning, however, he was with William and he could afford the break in ritual. Jerry was hesitant, almost afraid to offer his remarks. He spoke as if he had the complete morning planned . . . William suspected something like this to interfere. There may have been in his own busy life that he had to alter a time for a special meeting with Vivian. This time he could see the siituation in Jerry's face. "I'm afraid I shall have to leave you to yourself. "Oh God," Jair shouted mutely to himself, "please let Billy understand what it means to study for a stupid geologist." William remained quiet because he could not produce any comfort for this new friend . . . He simply did not object in the least The cab ride to Polk Street was numb, for William but more so for Jerry . . .

The small café was full of 'locals' who frequented the place. "When I come here," Jerry confided, "which is not often, any more, I like the omelet." He pointed to the menu. "That one there.". Jerry had regained his ability to converse as if he were the mayor. "After breakfast I'll have to get back to Reality." He reached in his front pocket and produced a drawing. "I drew a map for you from this point to where you will find the Civic Center for tomorrow." It must have taken him ten minutes to draw it. Jerry noticed that William was looking directly at him. He blinked his eyes. "What?"

The pianist, remembering his own necessity to ritual, to think first things first, he quietly interrupted Jerry's quiet dissertation between bites of food. "What time did you get up this morning?"

Jerry's answer was quick. "Six thirty. Aunt Urs has two bedrooms. She also has a third in the gable of her house and I slept up there instead of going back to Berkeley. It saves time." He cleared his throat when he noticed that William was listening attentively. and how he was judging each subtle move that he had with his fork . . . A short empty moment found his own eyes looking directly at the piano player. He looked down at the drawing before he continued. When William realized he would be alone for the balance of the Sunday. He also perceived a noticeable tear is Jerry's right eye. This was painful for him.

"I have to go," Jerry said, "believe me, I wish I could spare more time with you." They had walked a sort distance, standing at the impressive corner of Market and Grove Street just above the submerged rail stop of BART. A thousand regrets played on his face, obvious to both of them. William did not mention that he had the balance of the day without a piano. He watched as Jerry disappeared down the stairs. They would have Wednesday as planned, to walk across the Bridge and a café in Sausalito. He was a tired tourist. Jerry had given him a telephone number to call later that evening. William carried his brief case. He would have to find a piano somewhere. He went back to the hotel an was asleep in no time. He would call Jerry on that number he gave him later. Now, to find a piano, at a church, at a music shop, somewhere.

The next day, at noon, after a cab ride from Geary Street to Grove, William found the destination in a building that was part of the renovation. With the score of the Mozart in his briefcase just in case he needed it, he followed the direction of several poster signs pointing to the new areas for the symphony. He found the location he wanted. According to the letter in his briefcase he was on time.

"Come in, Mr. Kaplan," greeted the secretary at her desk. She rose upon seeing him enter through the wide glass doors of her reception lobby. She was impressed; two passers-by from the outer hall looked their way. This receptionist was a young woman with dark brown hair neatly pulled back with a tight clasp to hold it all behind her neck. "The guard downstairs telephoned me that you had arrived. I was ready for you." Then, as if it were part of her duty, she smiled an apology. "Please overlook the interior mess. Our entire Symphony offices were moved to the third floor here in the building. That's why you see boxes strewn all over the hallway and floors. The guards and security system were changed so no one knows what is going on for the moment." William listened. "The paint on the walls is dry and we do hope to have a fresh décor in a simple design." The large windows in the hallway opposite the tall glass doors to her area provided a panoramic view of the City Hall just to the west of the inner courtyard. She paused. Her introduction was complete.

William waited while some workers passed in front of him. "Mr. Preston, our symphony manager, is expecting you. Please, this way." She ushered him through a heavy inner door that opened to a large office much like that of Steven Young's, in Denver. It also had many pictures of celebrities on the walls, a piano, and a bar at the far end of a large open space. On a mahogany desk by the telephone was a name board which stated mutely, Arthur B. Preston. He stood beside a window and turned to welcome him. He looked to be fifty years old, clean shaven, in a colorful long sleeved shirt with French cuff links and blue trousers. His coat to match his pants was hanging on an old fashioned clothes tree. His red hair was obvious. His green eyes were, also. He looked efficient, much the same as any important figure that William encountered on his journeys and tours.

Raymond Hicks wrote him to be aware that this Mr. Preston was courteous but to beware of how thorough he is. Raymond's suggestion was not only part of the method of introducing yourself to such a prestigious orchestra, one to be remembered, but also to manifest a kind of sincerity of intent. Preston had a cup of coffee in his right hand and a piece of correspondence in his left. Seeing him for the first time recalled what Hicks had written him just before he left Young's office. "You are a brilliant pianist, Billy," Raymond Hicks had written this frequent remark more than once, "and the first thing I want you to do is, just tell him who you are, allow him to ask as many questions as he wants, and to leave him feeling great by the time you get back on the airplane and return to Denver. Just don't be too shocked if he asks the 'wrong' questions. This is *their* request that you visit them so you show them you can do whatever they want. And knock 'em for a loop with the piano!" That letter sounded like a father talking to a ten-year-old cub scout. But Raymond meant what he had written even though it was yet another repeat of the same worthwhile pat-on-the-back. That letter was in his briefcase along with the Mozart score. God bless Raymond Hicks. William hoped that he was still taking his pills, for whatever reason.

"We met in Albuquerque when you played, if you remember." Preston was unpretentious. "Right away I wanted you to join us in the '95-'96 season. I contacted Steven because I didn't at first care to go through your agent until I obtained Steve's opinion. We've known each other for a long time. So exchanging opinions is right down our alley." He glanced quickly at William's height and gestured for him to sit. "Steven seems to age comfortably. Is he one hundred four by now?" Arthur laughed. They soon were in large leather chairs in the opposite end of the room. William was relaxed but anticipating almost anything. His briefcase as on the floor next to his chair.

"You want some coffee? I don't drink martinis and delicious stuff like that until after four p.m. Doctor's orders." William was not surprised at the pace with which this manager spoke. He was used to the speed in which decisions were discussed and settled. Arthur Preston adjusted his right French cuff. Both his hands were rough, as if he wielded an ax or milked a cow in his youth. "We're glad to know you can play this Mozart masterpiece." As he continued to outline his plans, Preston appraised the pianist with those green eyes that scrutinized him. Arthur had already noticed his bearing, his stature, how he walked, how he spoke, his tone, his movements, how he crossed his legs when he sat in that chair. He did all that in Albuquerque. As a rule, Mr. Preston was always ready to determine if this pianist measured up to his personal qualifications. Originally he made his own notes in his little black pad to confirm later that he wanted to make sure of personal characteristics that never appear on contract sheets. He did not hesitate too long when he concluded that this man did not, in any way, manifest feminine characteristics of which too many young men in this City possess. It was well known in the Arts world, especially on the West Coast, that the Gay Element was prevalent. This very city was nationally, if not internationally known for *la gay world*. But Mr. Preston did not pass these thoughts to this guest. He was not here to begin an intimate discussion on that subject. He determined that right away. He could see it was not necessary. This person sitting next to him passed his one-minute test, one that began when he watched William Kaplan enter the stage and proceed to his piano in New Mexico. Preston could see, practically from the moment that William came through the door, that his hands were strong and his posture was perfect.

Preston was greatly relieved to view this artist up close, to verify the fact that he was more than pleased than when he heard him play the last of March. He was glad to pass that information on to whoever asked. "I'm to tell you right away that you will be busy with us. One reason that we brought you here today is to introduce you to the orchestra. After our first concert, they all take a long break. Now I know that sort of thing is done by all organizations—you've got to get the feel of the players and the attention of the conductor. But I like to think that our orchestra is somewhat better than L. A. or Seattle, or anywhere else for that matter. Tonight we will rehearse with you on several portions of all three movements. The practice room is here in this building on the first floor. It won't be a long session, merely to have you feel comfortable and for you to hear our organization and for us to hear your talent, your technique. Then tomorrow we'll sign contracts. By the way, there's a luncheon where you'll get to meet the Board and they are looking forward to that. Especially Miss Harriet Maybelle Hopkins. Yes, she is a direct descendant of the original Mark Hopkins bunch. She likes to shake hands. Just be aware, for I want you to know she is a charming and beautiful lady. Be sure to listen to her and what she says to you. If she mentions an invitation for you to go to the Top of the Mark, say yes." For just a split second, William noticed an affirmative nod which closed this interview. He had not said hardly anything.

Preston rose immediately, stretched his arms, and buzzed his secretary. "You can then go to a room we have for you to practice any time you want today or Wednewsday . . ." He laughed. A woman entered from another door. "This is Miss Bradley." He stopped a moment to recall more information for William. "You're free for the day. Have you been in our city before?" He slipped on his suit coat. "Do you know anyone here? We'll be expecting you at seven o'clock sharp today downstairs with our orchestra. Rehearsals usually are about two and one half hours with some kind of a break." He reached for his telephone. "Please excuse me, now. Miss Bradley will take you downstairs to show you the rehearsal room. I'll see you tomorrow. Be hungry. Miss Hopkins likes to eat a hearty lunch. If I have to reach you, I'll leave a message for you at your hotel. The Ambassador on Geary?" William nodded yes. "Goodbye."

On their way into the hallway, William nodded at the lady who welcomed him. "I'm used to the pace that managers have. It's not new to me." Miss Bradley smiled. "A lot of us do work fast, Mr. Kaplan." Presently, they were on the first floor with hardly any additional comment. When Miss Bradley unlocked the hall door to the large rehearsal area, William was surprised to see so much electronic equipment. "This room was a recording room until we moved into it. Our other room was too small." He saw the black concert grand waiting directly below the conductor's podium. He sat down, adjusted the seat, and struck several keys. "It was tuned, just for you." While she stood not four feet away from him, he began the third movement to hear it.

The acoustics in this space were perfect. While he was concentrating on this one passage, three men in the sound booth who were working had stopped to listen. Evidently pleased by what he heard, he stopped and stood and looked about the area. The three workers opened a mike and one welcomed him over meager applause. William smiled and waved to them. "I guess I can leave my score here since I'll be back tonight." To this, Miss Bradley agreed. "I won't be here. I'm not a musician, merely a stenographer. But I'll see you tomorrow at the luncheon." She shook his hand softly and said, "I'm glad to meet you, Mr. Kaplan. I have your recording of the Rachmaninov 'Variations on Paganini.' I guess it was your latest RCA. I would like you to autograph the album cover for me, please? I'll be at the luncheon tomorrow" To that he agreed through his smile. She smiled in return. "I'll show you the way out." He asked about a telephone. "I want to call U.C. Berkeley. Do I dial directly?"

"Yes. I'll show you where a phone is for you." She motioned in passing. "I have to go now. Goodbye." And she left.

"Hello," he began, is Mr. Champion available?" And to this, he was. "Hello, Jair. Can you talk for a bit?" To his surprise, William heard the voice of a contented geologist . . .

Jerry sounded more than elated. "Yes," he laughed, "It's great to hear you, I was sort of expecting your call. Did you get a lot done since . . . since I had to . . . to leave you? With that quick map." Before Jerry allowed him to say anything, he quickly continued. "Anything happening at the piano, I mean?".

William laughed . . . "I just llearned that tomorrow at one, there's a lunch and i've been invited." He waited. "I guess it's my turn to interrupt our visits." William was not certain just how Jerry would accept that.

"At one, you say? Jerry heard a quick cough on the line. "You okay?. "Sure!"

"Well . . . uh . . . I got an idea. If it's all right with you, then go back to the hotel as soon as you can. That's tomorrow, now, after that lunch business. I mean, please. So I can pick you up at the hotel at six. Can you stop everything and be ready by six? I want to see you before . . ." Apparently, Jerry stopped in the middle of an idea.

William said yes, that he could do that.

Jerry reiterated, "I'll show you the Bridge on Wednesday; that'll take four hours alone. We'll walk across and take the ferry back from Sausalito. We'll do that. Tomorrow night at the hotel. I can be there by 6:00p.m. Goodbye. Gotta go!"

William was able to detect yet another side of Jerry but for now, he had no time to sit down and commiserate. He looked at his watch and returned to the locked door to the rehearsal room and knocked loudly. He knocked the second time. One of the men working in the sound booth opened it. "I'd want to practice. About two hours. Okay?"

The man backed away to let him enter and smiled. "My name's Roger, Mr. Kaplan, nice to see you. Sure. I'll turn on some overhead light for you again." William stopped him with a quick question, "Didn't I see a nice restaurant about a block away, toward Market Street?"

"Yes, it's a hang-out for some of us." To that William nodded. With no one to interrupt as Roger returned to the booth William sat again at the Steinway and before he began to invade Mozart, he splendidly and joyfully struck into the dramatic emotions of 'Totentanz' by Liszt. Roger and the other two workers in the booth halted and listened. Then he relaxed and began his ritual, first with scales to warm his hands and to oil his brain. Then he plunged happily into Mozart.

And then after two hours, he waved goodbye to the sound booth crew and decided he was hungry.

Chapter Seventeen

THE COMPLETION OF THE renovation was almost certain to be soon. Instead of exiting to Hayes Street which would place him across the street from where he was directed, Willliam wanted to view the Civic Center more properly than when he was there yesterday. The day was bright and cool; he often wondered if he would ever get used to the weather here. The Symphony Hall just to his left and the impressive City Hall were practically opposite him. The late afternoon August sunlight made elegant shadows across the lawn to the library and for just a moment or two he stopped to capture this sight. Then, turning south on Larkin, he reached the intersection of Ninth Street which brought him to Market. He was starving.

There, in front of him, was the unobtrusive eatery. The moment William entered, a lady in slacks, a smock and an arm full of menus greeted him. She did offer him a smile but no recognition. Just as she was about to suggest a small table at the back of the crowded dining room, a man walked up to him. He immediately extended his hand for his greeting. "Mr. Kaplan," he began softly, "I'm here with two others from the orchestra." He dismissed the hostess with a wink and pointed casually to a table not far from them. "Please join us, because we're all here for the same reason—I mean—rehearsal at seven o'clock." He made his way past two tables through a narrow passageway where a few others glanced and smiled at the pianist. The guest was used to this sort of reception. The few people who did recognize him whispered to each other and one or two politely welcomed him. One nodded. One gentleman rose and offered to shake hands. "Nice to have you wish us," he replied softly.

The café was crowded. He followed this person and more people waved at him. The others at this table stood. The first one pointed. "This is Bertrand Wilson, oboe, and she is Estella Windsor, flute." They were ready with their handshakes. "And I'm Joe Jones, just plain Joe Jones, third row violin on the end 'next to the footlights'." Estella pulled the fourth chair and indicated that he sit. All offered their welcome and by the time the waitress appeared, the musicians all were chatting away as if they were old friends, surprised at the youthful pianist who would be with them. The oboist gathered his napkin and grinned. Estella extended her hello amid the noise. They laughed, much like William expected, for again he felt right at home. Bertrand Wilson was perhaps fifty, a thin long face with a mustache and large diamond ring on his right hand. A packet of oboe reeds protruded from his coat pocket. The flutist was too shy to join in on the laughter and she was the first to leave. William's food was quick and hot.

"You might think it strange that we have a rehearsal this far in advance of Thanksgiving." Joe Jones was vociferous enough for him and Bertrand. "I think that is because we have to get ready early for our first big show in October. Everyone is taking some kind of short vacation after it before we begin to work on Mozart . . . without you, I mean." Joe was not in a position to qualify anything else. I think you are due back three days before that Saturday performance. I think you're destined to have two runs-through with us, whatever!" With a mouthful of food, the oboist nodded. When he did have a chance to say something, he agreed. "Joe is librarian for all of us and he gets info more quickly than any of us does. "If we want to know what is going on, all we have to do is knock on his office door and look at the huge calendar on his wall."

Joe Jones laughed quietly. "I have an office now, with all the new decoration that is going on. It's in Symphony Hall. We're still in the old auditorium area for rehearsals. You'll see it, of course." The duo waited with him. "You look too young, William Kaplan," Joe announced casually. "I think some of us were expecting an Arthur Rubinstein type or maybe a Barrenboim. When I placed a picture of you on a wall in my cubby-hole, a lot of people were delighted that you are mid-twenties." William laughed at that. "Your agent sent the print to Mr. Preston and asked me to put in on the bulletin board. By the way, I have a second copy of the article that was in the *Chronicle* announcing that you were to be here with us for "primary rehearsals. I'll pass it on to you tomorrow at the luncheon." Preston sent us a memorandum which is on my bulletin board and I hope everyone read it by now. It said you were thirty-something. I would guess thirty, period. I think maybe I better warn you about two or three violinists . . . young ladies who already asked me if you were married," Joe continued while William ate, "As if I knew the answer." Joe smiled at his own humor. Several stood to make their exit. "There goes one of them, Mr. Kaplan. Did you notice how she eyed you ever since you entered. She shares my music stand and I know she'll have a million questions." Bertrand Wilson stood quietly, whispered something to William which he could not hear due to noise and then left. "I suppose it's time to go," Joe cautioned, "when Wilson leaves, you know you'll have about fifteen minutes because it takes that long for an oboist to check his reed and get ready."

By the time they arrived, the majority of the orchestra was seated. A cacophony of sounds greeted them. The moment William came through the door, the orchestra members stood and applauded. He returned their applause with a wave of his hand as he proceeded to his piano.

Carter McKissick, the conductor, entered from the far right side of this large room and came directly to William. "Well, Mr. Kaplan, it is nice to have you with us." His handshake and words were sincere. "This is the band, as Steven Young would say. I guess he's okay, I haven't seen him in a long time. Arthur told me he is very impressed by how his short interview went this morning. He did want me to explain that the entire organization is, at the moment, in a sort of disarray. I'm sure you're aware of it by now. We are at the moment redecorating almost every square foot. The performance hall where we have been providing concerts is all in turmoil." He was in the habit of talking about almost anything except the music that was ahead of them. Those in the "band" were used to the informality of his togetherness with them; they knew to wait patiently. "So now let us begin." He nodded to the concert mistress who sounded an "a" on her violin. William sat while a member kindly raised the cover. Mr. McKissick turned to him once more. "I want to play certain sections to verify tempo for you. William's eye caught Bertrand Wilson and the oboist very quickly returned a nod in affirmation. With his baton the conductor struck the music stand to initiate. "First movement," he said, "at fourteen bars before the piano enters."

Once again, William was immersed in his work, for he was comfortably waiting for his entrance cues, stopping when McKissick stopped for reasons pertaining to tone, to tempo, to volume when he wanted it, and repeats when he deemed necessary. The pianist was most patient because Miss Shriner trained him well. At one point, when the conductor discussed an important section with the violins, when William waited with his hands at his side, he allowed a strong reminder about Jerry to enhance his routine. He thought it logical that even though Jair may not know the subtle qualities of concert music, he was undoubtedly on the same plain in appreciating his own talent, that of science. He developed this trend when, during his own practicing, Jerry would invade his work and persist to stay mentally close to him. He would smile to himself, wondering what the geologist was doing at this time of day and how he became a recurring memory. William would never allow such an interruption to mar progress on the keyboard. Such as it was now, with this dedicated group of instrumentalists, he put aside Jerry and obeyed the orchestra. His eyes were glancing up quickly to follow this leader and to learn what he wanted from Mozart.

William was very much at home. As he expected, the beauty of the sounds, the musicians and their natural ability to give the soloist the proper background were all together providing the glory of the moment. Even during rehearsals, William felt immeasurably edified.

McKissick was a wonder. He looked at William often in this process of maintaining the coherence. At one time, they played the entire second movement twice, at separate times in that evening. After the break, the second half was devoted to the study of the concerto as McKissick was pleased to admit. "It is going to be a nice concert. Preston did well to locate Kaplan when he did." This was said while William was still seated on the piano bench. This brought an agreement and immediate standing of the total orchestra with appropriate applause from everyone. At the end, many members came to congratulate him. It was some time before he could find a moment to leave. McKissick did remind him that tomorrow was the luncheon for the Board to meet him. After a few members stood by him to offer their cudos, before the rehearsal hall was empty, William claimed his coat, his score and his briefcase, and disappeared en route to his hotel; it was all too exhausting. He managed to reach Jerry at the number he had given him.

"I'm all right, just tired but that's normal. I have that luncheon tomorrow. After that, then, I can see you. I don't plan on going back to Denver until Thursday morning. You want me to come over to Berkeley and meet you, tell me where. You want to see me . . . ?"

After a long moment of semi-silence, Jerry spoke quickly." I want to talk to you tomorrow. I mean a nice long talk." He sounded the same but a bit harried and occupied with his work. By now, Jerry possessed three, maybe four levels of vocal delivery, each for a separate purpose. This was his matter-of-fact voice. William imagined that he was standing in the hallway next to his lab, his left hand massaging his face as he spoke. "I'll call you early in the morning and tell you where to meet me. After four I'll have more time. You'll have that lunch business over by then. No problem. I have a lot to do tomorrow, so after four is best for me. I want to reserve all day Wednesday for us. Be ready to walk! It's a beautiful Bridge from up close." Silence.

"Wait a minute," William pleaded suddenly. I thought . . . I just thought you were going to hang up. You were talking about the Bridge Or about a nice long . . . talk . . . ?"

Jerry was tired, as usual. "It'll keep. Good night, piano player, I . . ." and he stopped.

William asked what he started to say. Another tone in his voice sounded. "Never mind. It can wait til tomorrow." And he hung up.

After his shower he crawled in bed. The phone rang. "Hello." It was Vivian. She wanted to know where he had been, that she had been trying to reach him for three hours. "Do you know a Gary Fuller?" Yes, he does. "Well, Dr. Young called me around dinner time and he said this Gary Fuller—whoever he is—was injured in a bar fight of some kind earlier this afternoon and he said Gary what's-his-name was in the orchestra and that you knew him. Whatever. This Gary . . ." and Vivian reread her notes before she continued, " . . . is hurt pretty bad, hurt his arm, I think he said. Dr. Young told me you'd probably like to know. I couldn't for the life of me figure out why Dr. Young thinks you'd probably like to know. In a bar, I think he said, The Ranger." William was tired but this made him sit up in bed. "Well, dammit." she continued, "Kevin told meThe Ranger is a gay bar." For the moment, she let that pass. "How's it going? When you coming home? Hey." She noticed the silence from his end. "I didn't think that this information is so desperately urgent but I guess Dr Young wanted to tell you and since I was calling, anyway." She took a deep breath. "I'm all right. Kevin wants a divorce or did I tell you before you left? Damn football player doesn't know what the hell is going on. Let me know when your plane arrives and I'll try to meet you if I can. Okay? Be good. How'd the rehearsal go? That's what you went for, wasn't it? Tell me all about it when you get back to reality. Goodnight, Billy!"

Chapter Eighteen

WILLIAM ANSWERED THE HOTEL phone. He was half asleep. A female's low-register recorded voice announced the time of six-thirty. He lay there for an additional moment having accepted long ago the modern technology of how a woman's charm can be duplicated so well. Presently he got out of bed, stretched, and went to the hotel closet where his suit was hanging. The phone rang again. Looking at his watch, he greeted the caller, "Good morning, geologist."

"How did you know it was a geologist?" Jerry was alert and ready. William sat on the edge of the bed. "Who else would get up at this hour and sound urgent? He giggled at his own remark.

"Listen. I've got lots to say because I have a class in forty-five minutes. Summer school early, like you said. Are you listening?" Yes, he was listening. Jerry was using his alert-and-ready voice. "After that lunch business go back to the hotel and check out and wait for me. I'll try to be there by five." This was alarming because he did not plan to leave until Thursday morning. "I know," Jerry anticipated what he would say. "You can stay at Aunt Urs' house until you go to the airport. You're still leaving from San Fran airport?" Yes, he is. "Okay. I'm sleeping on the day bed in the music room and you can have the big wonderful wide comfortable bed up in the third bedroom upstairs." William tried to say something. "Wait a minute," he said in his matter-of-fact voice, "I've got it all planned. Listen. Remember, I'm the one who is disciplined too. I'm a thinker and I think things through. I'm going to cook supper and I've already got it confirmed with Aunt Urs and Li." William grinned as he listened most attentively. Jerry switched to his jovial voice.

"Tomorrow is ours, just you and me and I'm walking the Bridge with you all the way to Sausalito just like I told you. Tomorrow, Wednesday, write that down. Then it's back to reality." He had heard that phrase from William. "Besides, I want to talk to you." He had returned to his specific voice. "I have something to say and I want to say it." William heard him take a deep breath.

"You've said a lot, already."

"Yeah, I mean, from me to you. Now, I've got a report to give to Dr. Clark and I'll try to remain calm. You heard me, piano player?"

"Yes. Yes, I heard you. You better get going. I'll be all right. I'll wait for you in the lobby. After lunch I want to practice on a real good piano where we eat that lunch. Goodbye, you rock hound." When he hung up the phone, he remained on the side of the bed just to piece everything together. He had not given much thought to his music, but Jerry was more on his mind this morning. Jair was much in charge of the plans as evident through the several colours of his voice. William was learning about the scientist's mind, the manner in which he said things and the way he moved, and the delightful way he would pick up a book from a table, thumb through it haphazardly but replace it carefully. His aunt told William that he was careful about books in general, that he enjoyed reading even as a child. It was by the aunt's proud remarks that Jerry had a well ordered mind. On weekends, when he escaped the confines of U.C. Berkeley, Jerry would sit on the front steps of the porch and lean against the railing and read. Li noticed this too when she brought a Dr. Pepper to him. He even ignored the pedestrian traffic on Green Street.

But that was all right. Both William and Jerry agreed that opposites attract. William told himself that time and again. At first, this was a strange new avenue for the music man; one similarity was the devotion each had for the other's talent. In these last days together he noticed this mystery that astounded both of them. That was the way it was. William heard this in just that one early morning telephone call. The geologist was more active, alert, vociferous. He even sounded different, using all of the changes in attitude in his voice. Evidently Jerry was never aware of this situation. He sounded different than how he responded on the wet porch on Green Street the other night.

This luncheon was organized and supervised by Mr. Preston's secretary. Miss Bradley. She wore a black cocktail dress, small ear rings and a matching necklace. She flittered and hovered over every phase of endeavor as the waiters finished preparing the tables. This formal get-together was situated in a new area that was not totally finished. But it already had a large golden chandelier hovering over the center of the room and a newly designed kitchen for such occasions. The head table, complete with a vase of flowers in front of where Miss Hopkins would be sitting, was stationed on a six-inch dais. It was she who wanted to order the menu and Miss Bradley graciously agreed. The seating cards were all in place. Miss Bradley read every one of them, marking some kind of an affirmative check on her clip board. The Board of Directors ambled in, one and two at a time.

Miss Hopkins found William right away. She was resplendent in a neat blouse and long skirt ensemble and wore a string of pearls with less conspicuous earrings. On top of her white hair was a small hat. As she came forward, William suddenly remembered the line he used to throw at a completely strange lady, whether he was waiting in line with her to buy a movie ticket or at the Union cafeteria. He had a charming habit of announcing, "Are these the earrings I sent you from Mexico?" Delightfully taken aback, the lady would inevitably answer, "Yes!" One lady once even said, "Yes, but don't tell my husband!" They sat at their locations, with the artist to Miss Hopkins' right. "Are you hungry?" she asked. "I'm always hungry," was his reply. "Then, dig in! My grandfather would always say 'dig in.'"

Carter McKissick stood, brushed the crumbs off his pants with his napkin, nodded at Miss Hopkins and looked at the main guest and nodded his head before his eyes meandered around the room. The conversations became quieter and the waiters carefully removed dishes. "Mr. Kaplan," he began, while using a fork to signal against a water glass. "I'm sure all of us do welcome you and we want to make you feel at home. A San Francisco welcome! Your August trip was necessary, due to our need for additional rehearsal time for the first selection of our season, *Carmina Burana*. The bulletin at each position on the tables will inform us of the rest of the season. As you can see we have Sibelius and *Beethoven's Ninth*. A full and busy season. I guess you might say we've got the Corps de Ballet and a large chorus to help us." He paused to wait for the sound of meager applause. "We appreciate your being with us at this time. By the time Herr Beethoven visits us, the auditorium will be completed, hence, will be available for another gem by Herr Mozart, as well, next spring with one of his several symphonies." By the time he had finished, his humor did not go unnoticed.

William Kaplan ate well, drank well, and successfully answered all questions put to him: his home town, his history of musicology, where he lived, how many hours a day does he practice, what is his favorite colour, is he married, and what his shirt size is. He was polite and charming. His favorite question came from one of the ladies who herself was a board member. "Oh, Mr. Kaplan," she gushed as he stood in the doorway leading to the newly finished hallway, "Have you ever performed on Broadway?" She may have been confused by the New York location and the street with the tunnel between Mason and Larkin. The one in San Francisco had one or two bawdy night spots near it. "Yes," he answered her, "I played the role of spectator sitting in the third row of the balcony of *Phantom of The Opera*. To that she displayed her enigmatic smile. "Oh . . ."

William grinned as he made his way to the rehearsal hall and to his Steinway. With permission and help from the three workers, he had well over two hours by himself at the baby grand.

He relayed the incident to Jerry who walked through the door of the hotel on time. He looked tired. He was using his exhausted voice. But everything was in place for a relaxing evening, a busy tomorrow on the Bridge, and to visit his favorite eatery on the shore in Sausalito. "I can't let you go back to Denver without walking the Bridge. We'll start at the top of Van Ness and begin walking there, due to the gradual incline of the street." Each sat in his chair, brown eyes peering into blue ones.

"What do you want to tell me?" was a legitimate question but Jerry was not ready to continue. He deterred. He was hungry. William understood and he confirmed that he could wait until they see Aunt Urs.

Jerry stood just four feet away from the two bags as William said goodbye to the desk clerk. "Very good, Mr. Kaplan," the efficient clerk responded, "I will make the adjustment before we submit the bill to the symphony." He then slipped a small piece of paper toward him with a quiet request, "May I have your autograph please? This is for a friend who just loves classical music." William consented. Despite how tired he was, Jerry grinned. Again, the clerk was grateful. 'Oh, thank you, sir."

An hour later, after a swift cab ride, they entered Aunt Ursula's house. The lady had been outside walking up and down her street always with Coit Tower in sight. She had already eaten a light supper and was sitting in the main room reading from *Gone With The Wind* for her second time in forty years. She found her book mark and placed both on the nearby table when William sat opposite her. Her reading glasses dropped in front of her on their cord. "Gerald told me you would be here this evening." Her eyes were still strong. He could see that in her smile.

"Is this all right?" he asked softly. Her nephew went directly to the kitchen with his bag of groceries from the little mart on the corner. "Of course it's all right. The bedroom on the third floor is small and we hardly use it only when Gerald stays over on weekends. He's very busy now." Again they heard pleasant sounds from Li's kitchen. Both she and Jerry were laughing.

The aunt changed her position in her chair. "You seem to be fairly good for my nephew." This was a sudden surprise, in that he did not know how to accept it, as a fair question or a genuine statement. He did not presume it, not from her, at least. She was such a nice lady. "May I say, Mrs. Griswold," he began formally, "that the pleasure is all mine. Your nephew, your house, this opportunity I have to play here in the fall have all been good for me, too." He suspected his answer was too diplomatic but it was true. His choice of words was a surprise to himself. He did not know how else he could reply. He did not think it necessary to go into any kind of detail how strong his friendship had become with her nephew. This relationship had just taken a stronger definitive shape. That seemed to have been the case. He knew what *pathos* is and he knew this friendship was without any considerable depth. That would be his tactical answer to her if she asked again. The whole picture had become more alive than he thought.

Mrs. Griswold smiled. "Yesterday he called and right away he wanted to know if he and you could spend the night here. He said he was taking you on a walking tour of the Bridge, something even I had been on with my husband." She laughed innocently. "Anyone may walk the Bridge. Just be careful of the wind blasts. Ask Gerald; he will explain how you should grasp the railing, if necessary."

"Excuse me, Aunt Urs," Jerry interrupted, and to William, "Soup's on in the kitchen, piano player."

"Go on, my dear, both of you." She reclaimed her book and replaced her glasses. "Scarlett calls me." She laughed at her own remark. "After all, tomorrow is another day." She continued reading as Li came in with her knitting and sat opposite her.

For just a quick moment, silence prevailed as Jerry dished the soup. They prepared sandwiches. William settled into a kitchen chair and watched him, often without his realizing it. But when Jair did look at him, both giggled quietly and bit into their supper. "What's with the business of talking to me? You sounded like you were ready to offer a prayer or a sermon." With a mouthful, Jerry smiled and laughed. He took a swig of milk. "No, no. But tomorrow's your last day here . . ." and he turned on his honest voice, "and I wanted to be . . ." but he did not finish the statement. Instead he took another sip of milk.;" . . . to be, Well . . . well, alone. With you, I mean. The best place to be alone is on the Bridge. I mean, to stop walking for a moment and listen to the wind and the seagulls . . . We have a wide sidewalk." To this, William raised his eyebrows. "Not very many people walk it. It's either too windy or nobody walks, anymore. A lot of traffic will pass us, and our sidewalk is on the east side . . . Just hold on to the rail . . . or to me. It's not dangerous, not at all." He added quickly. "Either one."

"Alone on the Bridge." William was half serious, but he did laugh. "Sounds like a British movie."

"Now, don't be facetious." Jerry took another sip of milk. "Just for that, you crazy piano player." He got up and took his dishes to the sink, "let's go upstairs, right now. Drink your milk and you can carry your sandwich. I'll grab the luggage if you grab the potato chips. On the way, they announced to Li, "We're going all the way up."

That one bedroom was small but handy, crowded as it was under the gabled roof that ran the entire length of the attic. Jerry dropped the two bags by the door and turned on the one table lamp by the tnarrow bed. He pointed to a narrow door. "The jjohn is through there." He sat in the one chair and watched how William slowly entered and looked around him to measure for himself exactly how small this attic was. He then sat on the bed by the table lamp. He finished his sandwich. "Okay, you crazy geologist," he murmured, "what's going on?"

Jerry stood up and moved the chair so he could have more room at the foot of the bed. For the first time since he had arrived, William saw a serious and astute young thinker standing before him. Not more than three feet away, Jerry grabbed the bed stead to stable himself. He waited a moment while they peered at each other in the dim light. He laughed, at first, to allow himself sufficient breath to begin. William peered at him, not knowing what to expect. Apparently whatever Jerry was doing would be quite a production or an easy display of a weird confession. Or maybe he could expect a lecture on rock formations in the State of California, or what the price of eggs in China is. Or maybe it was going to be a preview of his doctorate. There was one moment when Jerry altered his visual line and looked away from him into the darkness behind them.

The pianist was ready to hear from this scientist, for the first time in their four-month acquaintance, a lecture of the physical and mental breakdown of genuine friendship, something as ethereal as that. William decided not to be facetious, but to listen. Yes, he listened.

"I may have come on to you pretty strong, at the airport, maybe. Or that bear hug on the campus." No, William did not know what to expect. "At first, I really didn't know who you were or how you might accept the crazy way we started out." Jerry began to use his variety of sound levels that he often displays; William learned that trait just yesterday . . . "I didn't know very much about music, I still don't, except what my father tried to teach me. But I was glad I got to meet you, whatever that can mean. You were really nice . . . if that's the word I want to use here . . . and when you finally did answer my letters, not only the first one but all of them," and he paused and pointed with his right hand, "all of them . . . I've kept them . . . I felt like maybe it's time for me to square with you and the way to do that was face to face." He stopped again to clear his throat. "I was prepared to fly to Denver and face you but that was exactly when you told me you were coming here for whatever you musicians do to prepare for that Thanksgiving thing. God, was I happy!"

When William shifted his position on the bed, he extended his arms as if to guard against the objection Jerry might throw at him. "Wait just a minute, please." When Jerry realized he still had everything under control, he took another deep breath and looked directly at him despite the dim light. "Well . . . I may not . . . I just may not be worthy of your friendship." He waited again, for the loss of words was most apparent to both of them. He restated, " . . . Just may not be worthy of your . . ."

William suddenly blurted out, "Love," which had totally surprised the geologist who stood there and gawked at the figure in the lamp light. He rubbed his nose and tried to continue, " . . . worthy of your terrific friendship. You even used the word 'bonding' and I thought that was just great. But you see, my past history is not a . . . good one. I can see in you someone that I could really use as a good . . ." Jerry was at a loss for words. *Syntax* came to his scientific mind.

Again, William interrupted, "Love. That you could really love . . ." Even in the dim light from that small table lamp, Jerry could see the honest expression on the face opposite him. He had to pause while tears mounted in his blue eyes. " . . . that I could really love." He waited. "Oh, God!" He found strength to continue. "I was sort of a hell-raiser at MIT." He again shifted his position at the end of the bed. "I was a good student, don't get me wrong. But . . . ah, hell, I can't go into detail, not now, about what I did and how I guess I didn't live up to being a great guy, more or less—but, dammit, I want to tell you I was a great student and that is what matters to me. He sat at the end of the bed and grabbed the bed stead again. He turned away from him, frightened that he was unable to make valid conversation. "Oh, Billy, you don't know what I'm saying and I guess I shouldn't have even tried to tell you. But you are so much better than I . . ." He stood up and could not face him. "This is not going anywhere . . . ."

William stopped him immediately by barring any attempt to leave. "Hey. Stop it. Stop right there. This friendship-bonding-love business goes both ways, you know. I have to tell you right now that I just really did not know what to think of the crazy correspondence . . . those letters, back and forth, I don't quite know what is going on, myself. I've got a life too. I've got a past, also. Maybe you can hear what I can say. It's not all playing the piano stuff, you know." Jerry turned to him. William grabbed him by both sides of his face. "I like what I see. I don't yet know what a geologist is or does and I reckon you don't know a damn thing about sharps and flats. I've been thinking and right now I'm mighty glad God brought you into my life. It's as simple as that. He did that, you know! And if you don't understand that now, then you better start doing so. Right now."

Jerry stood transfixed, startled by the look in William's eyes. He blinked while a sudden thought raced through his brain, one that prompted him slowly to remove both hands that gently clasped his face. He slowly stepped backward and grabbed the bed again to steady himself. But in a nanosecond, without removing his own eyes from the pianist's face, he realized the strength in Billy's gaze. It was there, confirming the moment. Jerry recoiled. William's eyes never dropped their survey. Then again, Jerry had no reason, after all, to be discomfited, to step those few inches away from him.

William managed to grasp a shoulder when he saw stronger tears well up in Jerry's eyes that changed rapidly into weeping. He confirmed that even geologists can get emotional. "Don't worry about it, right now, Jair. You hear me? But I do want you to understand what I said about being extremely glad what God did. I just wanted you to know that. Five or six seconds elapsed. "Now let's go back downstairs and I'll play for you *Revolutionary Etude*."

"What's that?"

Chapter Nineteen

VIVIAN ANDERSON COLE STOOD in the area where passengers arrived. The mid-afternoon flight from San Francisco was on time on that Thursday after a successful journey of music and conversations. "I want you to go with me to Sterling. This is on the way and I have business with a couple of people." This matter-of-fact greeting was never new to William who was tired, eager to resume his practicing routines, and sleep in is own bed in the condo. "I really want you to go with me since the airport is on the way, already. This big landing spot that is far too bigger than old Stapleton Airport!"

William could see instantly that she had things on her mind. "I want to go to the condo. Please."

But silently and quickly, before he could object further, they grabbed his bag and fled to the parking lot. "I'm hungry. It wasn't a lunch flight. I only had a cup of coffee with a cookie . . . Permit me to go pee." He handed her his briefcase and disappeared.

Vivian sometimes displayed her tantrums and disgust with just about anything that did not go her way. William was used to this trait of hers. He did not particularly desire to hear about the football player. It was not often but he was used to this darkness of hers at a time when he did not expect it—certainly not now when she consented to meet his plane. "I want to go. Please. We can talk. We can stop at Marvin's Cafe because I haven't had much to eat and I'm hungry. They were finally away from the large airport heading east and escaping the Denver traffic. "I was expecting you yesterday. What happened? And who is this Gerald somebody?"

William managed a silent grin. "I walked the Golden Gate Bridge with Gerald Somebody." She did not believe that. "Well, we did. Yesterday. He said he wanted me to walk the bridge and we did." He was not unruly aggressive in that remark. It may be a long, long time for this really good friend, this wonderfully charming lady, to understand what has happened to him, to Jerry, to their new found friendship that apparently combines geology and music.

"Who is this Champion guy who's been writing you?" She finally asked her first question after talking to William for ftwo hours since his plane arrived. In the short time that he had been home, this was the first time she had another opportunity to talk. Despite her depreciating life as Mrs. Cole, Vivian fundamentally maintained her love of this celebrity. It was the first time, also, she ventured to question the delivery and the reason for that. She did not mind, at first, but the postman asked her on Tuesday if this Kaplan guy was living at her address. It was an ordinary question and was not meant to imply any other condition. She intended asking William a multitude of questions, anyway, with a preface that whoever this correspondent was, that he should cease using her apartment. It was as plain as that. William and she had been through a million and one arguments and discussions about a million and one other topics and she was used to his antics. Once even Kevin asked about the concert pianist.

They sat at their favorite table in Marvin's Café where no one would bother them. They could talk and argue and malign anyone they did not like. It was not often that they were together in this improved restaurant, long after their own rendezvous during high school and times afterward. Even now, both Marvin and Betty knew who they were. Marvin was getting old but he was acquainted with practically all the citizens of Sterling. He managed to drift by their table to say hello.

The one waitress who always managed to seat them had been there for a long time. This time, she spoke first on the strength that she knew who they were. "You may not know who I am, but I know you." She tried to be charming in her starched uniform and long dangling earrings. William was at a loss for words. Vivian stared at her and the waitress focused on William. "I'm Mayme Martin, Bobby's mother, Billy. I guess I can call you that. I've known you all these years. And I am happy to see you when you're hungry! I knew you were at Denver

University." Marvin called her from the kitchen window that bore two plates of food. "Excuse me, I'll be right back with your water." Vivian was spellbound. "Good grief," she whispered, "that is Bobby Martin's *mother?*" She hid behind her menu. "Excuse me, but she looks like she is old enough to be his grandmother! I forgot all about Bobby Martin. Where . . . I mean, what ever happened to him?"

The expression on William's face told her to shut up. If ever he was now ready to answer her questions, that time had passed. The mention of her son was totally inappropriate. The waitress returned with their glasses of water and took their orders. "Nice to see you two again," she mumbled, and departed.

Vivian decided to devote the rest of her Thursday to nothing but lassoing her good buddy to find out what in this crazy mixed-up world is going on. Their table was in a secluded corner where no one would recognize the local celebrity. She always thought of William Kaplan as a local celebrity and she often reminded him how proud she was of wonder boy. They stayed on a high plain of unique friends all the while. For thirty years they had palled around together and so she automatically asked him for any piece of information when she saw fit to do so, either discussion or argument. Actually, she did not realize that her question was for an intimate piece of knowledge. Bobby Martin came and went in William's realm of thoughts, with not much energy to solve any question about his comings and goings. Vivian Cole was intelligent to let sleeping dogs lie.

William was finishing some enchiladas with coffee. By six p.m. she did return to her original question about Jerry Champion. "Well." he started his answer but took the last bite of dark rice. "It's sort of a long story."

"That's what they all say." Vivian looked at her watch. "I've got time. But I'll take you out to your place while I take care of business." She opened her purse. "Let's go." She paid the bill "You can talk while I drive."

But he did not talk. Not about the interview, not about the luncheon, not about Jerry. He was tired . . . She had always been one to ask about his welfare, his health, his insistence on practicing every day, usually in the morning. But neither one wanted to talk, much. Not now. They were approaching the familiar gate with its new sign over the entrance. He saw the same trees, the same driveway to the house, and the same sidewalk to the porch. When they stopped, he noticed that someone had begun to draw a variety of lines with chalk . . .

"I'll be back for you in twenty minutes, I'm just getting a check, Billy. Be ready. He answered quickly as he made his way to the porch. His mother diid not answer when he called. He went to the kitchen but she was not there. He looked at the barn to see his dad but he was not there, either. Exhausted, he struck a few notes on the upright piano and heard that it was terribly out of tune. This was the first moment he realized that he was suddenly alone in a big old fashioned farm house with only a tall Grandfather's clock to tell him that it was six o'clock. He returned to the front porch to find Angus, a much older dog, now, than when, apparently, he saw him last. They sat on the front steps together when Angus quietly gazed into a familiar face. "Good ol' Angus, my ol' Angus. You were here. Where are they?"

After a half hour, William saw the old sedan and Vivian was driving.: "Hop in." And he did.

When she exhausted her repertoire of subject matter, she was forced to discuss her opinion of the price of eggs in China which was in the form of Kevin Cole. After William disclosed his careful explanation of this geologist—and he was careful not to explain too much—they managed to leave . . .

William added more to his summation of his two trips to California. "I guess you might say that Jerry and I have found a good example of what a few people I know said is 'bonding.'" To this, Vivian's face relaxed in a careless gesture of unbelief. To put that into words was William's next effort, for it was he and not she who had learned to wonder just what, indeed, was going on between Denver and Berkeley. "Bonding, you say?" was her next interruption. "I don't think you ever bonded with anything in your life except your piano."

She felt cramped in more ways than one and she began to doubt. Vivian was often too demonstrative with her gestures, but she was driving now. It was not she first time to ask if he was inclined to ignore the feminine side of life. He was surprised and he stared at her. "No." It was a definite negative answer. He was never shocked by what Vivian might ask, and so quickly and overtly. Practically all of her conversation which she could have with any one person, whether and old friend or someone merely standing on a street corner, would be direct and unsolicited. William looked directly at her while she used a quick gesture to question his reply. "That's just it, Viv, I'm beginning to think that I really enjoyed the entire four days. Jerry's aunt and housekeeper are really great people. The aunt is an intelligent and really great lady. Then, Jerry started to tell me all about how meeting me and how it changed his whole thinking."

"Oh, please. Don't give me that. Sounds to me like he is more weird than Kevin. Is that it?" This harsh word came from her store of knowledge about her hero. She stretched her neck. "Come on, tell me more." He obeyed and continued his dissertation. "Well, on the Bridge, for instance, he did talk about how he felt different than before we met. Don't pin me down, Viv. At the café and now, I've told you everything I want you to know. And if you just don't or can't accept what he had told me, then, maybe we just better shut up the whole episode. He's an academician, all right. And he's a scientist. And, dammit, scientists just don't think the way musicians think, at least, the way I think. At least, I've learned *that*. There's more to life than bread and butter and marriage and sex and I'm not going to carry on with this. I've yet got to practice tonight." Vivian was used to his change in tactics. By now they had entered the ramp to Highway 70.

With her driving she was most careful, but she wanted to talk, too "Yes, marriage and sex, and that leads me into the exciting adventures of Kevin and Vivian." She took a deep breath while they yielded to traffic. "I don't think you want to know about Kevin and Vivian." Her eyes became dark and she could not look directly at the musician. "At Marvin's I faintly mentioned the adventures of that Gary somebody that Steven Young asked me to relate to you, and I certainly didn't know who he was talking about." And I certainly did not have any idea why Dr Young should ask me to tell you what happened." She lifted her volume above the traffic as she pulled onto 70, "I know you don't go to bars, whether straight ones or gay ones. He is a cello player, I think Steven said. Do you know this Gary whoever?"

"He's Gary Fuller, yes, I met him once at the cafeteria, I think. Yes, he's a cellist. Good, bad, or indifferent, I wouldn't know. I learned that three guys assaulted him one night late and he has a damaged arm and I think it's his bow arm. I don't keep up with the band unless . . . unless it's music business." She managed a quick glance to her friend, while he thought of more to say. "I'm sorry, Viv, about you and Kevin. He's a great guy, Viv. Really, I'm sorry. I'm still haunted by how Jerry talked to me. Maybe I can explain the whole thing later when I set things in order for my Mozart in San Francisco. I have two whole months now to really work, plus the Paris opportunity. Want to go to Paris with me?" That brought new life into the worried face of this lovely woman. "Let me know if I have any more letters." He grabbed her chin and kissed her on her right cheek.

"Yes, from U.C.Berkeley, yes, I will." She did give him her best smile and then turned onto the exit that led to his condo. He became quiet while she wove through York Avenue toward Colfax. It was true, he botched the entire explanation he wanted to share with Vivian. She would understand him, more than anyone in the whole Colorado wheat farms, more than anyone. She had offered her honest version of what had happened to her husband. Why couldn't he have offered the same kind of explanation about Jerry Champion?

William remained quiet. Kevin, gay? He would never have suspected that at all. He had always developed a wide variety of people and emotions, their quirks, their intimacies, their personal lives, for some of them. It was simple, today, to be exposed to so much information that to include sexuality was just ordinary any more . . . a standard of sorts. While he was not wise in computers, he did know that he could obtain any information he wished at the drop of a hat. William can now include the trait that everyone seems to relax and grasp the knowledge of sexual promiscuity, even to accept it on TV.. It's the new standard of not being shocked upon hearing that one of his acquaintances is moving in with a sweet young thing. Marriage is not to be discussed. Please, don't worry one bit! By the time they reached the condominium, he had said enough and he certainly thought about it out loud for Vivian to hush. Once his door opened, he grabbed his bags from the trunk and waved goodbye as she pulled away. He was tired. He asked the guard to help him, something he would never think of doing. Mrs. T was home but he elected to discuss his trip with her over breakfast the next morning.

By morning, his gnawing questions that had no answers, at least, not after the drive with Vivian. They kept recurring in his mind. He began to question almost everything that ever had happened to him. He told himself that all those events, since he was in Junior High School with one boy, other than Bobby Martin, absolutely meant nothing to him. They were always taunting him, teasing him about having to go home to practice. The way they said 'music' with a twist of careless antagonism had remained with him in the back of his mind. This began to infuriate him as he grew older. That rendezvous with Bobby from time to time echoed. What had been forgotten was not forgotten after all. At least Bobby was far more furtive about their clandestine meetings. That was sixteen and seventeen years ago, when Sterling, Colorado was all, everything, each of them had ever known. Trips to the big city of Denver were always exciting dreams, always on their minds.

Once, maybe twice, Miss Shriner was able to enroll William in several contests at that time. William began to mature in his talent and he knew this. Still, he was often guilty of trying to understand what attracted him to the memories that persisted. So far as he could remember Bobby Martin had remained in Sterling and somehow became a handyman, a field worker in wheat, and, lately, according to his parents, a house painter of sorts and a high school failure.

After a quick call to the hospital, he was going to visit the cello player. He did not know exactly why he wanted to go, but the hospital beckoned and his indecisions would take better form if he would be able to see him. When he inquired from the main desk, a cloud of doubt arose in his mind. He felt like he was in a situation which was not altogether what he wanted. But he followed the nurse down a hallway and around a corner and into Gary's room.

The nurse vanished. Gary Fuller lay in his bed with his right arm in a strong sling. He was astonished when he turned his head and saw William standing in the doorway. William moved closer and stood beside the two blankets that rested at the foot. The patient spoke first, totally surprised by this visitor. "Hello, Mr. Kaplan." His voice was sincere. "I guess I didn't expect to see you coming to see this poor unfortunate cellist. I thought you were in San Francisco." William stepped closer. Gary extended his left arm and they shook hands. The patient's hair was uncombed and he needed a shave. "Nice to know someone cares to visit me."

Any kind of an answer to that remark was for the while lost. William was not prepared to devise any pleasantries to cheer this acquaintance. In fact, he did not know him well enough. Gary must have been a good student before he applied to enter the realm of becoming a professional at his young age with the Colorado Symphony. Steven Michael Young did mention to him that he endorsed this student despite the youthful image. The conductor knew of this man's sexual orientation. It meant nothing to him and to the position as cellist with the 'band.' Steven had investigated his application some six months ago. He was hired. So Gary Fuller, tremendously happy about this opportunity, moved to Denver and obviously found a bar he enjoyed. At first, in what may become a long period of questions and answers, some of which could become personal and embarrassing, William merely observed the patient from as far distant a vantage point as perhaps a sly detective could master. He wanted to solve this picture not for Gary's advantage but for his own knowledge.

He did not and could not bring himself to ask what he wanted. Somehow, conversation remained on the pleasant level. Why he was in the Ranger Bar had become suddenly apparent the moment Vivian announced it on the telephone. This cellist was attuned to discover his own reasons and answers as to why he fled the confines of "no-place" Wyoming for the big, fabulous, free and easy life style he was seeking. Denver was easily becoming a magnet for this Lifestyle. After all, Gary had heard Denver was the answer to his future so he gathered his wits and cello about him and began a strong chapter in his own life. And, based on how he reported to William, lying as he was with a damaged bow arm, three god damn hoodlums followed him into the street and practically killed him. So he said. So he reported to the piano player. And that is the way it was! Gary said that, whether or not William was prone to talk about it. It would be a long, long time before he could play his cello. First, the scars, inside and outside, had to heal. And with that, William, who had been listening attentively, smiled his best smile and shook the left hand once more. After providing words of consolation, the best he could conjure, he made a quick exit. By the time he reached the condo, he did not practice much of anything.

Chapter Twenty

JERRY WAS CAUGHT IN a maelstrom of indecisions, captured as he was in a world of doubt and ambiguity. His whirlwind through high school, with innumerable dates with sweet-young-things, as he called them, was just that—a busy fascinating trip from one incident to another. His confession to William upstairs was as much a surprise to him as it was to the pianist. This new chapter in his life was complicated. He could not afford that mental state. But time alone was cooperating. In one more weekend, he would be on a break between summer school and the beginning of his final two semesters. Jerry was confused by the fact that this man was more closely related to him than he could expect. For a while, earlier, he began to notice the subtle similar habits. Both of them understood the value of disciplined study, he, with his work, and William, with the daily necessity of practice on the keyboard. The sudden joy of seeing each other after a dry season of merely written correspondence was equally a boon to friendship.

A year ago Jerry found a small sign which read, "Study today— study hard." Someone had tossed it out in the trash bin behind the apartment. He captured it and now it was hanging near the medicine cabinet in his bathroom. He had stared at it every morning just as he was staring at it now. He was necessarily occupied with the habit of disciplined study. His advisors, especially Dr. Nelson, had complimented him more than once, although by now he was capable of easily comprehending just where he was and how much longer he would have to apply himself. Research and application to his doctorate was passé by now. He did not write any of these thoughts to Denver, not now, at any rate. He would be all right. He told himself he would be absolutely, exactly, specifically be a better person. Jerry did not confide anything to his aunt regarding how he felt. He could not account for what brought on the moment of that emotional incidence up in the attic.

The few days since William's return to Denver had developed into an agonizing valley of decision. No one realized the bittersweet series of events which prompted the outburst in the first place more so than he. The late August weather in the mile-high city was cool enough for a walk in the Chessman Park, just long enough for him to watch the teenagers at their soccer, just quiet enough for him to remember that Jerry would be taking that week-long break. The candidate struggled at times to keep his mind on geology. For one who does not ordinarily extend a request for personal correspondence with a stranger, especially a celebrity, he did begin to experience the complex alteration of his entire being. He could not account for reasons how this experience evolved. It was just evident, something that appeared. Even his aunt noticed the change during the weekend trip before the break between August and September . . .

At the time when he began that last week of summer school, he received a long letter from Denver. It was impressive and gentle in context, even beautifully complimentary. "Do not be alarmed at all, Jair," he wrote, "we have a lot to be thankful for. I am feeling strange, myself. The blunt interruption of my word, Love, just was sudden. I just said it out of the clear blue sky. But I meant it, Jair, I meant it." Jerry felt relieved, if anything, that he would have a complete week long break before the fall semester. He had not written him prior to that letter, so it was a total seven days that he used to prepare a decent reply. The letter that he did write in answer was not a good one, never organized in his good mind before he set it to paper. He was just intelligent enough to be confused and ignorant enough not to realize the extent of this change. Before he grabbed his overnight bag for a week on Green Street, he tore up his attempt to answer William's letter. He told himself that he waited to rewrite it when he felt more like being thorough rather than to let the words fall where they may. He would go up in the attic to be alone where he could think well and say exactly what he felt like writing. To be in the space where he heard *Love* which so astonished him that he was caught in that momentary nanosecond of time where tears came instead of a reply.

He was still a reader, much to what his family knew already when he was still in high school. He read a lot of texts at MIT and the librarian there was always kind to him. Shortly after she realized that he was not returning to Cambridge, she wrote him, herself, to wish him good fortune at U.C. Berkeley. How it was that he never did develop the art of writing letters was not a problem with him. And William, who conceded that he also did not build a talent for scribing anything other than a note, rested on the fact that both had no time for nineteenth century penmanship.

This was a week of pondering how William was getting along, how he worked each day, how he managed to find practice time on exercising and Mozart. Despite these premonitions and pensive attitudes with such progress, whether they be in Colorado or California, Gerald Champion, whoever he claimed to be, did set his mind to accomplish what Dr. Clark bid him to complete. He was to be ready for his orals, first in early December, next, coming up in March before graduation. That is what he set his good mind to achieve. That is what he instantly perceived when William cupped his head with his two hands and told him that God had a reason for bringing Jerry into his life. All of a sudden, the future fell into place. Immediately, despite the consternation, Jerry was joyous that he did send that first ill-written letter last April to Denver. After he sat by himself on the top steps of the front porch and after he watched the rest of the world go by Green Street, he knew, he just knew, he was okay, he was all right, he was a splendid young man who loved another man. At some point in recent time, Dr Clark mentioned *philios*, or something that sounded like that, among the Greeks—those who started thinking three thousand years before the Birth of Jesus. Jerry remembered that.

Five days of those next seven were at Aunt Urs's house. Jerry and she talked, they reminisced, they spoke of her brother she definitely remembered. They talked about Monticello and that she was pleased that Albert was buried there among the Catskills. He professed often that he missed those mountains. As they walked down Green Street together, slowly, she with her cane, he offered the curricula ahead of him. She was again the proud aunt and she reminded him of that. "I wish your father were here to see you and how you have blossomed into the fine young man." It was her time to talk. "I hope William is getting along fairly well, preparing, I mean, for his return in November. I like him. When we return to the house, after this grocery store trip, I want to read again his note about the vouchers you are to take to the symphony box office. I want to obtain the best seats for the three of us. I don't think Li has ever been to a concert." To that, Jerry quickly remembered, "Where we can see his hands." When he was in the kitchen putting away the items, he glanced at Li's calendar. "Labor Day is early this year—September third."

It was raining again in Denver this last week of August, bringing with it cool breezes that lasted three days. Up in the mountains west of the highway to Colorado Springs, the wind was more active and cold. Vivian did not go with a group merely for the ride. She became morose and cheerless but she did manage to speak to William again. It was to warn him that Kevin elected to converse with him but on the pretext to congratulate him on his work at San Francisco and Paris. It was the first time that Vivian noticed that Kevin appreciated the pianist's talent, if indeed that was the case. Vivian told William that this was actually to find out more rumors, if any, about Gary Fuller. "Just be careful," she cautioned, "I don't know why he would want to get information from you, in the first place. While I have you on the phone, I'll just say that he has applied for a divorce with his lawyer. Weird. At home, even since the age of eight or nine, I had my wonderful grandparents to explain what it meant to divorce someone who had been so explicit to profess love for each other."

A day later, at Kevin's invitation, William decided to satisfy his own curiosity and accept his invitation to meet at Danny's, a nice café in the downtown area which everyone called *Lo Do*, where business men and women congregated to eat and chat. Rain again was in the forecast.

William was expecting almost anything from this football hero who had become a new stranger to him. This luncheon business was not new. He often was asked to join the Rotary merely because of his celebrity-status and for no other reason. Kevin was dressed in his business suit and carried a brightly colored umbrella. Danny's restaurant was a divided room with the portion for conferences of any size upstairs to which customers had to climb on narrow stairs with no handrail. Kevin went ahead of him and only ordered coffee for both, to begin with, he said. "I don't know what Viv has told you already, I mean. I haven't seen you in some time. We're getting a divorce, as you may already have been told. And I'm sure she told you why." He looked furtively around the small quiet area but no one else had ventured upstairs yet. "My God, Billy, you're old enough to know just what went on and that I'm seeing a guy. And no, he's not ex-football by any means. William gritted his teeth and looked over Kevin's shoulder. He took a deep breath and started to object, but Kevin continued. "He's younger than I and that's all right. With both of us, I mean." William started to rise. "Sit down, please," he said softly. "It's great to see you and I just wanted to talk. I got us menus from the waitress on the way up."

But William was ready to object. He looked directly at Kevin and began his soft words. But he was not expecting to become so discontent that he would ignore this person. He sat to Kevin's left so he could speak softly. "Now listen to me, Kevin, I don't know what you're getting by with and yes, I know what gay means. I wasn't born yesterday. To me, being *gay* is a big misuse of that word" He decided that he was ready, no matter what Kevin had in mind or why he wanted to confide in him. Perhaps he was seeing Kevin only because Vivian mentioned that he would be calling him. "I don't need for you to tell me this guy whoever he is will 'meet all your needs' any more certainly than how Vivian managed." Kevin leaned forward and began by a soft whisper even though no one was with them. "All right . . . all right, I guess I don't really care what people think about it all. Viv is a wonderful gal, Billy, and we both know it.

"I Itold her this: I don't know what's happening to me. I don't know why I'm gay but I am. It could be that I've been this way all my life and I not know it. Billy . . ." but he stopped. He returned to his original thought. "I certainly didn't know it when I enrolled at C.U. I was really lucky—luck had a lot to do with it—was really lucky to get on the first team." William leaned back in his chair and practically knocked over his cup of coffee, but his face had a world of doubt.

To that Kevin was aghast. I'd give anything in the world to understand what the hell is happening to me. I don't have time to get to a 'shrink' to find out. Gary . . ." By now his vocal volume had increased. Kevin noticed this change in William. "What?" Kevin repeated it.

"What is it?" That name bounced in his brain and stopped the whole scene. "I know a guy name of Gary. He's in the hospital." Another couple was escorted upstairs by the hostess and Kevin made a point to wait and think. "No. My Gary is . . . . never mind." Kevin relaxed. "Never mind. You don't know him." Again he began to whisper. "I'd give anything in the world to know what the hell is going on. I don't know a damn thing about all this gay business." As an after thought, he paused and excused the waitress. Kevin saw instantly a question return to William. He leaned back in his own chair and placed his hands to the side of his nose to massage his muscles. The coffee date was not progressing like he wanted. He stood up. "Good luck with Mozart, Billy." He grabbed the check. "I guess in the long run, in the end, none of this really matters." Kevin turned and disappeared down the stairs.

Chapter Twenty-One

Early September 1997

JERRY WAS RESTED. HE said goodbye to five comfortable days on Green Street. Li prepared a delicious Labor Day dinner complete with a chocolate mousse and his cabernet. Aunt Urs wished him good fortune and gave him a kiss on his cheek; Li gave him a care package which contained some cookies she baked especially for his return to campus. "These look Chinese," he muttered and she said that the recipe was one of her mother's American favorites. Li had a new habit of standing on the porch to wave goodbye to him. The beginning of September was warm which was unusual for the Bay area. All across the gray sky was the threat of rain.

He had with him a letter that he tried to fashion in the time he was there. It was full of sentiment but radically constructed; the first impression he had upon finishing it was that he had to re-write it. He told himself he was capable of being an improved author. He re-read it as he whisked under the bay and nibbled on a strawberry delight. He had spent some time writing but he was totally unsatisfied. Despite the Tuesday schedule ahead of him, he promised himself to do a better job. This was the first item to complete as he entered his apartment He felt it more than just necessary so he set about to find paper and pen and concentrate. The idea consumed him that he was unable to form relevant thoughts for William. For reasons, now, which were still undefined, even with dimensions that escaped him, his mind was active but his ability to place proper emphasis where he wanted was weak. However he was writing this letter, it was all for strengthening his approach to his talent. It was all for completing the first draft of his major work, the dissertation. That was preeminent, but after the letter.

So he placed that first copy in front of him and began. By the time he had finished, he smiled at his effort, picked up the letter, patted it, and placed it in an envelope to mail in the morning. He slipped it into the pocket of his zipper rain jacket. He had thanked William for listening as he did to his confession, as he called it. He was not chagrined because he knew he would understand. Jerry knew that.

He sat at a table by a window where he could monitor the arrival of rain. He was by himself and started to piece together the plans for the crucial nine months ahead of him. It was seven-thirty in the morning and all he wanted was a cup of black coffee and a 'Bear's Claw.' He decided that was sufficient for him until he finished with the appointment with his new advisor. He glanced at the sheet of paper lying to his right on the table. The name printed on it in ink by a nice young lady was Pickering, Joseph, M.D., and not Ph.D. Jerry recognized this name because he was one of the five on his committee. It was normal for the candidate to have as many as three separate advisors in those three years. But what was surprising was that he was a doctor, the medical kind. His appointment was today at nine a.m. From several of his classmates, those with whom he had already 'suffered' through those first arduous months, Jerry had learned to set his mind to accept the fact that he is about to 'suffer' more sweat and tears, blood, very likely, also. This Dr. Pickering could very likely be the third advisor of three, the first two of whom had already given him the 'green light' to do well. Dr. Nelson and Dr. Clark both were highly complimentary. He knew that, too. Jerry's will to do well was greatly strengthened, more so, by the companionship he shared with the piano player.

His first adventure of this new semester was to mail that letter. This was to clear his mind for whatever Dr. Pickering was going to mention. Ahead of him was a battle royal with time, study, preparation, research, library, lab bottles of all kinds, analyses, aprons, gloves, late hours, more study, no more as an instructor for freshmen, hardly any time for falderal, fewer times to run across the Bay to Green Street, but never fewer times for letters to Denver, even if he would have to wait until one o'clock in the morning to write them. The one huge threat for him was to establish the subject of his dissertation. He took a deep breath and slipped the appointment announcement into the pocket of his rain jacket since he saw that sprinkles were falling on campus.

He made his way to Dr. Pickering well in advance of the appointment due to the rain. "Come in, Jerry," the voice was cordial. He opened the door and was welcomed by this pleasant advisor. Dr. Pickering was tall, the first time he had noticed him, since all the men on his committee were seated at a long table. But Jerry did remember the brown crew cut for a haircut and his dark horn rimmed glasses. His shirt was white but he wore no medical jacket. He had no tie at his throat. The office was not as big as others and one chair was placed, ready for business. "Take off your coat and hang it on the wall sconce. Make yourself comfortable." He appeared cheerful.

"I guess I was surprised a bit," Jerry started, "I didn't know you were medical. I'm so used to Ph. D. people." But he did notice the skeleton hanging from the sconce where he placed his jacket. On the wall to the left were three certificates properly framed and exuding pride. Dr. Pickering had a second room for consultation with a basin, mirror, an area for the gurney and a tall white cabinet.

The doctor pulled a chair around to Jerry's side and sat in it. In his hand he had a folder with Champion written on the label. He removed his glasses and began to clean them with a Kleenex from a box on his desk. "Nelson and Clark both spoke to me just last week—nothing but good vibes for you, Jerry." He paused just long enough to replace his glasses and glance at him. "I want to tell you that all of us seem to agree that you are a fairly good young man and great student. It's our business to keep up with you and to explain as best we can if you are not a healthy one." He stopped long enough to clear his throat and replace his glasses.

His remark, coming so quickly since he arrived, was exactly what he wanted to hear. It alone erased worry that he could easily have shown on his face when he opened the door and presented himself. Mentally he was running his scales and warming his hands, as William would say. A significant amount of energy was devoted to William being in San Francisco to play Mozart and Aunt Urs, Li, and he would be there to listen to him. But he must set his mind to his doctorate candidacy. That is what he had written so well, he thought, at the end of that letter.

You'll understand, I'm sure, Billy. Please say you'll understand. He listened to the doctor and that, too, was what went through his mind. That is what Jerry had written in that letter he mailed. We'll just have to wait for Thanksgiving. Write when you can. Play well Pickering was writing. He leaned over the side of the desk to retrieve a sheet of paper for the file and Jerry's attention returned to the scene. Dr. Pickering noticed that he was somewhere off in a reverie and he was not certain if Jerry heard what he said. "Jerry . . . ?" he spoke quietly. He decided that he had his attention. "Jerry, I wanted you to see me because I have a couple of ideas for you. Nothing unusual, you understand, just merely some good advice, mostly, from me to you." He could see how Jerry's posture became relaxed and his eyes were more alert, now. "I want you to remain the good student that you are, because all of us on your committee are one hundred per cent for you. Are you getting enough rest? You look rested now. I bet you went to see your aunt during our break. It's nice that you can have someone as important as that who can keep you pleasantly comfortable." And then, after glancing toward his window to see how the rain had increased, he added, "and to feed you well! Dr. Nelson said that he remembered your uncle. He's quite a funny Englishman at times. He even told me that you want to visit England sometime." He had Italy in mind but England would so. "Yes," Jerry said right away, "yes sir, I do. That's on my agenda." He laughed at that.

The doctor smiled. "I want you to be extra careful that you eat well and get plenty of good sleep. These next months ahead of you are crucial ones and both Nelson and Clark and I will be commenting on your progression from time to time. We want you to stay alert to your studies and not to be too worried about anything." Then he concluded after pausing to visually appraise his attitude. "Jerry, you'll do well, I'm sure. I want you to be aware of your own health and to be sure you give full attention to what we plan for you. I don't want to go overboard but your background, your bearing, your manner how you handle yourself when the committee sees you are most proper. I don't wish to be too premature, you know, but you have the ingredients to make a fine Ph D yourself, in your field. Geology, it is!" By that time he was standing which prompted Jerry to rise. "I shall make my notes for this appointment and place them in your file for all to see." He offered to shake Jerry's hand. He could discern a happy countenance more so than when he entered twenty minutes ago. "Don't forget to zip up your jacket. Looks like it will rain all day." His handshake was strong. "Goodbye!"

———————

Again, Steven Michael Young called William into his inner sanctum with the message to Mabel not to disturb them. The conductor felt like an important tycoon with such a word to his secretary. When William showed up after the semester started, Mabel was ready with a pat on the back, something she would not extend to just any one. Steven opened his door and welcomed him. "Sit down, please. I have some more news for you." William was used to almost any kind of message, situation, or unusual occurrence. He was relaxed. "How would you like to play the Mozart for *us*, after the Thanksgiving gig?" He waited but then he added because he detected a moment of doubt in his eyes. "No, I mean it. Here in Denver U.S.A." He had a smile on his bearded face which turned into a wholesome laugh. He started to sit at his desk. After a startled second or two, William took a deep breath. "What's going on?"

"I knew you'd say something like that." Steven came from around the desk and sat opposite him in a leather chair he pulled even with William. It seems that every time he is invited into this room, something different shines forth. "Now, I know how you may feel about this, but sit back and listen to what I have to ask of you. By the way, Arthur Preston was very pleased about your behavior with 'his' orchestra. He's a stickler on proper image of musical artists and is a good manager. I've known him since the Middle Ages. Anyway, here it is. After you play the Mozart for them, we want you to repeat it here in Denver with us. I will conduct, of course—I'm as much of an egotist as any other musician! It's the only concerto we'll present in this season and I'm eager to learn how a concert grand piano will fit in the space we have for the orchestra. The time slot is our concert in January. I've already talked to the committee to cancel a tone poem and place you on the stage with us. You will already have good experience and this shouldn't be too much of a challenge. Our orchestras sound just alike." He laughed at that last remark, and then he added, "But Carter McKissick thinks his band is the better one. Do you want to think about it? I'll give you one minute and then we will go to the restaurant on fourteenth street. I'm starved and I know you are always hungry."

William was concerned about an altogether different case, that of Gary Fuller. He had intended to broach that subject the moment he passed Mabel's desk. Steven was not glib about any topic that required serious comment, regardless of the circumstances or the subject. He could chat about the price of eggs in China or Maxine's Whorehouse downtown, a block or two from the Capital Building. "Of course it's not a whorehouse," the conductor would giggle, "but everything occurs in that café. Even I have been discovered eating a hamburger there!" He was interrupted a number of times when he was in the middle of a piece of vital information. Having to halt and solve a different brand of humor was never new to him. He would merely take a breath and return to his own lecture—if it were a lecture. This time, he stopped, looked directly at the pianist and committed himself to being a detective. He then commented, "You look disheveled. Do you want to tell me this before I pry it out of you?"

"Let's go," was his reply, "I'll talk as we walk." They were silent as they waited the elevator to the wide aisle that separated the two parts of the Center. "I went by to see Gary Fuller."

That was not a surprise to the conductor but he could not register a reason, at least, one that would satisfy both of them. Steven whispered when they stopped to stand in line. "I was horrified to learn what happened to him. Being mugged like that, left on the sidewalk to feel the pain in the arm and in his heart as well." He acknowledged two passers-by and continued, "The arm is not broken because I checked with the doctor when I saw him, myself, shortly after I heard about it. He'll be able to use the bow, I'm sure. I'm grateful it wasn't his left hand. With a mother killing her five children—did you hear about that?—we wonder why we live in such a violent society. What in the hell is going on?" He had not spoken about the cellist's personal life. Perhaps he knew and felt that William did not know or care to know about the other side of this cellist's personality. William stopped immediately just at the glass front doors. Steven halted as well to ask mutely what the reason was. William confessed, "I know *what* he is, Steven. He told me so when I was in his hospital room."

This whole scene was one to open a new vantage point. The conductor was chagrined. He realized again for yet another time that such knowledge had always been subterfuge, especially a condition wherein any kind of perversion of any musician whosoever, regardless of which century, was hardly ever overtly expanded in the history of music, either European or American. Steven knew for a fact that the present history teacher, the one with a forthcoming Ph.D. to his credit, had never felt it necessary to discuss Tschaikovsky's *other* life.' One day, a few weeks ago, here at the aisle of the Center, this very subject reared its handsome head and was a sidewalk subject to a conference between Dr. Young and this same professor of music history. "It is just that often I don't think it is absolutely necessary to go into detail about whom he slept with and whom he said he loved—whether it was true or not." Young disagreed vehemently with him. Especially dormant among the art world, and especially between instructor and student, this kind of reference just was hardly ever exposed, mentioned, yes, but not expanded.

But it was never embarrassing to Steven Michael Young. This conductor was well aware of this trait among those who were directly involved with his world, with a wide range of people who were sincere about their God-given talents. Several times, Steven had heard many students repeat a phrase that became consistent with brave young minds; "God gave me this talent. I am who I am and I don't care if anyone disagrees with me." This one attitude was extensive among those whose lives remained secretive behind a closed closet door. They were stopped at the closed doors, these that opened to the café. "Let's go in, William," Steven suggested quickly, "we're holding up traffic. I'm hungry and so are you." After a selection or two, they sat at a table against the wall where they could offer to each other various comments. Steven was pleased to hear that the pianist agreed to play with his 'band' and under his direction. Frankly he felt relieved, not because there was any doubt that William would not accept this gig, but because they knew, quite overtly, each had known for a few weeks, at least, that they were still among those who defended their natural order of things.

Chapter Twenty-Two

September 1997

TWO DAYS LATER, KEVIN Cole telephoned William to apologize for disappearing from Danny's Downtown Café. He sounded out-of-breath and obviously distracted. "That was totally unlike me, Billy," he said loudly because he was speaking from a phone that was in a room full of people. Once he was assured that William was listening, he continued softly with his hand cupped around his mouth over the receiver. "Please, let's meet again and I'll call you to schedule. Please." To that, no answer came but all they heard was background noise. A moment elapsed while William thought. Then: "Sure, Kevin. No harm done. Okay."

William was always surprised about this football hero's reputation. He did not have much inclination to follow the sport but he was careful to say some kind of answer to Vivian's enthusiasm during their tenure at C.U. Before they were married, she could think of no one else. William had seen him on the field during a game once when Vivian invited him to Boulder for that purpose. They ended up a threesome at her favorite eatery. The cafe was filled with after-the-game crowd. For one who had very little concept of how to play the game, William did know the rudiments and what the players were expected to do. Actually the overall appreciation of the sport was more than just that but it was sufficient for him to enjoy Colorado's team and Kevin, too. This was the last game of the previous season, when Vivian and Kevin apparently still had sparkling eyes for each other. Such was the only time William saw Mr Cole on the field. But all that was still in William's mind.

Recently, after that quick noisy telephone conversation with him, William began to think that only he was all alone on some island somewhere, away from the academia of the university where so many of his fair-weather friends were on campus. Those few symphony members often were happy to nod to him whenever they passed on the sidewalks. Once or twice, one or two would stop to chat. He was always ready to endorse his long-standing opinion that all he ever wanted to do was to play the piano. He even wondered if horn players or violinists reflected the same loyalty to their instruments. There was once after that practice with the San Francisco "band" that he thought he detected the same kind of opinion from Joe Jones. He remembered that he did profess a loyalty to his expensive violin before they separated. The librarian for the orchestra stipulated that his life was filled with the joy that only music had given him. Such an opinion of such loyalty may sound like that which a twenty-year-old piano student would declare. It was satisfying to hear that kind of remark coming from a violinist.

DuPres, that fabulous Frenchman, would be the one to endorse this idea of his. Ten years ago, that was very likely true for William. As he did grow older, though, he was forced to recognize, also, the daily schedules that came and went, full of agonizing enticements that mystified him. Kevin Cole was versatile on the football field. Maestro Young conducted. Gerald Champion had a healthy and strong mind. God had been good to others, too, like horn players and violinists, tuba players and cellists. Once, just once, at breakfast one morning with Mrs Tomassi, he suddenly professed his deep concern with music to her. She reached over, smiled, and patted his hand.

Sitting as he did on the front porch of the farm house, he had grown up with the idea that traditional Colorado Values were chocolate syrup over chocolate ice cream, mince pie, and football games on Friday nights. Those were obvious to him along with hard work, telling the truth, respect for neighbors, and the richly textured wisdom of Miss Shriner. With his parents sitting in the porch swing, rocking back and forth, with Angus at his feet, William realized some very important ideals, those that came and went with the beauty of the lives surrounding him. It was good to be home as often as he could manage his time. Ever so often, when he could, William would say, "Thank you, God, for Patty Allen Shriner." He had often mentioned Angus in the same breath.

When he reached the high school level in his thinking, he learned to include race or religion, and the most surprising indoctrination, sexual orientation. Presently, he could laugh at any surprise because hardly anything he wanted to learn was never in the curricula in a school room complete with a 'black board.' Lessons were bandied about among laughing boys who exchanged raw jokes and delightful opinions on the playground and never had time to appreciate music as Billy did. Further lessons in the art of this orientation were something introduced to him by Bobby Martin. Only Bobby could be the one to show him lessons successfully. Billy might have been awed by it all but now he frowned. If a few other classmates heard about this protocol from the Martin School of Thinking, then that was all well and good. The Martin guy became lost, forgotten, and was never, he realized, to exist.

William was older now, wiser, he presumed, more alert to geography, thanks to travel, and to the marvelous personality of Vivian Anderson Cole. Very likely she herself was the most inquisitive girl William had ever known That was true. He was known for a very long time at the university as one who was a strong believer in almost anything he had set his mind to investigate. That trait was most apparent to a great many of his acquaintances. He was capable of putting aside the practice book of scales once or twice to take up arguing with this inquisitive woman. He was not, however, one to be politic. The Reagan times came and went along with the first Bush problems. What did matter to him, more or less as a prying interest, was the growing threat of violence, either physical or mental. When Steven did mention, in passing, so to speak, of the mother who killed her children, he could not erase the fathers killing wives. One such incident was on a downtown street in Sterling. Often, when he was in his shower, or possibly sitting on the city bus going home from school, he strove to make sense out of the senseless. His only consolation is that children are unaccountable to God. "It's a dog-eat-dog society," he once heard Vivian comment off hand one day. At another time, when she was ranting and raving about almost anything, she said she was sick and tired of hearing about the so-called sexuality that is outside the Christian standard. That was most assuredly the only time in all the years William had ever known her for this vibrant and intelligent woman to show concern and interest about a topic that was at this time her defense of the man she still loved . . .

This delightful woman—delightful when she wanted to be— telephoned the condo in mid-September shortly after the semester began. She had already resigned herself to divorce proceedings which would take, more than likely, yet another month to complete. She was an intelligent woman, William had always known that, complete with a desire to put it all behind her and go on into her third decade of life with a smile and a grin. A laugh, she could not manage at the moment. She knew that Billy was experiencing his own growing-up and she knew that boys were different from girls, in more ways than one. What she was enjoying now was a full capacity endeavor to understand what was happening by all the letters that had been delivered to her apartment mail drop. In her opinion, William had not explained any of it adequately mainly because he was just now able to make some sense of it all. The world of music was foreign to the geologist. By now, the pianist was more than curious about the theory of 'stones and rocks.' Again, as if completely out of the blue, William thought of his rock garden and someone who took a chalk rock and decided to draw figures on the front sidewalk. It was a unique situation and Vivian was not a stranger to unique situations.

The incident in the attic surged in his brain again. His most surprising moment that prompted his study of this assimilation of two separate personalities came the exact second when he felt compelled to rise from the bedroom chair and envelope Jerry's face with his two hands. That was only last month. Right now, along with this fascinating study of thirty-year-olds, Vivian Cole wanted to understand just what was happening to Kevin Cole. "What did you two talk about when you were at Danny's?"

"I'm a musician," William kept reminding her. "But I tell you what I'm going to do! To help you, I mean." He really did not know at this point in time what exactly he was going to do to help her but he was not going to tell her that he was *not* going to do anything. Instead of given her a direct answer, he thought to himself, "I'll play this little game and see what happens." Then smiled, out loud. "Yes, I intend to help you. Let me think about it."

That remark really did antagonize her. She wanted a specific answer, meat and potatoes, and not a lot of psychological hog wash to which she was anathema. "This whole picture must be more than bars and hoodlums who go around clobbering guys only because they're *that way*. "Whatever made you take a geologist by your hands and tell him that God brought him into your life? God, Billy. Who is this guy you write to in Berkeley? Is he some kind of saint?" William saw that she was not ready to stop. "When you go to Frisco in November, are you going to see him again?" She knew her answer before she finished her question. "I think maybe I'd better start an investigation into the Life of the Cellist to try to come up with some answers of my own. I already know all about that of a football player." Later, when she was telephoning him, a pause ensued on the line when William heard in the background the siren of a passing ambulance. "Please meet me at Maxine's Café and we'll have a steak together. I need consolation." She was using her voice that insisted. "I'm sorry I was such a harridan. This is beginning to look like a Bette Davis movie. I promise I'll be sane. Seven o'clock. Now come on, Billy. Be there."

William looked at his watch and decided he should leave now for the errand that preempted her invitation. He set aside the score of Mozart's second movement, washed his face, and changed clothes. With the reference which Steven had given him for searching for the answer he wanted, once he was on the bus for the university library, he reread the notes which he was certain would supply that which he was seeking. Steven Michael Young was always helpful on practically every secret that he wanted to expose. "Go into the reference section just to the left of the main aisle on the first floor and ask for Miss Durer. Tell her I sent you and to take good care of you. She'll probably be tickled to death to get to see you. She always asks about you every time I'm in the library. She herself is a walking encyclopedia, full of tid-bits which she can display on any given topic. No, I'm serious, Billy. She knows everything. Just ask her."

And that is exactly what he did. Miss Durer, fastidious, remarkable, efficient, was on duty but she was going home in fifteen minutes. "I may not have time to help you, but let's go to the card catalog first." She took the slip of paper from him and proceeded down a narrow lane which had books and papers on all sorts on shelves that were eight feet high. The item they sought was just within sight beyond the last of the high shelves. The "A" portion of the cards took up two separate rows of the name, 'American.'

Miss Durer turned to William to ask, "It isn't music you want, is it, Mr. Kaplan?" She was looking at his beautiful eyes. "If it is music, then we'll have to go to another filing." To this, he said, "No. It's just as you see it there, *The American Psychological Association.*" He waited as she continued. "Yes," she muttered. After a short moment, she extracted her pencil from her hair bob and selected a tiny sheet of scrap paper from where the stack rested to her right. She wrote down the call numbers, replaced her pencil above her right ear. "Now," she motioned, "I won't be able to leave my area to go with you, but let me show you where the treatises are." She patted the card lightly with her hand. "This is in a bound album and you'll have to thumb through them all to get to the one that reflects the number you need." She pointed again. "Not very far. Evidently it is a new possession we have since it is dated nineteen-ninety-five. Good luck, and give my best regards to Dr. Young. You know, I suppose, that you are allowed to make a Xerox copy, if you want it, but you cannot take the whole album home with you. The cost is a dime per copy. Do you have a dime?" He did. He thanked her and she disappeared. Her perfume lingered for a while.

William stood quietly in a corner location with students all around him in cozy cubicles. He began to read. Yes. This is what he needed now. Dated 1995, and prepared in an extensive paragraph or two, the one treatise manifested the information he was wanting. *The American Psychological Association indeed stated that scientific evidence shows that reparative therapy does not work and that it can do more harm than good. Soon, with more independent study, The APA will again publicly caution against so-called reparative therapy, also known as conversion therapy. The APA therefore is opposed to R.T. and we will be able to state, most assuredly, that treatment attempts to change sexual orientation are ineffective. The American Medical Association states that it opposes this R.T. that is based on the assumption that homosexuality per se is a mental disorder or based upon the a priori assumption that the patient should change his/her orientation. The Surgeon General's Call to Action asserts that this condition is not a reversible lifestyle choice.*

William took the treatise to the copy machine and inserted his dime, pressed the required button, and out came one copy. In fact, he had two dimes so he printed a second copy. On his way to the main exit, he looked for Miss Durer to say goodbye but she had gone. He was hungry and he headed for Maxine's.

Chapter Twenty-Three

Late October 1997

THE LATEST LETTER FROM Berkeley was written Sunday but the date was missing, something Jerry hardy ever forgot to include. Coffee had stained the second sheet. William could easily imagine that his friend went to the café and that the waiter included some chocolate chip cookies which he wanted. Jerry had mentioned this in a previous note. He was writing, very likely, late at night. But his sentences were more than neat and comprehensible due most assuredly to his learned ability to compose for his dissertation. Both Wiliam and Jerry were in their mid thirties. Sly little jokes about that age were creeping into their everyday vocabulary. The note paper was no longer torn from a spiral notebook but was removed from a white tablet. With regard to his doctorate, "I'm no longer a vagabond." Jerry did have an editor whom he hired to review each and every page that he was creating. He made certain that he was doing what all three advisors would be monitoring. "I'm spending a lot of time in the library where all the employees know me by now. It reminds me of M.I.T.'s book stacks." William grinned at himself.

These past few weeks had been good ones for both of them. "I've got you marked on my wall calendar so be ready." Dr. Pickering met him in the cafeteria one day and waved a cheery greeting at him. Jerry recorded the incident most proudly in the letter that the piano player held in his hand. The letters from Berkeley were indeed much better in content, structure, and all smiles. His latest letter to William contained a rather good snapshot of him taken just two weeks prior. Jerry was standing on the steps of the Geology building managing a charming smile.

Mrs. Ursula Griswold and Li had begun to relay happy information to neighbors about the coming concert. In a recent article on the Arts page of the *San Francisco Chronicle*, the author's first mention of the forthcoming Mozart concerto was flattering. A small print of a recent picture accompanied it. Mr. Hicks, in New York, had sent a publicity shot to the newspaper for any and all such notoriety, with a short quip that "no, I won't be able to attend the concert, myself, but thank you for the invitation." The preliminary announcement did misinform everyone that the pianist's home was in Denver. Aunt Ursula picked up her telephone to make the correction that Sterling was his hometown out on highway something, she couldn't remember what Jerry had told her, yes, Sterling, like in silverware. A town out east of Denver. Anyway, the rest of that article was all right. And thank you. "Yes," Ursula answered the voice on the phone. "Yes, I do know Mr. Kaplan. How kind of you to ask. He has been in my home. That was a nice picture of him." Then she waited. "I'm not at liberty to discuss what you ask of me but he has an agent in New York." Another delay. "Very well, my dear, I can say that he'll be here four or five days before the performance. I can have him telephone you." But to that, the conversation was completed and she hung up the phone.

Li then began to assist her in choosing what gown she should wear. She planned no jewels, merely a lovely locket she wore around her neck to such occasions, even though she did not attend many of the symphony concerts. But this one was special. Maybe she could wear the earrings that Albert gave her many years ago.

Stewart Parker was an enigma to many people with whom he worked at the *Denver Post*. A man well past forty years, he had only been in the Mile High City for ten of them, "more or less," he told anyone who asked. He was an expert business man but he did have a knowledgeable following to whom he advised the Art of Music. Two other gentlemen wrote about the Cinema. By now Stewart Parker's byline was nationally recognized as a good arts reporter. "I'm glad to be in Denver," he told the mayor with whom he had brunch one day. "I'm more akin to the symphony and opera than to the three theatres on the other side of the Center." He was proud—if anyone asked— that his specialty was displaying his knowledge of music. Drama and Painting were all right but music was constantlly on his mind. It was fairly well known—which was a favorite phrase—that he often did not enjoy the rock bands nor the personalities who beat the guitars and depended upon electric amplification rather than their abilities to *sing* appropriately. Holding a mike and screaming lyrics to the crowds of youths was just not his idea of good music. Those were his very words in a recent review which he was forced to write because no one else wanted to tackle a well-known group. "They don't realize that they are loosing their hearing by the time they are old." He removed his horn-rimmed glasses and smiled at the mayor's daughter. One teenage who read his review of this group castigated him with a scorching letter to the editor that the old man was just too old to report period. He also said that the paper should get a new reviewer and put this old guy out to pasture. Even so, Stewart Parker still remained at his desk on the third floor and was content to depend on Steven Michael Young and his two assistant conductors to manage the coming season. After all, it would feature the local boy whom everyone loved playing a piano concerto with "the band" by Parker's favorite German, Mozart. He verified this juicy item with the conductor himself. "Dr. Young," Parker had learned long ago that politeness always won over any form of rudeness. He had no time to respond to that teenager with such a lesson.

"I'm glad to reach you, Dr. Young. I am delighted to learn that our local boy with be in the spotlight to play Number Twenty-One. I have before me the list of your complete season." Steven was at ease whenever he chatted with this well known journalist. "I understand that Kaplan will play it in San Francisco in November and will be with your band in January. I am glad to hear it. Yes," he said after a slight pause to hear what the conductor was saying, "yes, I hope to interview this William Kaplan soon. Yes, sir, I spoke to him some time ago with his opportunity to play in Paris. Yes, sir, thank you, I enjoyed writing that because I drew from my own trip to France two summers ago. I haven't been able to reach this Mister Raymond Hicks whom I understand is his agent. I think I shall go ahead and contact William right here in Denver and proceed with my own notes and whatever to make it all personal for him and for you, if I may. May I call upon you to ask the pianist to call me at the paper? Yes, to set up this interview. Any time. Yes. Any time. Why, thank you, Dr. Young for your courtesies. Goodbye, sir."

The very next day, at noon, William Kaplan made an appointment to see Stewart Parker to talk. It was to be for the following Monday at two p.m. at the Brown Palace Hotel Coffee Shop, at a table specially reserved for the occasion in a quiet corner. "Do they have quiet corners at the Brown Palace?"

Malcolm Forrester was a student of piano at the university, a bright overt early twenties who had never had an opportunity to meet William Kaplan. He never did mention this to fellow students in the music realm because a part of him remained shy . . . As time grew closer to Thanksgiving, his instructor and advisor, the Frenchman, discussed a time when Mr. Kaplan, Malcolm Forrester, and he should schedule the request that Malcolm was submitting. This instructor, Claude Dupres by name, was a fastidious Frenchman who had come to America sometime in the nineteen eighties with a claim that he hailed from the Loire Valley and had studied quite well at the National Conservatory. And he, along with a few other Europeans who lived in Denver, was most pleased to have endorsed the invitation that Paris offered. This instructor, long since having surrendered himself to academia and not performance, was a student himself of the art of Camille Saint Saens and of course was proud of his knowledge of Maurice Ravel. "And so therefore," Du Pres proffered the idea to Dr Young that the four of them sit down in Danny's Cafe, of all places, "because I should think it rewarding to Malcolm that he should have a tete-a-tete with Mr. Kaplan." This was decorated by a thick melodious French accent to which everyone by now was accustomed. "Oh, yes, I quite understand that it is best to wait until after the Holidays and the concert in San Francisco. Just a few minutes because I know it would benefit my student." Malcolm's age? "Twenty, I'm sure. S'il vous plait. Merci." This Frenchman really wanted to go to the Brown Palace Hotel for this lunch. He promised himself that he would think of something to get them out of the *Lo Do* area.

"Good grief," surmised the conductor, "seems everyone wants to talk to William!" Steven Michael Young had been the conductor of the Colorado Symphony for a number of years, how many only he and his buxom secretary knew. He once was quoted that he and Molly Brown were sweethearts. But, as everyone in the music field all across the nation knew, he had quickly become the most proficient musicologist and respected leader of his "band." Some people thought that he obtained that term from John Philip Sousa himself. When the outside world got to know him and to laugh at his jokes, his quips about sharps and flats, they soon realized that this genuine person was really a paragon. Before the Second World War he was able to talk his parents into supporting him with a lengthy study at the conservatory, for everyone who was anyone knew where the "Conservatory" was. The one element that superseded any degree of healthy learning was the fact that all of Europe was engulfed by that war. In early nineteen-forty he limped back to Reality as soon as he could find a cabin on the next west bound freighter. He wept all the way across the Atlantic. A legend was born and Colorado appreciated him.

Now, of course, he was at an age that defied rumors that he was one hundred three years old. "No, I am not, I am one hundred four." Down deep in his psyche where loomed a secret vault of thousands of answers to thousands of questions, he professed only he was able to provide answers to any and all the problems of the music student, the music world, the comings and goings of the devoted artists. Many others who came to his office wanted to know just what it was that compelled the artistic impulses to create, to the exclusion of almost every other endeavor. Why was it apparent that a great amount of devoted artists were absolutely loyal to the talent within them? Yes, he had answers for that, also. In many cases he had to ask Mabel not to bother him when a young mind wanted to know exactly what was happening to him. No, he was not a psychologist. That department with its wise doctors was elsewhere on the university campus. No, he was not on the faculty, but even so he knew all the answers. The entire city of Denver was his children and his children soon realized they had a gem of a conductor. And Almighty God was on his agenda every day. Steven Michael Young talked to Him when he could turn off the office radio and calm down. Mabel once heard him talking in his everyday voice. With her door open she thought someone was in the room with him. That was not the case; he was praying.

This business of Gary Fuller was not new to him. As a young man in Paris, he was subjected to the rigors of sexual activity, something his

American mind was shocked to learn. The so-called red light districts in narrow streets south—and north—of *Ile de le cite* were popular, oe might say, and grandly so. The conversations he began to have with William Kaplan were merely to call upon his storehouse of knowledge regardless of the concern. Albeit, it began to grow and mature as he entered into the time warp of being one hundred four. "No one, at first," he offered William as an incentive to investigate for himself, "can comprehend just what it is that tantalizes the impulse to promiscuity. The report from the *American Psychological Association* is a good one and I thank you for bringing me a copy. I heard about it from Dr. Rivera. He is Head Honcho in the Psyche building. He is interested in the orientation as it is obvious among the artistic community." Then Steven paused, thought about what he wanted to add dryly, "but not all artists are *that way*. The trait is found in other professions as well."

He rose to answer his phone and while he spoke at length, William found himself at the window again looking at the park. Soon, Steven hung up and asked the pianist, "and so I want you to know, as far as Mozart and January are concerned, that was Mabel on the phone. She has a confirmation and a schedule for December for you to consider when you return from The City out West.I think it's just an ordinary calendar for December. We won't demand much of your time. The band will start on its part along about now, I think." He studied William's face as he started to leave. "You be good, young man, and take care of yourself. Don't forget to put the date of our Christmas party on your calendar. No, it won't be in costume. Mable won't be wearing her helmet." He escorted him to his door., stopped him and looked directly into his eyes. "You . . . are going to be fabulous. I wish I could go with you and pester ol' Carter McKissick myself. Goodbye."

Chapter Twenty-Four

Thanksgiving Week 1997

FOR WHAT HE THOUGHT was the first time in his young career William Kaplan did not allow his personal contentions to interfere with his performances. He had a multitude of opinions based on anything pertaining to the world of music in general and the classics in particular. There were times when he was off the planet and into another universe, so excited was he in the way his life was going. He had equally many moments when he felt he could no longer give credence to anything *but* music. A few days he could not account for his laziness, his inability, he thought, to concentrate on any exercise. At other times he practically exhausted himself with his renditions of the Mozart that was ahead of him. And then the calendar could not lie.

Two days ago he arrived; with bag and exuberance he invaded the City. November in this part of the Bay was ideal. He reported to Mr. Preston immediately for the purpose of booking practice time for Thursday and Friday—not all day each day but sufficient time to mentally prepare. Li noticed his quiet self that Wednesday morning. Berkeley was quiet; classes were practically empty with just a few students scurrying through the usual moments when no one wanted to remain on campus. Li, Aunt Urs and he agreed Jerry would be here soon. From where he sat on the front porch he could see the intersection where city buses stopped to deliver passengers. That spot became his favorite. His feet were on the usual step when he faced Green street. Aunt Urs brought him a mug of coffee because it was still early. She knew where William was waiting. "Gerald will be here soon. He called me earlier and told me to have you sitting on the front porch. You must like the bed in the attic," she laughed. "It's yours while you're here, of course." She looked to her right, down the street where the bus came from Market. "It's a bit cool, I think I'll go back in." She patted him on the head and answered Li's call from the kitchen. He agreed with Jerry that Green Street was his street and the pedestrians who walked by the house waved at him.

Prior to this adventure into Mozart, he agreed that he had no dangerous antagonistic threats. His arrival gave him ample time to relax and appreciate yet another confirmation from Jerry to stay with him. "You don't need to check into the hotel until Friday afternoon," Jerry had written. Now, he waited as patiently as he was able for Jerry to arrive. He thought of Miss Shriner. He was always grateful to her for teaching him how to focus on the music within him, regardless of what occurred outside his realm of existence. Once he felt the strength of his work, in that he recognized his maturity in playing. He did so with the joy and beauty of his art form. Very few people understood this.

But now that he met Gerald Champion and accepted his friendship which seemed to proceed at an uncommonly swift pace, he discovered that he was thinking of him more often than he realized. Denver seemed so very far distant now when he viewed the Pyramid Tower, the traffic on Columbus Avenue, the noise of Green Street. The couple who lived next door, who were overjoyed to hear him play the night they came, passed on the sidewalk and waved at him. "Hello again, Mr. Kaplan," one called, "Best of luck on Saturday night's concert."

Over the weeks since April, William surprised himself with the number of letters he had written to Jair. The replies were equally abundant. The important lesson that he learned from all of this was that never did he presume that this vital Somebody was a threat to his playing in concert. Now of course he would be grateful for moments in time they both shared. For some strange reason, others may molest his reasoning but never Jerry. He did not allow this action to interfere with his talent, to supplement his work as a devoted artist. Practice continued, scales were still necessary, the rudiments of sharps and flats, all had never been ignored. That is why he wanted the extra time alone today and tomorrow with Preston's permission. Other than Vivian Cole, he had no one who could claim a deep and abiding adoration. There was something about this that he appreciated. He was no longer concerned about anything. He was going to play well and he was going to recognize this new empathy that would be sitting in the audience. He was no longer a loner. He was ready to perform. He was there with Jerry the day before when he reported to Miss Bradley that he was ready. It was she who was able to see the mysterious change that came over him when he asked to use the rehearsal room and the Steinway. Arthur Preston said "Sure thing. We'll pass the word to the three men who are working on the wiring in the booth. I think you already met one of them. In fact, they may not even be working."

New breezes came in from the Bay and swept across Market Street, down Grove Street between Symphony Hall and the big impressive City Hall. Jerry was ready to relax; his work was closed up for Thanksgiving, but he had to be back on Monday. "All is under control," This was the report to Aunt Urs on the telephone that morning. He was in the matter-of-fact voice again, "I'll see you soon. Today begins for us."

A bus stopped on Columbus Avenue going north. Jerry exited carrying his overnight bag. He proceeded East, looking for his aunt's house. William was on the steps. Once again they were laughing together.

Li was just as pleased and excited as Aunt Ursula. On Thanksgiving after their large dinner with wine, Jerry and William checked himself into the hotel. Then, deliberately they returned to Green Street. where they sat upstairs to talk about the price of eggs in China.

On performance afternoon Li. happily prepared a nice three p.m. steak just as William wanted. Jerry sat opposite him and watched him eat. Then, when it was time to leave, William grabbed the taxi that sounded its horn. He was ready. He stopped at curb side and signaled to Jerry who stood on the porch. "Come here!" That last bit of information that he gave was, "Don't forget the reception at the Hall. All of you!" And he disappeared. Jerry watched until the taxi turned out of sight. Ursula stood at the front door to observe how all of this registered in her nephew's happy face. She was pleased. Now their time did begin.

All this, including the outstanding performance, the noisy reception, the eager hangers-on which William expected, the tuxes, the splendor of matrons' gowns, the flash of cameras, this moment for William was new to Jerry, Li, and Aunt Urs. Together at the reception they felt that nothing indeed would be better in their lives than this moment, even though Jerry remained on the edge of the party. Aunt Ursula and Li were ecstatic. It was all just as he had imagined. He watched as young girls surrounded the guest of honor, their desire for his autograph, the young fellows who patiently stood to wait for their dates to laugh and giggle and vie for attention.

A man in his tux suddenly appeared at Jerry's side. "You must be the student from U.C. that Kaplan mentioned to me." Jerry could not escape him. "I'm Arthur Preston, the manager of the symphony." He offered his hand and looked closely at the short beard on Jerry's face. "You some kind of musician?"

"No, sir, I'm not. I'm working on my degree in science." Jerry replied simply because he already felt out of place earlier when the reception began, he in a suit and not a tux. The applause became overwhelming to him when William and Mr. McKissick were toasted by Arthur Preston. William made a point of acknowledging Aunt Urs—as he was able to call her, now—and Li, and personally to step over to the wine table with them to introduce them to Carter McKissick. Jerry was there, of course, and that is when Arthur Preston met the two of them. But as he turned to shake Jerry's hand, the girls got in his way with their pens poised. Preston tried to finish a conversation that was interrupted. "What are you studying at U.C.Berkeley?" Jerry was trying to drink his wine. When he spoke, the laughter and noise obliterated his answer. Preston only nodded his head, smiled a weak grin, and reached for a glass of wine for himself and vanished in the crowd.

Gerald became weary of it all and in a short moment when William found time to look at him, he realized this. "Let's go, Jerry," was all he needed to set his wine glass on the table and follow the pianist out of the room. "Good night, Aunt Urs" They obtained a cab for the two ladies and watched them depart.

In another moment they were in the Ambassador lobby. They sat on the big sofa in the center of the room. "Now, you've been through the mill," William smiled. Jerry looked at him silently with tired eyes. "The hotel restaurant is still open and I think it's time for a sandwich. Remember?" William waited for an okay and continued. "I've got a room with twin beds and a nice shower." He stood up and handed him the door card. "Let's order room service and call it a day. Come on."

———————

Despite the late hour they sat on the beds facing each other with the narrow space separating them. They finished eating and William poured a cola into two glasses. He could see that Jerry was exhausted. In fact he yawned twice. The pianist was used to this process of concertizing. But it was late, especially for Jerry who usually had to rise early any morning. "I have something to tell you, Billy. I've got to tell you before you go back to Denver tomorrow." This was all so unlike Jerry, to commit himself to his own approach to a talk. He spoke with his serious voice; he was too tired for any other type.

William took a sip and put the glass on the table by the telephone. He removed his tux tie and shirt and threw them beside him on the bed. They looked at each other for just a moment before Jerry blinked and began. "Aunt Urs is going back to New York State, maybe to settle in Monticello. She and Dad were born there. I think she really wants to do this, Billy." He removed his own suit coat and laid it on the other bed. With his feet on the rug he stared directly into brown eyes. "She has always liked this part of California, I know that, so it all came as a big surprise to me. To Li also. Li has been with her for a long time." While Jerry stopped to take a big swallow of his drink, William took off his shoes and pulled one leg upon the bed. He was expecting anything. "I really think she wants to go back. She told me once that she misses the hills around the town." He stopped, stood up to remove his tie. He waited for another moment, peering into William's face to see how he was accepting all this. Right away he asked. "You listening to me?" William was non committal but grinned. "Billy, my aunt left me the house, including Li if she wants to remain with me. I've got a house now. It's all mine. All she and I have to do is go to her lawyer's office next week to sign papers. It's all set. Li knows all about it. She knew about it before I did."

With this 'bit of news' as Jerry put it, William took a deep breath and wondered just why this was affecting him so drastically. He reached for his glass to take another swallow and he looked at Jerry again, seeing a frown appear. "Well, say something," the frown said, "Say anything."

All William could do was to smile and with this smile, Jerry's face changed from that frown to a broad grin which broke out into the smile with his dimple that William had always known. "Well. It's true. I got a house on Green Street next week and I don't know what in the hell I'm going to do with it. Billy: I've got to finish my doctorate. I won't have time to adjust to this falderal." Jerry stood again and began to pace in the small space that the room afforded. His voice manifested all the textures he had, repeating, "I've got a house" as if he couldn't believe what had happened. He came back to the beds and pulled William off his twin and grabbed his face much as William had done to him some time ago. "I got a house, Billy." This, the second time, was repeated softly while he stood opposite the piano player to gaze directly into his face. He grabbed him joyfully and for just an additional quiet moment, William could see how buoyant Jerry's joy actually was! Now, William thought, Jerry had to work. This crazy joyful geologist—somebody was really important to him, and they both realized it.

Chapter Twenty-Five

December 1997

WILLIAM HAD TO STOP what he was playing and sit back from the score and think about another matter. The concept, appearing and reappearing inconsistently, was forming into a stronger dimension. He still gazed at the notes, he still was half-immersed in the mood of the second movement, but he waited for the thought to dissipate, if it ever would. It reminded him of movie music, written to assist the scene but never to become predominant enough to be too noticeable. It did, however, halt his practice for just a while. Mozart was haunting him, in that San Francisco was an outstanding success. No, it was not Mozart. The concert in January was not necessarily a problem.

For the first time in well over two weeks he felt this urge to separate himself from Saint Saens. That was a threat, something he did not ever dare to acknowledge. He could not afford to separate his mind from the score. He did not move, he did not rise to look at what new Christmas lights may be on the street below the condo. The thought became persistent to a degree but was never harmful. He decided that whatever was haunting him had nothing to do with the theory of music or the notes on the staff pages in front of him.

For all that went before him in his thirty years, he did not or he could not allow different areas of his previous existence to interfere between him and his gift. He was not arrogant; he was never selfish about his talent. That was just the way it was. He looked again at the score. This was some urge which had been with him for a good length of time. If he did encounter strange quirks while growing up, if he did meet with puzzles of any kind, these incidents were either too miniscule or they did not register with him until this moment. He realized that something invaded his mind and blurred the notes on the pages. He was passing from having completed thirty years of age and now, regardless of what the culprit was, he was now thirty-one. He still had his affinity, his joy, his impetus for music.

This came at a time when he did not hear from Berkeley in two weeks. That fortnight was well into December, when winter finally arrived in Colorado. Perhaps that alone was the main reason why all of this thinking interfered with his concentration at the keyboard. All the previous twenty years, since he realized that his music was the only undertaking that was preeminent, he was content to live such a life. Prior to this moment, this new serge of piecing together the puzzle of it had never bothered him.

Miss Shriner had been for him all this time, had encouraged him to "study hard" as she insisted on reminding him. "I want to tell you, over and over again, Bill, of your prowess. I want to commend you for your consistency in your progress." Her words were forever at the frontal lode of his mind. "If I teach you anything, then it is that you should be grateful and you should be persistent in your practice." Even when he enrolled at the university and became astounded by the variety of other people, he still was piecing together this puzzle of what he had done for himself. And what he had done was to underscore a way of life that meant more than anything else in his whole universe. Some secret ingredient of his thinking was there and he really had no time to investigate it, until now, on this cold and blustery morning. It was all because he played a concert while on tour in Berkeley one evening eight months ago. He dared to agree with himself. He did agree. This weird panorama pointed to Jerry Champion.

He rose from his piano bench, stretched his arms and hands, and stepped away from his piano and from the Saint Saens masterpiece. He went to the window and looked at the Christmas lights in the apartment building across the street. He watched the traffic. He doubted that snow might fall before nightfall. He had been working on a difficult portion of the second movement and it was time to walk around the room. He stopped at another window, looked down, just in time to see that the mail man was leaving in front of the condo. In a sudden and delirious thought, he raced down the hallway to the elevator and went down to the main lobby. There, waiting patiently was a letter postmarked Berkeley in the box. And in it he learned that Jair was working extremely, diligently, and had no time, no long moments to write before this note. Of course, Jerry was sorry he hadn't written any sooner but that, as he knew, he really didn't have time to say what was far more important than to admit the price of eggs were in China. William grinned and laughed at the rest of the crazy words. On the way back upstairs, he felt a strong impulse serge within him, one that obviously could be the essence of what he felt. He was at the intersection of this new and mysterious valley of decision, this complicated avenue down which he was speeding. What, indeed, was happening to him?

William picked up the phone when it rang. It was Kevin Cole. "I've been thinking about you and hope that we can meet." Those were the first words he heard. The fact that it was Kevin, and not Jerry, calmed him considerably. William sat immediately in the nearest chair. "It's really nothing," he admitted, "other than I haven't seen you since you got back from San Francisco." Hearing from the football star was a genuine surprise, one that erased the maze that was growing in his mind. It was time for William to take another break. He had never given Kevin a second thought since the divorce was finalized. "I know you're working on the French thing for Paris. Frankly I wish I could go with you. Vivian told me you're going to play the Mozart thing in two weeks. Or is it in January?" There was an awkward silence on the line when William heard him clear his throat. "Maybe I can go hear you play the Mozart thing." Kevin paused. "Listen. I was hoping we could meet somewhere for a break. You need a break from all that practicing you do." This was so like Kevin, to call him infrequently and then, when he does, to act like they're old drinking buddies. "You want to meet me for a drink? I'm buying." Kevin cleared his throat again and William could hear a clock chime five o'clock in the background. This interruption warranted an explanation which William felt he could afford. "Okay?"

William looked again at the letter from Jerry and placed it on the table by the phone. "Someplace where I can eat," he answered. "Mrs. T went to Chicago to spend Christmas with her family and I don't want to fix anything here tonight." To this, Kevin agreed jubilantly. After he suggested that he bring something to the condo which William negated, they did decide on a café other than Maxine's. "I know a place, really nice place. In an hour, say, and we can sit and talk. Viv said you like Mexican. Okay, it's Carlos' Cabaret. Thanks. See you just after six." William said okay and hung up. He looked at Jerry's letter once more, put it back in its envelope. He could answer this when he returns. Then he took a shower. He did give a thought to why Kevin called. But such a reason was inconsistent, anyway. Kevin was hardly ever on time since his football antics. He was always the first into his scrimmage uniform and last one out of the showers. Vivian told William that once not too long ago William again thought that Kevin was diligently trying his best to be a friend when he was, most assuredly without friends.

The bitter wind was still brisk but that was typical Denver. He wondered just what Kevin was doing. Vivian had mentioned him as usual. He could discern that the woman still loved this hero. To him, her best buddy, she was always showing some degree of care for this 'hunk,' as she stated. She had often told William that she would spend the rest of her days trying to decipher just what in the world was taking over her ex-husband's mind. In all her born days, as she had put it, she had encountered every deviation of brain waves, especially those that pertained to her bedroom. She had had more than one honest conversation with this piano player in an attempt to analyze how Kevin was still Kevin, having wept genuine tears in their apartment so very long ago, walking around in Denver with a huge question mark above his head. And when William either could not or would not analyze with her, she looked at him and her anger took the place of her patience. "Okay," she retorted, "If you refuse to discuss this, I won't bother you any more about it. You are undoubtedly out in left field yourself that all you care about is your dumb music." The moment she said that to William, she admitted a sorrowful and agonized denial... This may have sounded mean but it really was not, because Vivian could never be mean. This woman also knew when to make a joke and when to walk away from a problem. To her, her ex was most assuredly the number one in her life. Possibly Kevin wanted to hear that.

William waited inside the lobby of Carlos' Cabaret. He had eaten there a number of times, once with the Frenchman. Its interior was typical Mexican, low hanging wooden parrots with purple feathers, wildly yellow walls, and the best burritos mojados in Denver. And, too, because he learned Kevin was never on time. Carlos himself welcomed him with a wide smile and delightful Spanish with his accented English. "Don't worry, Senor Kaplan, your friend Senor Cole will come. I know him. His friends also tell me he is late." He claimed two menus from the counter to his left and laughed. "Look—there he is, now!"

Carlos escorted them to a square table with a checkered oil cloth for cover. Kevin hustled in and unbuttoned his Mackinaw. The wind had increased and his hair was mused. "I'm hungry, Carlos," he said, and then to William, "Thanks for coming." In a moment later, they were seated, all alone at the far end of the room by the side windows with wine. "Merry Christmas and all that jazz." Kevin lifted his glass in a quasi toast. "You look great, Billy. Vivian told me you did well in San Francisco. Why don't you move to the City?" That last remark was so sudden that William did not have time to sip his cabernet. "Vivian tells me you've been getting letters from Berkeley, a lot of them since God knows when." Kevin did not surprise William in many respects, his droll sense of humor, his insistence on meddling in other people's personal letters.

Vivian was always discreet that Kevin was able to add a lot to his own ideas to bolster up any situation. "The last time I spoke to Vivian she told me she had mentioned to you that this Gerald whoever guy should write you at the condo address, now." That was Vivian's latest subtle suggestion during one of her last telephone conversations. She knew when to be subtle at times. When Kevin heard this, he agreed. He did not know what he wwas talking about Besides, he was actually not seeing Vivian much these days. Well, it worked. William got his letter.

But Kevin did begin to wonder during their dinner. He was content to sit and eat and try to ascertain just what William was thinking, for he wanted to ask far too many questions. "A good looking guy like you, in your early thirties, a terrific pianist, still single, with all the sweet young things hovering over you after each concert, pleading for autographs, wanting . . . a lot of things, very likely. In this day and time with all the raucous music I hear on the radio,—God, it's so damn loud—your kind is still popular!" William let him carry on from one topic to another for he commented radically on several. He had yet to learn why Kevin had wanted to talk to him in the first place. "Vivian has always been a real good pal for you. I just never did know how it was that you and she were so close and yet you didn't marry her to begin with." William answered quickly. "Why don't you ask Vivian?" That stopped Kevin. He took one more bite of enchilada, leaned back in his chair, and grinned while he sipped his wine. "Well, I actually did, at one point in our life together."

William countered, "I could ask you a question about how anyone could appreciate the sport of football. I got the idea that it could become quite an addiction, for a lot of people and such. With you I always thought you cared more about Monday night football than you did about anything. With you, football was all you wanted. I once heard about Football University at Boulder." That was true for Kevin and the team. William studied his face before he continued. "I can understand that. With me, it's my music." That remark was new to Kevin. Much like an addiction. Evidently William did not ever think of music in the same light as Kevin's precious teammates. William's statement was closely akin to something one of the high school players—maybe it was the Martin kid—had shouted out one afternoon a long, long time ago in the school showers. "I wonder what the football team thinks about when *they* take showers." William smiled to himself; only a Jock would think of something like that. William remained ignorant of the theory of the sport and now was a good time to cease that approach.

"You never did date, did you?" Kevin leaned close so that his question was directed intimately. "I always wondered why." William put down his coffee cup and replied in the same soft tone. "I didn't have time." This was not the answer the inquisitor expected. He continued his gaze into William's stone face which did not change in the least. Kevin wanted another answer, one he could write on one of the paper napkins. For just yet another long moment, he bargained for a specific word or two but apparently he was not receiving what he desired. Kevin was still very treacherous. He had known this pianist for as long as he had known their mutual friend. He presumed he knew all about why good looking young college guys never did date or never did get married or never did do what normal ordinary football players did. But Kevin was not an ordinary football player. Kevin was a *different* football player and whether Kevin knew it or not, William would never encroach upon his personal life with any such questions similar to those Kevin was throwing at him, either directly or subconsciously. Kevin began to laugh softly as he stood and signaled the waiter for the check. He said nothing as he paid the bill and followed William through the front door and to the sidewalk. "Gracias, senores," was Carlos' goodbye with a nice wave of his hand. "Button up, it's cold out there!"

They paused at the first intersection. "You are a really nice guy, Billy." They waited a second or two before he added blatantly, "I just thought that you might be like me." Hearing this from Kevin did not shock the pianist, but it did startle him. He glanced at Kevin who buttoned his mackinaw. He produced his business card and printed his personal address on the back. With a sincere smile he gave it to him. Silently, they walked together for an additional block when William stopped, removed his glove and placed his hand on Kevin's shoulder. "You are really a fine guy, Kev." He was careful with words that he chose. "Actually," he hesitated, and then looked directly into his face, "You are . . . really." Kevin was not one to ignore this moment. "Thanks a million for tonight and for dinner. Mozart is coming up in two weeks." He waved the card. "I'll get a free voucher to you." He stuck the business card in his pocket and replaced his glove. "I hope you enjoy it."

Chapter Twenty-Six

January 20, 1998

DENVER WAS ALWAYS SUBJECT to snow in January. Bleak and cold, the city tolerated it as well as it could. Despite this threat, the symphony prepared for its performance as scheduled in the last week. Steven Michael Young gallantly wore his snow boots every day to and from his office whether the weather man was honest or not. Mabel perennially complained with her own threat to take a Mexican vacation and go visit her sister and brother-in-law who lived in a little Aztec village south of Guadalajara. "One of these days, I'll do that, Dr. Young, and I'll leave you to battle the snow plows." In this year, she elected to remain because William Kaplan was playing Mozart. "We're just lucky to have this young man!"

She was capable of providing a noticeably stronger image than merely being his secretary. A native of western Wyoming, she was the only daughter among her four brothers who decided that she would not milk cows for the rest of her good days. That was all well and good with her family, especially her mother who was overjoyed when both parents sent her on her way to Laramie to escape the drudgery that her mother had. Mabel had always been strong and healthy. Her height made her a standout in the entire complex. The offices for the symphony was on the second and third floors of the Center. Only Dr. Young's area was in a location that commanded the view to the Sculpture Park. Her study of music history was without singing. But all that was in her past. Some time ago, when she knocked on the door to Dr. Young's place of business to become his right hand man, so to speak. She told him she was a left-handed woman, however. She knew every member of the orchestra, the majority of the scores in the music library and she confessed to Jimmy, the 'gofor' that she loved him. Jimmy was seventeen and only adored being the volunteer after school when he could learn all about symphony business. He played the saxophone in the high school band. He also was able to obtain vouchers for performances.

Mabel saw to that. Both Mabel and Jimmie were in awe when they first beheld Boettcher Concert Hall where the symphony performed. The interior architecture was fascinating, built as it was in allotted egg shaped sections. The orchestra was curved in three separate units with eleven surrounding portions designated as Mezzanine one through eight with one curved area directly above the stage which Jimmie learned as the Parquet. He was taking a second year course in French at his high school.

In the four or five days before the concert, no snow appeared and the streets were clear. Even so, the weather remained very cold. With permission from the manager of this Hall William was able to practice by himself on stage, seated at the piano which he would play at performance. He was surrounded by this unusual interior design; he marveled at the acoustics and the sound as it permeated the entire space. His playing would sound better when the seats would be occupied. On his way to the stage right exit, which led eventually to the large lobby with the box office, an employee stopped him with a cheery greeting. "We're ready for you, Mr. Kaplan," she announced from behind her counter, "we're selling balcony now, lots of seats in any one of those Mezzanine units. That's great for a January concert. Dr. Young was happiest I've seen him in a long time. Are you coming back tomorrow, same time?" To practice, I mean?"

"Tomorrow morning is my last time by myself," he answered, "before the orchestra joins me. Thanks," and he threw his scarf around his neck as he waved goodbye, passed through the glass doors and into the wide center aisle to brave the weather.

The next afternoon, he found a moment to write Jerry. It was a nice simple note reflecting that he did not have time to elaborate on all the rituals of getting ready, but that he was with him, on his mind. He placed a copy of the program in the envelope I sincerely wish you cold be here with all of my family. But I am overjoyed that you will be here in my heart . . . He wrote it just like that and he gave no heed to how surreptitious it sounded. He mailed it immediately.

The weather cooperated. No snow appeared on the night of performance. The concert mistress sounded her 'a' for the orchestra and a cacophony of notes penetrated the stage. Then, everything was ready. Steven Michael Young, with his flourish of a first entrance with his smile as big as his black tie nodded his fabulous greeting to everyone in the House. The evening was another sell-out! He shook hands with the concert mistress, took his place at the podium, turned to bow at the audience. He quietly raised his baton. He and his 'band' first played an overture and then a short number while William waited off stage right. This evening belonged to him. During a lengthy intermission, Steven approached William. The concert grand was rolled into place. "Okay, my boy," he congratulated him, "let's do it! Let's show them what Mozart sounds like!" A member of the Cello section raised the lid to the piano. One second elapsed, the house lights dimmed, the audience quickly was receptive. When he did make his entrance, they offered him a sumptuous applause, and he smiled as he made his bow and sat on his bench.

Vivian Anderson Cole and a sorority sister were on the third row center of Orchestra at a location where they could view his hands. Kevin Cole was seated five rows to their rear. He brought no one with him. Immediately after the artist and orchestra concluded, the ovation was deafening. Dr Young grabbed William's hands, shook them gladly, with a big smile and the orchestra in turn sounded their applause. William was ecstatic The joyous guests slowly departed, elated by what they experienced. Kevin mumbled to himself, "I don't know too much about this Mozart fella, but I do know the guy who played the piano." Kevin managed to look around the area where they were seated to determine if he could see anyone whom he knew. Vivian Cole did not attempt to do the same.

The reception was by invitation only in a large room reserved for such a purpose. A variety of well known personalities were there, including the mayor and his wife, the Fire Chief, because he appreciated classical music, and a few other notables who always received cards to these events. It was a comfortable evening for the pianist. Vivian had a nice remark about her sorority sister. Before they did leave, she pulled William aside beneath an archway that was framed with tall foliage which was out of character to the rest of the interior décor. "Just how come," she softly mused, "that I looked around and saw the football hero. I saw him at intermission in the crowd around the bar. No, I didn't speak to him. Mary Alice knows him, too, and I didn't want her to know anything, not yet, anyway." She teased him. "I bet you gave him a voucher for his ticket. You're like that. By the way, thanks for mine! And perhaps, I should be corresponding with that friend of yours, Gerald Whatever. I got a letter from him just today. I'm going for champagne right now. Keep smiling, sweetheart, you're great!" "Before I do go drink up," and Vivian was cute and wistful in her smile, "Here's a letter for you, my dear, the last I will deliver to you." And off she fled to the wine table . . .

Fans swarmed around him. Of course he was used to this procedure. With Mozart being history, so to speak, he was now free to concentrate in the next two months on Paris. But that was not all about which to give more thought. He professed to no one that, also, he was thinking about Jerry. The noise was loud but he did think what may be in that letter that he placed immediately in his tux pant pocket. It undoubtedly passed in the mails that he just wrote to Jerry.

The reception area was well decorated. The food line was long and crowded, with the wine table at the end where an attendant stood and poured. Stewart Parker appeared from nowhere. In a whirlwind of questions, his rudeness was unforgivable. He did not wait until a matron had finished her kind remarks to the artist. "Excuse me, dear," he blurted, and to William, "I just wanted to check with you on minor answers you can give me quickly." While the pianist was aware of this person who demanded interviews on the spur of the moment, the critic was often impertinent regardless of the occasion. "I have a photographer, Mr. Kaplan, if you will stand where you are . . . oh! There is the Lieutenant Governor and his lovely wife. If you will, please, allow me to take a shot of all three of you." He beckoned to them, pointing to the camera and for them to join the pianist. "Thank you, sir, madam, and thank you, too Mr. Kaplan. You'll be able to read my review in the paper on Monday. Complimentary, very nice. I will go into detail in my preview I might add." He forgot to say thanks and was gone just as quickly as he had arrived. The matron, who had not finished her own comments, was pleased anyway. She made certain to be in the picture, that she stood to William's left in the photo while the lieutenant governor and his wife were to his right.

Between the plaudits and best of luck from those who remained after the majority of well wishers departed, he was able to respond gratefully now that the obtuse critic had vanished. As the crowd dispersed and only a few were standing around drinking the rest of the wine, William's eye caught just a glimpse of Kevin as he stood in the hallway outside the door. He realized that he forgot to place Kevin's name on the reception list. The hero waved very quickly and then was swallowed up by the crowd.

Vivian spoke just as quickly. "Please come with me and Mary Alice. We're going to Maxine's Bar and Grill and have a drink. Join us, Billy." Then she added surreptitiously when somebody asked her sister a sorority question, "She'd like that, if you know what I mean." When William hesitated and waved goodnight to two passersby, Vivian laughed and gently touched his pocket. "You can read that letter after midnight tonight." Camouflaged by his tux coat, she gently placed her hand on his inner thigh and winked at him. "Is that a banana in your pocket or are you glad to see me?" She giggled and then the two of them departed.

So that is what the three of them did. It was a nice moment, full of laughs and easy talk and a pleasant nod to the few who were hangers-on in the elevator. He leaned against the far wall and closed his eyes.

It was late and Mrs. T was already abed in her suite. He opened the drapes to one of the big windows in the living room and collapsed on the sofa after turning on the small lamp.

Before he could successfully rest, before he could reach decisions whose questions began to haunt him again, he reached in his pocket and extracted the letter but he did not open it, not just now. He laid it aside, went to the kitchen where he stowed his wine and he poured for himself a small portion of his cabernet sauvignon, took a sip, and then returned to the living room sofa. At that late hour, he heard only a few cars far below the window. Here, it was quiet. Again, he claimed Jerry's letter; again, he hesitated to open it.

He stepped into his bedroom to hang his tux coat. It was then that he saw a note anchored on the bed table. It was from Mrs. T. "William. The Frenchman, M. Dupres, called to wish you Bon Chance for tonight's concert." That was not all. Added quickly was another remark. "You did well. I couldn't remain for your reception, I am too tired. Have gone to bed. T."

Oh, yes. M. Dupres. Steven had mentioned earlier that he wanted to schedule an appointment with him to meet a young piano student of his. All right. He'll check on it tomorrow. Malcolm somebody. He was too tired even to read Jerry's letter. He was too tired even to piece together the few scraps of thoughts that scampered wildly through his mind. One was that fact that his own parents were unable to come to Denver to hear him play tonight. He has to call them. He must. He remembered Kevin's grin when he waved at him from the hallway. Vivian was lovely tonight in a dress that, she said, she purchased just for the occasion. He placed Jerry's letter on the bed table, unopened. After his shower, he collapsed into bed.

Chapter Twenty-Seven

Early February 1998

WILLIAM CAUGHT HIMSELF PEERING casually at Mrs. T's kitchen calendar. As organized as she was, with another reference calendar on her desk in her "correspondence room" as she calls it, she placed reminders on this *Norman Rockwell* with a gentle check mark as each day closed. He had just made his morning coffee. He answered the phone; Mrs. Ethel Tabor was calling. After explaining that Mrs. Tomassi was out of the condo, he had a difficult time trying to terminate this call. He had known for a few months about Mrs. Tabor. She was a persistent conversationalist who did not know when to hang up the phone. Mrs. T told him about this lady whom he had never met. "She is compulsive and even *I* cannot shut her up!"

Her call was easily explained, she said. "Oh, it's you, Mr. Kaplan. Well, then, I can tell you how much Donald and I enjoyed the concert last Saturday. Or whenever it was . . . I had heard about you and I must tell you that you played exceptionally good." She coughed. "My husband and I have season tickets. After all, we're both native Denverites. My Goodness, this city has grown!" While he tried to listen, William's attention was not with this odd conversation. This woman persisted. "I understand you made a trip to Europe! Donald Ray and I visited Italy and we tried to locate Mr. Tomassi's relatives and this was before he died and we couldn't find them. We want to be sure and meet you before you go. Please tell Amelia I called. She is so busy it's hard to find her at home some times. My husband is calling me so I have to say goodbye." With that he heard her yell at Donald before the line went dead.

He poured his coffee and sat with his piece of cold toast. Jerry had been the bearer of what was already manifested in a previous letter but now less urgent. He had long ago learned to pen only reliable and meaningful references that pertained only to their personal welfare. He was more than thoughtful about his Mozart reference. In this latest letter, William realized Jerry was becoming more important to him than he would have expected when first they met. That seemed so very distant. And he promised himself to answer the short note this very afternoon. This very afternoon, he thought again. Before he poured another cup of coffee, he sat, pleasantly aware of how this geologist had progressed. Beside Mrs T's calendar without a frame was a piiciture of Mr Tomassi which was taken three or four years ago at the Grand Canyon. Beside it was a quick snapshot of Jerry with his typical smile with dimples. That picture alone always prompted William to write him, even when he desperately needed to practice Saint Saens. The music won out. William folded the letter and slipped it neatly into its envelope. He was obliged to go to the next errand.

William erased the question of when he would have time to answer. The Frenchman won but afterward, at a moment or two which brought security to the pianist, he found an envelope and stamp. He wrote a nice letter because Jair had told him that he was finishing his papers—two of them—but that he did not want to sound premature with his added bit of good news that all was well. Dr Clark with the other four advisors confirmed a doctorate for him. Jerry wrote this information in the letter that passed that other letter from William. So Dr Champion had learned to be specific, even in his personal notes.

The following afternoon, he bundled up against the weather and met his French instructor and Forrester at Maxine's Café, as scheduled. Going to the Brown Palace for lunch was, for Dr. Young, out of the question. According to M. DuPres this was to be more of a social rendezvous and certainly not one for any location on campus. But even so the conductor could not be with them as he had previously planned. M. DuPres was one on whom to depend for French protocol. He was one on whom to depend for valuable directions in Paris when it came time to make all kinds of enquiries. M. DuPres had always been a gracious and explicit instructor regarding French musical history especially Camille Saint Saens. This Frenchman insisted, also, to have weekly sessions with William in preparation for the intricate and glorious melodies this French composer wrote. He wanted to make certain that William would be ready to play in his capital city.

M. DuPres's conferences with Dr. Young were equally valid, for the conductor was happy to review lessons with the Frenchman. At Maxine's Café, he was there only to introduce the pianist to Malcolm Forrester. Then, without hesitating, and in a style only the French could appreciate, he smiled at both the men and quickly took his leave.

Malcolm was, at twenty-two, a protégé with the Frenchman's blessing. He was tall, with a whisp of black hair and brown eyes and broad shoulders. William's eyes immediately went to this young man's hands. They were strong, not effeminate at all, and today he wore a small friendship ring on his little finger of the left hand. Why this social moment and not an academic conference, William did not understand. He considered this as part of the French Way of Doing Things which he must learn.

This rendezvous this afternoon in Maxine's American Bar and Grill was his first lesson. Maxine herself escorted them into the busy afternoon crowd. She smiled a nice greeting to the celebrity and his guest. "I'm glad you waited until now to meet because I was busy with the symphony and Mozart." William tried to find a less serious way to begin. "But I guess you realized that." Maxine pulled back a chair and removed the 'reserved' sign from their table. She greeted them both with a nice smile.

"Oh, yes," Malcolm agreed, "and I fully enjoyed the concerto. Hiroko Adachi did too. I've got a big appreciation for Mozart. I seem to always have it, for a long time. At first, he didn't sit well with me. But that was when I was a young guy, a long time ago." William smiled silently at this remark. "Maybe I can attempt the whole score some day." A wine Steward brought them a small bottle of cabernet. "Complements of M Du Pres." He opened it, poured into two glasses, smiled, and departed.

Malcolm was careful to try to find words that were appropriate for what he was asking, in the first place. He was less nervous than he expected. "I usually drink wine in the evenings after I get tired practicing. I . . . I better not drink . . . maybe just a sip." Seated opposite him near a window to the side street, William was the first professional concert pianist he had met. The student did not, in the long run, want to appear as if he were some campus journalist asking peculiar questions. "I hope you don't mind talking to me. I just wanted to meet you and I had asked M. Dupres if I could sit with you and get the feel . . ." No, that was not the word to use, "to get the opportunity to do so." He stopped, selected his words. "I really wanted to meet you."

William thought for a moment how immature even he may have been at twenty-two years. A girl with an apron and long earrings suddenly appeared. "Your order has been arranged by the man who just left and I'll be your waitress. My name is Gladys and I'm new here. I was told by that man with the French accent—what a nice accent—to take good care of you." She curtsied and left.

William fumbled with his napkin. "Yes, well . . . Malcolm Forrester, I'm glad to meet you. I don't know too many music students any more but this is a good time to start." He did notice Malcolm's slight nervousness and how he listened attentively. And so it began. The episode was pleasant. He saw that Malcolm was content but eager. He surmised that he came from a good family. "I just realized," William grinned, "that you are to play for me at a master class in April some time. Freddy Graham thought I would have time to do it, and I said, yes, sure, of course. You, and another student." And while Gladys brought their lunch they settled down to eating and laughing. This lunch arrangement was quite out of the ordinary and both Malcolm and this mentor were there to enjoy and that the surprise element quickly dissipated. William noticed secretly how the young man hesitated in beginning. But he did realize right away that this informal get-together was exactly what both of them needed. Secretly he recalled how he was able to be the recipient of the same kind of occasion with Van Cliburn

When William became more comfortable, he offered a quick comment about the hands. "I noticed that you're left-handed. I . . ." And Malcolm was quick to answer. "Yes, and I knew that you are, too." Malcolm decided to add an additional word or two about this trait. "It's been a hobby of mine, almost, to try and study this left-handed business." He was pleased to find that William did not object, even when he felt comfortable in talking more than the professional. A lot of artistic people are, you know!" That was not too forward, he thought. Again, William did not seem to mind. "A lot of well known people.

Ringo Starr, Marilyn Monroe, Judy Garland, Paul McCartney—
another Beatle. Oprah." He stopped to take a bite of his salad. "I think
I knew about some of those," William put in his quick remark. He tried
to change the subject as politely as he could. "M. Dupres left me a note
the other day. He said he wanted Forrester and Adachi to plan for a
master class, and for me to adjudicate."

Malcolm took a drink from his water glass. "Oh, yes, and that's
another thing. I'd like your opinion on the piece I've chosen to play
for you. It's going to take a month or so, but I want to be sure before I
start. M. Dupres wants me to try Liszt or maybe a Chopin. He seems to
think I'm ready for something mature like a Liszt."

"I'm sure you'll do well, Malcolm. May I call you Malcolm, now?"
The student did not register any amount of embarrassment and he felt
very compatible this afternoon. "You might try Chopin's *Polonaise in
A flat*. You better check with the Frenchman on that one." Malcolm
was grateful for any word of advice about the master class, but he
secretly wanted a selection from Liszt. "I'll see what he will say. He's a
great teacher and is always after me to study French. I grew up with a
Mexican-American who pestered me with his lessons in Spanish. I'm
fairly good at Spanish."

After a small dish of chocolate ice cream, Malcolm stood, smiled
broadly and shook William's hand. His eyes reflected a genuine
gratitude. This reminded him of the honest look in Jerry's eyes when
the geologist and he first met. Again, William's memory resurfaced.
Again he could see Jerry at his desk, with his million questions flying
around him.

But just as easily as Malcolm came into his world, with his *joie de
vivre*, William did remember so very well the same kind of *esprit de
corps* he once professed, and not so long ago. Something this student
possessed was so closely akin to his own mental make-up. In his coat
pocket was his letter to Jerrry still snugly fitted in its envelope. He
found it when he reached for his wallet. The cashier told him that the
lunch was already paid. So he held the letter until Malcolm shook his
hand again and disappeared down the street.

Then he slowly opened the envelope and reread its contents. Two
events were important. His aunt finalized the paper work and the
house on Green Street now belonged to Jerry. Secondly, and this is

the happiest William had seen Jerry in a long time: the doctorate is confirmed and the moment to grant it was a coincidence with William being in Paris. The celebration of the two French composers had already been secured for the last week of April, just two months away. In the ensuing days when he and Steven Michael Young were to be in conference, he will explain to Vivian. She wanted to know more about this secret character at U.C.Berkeley, now that she was no longer a letter carrier.

William's considerable time was with the conductor. The symphony was rehearsing by themselves for the next two weeks. It was finally decided to wait until after the Paris Celebration that the Saint Saens concerto is to be repeated in Denver. In the next few weeks eventually the soloist will join the orchestra in preparation of much the same reasoning of what Maestro McKissick and he accomplished in those two days in August. Jerry will then be expected to be in Denver to attend. All this was foreign to the geologist but William did manage to type it all out for him and to apologize for the closeness of time.

To close this letter, William did mention Aunt Ursula. In response to the fact that her house was now Jerry's house, he was greatly pleased and happy for him. For the first time William's ending was a large printing of "Love." He sat there and stared at it. He had never really thought to finish all his previous letters to Jerry in that fashion. But with the incident in the attic that was still relevant, it did, after all, appear logical and most appropriate. William re-read his type and realized that it did look far too impersonal. He did not have time to hand write it. At least, that is the excuse he gave himself. He wondered just what Jerry would think when he received it. He mailed it, anyway.

On the weekend, William rented a car and drove the long highway to Sterling. The weather had improved with a bright sun and he needed to find why his parents did not contact him for the Mozart repeat. Vivian elected not to go with him. William knew her too well to object. The divorce was too much on her mind these days and her adjustment was not too secured.

Herschel Kaplan was in the kitchen talking to Bobby Martin and Bobby Martin was not to be expected. Julia Kaplan came down stairs when she heard the car come down the long drive from the main road to the front door. The sun was out. Angus ran down the steps from the porch. William stopped just to the left side of an old pick-up truck with a sign, "Martin's Paint Shop" on the door. She was the first to greet her son at the screen door as usual. "Where's Vivian, Bill, didn't she come with you? Where did you get the car?" She greeted him with a big bear hug. "Come on in. Guess who's here!" She was in a faded house dress on this Saturday morning with a piece of cloth tied around her head.

By the time they reached the kitchen, only Bobby Martin stood to say hello, the first to speak. "Well, by golly, you ol' so-and-so," he grinned, "it's been a whole year or so since I've seen you." He had on his all white costume as the town painter complete with a spattering of colorful specks. He had not removed his cap since he had arrived. Herschel merely nodded his head in greeting. Bobby appeared to be years older than he, with long straggled hair with just a streak of white above each ear. "You mother wants me to paint the kitchen!" He picked up a sample of what she had chosen. "It's going to be yellow. I can't start until a month from now because I'm busy. But I'll get to it." Bobby Martin was always the talker. But now He talked whenever he had a chance to explain almost anything. His voice suddenly became foreign to William. This time, it was Julia who interrupted. She noticed how her son stood, surprised to find him there. "You asked me to tell you when it was noon, Bobby. Didn't you hear the chime from the Grandfather in the hall?"

"Oh, it is?" He feigned surprise, suddenly collecting his sample case and moving toward the hallway. "Well. Mrs. Kaplan, thanks for making the choice. You'll be hearing from me soon." He did not shake Herschel's hand but he did smile at Julia on his way out. "Walk with me to the truck, Billy. It's been a long while since we've seen each other. The front screen door bounced against the door jamb as they stepped onto the porch. Bobby walked ahead, down the front steps. William paused, unable to follow. Angus stopped and looked back at his master . . . but followed the stranger to the truck.

William did not care to talk to him. He looked back at his mother who had paused inside the front screen to close the door against the cold breeze. With his sample case in his right hand, Bobby Martin returned only four steps as William paused at the top of the steps. With one additional step closer to William, Bobby swung his left arm around William's neck and laughed. "My God, Billy, it's been a long time." William slowly removed the arm and waited . . . He began with a few soft words. "I don't care to talk to you, Bobby."

That quick remark was a bit caustic. It made the painter stop in his tracks but he proceeded down to the driver's side with his normal insincere grin on his dirty face. "Oh," he cajoled, "I really don't think you mean all that, Billy, especially since we've been more than just good friends." Bobby noticed how the pianist stepped backward slightly to escape the narrow closeness of the cars. "You can't kid me, Billy Boy! I could get cleaned up and be back to get you by five. We could go to Maxirie's Bar and drink up some of her beer." He did notice also the sudden increase in breathing and how William shifted his feet. He reached for the door and tossed the sample case into the seat. He stepped closer to William and his lips started to produce his insincere smile. His right hand touched William's left shoulder lightly. But just as quickly, he brushed it off.

"Let me tell you something, Bobby." In a matter of seconds, William gained strength he never thought he possessed. He was face to face, eye to eye in a manner he would never presume to have. Bobby was stone-faced. "I don't ever want to see you around here anymore."

"But I got to paint your mother's kitchen." The quiet response was surprising. "What ya say? Just you and me and old times. Come on. You still playing the piano, I bet?" It was as if all the hatred apparent to both of them was nothing more than merely simple lines of dialog from a play. "Dammit, Bobby," William continued, "you get in your truck and you get going and I mean now." The darkness in his voice became more valid. Again Bobby ignored the whole scene. "You want to spend some time alone, just you and me like we used to do? Huh?" To that proposal, William had his negative reply. Bobby Martin stood there for a moment and looked directly at him with a smirk only in his eyes. He leaned against the open door, climbed into the driver's seat and slammed it. "Hell, Billy. Back in high school you and me had a ball and by God I taught you a lot, didn't I? You can't deny that, can you?" William realized his words were only manufactured out of nowhere. He waited for an answer that never came. "Did you hear I had been in prison? Three years, Billy. But, Hell, Billy Boy, you just don't want to hear what I've been doing. You're the big high-falutoned piano player. He looked at the front porch and waited. Then he added, "I used to have a lot of fun with Sarah what's-her-name, hell, I can't remember any of them no more. I'm not going to tell you what I did to get into prison. here. I guess that's out of your league by now. I used to have a lot of fun teasing you whether you realized it or not. We can still have fun. But you just disappeared, you with that damn piano of yours. Oh well. What the hell." He started his engine. "I always did wonder just how you made it without me, you and the boys. Christ, Billy! You can't kid me. Not ol' Bobby Martin. When I come back to paint your mother's kitchen, you show up from Denver and we'll paint the back bedroom." To that, he laughed and reversed his truck, turned around and without waving goodbye sped off back to the main road.

William watched him go. It frightened him. He suffered this whole scene. He hated Bobby Martin for what he had done to him and with him. He despised the idea that Bobby could come back into his life after all this time. He felt scared, the part of him that was shocked to find him here in the old farm house and to presume that he could be strong enough to startle him, simply to knock him off his feet again, just like high school. He was practically in tears.

Julia reappeared at the screen door. "Come on in, Bill," she beckoned, "I've got some coffee and a sandwich for you!"

Chapter Twenty-Eight

Mid March 1998

URSULA ELOISE CHAMPION GRISWOLD was a wise woman and her nephew was most assured of that fact. She had always been wise, even when she was eighteen years old. She was a great dancer in her day who was guilty of having far too much fun on the dance floor in Monticello New York. She came from "good stock" so said Albert Griswold who decided to marry her before any of the Champions objected. "What I'm going to do," he shouted from the dance floor, "is to marry this young gorgeous creature." And Ursula's family did not object. It was slightly premature to presume that she would marry him in the first place. By 1950 she had reached her nineteenth birthday and Albert, being only four years older, was content to tease her, her sister and her brother.

The Griswolds lived just down the street from the Champion flock. Ursula thought highly of her two brothers. She knew that Charles was more handsome than Arthur and her sister agreed but all was a happy group. The brother that Albert was always teasing in one way or another turned out to marry Anna Maria Cerna, a lovely woman whose ancestry was pure Italian. By the early nineteen-sixties, Anna Maria gave birth to two boys whom they named Gerald and Geoffrey. Arthur went to war first and never married. Ursula's sister, Ella, stayed in Monticello and became the proprietor of one of the large tourist hotels. Ursula gave thought to marrying the Griswold boy. She was happy she did, even though they had no children. But Ursula had Gerald and Geoffrey, her two favorite nephews. It was all well and good, she said. The Champion family was a happy family.

Ursula said yes to Albert and before they realized that war was to change everything they did hold dear, very dear, Albert, older than she, survived but not very well. They all came from the geographical area in and around Monticello. Albert Griswold, having suffered too much from the ravages of WWII and his lovely wife moved to San Francisco where he obtained a good position with an airline. The beauty of that area and the weather of the Bay eventually became the selling factor of any who followed them, anyone, that is, except the Champion relatives. This had all been Ursula's story. She had relayed it to her nephew whenever he had time to listen. His Italian mother was too busy cooking his favorite foods when he was in high school and at MIT. Geoffrey disappeared as they thought he would and became enamored with New York City. Ursula was a strong woman when Albert died. She decided to make a decision about her own future. She was pleased by Gerald's commitment to his doctorate.

So in the autumn of the year two thousand, at the time when Gerald was near to completing his doctorate, she made a point to bring the two of them together one Saturday evening. After dinner, with Li as a witness, she confessed that she would give her house to Gerald with the promise that her loyal Chinese housekeeper would remain. "I know how busy you are, Gerald, dear, and I'm proud of you. I think I shall always be proud of you. I just wish that I knew whatever happened to Geoffrey." Her antagonism about this question did not bother her, not too much, because he had simply gone to the Big Apple and disappeared. She had too much East Coast blood in her to remain in the City by the Bay and that was not difficult in any way for her to explain to Gerald. Li had brought them each a glass of cabernet and placed their glasses on the coffee table next to Ursula's favorite chair. "Thank you, Li." And Li retired to her kitchen.

"And now, my dear Gerald, I want to ask you what you think of your new friend, the concert pianist?" She waited a moment and watched her nephew's mind begin to form an answer for her. He held his glass in mid air and took a deep breath. Ursula changed position in her chair while she waited patiently. She wanted to make a suggestion or two but she could see he was on the point of answering. Before he did, she added, "You are a scientist and he, a concert pianist. There is a difference, you know!" In the last two months and especially since last November, she was certain she saw a virtual change in his own personality, his commitment to his own studies, that being a noticeable improvement in his willingness to complete this chapter in his life. His five-man committee smiled on him. She was happy to be able to claim Doctor Champion and her nephew one and the same person. She took one more sip of wine and looked directly at him. This was all a part of her plan. She was thinking ahead. While that plan included her return to her birth place, it also included her concern for Gerald's welfare.

Jerry was ready to offer his "dissertation". He had been ready for some time. It just was shelved and placed on 'the back burner' as someone told him during a class experiment. "Okay," he took another deep breath and smiled weakly. "He doesn't know too much about me, Aunt Urs. I haven't been able to explain any or all of it, actually, even to myself." He paused, and then rapidly, "I haven't had time. He knows how I've been working. You know it. It's been sheer luck that I've been able to come to have Saturday night dinners with you . . . and I've loved every minute with you and Li, don't ever think I'm not appreciative for all you've given me, especially this house. My God, what am I ever going to do with it?" Ursula mutely took another sip of cabernet and proceeded to listen to him before she committed any more remarks. "Billy is a good guy, Aunt Urs. There was a time when I really could not say just why it is that we've latched on to each other. Here I am, opposite to him in many ways. But he and I bonded. I mean, we *bonded*. I don't know what went on and I can't explain what happened to us but I guess opposites attract. That's the only thing I thought for a while. Then, our letters started up and there I was, writing him at one o'clock in the morning and his letters to me were coming just as thick and fast. He . . ." and again he paused to think, "He just is my best friend and I don't know a damn thing about sharps and flats." They could hear Li in the kitchen. "I guess that is what I mean."

Ursula secretly laughed at that musical reference. Jerry rose in defense of what he had said. He took another sip of wine, placed his glass on the table, and paced to the front window but turned immediately when his aunt called to him. "Gerald, dear," and she pointed to the hearth, "Bring me that folder resting on the table there, please." He responded, claiming the only item on the small lamp table where he was sitting. He brought it to her and returned to the fireplace.

"Sit down, if you will, I want to show you a piece of a letter written by your uncle Albert to me during the war. It was a long time ago. I think you'll like it since you write letters, too. I don't think you've heard of this one." She found what she searched for under some flat papers. Jerry sat down in his chair to hear her comment. They heard the mantle clock in the hall strike nine.

"First, let me say that Al met a nice soldier when they were together through basic traaining. I can't remember at what camp they were, somewhere in one of the Carolinas. They took their leaves at the same time, his friend going to his home, and Albert, to Monticello. Then, later, they were together at Fort Ord when they shipped over to the Pacific. This, you know." She unfolded a piece of paper, placed her glasses on her nose from where they were dangling in front of her on a cord. "Before I read to you, I will say that this other soldier had the same last name, Griswold. He was from Oklahoma, I believe. They had similar army numbers, they did appear quite similar also in height and looks and hair color. Albert told me all along the whole incidents that they experienced were quite unusual. They were together in the same training unit. They came to the West Coast together. They were on Guadalcanal, and in the same outfit." Then she began to read. "Urs, sweetheart, I don't have much time anymore, it seems, to write you. My friend, Hal, you remember, the one who has the same last name, well, he's still here with me. He's going on patrol. He says to tell you hello and hopes to meet you some time. I'm sorry, I have to go. I'll finish this when I can." And then Ursula turned the paper over to continue. She looked at her nephew and interrupted her reading. "This next," she whispered, "was written much later, about three or four days later. "Urs, oh, God, we just heard. Hal was killed last night. I can't write any more please forgive me but I'm crying as I write this. Goodbye for now I love you, Al." She quietly folded the paper and replaced it in its small envelope. She glanced quickly at Jerry and then continued. "Albert had told me more than once that he and Hal were just plain buddies, I think he used that word. It was exceptional that the army kept them together all this time. The army probably thought they were cousins, but we never knew for certain just what the army thought." Jerry stood up and returned to the window. "So I know, now, what this pianist means to you. At least, I have a pretty good idea." The Manila folder rested on her lap. "Come back and finish your glass." And then she also stood and stepped toward the hallway. She waited while she mused but then she turned to him as he finished his wine. "Have you ever told William about your health?"

This was always on his mind from the moment he began to feel a closeness to this pianist. He had never mentioned it to him, had never intended to bring the subject into the friendship. He had been tired, of course, when on campus and elsewhere. But he presumed that it was because Dr. Clark and Dr. Nelson were always the good counselors and were keeping him studying all the time. Jerry was often tired but he was assured nothing was wrong with him, by any means. "No, Aunt Urs," he turned and smiled at her, "my health is just fine. Where did you get the idea that I may be sick?"

The sweet lady that she was prompted her to assume too much. "You did tell me that Dr. Pickering, the medical doctor, was urging you to take care of yourself." She paused and stood. "Gerald, darling, I'm glad you don't smoke. I know you never did." Jerry's father died at the age of fifty-eight but both of them knew that he smoked too much. "I guess I worry too much. By the way, effective the first of the week, according to this helpful lawyer that I have, the house is yours, lock, stock, and barrel, to coin an old New York phrase. My plane leaves in two weeks. I'm packed and ready to go." She was aware that Jerry was ill at ease. "I want to be home by Christmas. I guess this leaves you and just Li together." Then she returned to stand directly in front of him and she took him by his shoulders. "Gerald, my boy, it won't be long until I can tell everyone you are Doctor Champion. I won't write you a letter, I'll telephone you." She kissed him on the forehead and gave him a bear hug. "See," she laughed, "I'm pretty good at bear hugs, too." She slowly went upstairs to her bedroom as Li followed her.

Jerry watched them as they turned to the final two steps at the top of the stairs. Then he extracted a letter from Denver that he had stowed in his suit coat pocked all this time. He re-read it as he walked back to the front window to watch the rain begin.

Chapter Twenty-Nine

Late March 1998

MABEL KNOCKED ON STEVEN'S door and called, "Dr. Young! Mail call, Dr. Young!" In her hand was a manila packet postmarked New York. "May I come in?" When he answered yes, she opened the door and discovered the conductor on the telephone. He motioned to her with a hand that held a pen. She was excited because it was heavy, probably with all kinds of information he was seeking about France and related environment. He opened his lap drawer, produced a pair of scissors, and indicated for her to do the honors and tear open the end. As he continued to talk to whomever he kept his eyes on the contents as they appeared. Inquisitive as she always was, Mabel waited. M. DuPres, who had been waiting for the maestro to complete the telephone business, patiently stood beside Mabel. He was pleased to see that much of the material was in French. "As it should be, of course."

Additional correspondence in English was the first to gain her interest but several French brochures met with approval. Steven ended the conversation and verified to see who had sent it. The whole packet came directly from Raymond Hicks. The agent included a small note that the committee to organize the celebration of the two French composers sent it from Paris. The manila envelope contained a map of the City, some highlights for tourism before or after the three day event—which Raymond Hicks was glad to have—and a list of hotels, some expensive, others, more practical. Hicks' hastily written note mentioned that his passport finally arrived. He was relieved because he had never ventured beyond the protection of the Island of Manhattan. In the last paragraph of the business letter from someone whose signature was illegible was a welcome to Paris, partially in French. Someone will meet your Air France plane's arrival at Charles de Gaulle Airport. Kindly tell us on which day you are arriving. Maestro Young carefully replaced all the correspondence inside the packet. He was pleased with everything, including M. Dupres' excitement despite that he was not accompanying the pianist himself.

"Thank you, Mabel, dear," he chortled as he motioned goodbye to her. He did not know this Mr. Hicks but he was nevertheless happy that William Kaplan would be so honored. Before the Frenchman left the inner sanctum, he serenaded everyone, including Mabel, with one full minute of French gratitude with kisses and American handshakes.

The maestro was more concerned for time spent with with William. "The time is so urgent, now, that you are to concentrate, with me, on the music at hand. I'm not saying that you can hustle off to France with the work we've already helped you with. But with the appearance we've arranged for you upon your return to reality, after the fact, when you step off the plane at our infamous and new Denver airport, you will then be expected to play and display the same talent with our 'band' as you will accomplish over there, across the pond." He was excited, himself, merely to count the days between now and when William does leave. Once the Frenchman departed, he was pacing in his office, glancing out a window, looking down to the Sculpture Park, rearranging items on his desk top, or fidgeting with his new BIC pen. Then he had to stop and analyze William's posture. The pianist sat in one of the chairs over by the sofa at the far end of his office. His head was lowered and his hands were clasped in his lap. "Bill," the conductor spoke quietly, "Have you been listening to what that crazy Frenchman and I have been saying for the past thirty minutes?"

To that, William could answer yes and no. Together with the 'band' both had been working twice or perhaps three times a week in the past three weeks on Saint Saens. It was not an easy task for Steven Michael Young to convince the powers that be that the orchestra may present a special program just to honor the local pianist. Steven had used 'genius' only once. Stewart Parker had already written an exceptionally vociferous article. Everyone will know now that they will present him in concert in Denver upon his return and they should announce to the world that this is a great moment for Denver, for

Colorado, and anyone else who can make it to Boettcher Concert Hall. The exact date is to be selected as soon as they settle down and establish the information for the newspaper. It was to be a 'Plus' for the symphony. Stewart Parker had been writing a paragraph or two about this affair. Each day, with new incentive and elaborate compliments, the columnist would add more to his article. "I hate to interrupt you again, Dr. Young," he said, "but I'm ready for your additional number or numbers you intend to play. I already have the overture and the number you want just before the intermission. But you told me three days ago that you don't want *Afternoon of a Fawn*—all right, thank you, I can wait." Dr. Young did not enjoy interruptions and Stewart Parker was always an interruption. He turned once more to William. "Did you hear what we said?"

William did not answer but merely blinked his eyes as if awakening from a trance. His friend joined him at the end of the room. "William?" He grabbed a chair and sat opposite him, leaning over with his hands on his knees. "What's wrong? What is it? It is the work? Are you tired?"

Since that morning, when Mrs. T asked him the same question, he had refused to mention, either to the lady who had been his close friend or to the conductor what exactly was on his mind. The music was secured, the tempos were correct, the orchestra, all of them, was pleased to be playing; they all were more than exultant.

What exactly was on his mind had nothing to do with preparation of the program. It was Jerry. It was what was on Jerry's mind, and his frantic effort to complete the doctorate, just as frantic for him to secure the concerto. In a flash, for as long as it took to count a nanosecond, his mind was back in the room and he faced the maestro. "I'm okay," he answered quietly, "My mind was somewhere else." But that did not satisfy Steven. For two or three days, despite the fact that they stopped and started, the moments when one or both were not satisfied with the correct tempo, that perhaps the strings were too loud, or that the French Horns did not come in when they should, they were still together as it should be. But afterwards, at the end of a grueling three or four hour rehearsal, William plunged into a quiet and subdued farewell before he ventured home. For one who was energetic and always ready, always listening attentively to Steven, he sat in that chair opposite the maestro and said again, "I'm all right."

Steven leaned back in his own chair. "All right, so you say. We want you to be more than ready, my boy! This whole business now is not only for you but for our symphony and everyone who loves you and that means a great deal of people." He patted William's knee and stood up to meander to his desk. "It's late and you go home and rest. I remember you said that tomorrow Miss Patty wants to discuss with you so you play for her the second movement—without us, of course—there's nothing wrong with it. It sounds great but she may want to give you some hints. Obey her. She's the best. She'll give you some pointers, I'm sure." He stopped at his telephone and waited. "Go now, Billy boy! You sounded great and it is great. The concert mistress told me so. And you can't forget the ovation the entire orchestra gave you tonight when we called it 'quits.'" With his hand once again on the telephone, he waited until William left his office and closed the door.

Tonight, William reserved those moments to be with Jerry. He walked by the bus stop and proceeded into the section where Fourteenth Street became less occupied with traffic at this hour. Near the end of that part was the Ranger Bar. Its facade was secluded by an alley but its window had one neon sign lit in two colors. A large parking lot full of cars was south of it. It was a late hour but not for the patrons who came and went. He dodged three cars when he crossed the street.

One customer, just ahead of him, halted before he opened the wide door. "Hi," he smiled, "Coming in?" To this William was not sure. He never did know the location of this bar. He was surprised to see that it was in this section of the city. "Aren't you . . . ?" the man stammered, "You're Kaplan, the pianist!" He ignored the others who passed them. "I read about you. I'm Rick." He offered his hand but William shook it lightly, still somewhat hesitant about entering. "I'll buy you a drink, if you're game. Want one?" William saw two others enter; one said hello. "No. no thanks. I just . . . I was . . . I'll just . . . ." He was at a loss for words or maybe he did not quite know what he wanted to say. It was Rick who spoke softly. "Could I have your autograph? Not very many times I run into a concert pianist in front of a bar!" To this, Rick laughed at his own remark. "I've got a pen and paper somewhere," he said as he fished in his coat pockets. "Okay, here." He blew hot air into his hands. "Damn, it's cold. Come on in where there's a light." William hesitated but finally followed him. "I've got to tell you I don't know too much about music—I mean, your kind—but I'm mighty glad to run into you." William signed quickly. "Okay?" That was a meager remark for he did not know what to reply.

Rick grinned. "Just for that, I'll buy you a drink." He took the paper, folded it neatly. Looking at it as if it were gold, they followed two others. Once at the counter, Rick anchored the signature under an ash tray. In the garish interior light above the counter, William saw a line of counter stools. Rick patted one of them and announced softly, "What'll you have?" William looked at him and sat in the nearest. A little wine would help him relax and sleep tonight. "Red wine, Cabernet, if they have it." A few other customers began to glance his way. Some recognized him. Others exited through a wall of ribbons hanging down from an archway when the D. J. began a loud dance number. Rick got a beer for himself and placed the wine in front of his celebrity. "I have a feeling this is your first time here. Where have you been, off to Europe or some place?" It was meant as a joke but William did not laugh. He took one sip and glanced about the large room. A few customers sat at a table across the room. "Oh, I knew about this place. I just hadn't been here. In a long time." William took another sip of his wine and noticed how Rick moved his stool closer. "Well, welcome to the Ranger, stranger. I guess we just better get acquainted. Maybe you can teach me how to play the piano." His humor was not the best. Rick bent forward to offer a kiss on the cheek when a strong hand grabbed his right shoulder and pulled him back.

Kevin Cole practically slapped Rick's face. William was stunned. He turned from Rick. "What the hell are you doing here?" he shot the question. "My God, Billy, I would never . . . never expect this from you." William, totally surprised to see Kevin. Rick straightened up and his mouth flew open when he felt Kevin push him aside. Kevin's attention was immediately upon William. "Do you know this . . . ?" he tried to ask. But William could say nothing. "Come on, Mister, I'll take you home." Kevin picked up the autograph from under the ashtray.

Rick tried to grab the paper. "Hey, that's my autograph."

"Not now," Kevin replied as politely as he could while William climbed off his stool. "Not . . . now." The whole incident was over and Kevin marched behind William through the front door and into the cold brisk air. "I would never expect to see you here. Not . . . ever. What in the hell were you doing? Viv is not ever going to know about this, you hear me? Not Vivian. I don't know what you want, maybe something you want to do or say or . . . learn. Maybe that." They walked to Kevin's car. "If you want to know about anything . . . and I mean, anything. Ask me, you hear? Just ask me. Dammit, I'll tell you right off." William climbed into the passenger side and slumped against the window. Kevin slid under the driver's side and slammed the door. "Now, you tell me . . . you ask me right off, you hear. Just don't . . . just . . . ah, Billy, why did you have to show up at Ranger? Why? Dammit." He started the engine, pulled away from the curb, and for the entire trip to the condo, William did not say a word, ask a word, or make any kind of reply.

The next morning in the kitchen, he tried to piece it all together. The calendar to the left of Mrs.T's refrigerator was crowded with his own scheduling with rehearsals and the proposed date he was to depart for New York. Over his coffee he could not erase from his mind the loud noise, the eyes of so many guys who looked at him and were pleased to say hello to him last night. He would not have been too surprised if he had not seen Kevin there. But Kevin did show up. Kevin *was there.*

William was concerned with Jerry's own time frame. He was counting the days, too, for his own celebration. He picked up a pen from a table in his bedroom, selected a sheet of paper and an envelope, and went into the living room to sit at the desk by the window. He wrote a good letter to Jerry. He re-read it, folded it, placed it in an envelope, sealed it, addressed it, put a stamp on it and mailed it.

Chapter Thirty

April 1998

"MRS. GRISWOLD!" THE PRIEST jovially welcomed her. He stood with his right hand on the door knob and he was happy to see both the kind ladies. They stood just outside his office door. "Come in, dear ones." He moved swiftly to his desk. "Just let me," he continued, " . . . clear up this paper with my signature and give it to my helper." Two nuns were waiting. His working area was not cluttered but it appeared busy. He signed the letter, and handed it to one nun. "Now. I see you have Li with you. So good to see both of you again. Please. Sit down."

"Good morning, Father Joshua," Li spoke quietly, shaking his hand. The church on Washington Square had always been handy for both of them, situated as it was so close to the house and to the grocery store on Columbus Avenue. The proximity of church, store and bus line was the main reason for Albert and Ursula to buy their house.

"I'm glad to see you, Father, because I shall miss this church and you." Ursula Griswold settled in the leather chair and repositioned herself when the priest came around to sit in a corner as a trio. "This appointment to talk to you came at a good time." The Grandfather clock chimed ten in the hallway to this old addition. "Oh dear," Ursula interjected, "Albert loved that clock. He was really pleased to offer it. The sanctuary itself was just to the south beyond a lovely courtyard with its twin bell towers.

The entire area was a great calling card for many worshipers. "This is a good time, I presume, for all of us." While Ursula and Li had been in the main church, this was the first time in forty years she had been in Father Joshua's office. They had been in this office only once a year ago when the two of them introduced him to Gerald. "We have no problem walking such a short distance from the house on Green Street. We usually walk a little every morning." Ursula added, "When we come to church, for this jaunt, we hike to Union Street and then down to the square. A mere five or six blocks. It's good for us!"

Father Joshua was fifty years old, a tall and gallant messenger of God, with a ready smile and a hearty greeting. He enjoyed calling himself a disciple of Christ. He was German by birth. Hardly any of his parishioners ever inquired about his youth. He was a good listener and a marvelous prayer consultant. Today was a sad day for him. He had to say goodbye to Ursula Griswold.

"Yes, Father," Ursula waited until she felt more comfortable, "the time has come when I wish to return to Monticello" Peering at Li, she added, "Or as the Chinese would say, the place of my birth. I guess I got that idea from my housekeeper. I don't know that it is a Chinese belief of some nature, but I like it, nevertheless" Li laughed and then smiled. "I guess I shall always have Monticello blood in me."

The priest smiled and nodded an approval. "I was in upper New York State for a short while before I was called to move to California. I do remember the mountain ranges of that area." A knock on his door brought him to his feet and he opened it to accept further correspondence. He returned immediately to his chair.

"I leave a week from today. I'm all packed. I've already shipped some things, and I'm flying. I have no automobile any longer. After Albert died, I sold the car. I never did need a car here in the City." She smiled at Li again. "Li is staying here. She remains to be with Gerald because my house is his legacy now. That's all settled."

"I do remember the young man." In his German accent which was still evident, Father Joshua said, "and I shall be pleased to welcome him to the church. Has he completed his work at Berkeley?" To that, she went into great detail about his study, his degree, and his own plan for remaining in the City. He even has a strong promise of a job in May. The doctorate was confirmed, the move to occupy the house was forthcoming; the future is secured." She was joyous. Despite the happiness, Li silently looked downward to her gloved hands, and then with a sad countenance she tried to smile. Father Joshua noticed this. They heard the stately clock in the hall chime the quarter hour. Several people passed to the main door.

"Please pray for me," Ursula asked softly as she looked again at this kind priest. "I ask it in the name of my savior, Jesus Christ." "Of course I shall," he answered, rising to the occasion. They remained seated while he placed his right hand on her head. "Gracious God, look down upon this, thy servant, and give her your blessing now and when she departs for her journey. God bless her and keep her safe at her new home." Then, with his left hand, he covered Li's head scarf and he added, "And bless this, thy servant now and forever more. We pray en nomine et patri, et fili, et spiritu. Amen."

Father Joshua opened his door and followed them into the hallway. "Goodbye, dear ladies. God bless you both."

————————

In one great breath that he took, Jerry Champion relaxed for just a short minute before he entered the Science Building hopefully for the last time. Oh, of course, he would have millions of memories going in and out that trio of front doors. Carrying texts from the library, protecting lessons in the front of his mind, bearing joy and hope within his breast, he traversed the granite aisles of both floors. He was lucky. The people with whom he was in contact were really for him. This late April morning was very much on his mind, for he was to say goodbye to Dr. Nelson. He then would step into Room 105 where he spent too many hours in the lab with his lab friend Mark. First he knocked on the hall door.

"Come in, my boy," Dr. Nelson was cordial. He was wearing a bright tie for this occasion, but he was known all over campus for the variety of ties in his possession. This tie, today, was unusual for it had Mickey Mouse standing in a Disneyland background, waving his four-fingered hand to everyone. "I was wondering if you would be in today or tomorrow." Jerry was spellbound and his joy was most apparent in a wide smile and strong handshake. "I shall always remember you and all the other instructors who helped me along. Maybe I'll get to England one of these days. I really did like your description of Kent that day when we had lunch with Mrs. Nelson." That was the one time Jerry had to meet her with her accent that was more distinctive than her husband's. "And that photo of York Cathedral she gave me is framed on my wall above my desk."

"Yes, of course, I do hope you are able to be there. You should like Emgland because I like America. History abounds in every nook and cranny of Britain. As far as America is concerned, my wife just adores this whole Bay area." "She is from Yorkshire. I do hope you get to York."

Jerry's work had included radioactive waste disposal, a subject which William would not necessarily understand in the overall definition of his dissertation. Dr. Nelson and he reminisced, bantering back and forth, joking now about the intricate explanations Jerry had to clarify. Much of the beginning of the work at Berkeley was cemented at MIT. When he agreed with Dr. Clark on the title, the whole process could easily have been totally foreign to William. That was why Jerry had not stressed what he was doing nor to offer any detailed analysis of his work.

Jerry noticed that Dr. Nelson had a copy of the final version on his desk in front of him. Its title was printed in bold black letters on the cover, *The Transport of Radioisotopes by Fine Particulate Matter in Aquifers*. It was his personal copy and he opened it to the first inside page. "Please sign it, Jerry, if you please. It is a great contribution." Immediately, Jerry turned it around to face him while he produced his pen. He took another big breath, closing his signature with 'and a great big thank you to my favorite advisor.' Gregory Nelson was amused at this. One of the American traits he had learned was this informal manner by which many of the students related to instructors. "You must step into the lab and say hello and goodbye to Mark. I think he's expecting you." Dr. Nelson decided to try his luck on being less formal-British and more informal-American. "But before you do leave me, I have what I think is a good surprise for you . . . I guess you do appreciate San Francisco. Most people do. Do you still have your aunt living on Green Street?" This was not the surprise he was thinking that he would mention, for not much in the way of delicate conversation took place between them. Even so, the advisor was often curious about his life, having come from England. At first, there was a world of differences which Californians were always able to discern. Dr. Nelson tried to recall a phrase he had heard at a cocktail party about a year ago. It had to do with the adage that America and Britain have much the same living style, separated only by language. The good Ph.D. elected not to throw that out to him, not until he was sure of the way to say it.

Jerry explained. "My aunt is elderly, sir. She wishes to return to her place of birth, that being a city in New York State. She is flying back soon, next week." Jerry elected not to go into detail about his possession of the house. Dr. Nelson then offered his surprise. "Well, Gerald," he grinned, "I think I have something for you if you wish to pursue it, that is, if you intend to remain in the Bay Area and not return to the East Coast." He opened his lap drawer and extracted an envelope. In its upper left corner was a stamped return address of 'The Placement Bureau, U.C.Berkeley.' He extended it to him. "It's a job opportunity for you and you may want to investigate it. The company advertised for a geologist a month ago and I thought of you. It came at the right time for you, I'm sure. Things like that just don't happen for no reason." The Brit smiled. "I'd call it a 'Divine Appointment.' The advisor saw in Jerry's eyes gratitude that was boundless. This was going to be worth a long distance call to Denver, before William leaves for France. The advent of employment was worth something very special. His hand shake was strong. "And don't forget to hop in and say good bye to Mark! God Bless you, my boy!" The last lesson he learned from this man, that things just don't happen for no reason, echoed as he walked to the stairs and down to the first floor. Grateful as he was, with all the years in classrooms behind him, he was more aware now of what had happened to him in these last twelve months than before them. Mark was joyous to walk with him when he exited the building. In a warm smile and a great handshake, they smiled at each other; Mark remained on the steps when Jerry disappeared around the corner.

Li was with him when they accompanied the aunt to the departure gate. This had been in a huge mental fog, after the two or three days of packing and saying goodbye to the neighbor couple. Li was in tears, having said farewell in English, Chinese, and any other way in which she could retain her composure. Aunt Urs was the one who remained calm throughout her ordeal. Gerald had said 'thank you' so often that he stood aloof for a short moment, trying to piece it all together. The gate agent was more than kind. She assisted Mrs. Griswold first, allowing her to disappear through the cabin door. Jerry then, with his arm around Li, escorted her slowly, away from the other passengers. They proceeded to Green Street with hardly a word between them.

Gerald B. Champion sat alone in the kitchen of his house while Li went about tending to some business that was required on the phone. His attention then returned to the item in front of him as he tried to solve the time difference between San Francisco and Paris. Later he tried to make that telephone call but nobody was at home in the condo. So he waited.

Before him, resting on the old place mats that his aunt still had after twenty-five years was a professionally printed hour by hour schedule of the twenty-four hour clock of the world. He poured himself more coffee. After dutifully comparing the space around GMT and NYC, he surmised that he would have no problem in wondering just what Billy would be doing: rehearsing now, sleeping now, talking now to an interpreter about sharps and flats or with his emotional agent in the lobby of the expensive hotel paid for by RCA or probably by the committee that arranged for this international concert. And Billy had not even left Denver yet.

He stood, moved from the table with coffee cup in hand, and stepped into the hallway. He glanced at the telephone for the third time, took a sip, and opened the front door. Once on the front porch, he took from his coat pocket the placement announcement from the university. He read it for the fourth time. The company was in the Justin Herman area near the Maritime Plaza on Clay Street practically the point where Market and California streets intersect. He knew that area fairly well. He had stopped once on this plaza to admire the spectacular view of the Oakland Bay Bridge. From Coit Tower and Green Street this view southward included that entire portion of the City.

His life had been filled with a variety of circumstances. By now, he had learned what emotions were his. Those had become prevalent. A scientist, even one who had survived seven years or more of earning his own education, had learned also to identify them, a fact that he would be pleased to report to the pianist himself. He looked down to the first step from the porch. The memory of where he and that pianist sat some time ago returned. He sat down again. He wondered just what Billy was doing on a Saturday morning. He remained there to feel the cool breeze against his unshaven face. He had an idea. With his empty coffee cup in hand, he returned to the kitchen. It was a beautiful morning in San Francisco.

Chapter Thirty-One

VIVIAN WAS DRIVING HER '95 Buick Regal on this Saturday before William was to fly to New York. She talked him into taking this short trip; he had told her just yesterday that his mind was not set on going to Sterling with her in the first place. He did not care to sit and argue with his father about anything. He did not especially elect to visit his parents for any reason but she insisted. "You would be across the Pond at least a week." Her argument was more valid to her than to him. "This one-day jaunt to this momentous place of our births was a 'must.'" He sat in the passenger seat morosely looking at the passing terrain, through the few small towns which comprised the old road from Denver to Sterling. *What difference does anything make, anymore?* He had argued the theory of the universe with this lovely lady. Time and again they had promised themselves never to go beyond the norm in their thinking. Their 'norm' was almost anything they would care to establish. The subject this morning was nothing pertaining to music for she had more than once agreed that such a topic was always foreign to her. At one time, just recently when she was in a fit of pique more closely related to her divorce than to the theory of music, she argued vehemently. She would listen to him play and she could enjoy it, whatever it was. A sonata, a prelude or even a tone poem someone had transcribed for solo piano or any lengthy piece with which he could charm her. But that was all. Today it was whether or not they would enjoy seeing Herschel and Julia, especially since they did not come to hear him play Mozart. "Never mind that," she threw at him, "they probably had a great big honest valid excuse."

One thing they did agree upon right away and that was this whole stretch of road was boring to them, always, to anyone who had been unlucky to live in the wheat plains. It was the same two-lane pavement that had been there since the Year One, complete with broken signs along the way, including Marvin's Café and Martin's Paint Shop. The Buick radio was playing a D.J. whom they had known since forever. He was a product of 'Popular Tunes' College and he could not say anymore than 'welcome to Saturday morning, Mr. and Mrs. Colorado, this is your favorite D.J. and here is the latest.' She turned off the music and quickly glanced at him. The drive east had been too quiet far too long.

Vivian had to speak. She could not bear the silence from this man with whom she had argued since junior high school. "All right, Mr. Piano Player, say something. I'm not along for the ride, you know." He remained adamant. "You want to turn around and cancel out? I can, you know."

William waved at a farmer on his tractor and slowly turned his head to glare at her profile. Her hair was still a natural blonde and she still had a voluptuous figure. Today she wore a terrific blouse which advertised her ample breasts. His eyes gave her the answer. They were sad and damp with tears that told her he was going to be all right, after all. He produced his dark glasses and hid.

"Okay, what? I have my own eyes on the road." She smiled her same smile he had known all these twenty-five years. "Okay, Billy-Boy. Tell me again. I can listen and drive at the same time."

He struggled with the only answer he could manage. "I'm going to visit Mom and Dad because it's the thing to do because it is the only thing to do." He sounded belligerent whether or not he actually was. "I asked you along mainly because I don't feel like driving and I really don't feel like this trip is absolutely necessary. I didn't have time to rent a car and I like the Buick and I love you. I ought to, you've known me for a hundred and two years . . ."

She interrupted with "Known both you and your sister, don't forget."

"Yes," he agreed, "and you ought to know by now I don't especially like to go home." He started to say mom and dad but was more diplomatic. He was old enough to master his own realm of things. He was frightened by these rural towns. He learned to dislike the winters but that was only in the last ten years. Since then, he had told himself to visit only in the spring time, like this spring, this magical time when he would be able to hear all about wheat and barley and sweet corn and what-have-you from his father and nothing about his music. For those past twenty-five years, his father became impenetrable. Talking to him, whenever he did visit, had become difficult with just ordinary conversations, much like farmers talk about when they go into Marvin's Café on Sunday mornings after they drop their wives and kids at church. They try to talk and think about politics and that is not very much for wheat farmers anymore. It is a wonder how Patty Allen Shriner and her family lived in Sterling. Once, his teacher told him, "I like to say hello to most anyone, because someone may be an angel."

"Sterling is my hometown too, you remember." Vivian could detect his antagonism. She was used to his moods, his mild theatricality, his hesitancy in having to tolerate any activity that did not have anything to do with his classical training, his devotion to his art, his piano-playing, as his father called it. "I thought you were going to call Jerry before we left. I'll be happy when I get to meet this geologist. Frankly, I want to tell you this—that I'm glad you're taking him with you. If you haven't already told him, he is going to be surprised." Only with a short glance to her companion when she stopped for traffic at an intersection, she caught the complete change in his attitude at the mention of Jerry.

As long as William was quiet, she continued. "I think I'm having problems with Kevin, you know. About the divorce."

William still remained quiet, relaxed, but quiet. The event in that bar was prying on his mind. He did not reveal any of that incident to anyone, for there was actually no one to whom to disclose the details of it. On that, he agreed with Kevin. He did remember, for the good of it, that he wanted to ignore everything and move on his way. The fact that he was curious led him to accept Rick's invitation. But Kevin did tell him to keep it quiet, for his sake as well as the guy who opened the front door.

"Now when we see mom and dad, be nice. You can do it. I'm there, standing beside you. If the upright is still needs tuning play it anyway. Your mom wants to hear you play. Play anything. You're a big star, now, on your way to Paris to play that composer whose name I can't pronounce correctly—his concerto piece and record it with RCA. Tell her about RCA, she'll like that." She stopped her recitation to smile at him. "Okay? Just don't get entangled with your dad." She changed her attitude. "Just what is it that's eating you? My God, Billy, you've been like this ever since we left the condo."

He relaxed and waved at someone who recognized him. They were crossing the railroad tracks and slowing to meet the growing traffic of Main Street. This bustling metropolis was Sterling. William adjusted dark glasses as they passed through this busy thoroughfare. "I'll be all right."

"Of course you will. They're proud of you. I'm proud of you. I can only play 'Chop Sticks.'"

"Mom is proud." He hesitated again and then he added. "Dad never was." The agony of too many arguments with him suddenly filled the space in the car and both of them felt it. William's power with the piano, his talent for every conceivable dimension of music, the natural ease with which he undertook the scales, the depth of emotions that permeated every piece he possessed, all remained a great mystery to the man who fathered him. The man absolutely did not have any comprehension of who his son came to be. "My dad is a mystery to me. I have no idea what I'm going to say to him." By this time they were out of town, on the same rural road that had been there since William, Sis, and Vivian were in the same school building. "I've got to go and see Miss Shriner. She's expecting us because Mrs. T told her I'm on my way to New York so she knows to expect me." He dried his eyes. He erased the Ranger scene. Kevin Cole was still on his mind. He was glad, really glad, after all, that Kevin had still been in that bar.

Vivian slowed the car as they passed through the entrance. Somebody had already opened the tall wide gate. Angus slowly rose from the front porch and sauntered to meet them. Vivian was the first to step from the car. "Come on, Billy," she urged, "you're home now."

He paused before opening the car door. For as many times as he and his sister had sat on the narrow front steps of this old house, he could not remember how wide the two-storied home was. But the Collie remembered him, for the dog waited patiently for that door to open and for William to greet him avidly as he always did. "Hello, Angus!" was the call which sent his tail wagging. William looked around the drive way, the front of the house. He saw the old tractor in its parking area with an old blanket thrown over the metal seat. The barn, constructed first before the two-storied house, was just beyond the fence.

The screen door opened and banged shut as a tall slim lady appeared wearing a clean cotton dress with no apron. Her hair was freshly combed, her bright hazel eyes flashed her smile as she stopped at the top step and laughed. "Oh, William, my darling boy, come in, come in." And then she turned to Vivian. "I'm mighty glad to see you, too, Viv. My, you look pretty." And so this was how she always met any visitor who came her way, to her house, to the farm. It had always been the same, the sweet, charming manner that accompanied this bright and busy woman. "Oh, how I wish Mary Louise could be here today."

"Hello, Mom!" He walked up the few steps to be there by her side, with a warm hug and a kiss on her cheek. It had been a year since he saw her. And inside, with the worn rug at the door, with the tall hall tree standing where it had always stood with his dad's leather coat with the bill cap, nothing had changed, nothing at all. Vivian waited patiently behind him as his mother directed them into the hallway and parlor.

Julia Kaplan, this lady who, across the years, had married the man she loved and bore him two children, and came with him to Sterling to work his wheat farm, this lady who surrendered her own impulse and talent in music, now greeted her son gladly, knowing that he was her music, her own happy soul. "I had the piano tuned about a month ago," she announced with a joy she hardly ever expressed any more, "just for you."

They heard the kitchen door swing open and slam shut. Julia turned to welcome her husband. "Oh, Herschel, it's William," she called brightly, "With Vivian. They arrived just now." She turned quickly to her son. "You look just spiffy. Real handsome in those dark glasses!" She turned to the man who joined them. " . . ." he just got here this minute, Herschel. Drove in with Viv."

Mr. Kaplan—Herschel to everyone who knew him—nodded his greeting silently. He looked tired and older than he was. Sweat stained his rugged face and he used his bandana to wipe his neck.

"Hello, Dad," He was as pleasant as he could be with his handshake. Herschel spoke quietly to him and to Vivian, too, making no obvious happy gesture of it. He was still the robust farmer, tall of frame, with dirty hands and his old hat which he removed immediately. He eyed his son with an aloof blink of his eyes that told William he was still taciturn, one quiet person who hardly ever offered his opinions on matters that were even of minor importance. "Did Mary Louise come with you?"

William decided to answer. "No, Dad . . . . Sis couldn't make it. She said she was too busy. Just Viv with me." It was better to leave it at that. His older sister by seven years had a husband who was a successful doctor with a grandson and granddaughter much to the delight of their mother. Mary Louise, who had always been called "Sis" by everyone in Sterling, was somewhat at a loss to comprehend the abyss that existed between her father and her brother. She noticed odd personality traits ever since little Billy sat down at a piano in church and manifested a gift that eventually brought about the gulf between them. Herschel waited while the trio disappeared into the parlor.

"Herschel, dear," his mother called as she sat down, "come join us, will you?" Julia long ago learned to ignore the dirt on his overalls.

"I'm going to make some coffee," was his reply. And so the atmosphere was the same, much like the upstairs that led to the three bedrooms that were still there, the gabled roof, the twin bed in one of the rooms with the picture of little Billy Kaplan all dressed up in his sailor suit, the hardwood floors that squeaked when even old Angus walked on them, the old water well in the back yard with a bucket that had been there for forty years, the tractors, the old barn, the strange way Herschel silently worked his wheat fields with hardly anyone to help him. So he went to make some coffee.

"Mrs. Tomassi told me you are flying to Paris." Julia was elated. "All the way to France. Oh, my, how I wish I could go to hear you play." Vivian smiled at her innocence while William remained standing. "Sit down, son. When are you going to leave?" Her innocence was enveloped by her smile.

He heard his dad in the kitchen. With a nod to Vivian he replied, "I'll just go help Dad." He bent down to kiss his mother's cheek.

Vivian reached to pat Mrs. Kaplan's hand. "We're glad to be here. He has a rough schedule to follow, with the stop to see you. He's flying out to New York day after tomorrow. He'll be there for an additional three or four days. He'll see RCA during that time there to meet the two men who will fly with him to Paris. It's a little complicated but he knows what to do." Julia's frown changed to a gleaming grin. Vivian felt like she helped her. "He'll be playing in the concert about two weeks from now, back in Denver. It's all arranged." Vivian could see the questions already on the lovely face. "The concert in Denver? That's after the Paris trip. He's to repeat the . . ." and she had trouble in pronunciation again, "concerto in Denver, as scheduled, on his return trip." She walked over to a Norman Rockwell calendar on the wall and pointed. "That's on a Saturday night coming up. This one."

"That's when Herschel and I plan to be in Denver," Julia confirmed. "Oh, I'm so thrilled. I can't wait." She heard the men in the kitchen so she called loudly. "William, look in the bread box. I made some sweet rolls for you." She tried to sing. "'If I knew you were comin' I'd have baked a cake . . .'" Then she returned to Vivian. "I'm glad you telephoned me this morning that you were coming. Gave me a chance to bake the rolls. Herschel likes sweet rolls on Saturday mornings."

Herschel stood near the coffee bar to monitor the brewing with his reluctance to speak. It had always been that way, with hardly any conversation between father and son. With William away to study in Denver at the university, visits to Sterling had become limited. Few and far between were they to the farm, to the parents, even with Sis when she could get away from family.

Herschel turned to the table, pulled out his chair and sat down quietly. He was tired. "I forgot to pull the cups and saucers." He pointed to a cabinet. "They're up there."

"I'll get them," and William used this as a hopeful means to broach a conversation. "Looks like you painted the cupboards. They used to be a sort of dark color." In fact, the whole kitchen was redecorated. The one window over the sink had a new set of curtains with a bright yellow background with small references of knives, forks, and spoons. He remembered the paint job but he refused to mention it. The coffee was ready so he poured two cups.

The painter came out to do the painting about a month ago. "He lifted the top to the sugar bowl on the table. "You use sugar?" William shook his head. "He said he remembered you because he was in high school with you." Herschel spilled a spattering of sugar on the oil cloth. William noticed how his tremor had become more prevalent.

As he sat down, a flood of memories invaded his head. He did not mention name, with a reason or two that he had practically forgotten, or wanted to forget. When Herschel rose to place Julia's rolls on the table, they talked of the Pacific war and the one in Vietnam. "You remember Wilber Duggan. His father and uncle had to fight in the South Pacific. Wilber died last month," Herschel added.

While his father softly tried to make some kind of conversation, strange as it was, William's mind was not hearing what he said. It was a repeat of what Herschel had told him the last time he was here. He did remember that few times, he and a lot of others had discussed a myriad of ifs, ands, and buts, which ordinarily transpired with adolescence including sex, basketball, even rock-and-roll. William often did not have valuable time for bantering and arguing even when Vivian insisted. She would be intimate all too often. Her bright blonde hair, William remembered. She would stop in the school hallway with her arm tossed around William's neck. "Billy," she would plead, "You're my favorite friend. Dammit, I wish you didn't have to go to that music lesson." But he did go to his lessons with Miss Shriner. Once out of Junior High, all his friends would change for one reason or another. Even Bobby Martin eventually disappeared, until now. "Yes, I know Bobby Martin, at least, I remember him." He tried to remain attentive to what his father was saying. "Oh, yes," Herschel concluded, "Bobby was here, I remember, to paint the kitchen." The son politely agreed. In the long run, so much of anything, any more, turned out not to matter.

Herschel made more coffee. "Go tell Julia and Vivian coffee is about ready."

He looked at his father. "I will in just a minute. I want to talk."

Herschel cleared his throat. He looked down at the table where he noticed that he had spilled a drop. "Okay, I guess. What do you want to talk about?" William thought that his father feigned indifference. He heard the loud clock in the hallway strike the eleven o'clock hour, another item in this old house about which he had completely forgotten. "I want to make sure you and mother will be in Denver to hear me play, when I get back from France." This reminder did not exactly set well with his dad. This was just another example of how his father somehow ignored his talent. "Will you, please, Dad?" William took a quick sip of coffee and with his left forefinger traced the top of the old cup. Desperately he was trying to mend a weak conversation.

Herschel stood immediately and placed two more cups and saucers opposite them and sat down again. "Go get your mother and Viv." He glanced furtively at his son. "I guess we will. But I've heard you play before."

This was a gleam of hope. "But not with the Colorado Symphony. I'm playing a concerto which I'm recording in Paris next week. I'll be done after a week when I get back to Denver I want you and mom to come hear the whole thing. I have a room for you at the Brown Palace. You remember meeting a lady name of Amelia Tomassi. She says to tell you you're invited to the Tea she's giving in her condo on the Sunday afternoon, after the concert. Mark it on your calendar. Tell Mom."

Herschel spoke without looking at him. "I got the idea from the painter that you and he were fairly good friends. He wanted to know where you were and I didn't quite know, other than in California." William's jaw dropped. "How did you ... guess ... ?" Herschel said softly, "I think Julia heard something about a university from Vivian one day."

Suddenly Vivian appeared, escorting Julia into the kitchen. "We could smell the coffee so we came on in." Julia offered a chair to Vivian and took the one next to Herschel. "I bet you have had a nice conversation, too. I know we have!" She looked directly at her son. "We'll be there, dear, for the concert and that lady's Tea."

Chapter Thirty-Two

LESS THAN ONE HOUR later on this same Saturday afternoon, after deciding they should return to Denver, Vivian condescended to make a short stop at Mildred Stanton's house. William wanted to say hello to Miss Shriner. "It won't take long," he said as he stepped out of the Buick. "Milly is her sister." He knocked on her front door. "Oh, Billy," she said quickly, "Patty went to Denver this morning early. I bet you forgot she has some kind of a meeting on Saturdays with Mrs. Tomassi."

Yes, it was true. The teacher and the wealthy widow had become great friends across the years. Of the many Saturdays which they spent together—and there were many—this particular one in April was the most anticipated. Their 'desert and tea' had begun merely as a get-together, just the two of them, at Maxine's Bar and Grill because Maxine made the best scones in Denver. Then, with the insistence of Mrs. T, they moved to her condominium where they could invite others. They had the wonderful habit, so said one of the ladies, of discussing the history of music or, as Mrs. Tomassi heard William announce, to discuss the price of eggs in China. Either way, their Saturdays were a success. Dessert with tea remained a delightful social event because Mrs. Tomassi and the piano teacher both liked Earl Grey, among the others. On their minds this afternoon was the forthcoming trip to Paris for the Colorado Celebrity who was out of town, or he would have been invited. "It's Paris, France, not Paris, Texas," soon became a standing remark that was bounced around the music department.

Downtown somebody drew a large poster and placed it on the wall next to the door leading into Dr. Young's office. Mabel insisted that she knew nothing of this gesture. Being the type of lady she was, she winked when she announced that. M. DuPres was delighted! The other employees at the Center, those attached to the theatres on the west side of the public aisle, were equally as proud of the Coloradoan.

Patty Allen Shriner was a statuesque lady of seventy years who once lived with her large family of four siblings, a mother and father in a large farm house not far from the Kaplan family on the southeast side of Sterling. She was fortunate to be surrounded by the joys of her unique siblings. At the time when they were all growing up, they were hardly ever aware of the kind of joyous love that permeated this happy group. Mildred, her older sister, somehow learned to play the violin and she played it well. Many in the Presbyterian Church commented from time to time that Mildred had the gift of the Gods, although a few recognized that this gift came from God, Himself. Of her three brothers, each was thankful of his own inspirations separately; Ben, on every athletic team he could think of without much of a success, John, the clown of high school in his hey day, and Marshall, consistently the best half back on the football team and the first to get married at nineteen. No other family either here, or in Fort Morgan, or in the smaller town of Brush, could claim such notoriety. They all became, sooner or later, notable people.

But Patty Allen, whose middle name came from her grandfather on her mother's side, suddenly found her self at a piano. She studied diligently from as early as seven. She studied and all of Sterling began to realize that the Shriner Family was blessed with two athletes, a clown, especially in church, a virtuoso violinist who captured the hearts of all the boys, and a young miss who grew up to become a nationally well known piano teacher. Somehow Patty Allen never married. Mr. and Mrs. Shriner were destined to tolerate this vivid menagerie. Along with their various interests, each had a cow to milk or a hen that provided eggs, two dogs and three cats. John at one time wanted some Guinea Pigs but he outgrew his passion.

This must have been the day for remembering. For just a split second all the memory of desert and tea reaffirmed itself. Of course William remembered. He had been invited at one time. "Vivian is waiting in the car, Milly, nice to see you again. Goodbye. I'm leaving next week. Check with your sis."

He slid into his seat while Vivian drove all the way back to the condo. He said hardly anything; his mind was elsewhere, on Green Street. Later, it was imagining what Paris looked like after half a year since M. DuPres first mentioned the city to him. "You will like it, I'm quite certain," was his recommendation. "With so much to see and do, you hope you can see it all. The one place I want you to observe is the area directly in front of the main doors to the Sacre Coeur church—the one on the highest position of the city, higher than anywhere else. Walk up the steps. Stand there and look out on the entire city before you. The view is magnifique. You can't miss it. Do this for me!" William's mind ignored the landscape rushing by them. Vivian realized that he was so quiet, so unlike the temperamental soul he was when they were east bound into Sterling.

He returned to a moment at the Shriner farmhouse during one of her lessons. The lady sat alone in her makeshift studio of one room, complete with her upright piano and her thorough knowledge of 'sharps and flats' as William soon learned to call his lessons with her. She decided to enlist the help of the Almighty—as her parents taught her. "It is God given, my boy," she told him often between the years when he was somewhere between an awkward adolescent and a twenty-year-old. "I want you to learn that and respect that, for it is merely not my own decision," and she made certain that he was paying attention to her, "but that it is a gift which must be treasured." She had his undivided attention, that was certain. "From now on, Bill," she ended her sermon with a specific edict. "When you are working with M. DuPres at the university . . . and I recommended M. DuPres to Dr. Graham, for your classes, he is the best. Being French he knows piano very likely better than I do. Don't get the idea that you and I are finished. We are not. I intend to be at your side, so to speak, and I intend to help you when you need it." So this was imbedded in William's soul and mind, thoroughly. It became the cornerstone of his belief that God brought this fabulous Shriner woman into his life. William called her his angel.

Mrs. Tomassi was sixty years old with grey hair, always immaculately combed no matter what. She was a widow of ten years and her legacy was the lumber yard of her late husband. "William told me he and Vivian would be back just so he could tell you goodbye. He's flying out on the morning plane day after tomorrow. It was nothing to be worried about." This gracious lady and her guest learned some time ago never to be too disturbed about the pianist's comings and goings when he is in Denver. They were sitting in their quiet atmosphere. It was late; the other guests had gone. The sky was a dark gray with heavy clouds and several peals of thunder with sheet lightening, a typical Denver Spring.

A definite concern for William always was obvious on the mind of this teacher. Mrs. T was used to this sort of reaction but with William her whole devotion was more evident for him than for her few other students. She could not take more students, now, those few who enrolled in a curriculum at the university. She was frail, now, with a kind word for everyone and a wisp of a smile, no matter what. "Did he seem relaxed," was the next question the teacher offered, "I mean, ready?"

It was a question which even Mrs. T had asked herself time and again. In this day and time, with all the noise and confusion of just merely trying to live comfortably, William did manifest some kind of nervousness about himself. "Actually, in the long run, nothing to be too concerned about. Everyone nowadays, to some degree, fights his own battles." Even so, Mrs. T was always able to remain calm in thought, appearance, and bearing. "Oh, yes," she conceded, "our William is very much the sane gentleman and human being. I don't think you have anything to fret about. He knows the Saint Saens very well."

"Did you hear him?"

"I usually don't pay attention when he is at the piano. The door to that room is not only closed but it is now designed to be soundproof. That is because when I am here, I'm either in my own rooms or I'm in the kitchen. Yesterday, for example, I told him I was going on some errands and not to be too distracted because no one lives in the condo next to me on this floor. He can be as emotional as he wishes. He's a happy, curious soul." She rose and collected the empty tea cups and plates. She looked at her clock on the mantle. Mrs. T spoke from the kitchen. "Did you have a good conversation with him yesterday?"

This teacher who knows him only too well sighed deeply and gathered her purse. "Yes, we did. I was concerned, because . . . well, I thought differently. He played in San Francisco last November. He's been very nice about e mailing me. My nephew has his new computer but I haven't learned to use it. He comes by to deliver my mail for me. William just seems different a bit, that's all." She walked to the door. "I shall wait with baited breath to hear what occurs in Paris. I wish I could stay to say goodbye again but I'm tired. I think it's going to rain and I want to get home. Goodbye, Amelia." And with a nice gesture and smile she made a quick exit and softly closed the door.

William arrived two hours later, too tired to discuss anything with this dear Mrs. T. He sat down opposite her in the dinette where she was preparing something to eat. She discerned a somewhat flustered appearance; it was nothing more than what he usually felt and encountered every time he tried to revive a warmer relationship with his father. He refused to allow any depreciation of his energy.

She smiled a greeting and inquired about his disposition. "I was wondering about you." She paused when she realized he was indeed tired. She produced a sheet from her note pad and passed it to him. "Your friend telephoned from Berkeley—here's his number. He'd like for you to call him."

That alone aroused new interest. "Excuse me while I make a call." He slipped into his bedroom. In a few seconds he was speaking to Jerry. "Hi, Jair," William began, in a habit of not wasting time, something which he had learned from the man to whom he was speaking. "Everything here is okay. Freddy Graham is taking me to the airport. I packed yesterday. We just got back from seeing mom and dad at Sterling." He waited to hear what Jerry was saying. "No, it was a trip I had to have, I suppose, so Vivian told me. Did everything go all right?" He waited while Jerry dominated the conversation. "You what?" He was suddenly more alert than ever. "Wait while I get a pen and paper—I have it now. Go ahead." He became more excited as the words spilled out from the message. First came the affirmation that he is now a Ph.D. and that he is going to a banquet this very evening to celebrate with those few other candidates and his advisors. "But that isn't why I called earlier. Are you sitting down?" Yes, he was. "I have the job but it doesn't start until two weeks. Yeah. Two weeks. So—and get this—I'm coming to Paris with you." This was like a bombshell. William stood up immediately hardly believing what he just heard. "You're *what?*" Listen to me and write all this down. Give me the name and address of the hotel where you'll be in New York. I am flying the day after tomorrow and I'll join you *before* you fly out to France." William could not believe what he was hearing, yet it was true, for in the balance of the message, Jerry said again what his plan was for the rendezvous. He needed a vacation and this was an opportunity he could not deny. William was to call tomorrow and give him the pertinent information. *Yes, he has a passport.* He has had one for seven years when his brother and he were to go to Italy after graduation from high school. That trip did not materialize.

William was too ebullient to speak. He heard the affirmation and jumped up from the chair at the telephone stand. "Oh, wow! I can call you Doctor Champion, now. Oh, God, Jair, that's wonderful. Yes, I'm happy for you of course. I'm just happy! Oh, it's you're birthday. No, I didn't forget that. You'll be here for your birthday and we'll have a party to end all parties. You've heard me mention Vivian Cole. Well she said, today, she'll be pleased to meet you. I'll tell her to rig up something special. It'll be special just for you." He waited, again while Jerry laughed and answered him. "Okay. Okay! I guess I forgot about the celebration banquet tonight. You get yourself in your tux and go to that banquet. What?" He waited until Jerry finished his thought. Then he answered quickly before he stood up again. "Jerry, you're just fine. You'll be the best guy there at that banquet. When we get here, after Paris— Oh God, I can't believe it—you'll meet everyone and I want everyone to meet you. It won't be long, now. I'll get the info for you and I'll call you tomorrow. I can't believe it, I just cannot believe it!" Then he held back his tears of joy. "Goodbye, you rascal!"

A knock on his door sounded as Mrs. T opened it slightly. "You all right?" She inquired? He turned to her, grinned, and all exhaustion had disappeared. "Paris! Paris, Mrs. T! I'm ready for Paris.

Chapter Thirty-Three

FREDDY GRAHAM HAD AN unusual business relationship with Dr. Young. He had been head of the music department at the university for twelve years. Since the campus was well over five miles from the downtown Center for the Performing Arts, they were unable to see each other readily enough to make decisions as rapidly as they wished. One of the subjects which took precedence often was the curriculum to develop a program for professionals. The university orchestra that already was of great concern was most suitable, but the overall plan, now, was to enhance the whole school. Originally Dr. Graham gladly spoke to the university president. He outlined his plans at that time; with the agreement and endorsement from the conductors at the Center. Together they quickly became the men to do the work in so short a time. One morning not long ago Freddy Graham and the conductors congratulated themselves over an improvement for both.

After all, the city had a symphony orchestra of its own. Both the Colorado Symphony and The University of Denver's orchestra became well known statewide as a result. At a banquet to honor recent graduates Dr. Graham included William Kaplan as a good example of a local talent who had successfully developed a strong image for himself and for the department. Just in these last three years Raymond Hicks rejoiced even though he had always wanted William to move to the Big Apple. Nevertheless he promised to include these remarks in all the forthcoming publicity. The agent made certain that information for all bookings, anywhere, would be instantly sent to both Graham and Young. The *Denver Post* hardly ever received news from Hicks, something Stewart Parker did not appreciate. Once, when Parker accidently encountered Dr. Young in a Lo Do Cafeteria, the journalist mentioned this little tidbit to him and provided his own scalping opinion. "I have to be careful right now with Kaplan going to France." Stewart Parker suggested to Dr. Graham. "I want to make sure the publicity points with pride to the artist as well as the university and our C.S.O. I have tried to correspond with this Mr. Hicks but I get the idea he is on a break and probably is satisfied with the status quo."

All that was well and good, Freddy kept reminding everyone within ear shot. He wanted to broadcast the fact that this young Kaplan not only was a local sensation but also an individual who lived and breathed music. He was a splendid example of one who lived alone, so to speak, and hardly ever ventured to befriend anyone. Eight years ago, when young Kaplan enrolled, the lad from Sterling who invaded the premises and shyly explained to Dr. Graham that all he ever wanted to do was to play the piano well. One of the fraternities extended an invitation to him. The current class of pledges was too rowdy. Vivian Anderson was in Boulder at the time falling in love with her football star. She negated the call from the frat. That is, until his tour last April.

Both Young and Graham began to notice an obvious change in the pianist's composure, his personality, his demeanor. One day recently the conductor and the instructor both looked at each other in the hall leading to Mabel's desk. She was not there. They stood and talked quietly. "You know," Freddy Graham began to admit, "I think it is natural for our celebrity to show a healthy degree of excitement. I noticed this right away about three weeks ago. I'm not really concerned about any of it. It's just natural for him to be eager—if that is the word I want." They waited until two students passed them. "I heard this from the Frenchman, but you and I both know the Frenchman is more excited about this Paris trip than anyone."

Dr. Young waited a moment before he spoke. "Yes . . . I do agree and it's nothing to try to solve—if we're to suggest anything else. William was tired the other evening after a thorough run-through of the third movement. You know what: I think it's just euphoria. Nothing drastic."

On that Sunday before he was to fly to New York, William talked to Maestro Young. The conductor was curious from more than one standpoint. He wanted to ask the pianist outright just what was the impetus that brought about this change especially in the last six months. Dr. Young then decided that this was not the actual reason for seeing him. He was gracious to make the visit merely to say goodbye and to wish him 'bon chance.' "You go to Paris and you play well. Upon your return to Reality we'll discuss interpretation regarding Saint Saens. We will have plenty of time to rehearse the whole concerto here. I'm not the least cautious. I appreciate what Freddy told me of your *elan vital*. I like the way you think, now. I say 'now' because—and he started to mention what he promised himself that he would not mention— well, I have noticed the great improvement in your own personality. M. DuPres noticed it, too." Then he looked at William in the eyes seriously. "I have always agreed with Graham that we have a splendid artist." William looked the other way. "No. Wait. Hear me out. I must tell you, it is one thing to be elaborately aloof from the things that are going on around you. Five years ago you were in your own little world. Now in certain cases, I suppose that is more evident in musicians than in actors or painters. Five year ago I was just getting to know you. I didn't doubt for a second we had a developing artist who would prove his worth." Steven manipulated him to escape the hall and to descend to the public aisle below them.

"I'm here to tell you now that all of us are extremely proud of how you have blossomed in the last year. I'm talking about your total image; your talent has greatly improved too, so says the Frenchman. That tour you went on must have been the key to unlock a treasure chest." This brought about a gaze from William that surprised both of them. "Whatever it was, I want you to remember it and take it to France with you." The conductor stepped down from his 'soapbox' and grabbed him by the shoulders. "This is the time for me to tell you these things mainly because I feel you must know what I think of you and how all of us here are elated and excited. You are a fine young man." He took a deep breath and laughed at his sermon. "My God," he chortled, "did all of that come out of poor little me?" Then he shrugged his shoulders. "Well, so it did. I've said what I guess I wanted to say. Take it for what it is whether it is B.S. or not."

"I have a favor to ask." Dr. Young waited until two women passed them in the wide aisle. "There's a nice book store on the Rue Rivoli. I have the address for you." He supplied a note paper with the information. "If you have time, go in and buy a book on Ravel and bring it to me. Oh. M. DuPres says au revoir. You might send him a card if you have time." They shook hands silently and William turned and left toward the steps that led to Fourteenth Street.

————

Freddy Graham came by the condo at seven o'clock the next morning. He announced that he was fifty-five that morning and felt that he should be going to New York and points east instead of this thirty-something-year-old upstart. He parked quickly at the depareture sidewalk. "Somebody from RCA will meet you, probably carrying a small sign with your name on it. You might look for that. No doubt you will be whisked to Manhattan in a fashionable limousine, but you've probably been used to this for some time, now." Graham even manifested a bit of jealousy. "I wish I could go with you but duty calls and I have a Valkyrian secretary who keeps me busy. I shall expect to hear from you before you leave Kennedy. Steven wants to talk to you about Saint Saens. He couldn't ride with us this morning. He says it's too early." William opened the passenger door, got out with his carry-on case, and reached over to shake his hand. Graham, however flippant in tone, was really quite sincere, and opened the truck for the suitcase. "Thank you, my wizard. We wish you well. Wow them in Paris. You can do it." And with that, he sped away and left William to his future.

"Mr. Kaplan?" sounded a voice from behind him. He turned to see a tall woman carrying only her handbag, a tablet and pen, wearing a smart black dress but no sign with his name on it. "I'm Sybil Connor from RCA." They shook hands. "Once you checkyour bag, we can go to celebrity parking. It's not far from baggage carousel. I'm glad you can make it. My boss has a lot planned for you." She was efficient, and she walked just ahead of him through the crowd. "Your hotel is the Ambassador and here is your schedule for the two days you will have in New York. Mr. Hicks's new telephone number is there on the top of page two." She managed to give him a folder with some papers in it. "Day after tomorrow you and he will leave with one of our French interpreters. You're flying Air France. Have you been to Paris before?" She ushered him down with his bag and did not hear his reply.

He had mixed opinions about the Big Apple. It has been like this every time he was in this hectic city. Hicks usually met him or made sure he was treated well. But the noise and confusion, the traffic from LaGuardia, the taxis, the continual feel of the people around him all were so unlike where he lived in Denver. He just did not like New York and he made an effort not to let this city undermine his artistic energy at this point in time. His mind was on Jerry. He was expected in the morning after an overnight flight which was non-stop.

He wanted to relax in his room. He hoped that the hotel would have a piano ready, just as Mr. Hicks had ordered, somewhere, away from the crowds, a quiet place where he could work some solo portions. Miss Connor was nice, courteous, but she reminded him of this huge island's nervous populace, complete with a noticeable local accent. Maybe tomorrow will not be hectic. Maybe, once they get on the plane and say goodbye to New York, that he will be ready to meet all those other people in the City of Light, and to play Saint Saens's masterpiece. That is all he wanted to do.

Before this ritual began, he was alone, at last, in the Ambassador Hotel on the twelfth floor with no other guests. In the one large room at the end of a corridor, the piano was waiting as promised so he could play as much as he dared and as passionately as he could manage. Two employees who monitored the activity were told not to bother him. But they did stop in the hallway a few feet from where he was playing to admire the music and to make certain all went well. It wasn't everyday these two maids were able to hear any famous concert pianist, even if he did not play long. He stopped because he was tired. He opened the door suddenly and appeared in the hallway before the ladies were able to excuse themselves so they applauded. He smiled, waved a hand, and disappeared into his room. At a window he could see the momentum of the populace and the stretch of lights on the streets below him. He was too tired to try to reach Jerry even though it was still early evening there. In another few minutes he was asleep in a bed that had two small pieces of chocolate on the pillow.

The day began with yet another surprise. By mid-morning, when William had already confirmed itineraries with RCA Victor, he opened his hotel door and there stood a sleepy Jerry Champion. The *Red Eye* flight that was slightly late was not good to him. But Jerry's smile quickly endorsed the fact that he was indeed peering into a happy face. With no one else in the hallway, William grabbed a crumpled tie and pulled him into the room and slammed the door. Jerry started to say something but an embrace was sufficient. They backed away from each other. In yet another silent moment they awkwardly stood to look at themselves, enveloped as they were by sheer joy. "I'm tired," Jerry announced breathlessly. "Yeah, well, I guess I didn't sleep well, myself . . . waiting for you to get here. Look. Take a shower while I tend to some business."

In a split second they both laughed uproariously.

That evening when it came time to board Air France, Hicks was flustered by all the last minute paper work and what-have-you. He said he wanted to see where Napoleon is buried, inside some big building where tourists stand around on a balcony of sorts and peer down at the tomb. Just before they boarded the plane, he dropped his passport and William bent down to retrieve it.

Chapter Thirty-Four

THE EUROPEAN SUN APPEARED on the starboard wing of Air France. Its rays, peeking through a dozen clouds, made the overnight flight seem short. Once William opened his eyes he was astounded at the clouds over the Atlantic. Having experienced a mere seventy-two hours of minimal sleep, from the West Coast to France, Jerry Champion was still dozing in the aisle seat next to William. But in the short day from the moment he greeted the pianist yesterday morning, he tried to find time to snooze while preparations were finalized for this trip. A flight attendant was at his seat and offered him a fresh warm towel to wash his face, one to William and one to the geologist. They looked around the cabin. Raymond Hicks was still asleep and the interpreter was returning to his own seat. Jerry had a difficult time trying to open his eyes.

William did not need to ask for coffee because the attendant was there with a demitasse and a croissant with strawberry on a plate. She smiled as she lowered the tray for him. "Bon jour, M. Kaplan." April in Paris became more than just the old ballad that he had heard since well before he realized that song would become a part of his history. The plane hovered over the Loire Valley as it neared Paris. From his window seat, he saw the splendor of the City of Light, welcoming the jet as it circled well above Charles de Gaulle International. The sun was bright on this morning of mornings and even though he saw this for the first time, he did not deny the tears in his eyes. An announcement, first in French, then in English sounded over the loud speaker as the huge plane dipped to the left to make its approach. Music followed. *April in Paris* surprised everyone, especially when sung by Sinatra. William removed his flight socks and slipped into his shoes. In another twenty minutes they were at the arrival gate and ready to disembark.

The quartet found two hosts waiting for them to go through customs. Raymond Hicks was half asleep. He glanced at is watch; "My God, no wonder I'm sleepy, it's ten after two in New York." The third party, the silent escort, spoke fluently for them. In a matter of ten more minutes, all were seated in a black limousine. With the driver in his black hat and a gorgeous lady dressed in a black gown, French, of course, who had stood in the crowd with a large card with Kaplan scribed on it, they sped to the City.

"It's a pleasure to meet you, Mr. Kaplan," said the lady. Her cleavage was most obvious. She had a manila envelope full of papers which she held in her lap. Her hair was combed neatly and her fingernails were immaculately groomed. Raymond Hicks was awake by now, starring at the lady and the terrain. "We're going directly to the hotel where you will perform. It has a large auditorium big enough for orchestra and an ample audience. You may rest before your lunch gathering." From the envelope she handed him a paper with a multitude of schedules printed in English. "In order not to confuse you, here is your list of activities designed just for you. Please carry it with you at all times and don't be too worried about meeting rooms, lobbies, and such. All the desk clerks speak English—or do you speak French?" To that, he said "no." She continued: My name is Deseree. When I see you, please ask for help if you need it." She pointed to the paper. "Oh, and please note number six. You have at your disposal a concert grand piano in your suite of rooms at the hotel. The room is sound proof so play all you wish. Item number twelve manifests your time frame when you are to be introduced to the orchestra and when you meet the maestro. You will play with the French National Orchestra. He speaks little English so be aware of this. He always has an interpreter with him by the podium." Their own escort frowned at this lovely lady. "Your rehearsal times, both of them, are one and one-half hours in length. A tux is available if you prefer but please offer your sizes as soon as you can." His interpreter announced that he already has one.

The car pulled into the drive and immediately two bell hops were there to assist. "Here we are." They stepped quickly to the sidewalk. "I do hope you had a pleasant flight. I must leave you now, Mr. Kaplan. I hope you can see some of our city before you return." She looked at Jerry. "Turn yourself into a tourist. Au revoir." She smiled elegantly, shook his hand, nodded to Raymond Hicks and the escort and left them standing amidst their luggage and two bellhops.

The schedules were specific and in French with English directly below each sentence. William was more tired than he expected, having crossed the Atlantic from Kennedy in a mere seven hours, more or less. Jerry mumbled that he had to lie down and sleep. A large world map in the main lobby described the answers for him with half the map lit up, as day, and half in darkness . . . Lunch time came suddenly immediately but Jerry elected to sleep.

After lunch, on a specific concert grand reserved for him in a large conference room with two elegant chandeliers he felt better and practiced his scales. The room was elegant with a ten-foot ceiling and red drapes surrounding three tall windows. Hicks discovered him and closed the double doors as he interrupted him. "My God. Billy," he whispered, "this place is a castle. Two staircases going up to that balcony from the lobby. I've never seen anything like this place in my life. How you feeling?" William found time to stop to try to find an answer for his agent. Hicks continued. "I had to hit the sack for a while to catch up on sleep. How was lunch? What did you have?" William banged the keyboard with both hands. "Okay, okay, I'll leave you alone." At the doors, he turned with a final remark. "I knocked on your door and that Jerry somebody was awake. He told me he came all the way from Frisco." Hicks noticed that he wanted to be alone so his departure was without further comment. "Thank you, Raymond," but his agent had already disappeared.

The first movement was crisp and still fresh with its long and involved passages. After practicing for two hours, he was too tired. Upon leaving the room, he moved the sliding indicator by the doors to the *unoccupied* position and softly stepped into the hallway and to the elevators. He found Jerry in the shower so he sat in a large elegant chair by the windows. When Jerry appeared, William made a suggestion. "I think it's time to go do something. I don't have anything scheduled until dinner time at seven o'clock." They both were quiet. William sat with his eyes upon Jerry who was yawning. The Atlantic crossing was the first for both of them. All they could do was grin at the moment . . . In another ten minutes, they were ready. "I want to talk to you, anyway."

Jerry noticed a reluctance in his friend, a hesitancy that he had hardly ever discovered before now. Maybe it was because of the French atmosphere, the imposition of less sleep than usual for both of them. They were quiet as they walked through the impressive lobby. One desk clerk nodded to them and smiled. He was occupied with another artist who had arrived that very afternoon, the Russian pianist who was to play the Ravel *Left Hand*. She and her escort turned to observe the Americans and to venture a 'hello' to them but they already passed the desk.

The hotel's courtyard was wide and in the center of the building. It was surrounded by ten floors of an atrium, complete with a few small ornate tables and chairs where coffee was served. They found a secluded area with palm trees. Instantly, a waiter was there so they ordered. A group of well dressed Frenchmen walked by them; one extended a welcome to the Americans. Another moment of silence was most apparent to both. Then, after one or two sips in delicate demitasse cups and a quick bite of ginger snaps from a large plate, Jerry spoke first. "All this time, since Aunt Urs left, I really haven't had time to tell you anything. Anything of value, I mean." William eyed him closely. "She's happy in Monticello now, Billy. I'm glad for her. I know she wanted to go back to New York. By the way, Li says hello and good luck. She's there at the house until I get back."

It was then that they realized how tired they both were. William reached in his coat pocket to produce his copy of the schedules. But it was Jerry who spoke first. "That's what I want to talk to you about," he said, pointing to the list of rituals ahead of them. "When I get back to Denver—with you, of course—I want to get back to the job." He was speaking in his matter-of-fact voice. "Mr. Lemmon, my new boss, wants me back as soon as I can make it. It was sort of . . . well, embarrasing." But Jerry was not hesitant in what he said. "I got the jbb, all right, right out of the clear blue sky, so to speak. To tell him I'm going to France for two days . . . well, not very many people suddenly say that. Both he and I agreed that my work wouldn't begin until possibly two or three days *after* that concert in Denver . . . a repeat of the one you're playing here".

William registered complete understanding. He waited until another crowd of people passed them before he spoke. "Sure." It was succinct. He opened the folder of information. "Tomorrow night, Saturday, is when I play. The Russian lady plays the Ravel on Sunday night. I just hope that Hicks and that escort will leave on Sunday's plane . . ." and he noticed that Jerry was ready to interrupt but he continued, "because I want Monday here." He pointed to a small calendar among the papers, "We can leave on Tuesday if that's all right. My repeat of the Saint Saens in Denver is not until the following Saturday night. Young wanted to have a couple of days with me to rehearse."

Their eyes met and William could see that this whole plan was valid with both of them. When the waiter came with more coffee, both waited for him to leave. They wanted to prolong the moment, because William could account for their eagerness to be together, comfortably, sitting as they were at a distant table, away from the normal crowd . . . After another prolonged moment, he added quietly, "I guess I haven't had time to talk to you." He watched several people enter the coffee bar. "Jair . . . I'm extremely happy you are here. I don't know what it took to get you to do this—flying as you did on the *Red-Eye*—man, was I happy about that!" Jerry started to push his chair away from the table. "Hey—just a minute, please Jair, please. I . . . I want to say something else. I know you're tired. So am I. But . . . please." More guests passed their table.

Then William continued. He leaned into the table and moved his demitasse to one side." I am a bit nervous. You may not see that but I am." Jerry took one sip of his coffee and with the cup in midair, his eyes moved to William's face. "God, I hope you can appreciate that. Here I am . . . here *we* are . . . and I want to do a bang up job." Jerry sandwiched in a quick retort: "you're okay. You'll play just fine." To that, William took a deep breath. "Yeah, sure, I know. I just can't get over the fact that these people wanted *me*! I tried to ask Dr. Young why me but I never could find the courage, so I got on a plane and came to . . . this place." He noticed that Jerry was sitting there, listening attentively, listening to what he wanted to say. William folded his hands before him on the table after drinking another sip. "This whole big wonderful city is kind of important to me. Dr. Young was here before that war. Here I am sitting in a fabulous hotel drinking coffee with a guy whom I did not know one year ago. Paris, Jair, *Paris*. This whole trip is really . . ." and he searched for a word, " . . . important to me." He likened the city to a most compensative act that any artist could envision. Paris was full of artists of all kinds. William wanted Jerry to understand. The geologist blinked his eyes as he sat and peered at him. "I just want to be good . . . the best. It's . . . the epitome of where any artist wants to be, at least once in his hectic llfe." Then, as if he quickly compared Jerry to any other scientist, he said, "I'm proud of you, Jair. I *am*. I'm so damn happy I could shout it from the housetops," and he suddenly noticed several people glanced their way because his voice level rose. "Or from the courtyard even." A man and a woman at the next table smiled and applauded them. William became calm. "I just want to be good, Jair, tomorrow night. I just want to play really well. The best." He leaned back in his chair, took another deep breath, nervously glanced at the couple who smiled at them again, and relaxed.

Jerry was seeing another William whom he may not have realized was there, inside this person sitting next to him. Yes, he could understand, because time and again, Jerry had travelled the inroads and byways of his own doubts and fears and turmoil. He often wondered, himself, if he ever would be able to be not just a good geologist, but the best. That propelled him to the success he gained in just this last week. Yes. He understood. He drank the remaining drops in his small cup, sat back in his chair, and reached over to pat his friend on the back. He waited until William turned to him and saw in him the confirmation of the future that was ahead for both of them. Jerrry grinned. "You're okay, in my books, rascal." He hit the schedule with his index finger. "You're going to wow them tomorrow night."

William's first rehearsal with the conservatory orchestra was that evening. Their rituals began. He was confident and ready. The conductor was a young man, somewhat older than William. When he entered alone, with no interpreter with him, the orchestra members stood and applauded, much the same as what happened with the Mozart last August. He shook hands with the conductor. "Shall we begin, M. Kaplan?" was an immediate greeting. The interpreter standing near the piano followed the French of the conductor, "We will take the first movement, first, I mean, and then we will see what we need."

For William, Raymond Hicks, and the escort, everything began. Once, after this first rehearsal, William waved his hands, thumbs up, to Deseree as she passed him in the lobby. Another practice session was for the next morning, that being the day of the concert. Jerry sat alone to watch and listen. He and William had no time for tourism, as much as they wanted. That would be later, after the celebration concluded. Raymond Hicks did make sure he saw what was to be seen, complete with his small camera and the escort who helped him from time to time with any French word he was learning. Their tours went well. When they returned they found their seats and were ready, too.

The printed programs were prepared in three languages. 'The French National Conservatory of Music proudly presents its fourth annual celebration of French composers, with the American, William Kaplan, and the Russian, Olga Smirnov. M. Kaplan performs Camille Saint Saens Concerto #2 in G Minor for Piano and Orchestra, Op. 22, this Saturday evening. Ms. Smirnov will perform Maurice Ravel Piano Concerto in D for the Left Hand. Each program was available on a table draped in red satin. After each performance, each evening, a reception was in the large ball room. It was all congested with French language, a French quartet, and multiple waiters who made sure everyone was drinking champaign. Deseree did manage to wave hello to him. She was surprised and she told him so. A tall gentleman stood beside her. "M. Kaplan," she laughed, "this is my husband. Don't worry, he speaks English because he is British." He graciously agreed. "Mr. Kaplan," he began, "I am totally in agreement with Deseree. I was surprised indeed, and you played it so well. Thank you for a job well done." They disappeared in the crowd before William had an opportunity to talk to them. Other people surrounded him. All he could do was to smile and grin and laugh. The escort stood beside him to translate.

Jerry's eyes captured the entire room. He grasped the high ceilings with their glittering candelabras hanging dramatically from their ornamental centers. The musical quartet was often smothered by the happy crowds but even yet he was captured by the moment. Once, maybe twice, his attention was riveted on the spontaneity of his great and good friend. Once, when their eyes met amid the crowd's glee, William signaled to him to join them but Jerry only hesitated. This was Billy's moment.

Jerry stood aside and merely watched as the crowds swarmed around the American. He grabbed a glass of Champagne as a busy waiter passed him. He raised this glass to his own toast. "You were okay in my books, rascal," he muttered very softly to himself, *"You done good!"*

Chapter Thirty-Five

"I WANTED TO BE sure and give him my regards." Stewart Parker had never been in Mrs Tomassi's condo. He searched for William on the verandah just through the two doors from the main room. The weather was too cool to remain there long. He arrived not more than ten minutes ago at Mrs. T's Sunday afternoon tea, paid his compliments to the lady and began moving through the remnants of those who were still present at this late hour. He ignored a few who said hello as he found the pianist immediately. The hostess was never surprised at this man's rudeness for his reputation was widely known around town and at the *Post*. Despite the unseemly reputation, somehow he succeeded in being a fine critic, if such a mark of character is a foundation for honest criticism. He was blunt with the first request. "I wanted to schedule an interview with you. I just learned you are leaving for the West Coast. You're moving, I hear." Often he worked on a moment's notice as this was the case. "You don't mind my asking some questions? Now, I mean?" William had never had even a moment's notice to say yes or no. "You're moving, I take it? Bag and baggage?." William glanced through the doors to see his sister. She disappeared when she saw Parker. This was the first opportunity he had to greet her.

In such an informal interview, and William was used to all kinds, he volunteered, "I . . . yes, I'm moving." He immediately enjoined his thanks before the journalist had an opportunity to say more. "To San Francisco. And thank you for your kind words about me and for my going to France." I made my decision for San Francisco almost immediately after I repeated the Saint Saens here. I won't be here

243

much longer." He realized the critic was working without pad and pencil.

Parker hesitated. "I would like to see you sometime, tomorrow, possibly. Can you spare an hour with me? It would be a nice 'follow-up' on how busy you are. I'm trying to beat 'Sixty Minutes.' Or did you know? Bradley wants to do a segment on you to come out next fall, I think it is. I know him fairly well and he is planning it. He told me he wants to contact your parents in Sterling to do a "back-up" with pictures of the farm. You were born in that house, I learned. My questions won't take long." William was startled by this man's abruptness. He saw Jerry through the glass doors and nodded his head quickly. "All right, I suppose so." He surrendered his time. "Make it ten o'clock here, please." To that the critic answered affirmatively. "I'll have a photographer with me." He signaled with his thumb up and smiled. He left without saying thank you.

The jovial manner William enjoyed since he got out of bed that morning was lost the minute Stewart Parker arrived. It returned when the critic departed. He came through an archway and stood face to face with his sister. "He looks like a sly fox. I know sly foxes when I see them." She escorted her brother through a double door and into the library. "But he explodes in his columns. You're just not aware of his journalism as I am. Usually it has to do with personality clashes. Freddy Graham calls him a snake in the grass, but he does have a remarkably good education with classical music." She paused to see that he was rested and ready for the next big move. "By the way, Mom and Dad are tired, I think. I've got him sitting in the kitchen with a cup of coffee and Mom is around here, someplace. Vivian is plotting a million questions to Dr. Champion over there in the corner. She wants to know everything. But that is typical Vivian." William looked at her with his own questions obvious on his face. He still had a tired expression after having slipped through New York and onto a plane for home. Yes, Dr Champion went to France with him. I guessed you wanted to know. Sis made him sit next to her on the sofa. She was bound to remain alone with her brother for as long as she could manage.

"Okay," Sis said, "this is the first time I've had to sit and talk since you two got back home. Let's just hope that no one comes through that library door." She took his hand and looked directly into his face.

"What's wrong?" She was always good at playing the good doctor, having been married to one for ten years. He did not reply. "You want me to repeat the question?" He responded with a question, himself, about how her husband is. She did not feel any compunction in a delay. She took a deep breath and found words. "My husband is the practical side of the family. He thinks things through pretty well. He is a paragon. I have learned to think things through, myself. But I grew up with you and I also learned long ago that for some strange reason which I have yet to fathom that you are not practical. That can never be. Now." She smiled and repeated her own question, more directly . . . "What is wrong?"

"Fair enough," he agreed. "All right." He was choosing words for her. "I'm a pianist. I'm a romantic."

She leaned back in the sofa. "I never could make heads or tails of your romantic side." She thought before she said anything else. Then her remark came easily. "I'll never be able to figure you out." It was not difficult to say that.

"Ah, but you always see through me, don't you?" He was more serious than she could imagine. "Yes, I'm a romantic. And I'll tell you something else. Let's just hope Jerry doesn't come looking for me! He has to be back to go to work in about four or five more days." Sis was totally surprised at that. "Something I discovered in France." His elbows rested on nothing as he folded his hands before his mouth and touched his lips to his thumbs. It was a manner he developed a long time ago. He waited so long that Mary Louse began to wonder. "I wish I could live in France." To her this was a surprise. "I felt quite at home for myself. Like Saint Saens and Ravel and Alice B. Toklas. I managed to get away from Ray Hicks. Jerry and I walked down a street and I knew I heard a million footsteps behind me. I turned a corner and I swear I expected to see Toulouse-LaTrec sketching. People like that. Through a shop window I saw a huge poster of Claude DeBussy staring right at me. A big colorful poster of Claude DeBussy! And Monet said hello to me and Bizet was right there walking with us. I know who they are and what they represent. I can see it in their eyes. The French adore *Les Arts*." He left her there on the sofa and strolled to a window. "Oh, Sis, oh! I long to know who I am. Without any pretense. With no masks, no disguises. I feel that way when I'm playing. Often . . . I feel that way." She joined him and placed her arms around him. She turned, saw Vivian and waited.

It was not Jerry who interrupted this scene, but Vivian carrying her own glass of wine. She curtailed her vivaciousness when she sensed what she saw. "People are leaving. It's late and I want to check with the crew at my apartment." She patted William on the back. "Din-din is at eight tonight." And as if it were a good tonic, she added, "I'll have some good people who want to meet you, sweetheart." And she added, "The invitation includes the good doctor."

Sis stepped to the door. "Bill," she said softly, "Mom and Dad will be leaving. I'm taking them home for dinner and then we're driving them to Sterling tomorrow. Come say goodbye."

Alone now near a telephone, Vivian dialed her own apartment. "Hello, Ruth. Dear. This is Vivian again. Is everything under control? Good. No, I was just checking. How does the cake look?" While she listened to this voice that described the chocolate cake, with all the glitter of the trimmings, the icing, the capital letters that spelled 'Congratulations, Billy', Vivian nodded an agreement. "Put the cat on the back porch, please, will you? He's used to you people by now. I forgot to tell you about the candles. That's why I called. The big tall white ones. I just got them yesterday. Pull open the top drawer in the cupboard and you'll find them. No, you don't light them right now, but I do want the dining room to sparkle when we get there. Oh, and how does the top of the cake look? I mean, does it really say "You done good!" on it. No, this tea party is winding down and we'll be there in another thirty or forty minutes more or less." She sipped her wine. "Ciao." She heard a knock at the door and looked to see Jerry come in rather slowly. "Hello, Doctor Geologist! Want to use the phone?"

For the first time since she saw them get off their plane, he was dressed in coat and tie. Jerry was a bit hesitant. "I saw you come in here. This is the first time I've had to thank you for meeting us." He glanced at how her hand was still resting on the telephone. "No, I don't know anyone to call in Denver." Since then, Vivian had been trying to piece together the events of that afternoon just four days ago, in a busy time before they arrived from New York. Mrs. T went with her to wave her welcome sign. Freddy Graham and Steven Michael Young missed their arrival. They had it the next day on their calendars.

"Come in and sit down. Away from the noise." She had wanted to speak to him personally, alone, away from that crowd. William had already told Jerry that Vivian could easily fill up the room with her asking all kinds of questions. Now that she actually was speaking to the secret correspondent from U.C.Berkeley, she was more than pleased to discover that this new doctorate recipient was really nice looking and the same age as she. "Yes, I'm the one who gave all your letters to the Boy Wonder. He didn't say very much at first, just thanks, each time.

"Vivian relaxed in a chair. Her appraisal of Dr. Champion was never at an end. She managed a deft conversation with him on the long drive from the airport but she could not look at him sitting beside her in her Buick with Billy in the back seat. Now, she saw his fresh haircut, the nice suit he wore, the gleam in his eyes. Her questions did not include anything about his new career. She confessed she was ignorant of geology. En route to town, Jerry reviewed for her all the hard work he had just completed. This included credit hours, research, the GPA that haunted him all the time, qualifying exams, both written and oral, the writing of his dissertation, coupled with the departure of his aunt who flew back to Monticello. Once they got to the condo, Vivian made him a frozen daiquiri. Now, after the tea thing, which Vivian told him flatly that she did not care for such, she told him she would make another drink for both of them. This made Jerry feel more at ease. "He sent me in here. I think you are to meet him. He's on the balcony talking to Mrs. Ethel somebody. I think he needs some help."

She started for the door. "I can imagine. With Ethel Tabor, you need help." She stopped at the door. By the way, are you two still flying back as planned?" Jerry moved nearer the piano. "He has a master class. We have three more days here. Leaving on Wednesday."

Vivian laughed. "My welcome home party tonight for Billy should be over by then. The party at my place is your birthday party. too. I realize it's not until the ninth but that's coming up." She smiled and closed the door.

A part of the new image that Jerry seemed to promote for himself was a carefree attitude that he did not realize he had. Possibly it had to do with the total release of living with stress. Maybe it had to do with a new city, one that was a stranger to him which he had to depend upon William to show him. It had to do with this Vivian Cole, whoever she was. It had to do with the orchestra last night when Jerry was able to see up close exactly what the players looked like, what they said not only to William how happy they were for him, but what the conductor earlier told everyone at the reception. It was even a better performance, so Jerry thought, than the one he witnessed in Paris just days ago. It was important for everyone, not just for the honored recipient.

William Kaplan, in a short matter of twenty years, became a concert pianist. This was something completely out of the scientific realm with which he had involved himself in his own little world. Mrs. T understood all too well. "Oh, my young doctor, nothing surprises me, anymore. I am one to believe in what God Almighty can and may do for any of us. May I say, right away, at the end of a busy afternoon for us all, I'm sure that I want to have a moment with you some time if you may. I have several questions I want to put to you. And they have nothing to do with geology. Alas! This can never be."

Jerry began to understand the people of music in Denver. He met the maestro, the head of the music department at the university, the concert mistress, *and* Vivian Cole. "Cloak and Dagger? What you may learn from me may shock you."

"Oh, young man," she laughed, "not anymore. In this day and time, I'm unshockable, even about the ugly Vietnam War. I may be choronologically sixty years but I've been known to shock people with my own answers. I've encountered a whole new vocabulary. Everyone on the board of directors for Dr. Young's troupe of players thinks nothing of my caustic remarks. Some of them are too tame, even for me." She smiled enigmatically. "I think you have an influence over William, if I may say so. To that sudden word Jerry said, "You're psychic." Her reply told him she was not finished with this conversation. "I don't believe in spiritual matters, mind you. Vivian says that I do. But I don't. You're one to set a goal."

"A goal, huh?" Whether or not this had any scientific approach, Jerry was himself intrigued.

"All scientists have goals. And a few other professionals, just as noble as your doctorate. By the way, congratulations. But I don't know a thing about geology."

"I tell you what! While Bill practices here tomorrow, you and I will go down town and sit and talk over lunch and I'll tell you everything you want to know." Mrs. T paused. "Everything?" she asked. "Almost everything." "Too bad, kind sir. I have several errands which I must do. I leave for Chicago to attend my grandson's christening the day after you two leave for the West Coast."

Mrs. Ethel Tabor interrupted their chat with her unusual questions. "Is Mr. Kaplan still here? I hope he'll play a number, just for me. I tried to talk to him." Jerry meandered away from them. She turned to Mrs. T. "Did I ask him?"

"Well, I really don't know, Ethel, did you?

"I get the idea he's kind of stand-offish." Ethel was resetting her hat. She was the only lady at the tea who wore a hat. "He doesn't talk much, does he?"

"I tell you what I'll do. You go into the library and wait and I'll ask him to come in and play for you."

To that she had to think a moment. "Yes, I shall." She started, but stopped. "Did you read that article in the *Post* last week? All this publicity about Paris and about 'the young genius' I mean, all this 'devotion' to his art. Look at all that standing ovation last night! I couldn't stand, myself, because I took off my right shoe because my foot was killing me. And another thing as long as we're talking. I don't think I quite understand any of this 'artistic impulse' that everyone seems to identify with Mr. Kaplan. What else do you call it?" Mrs. T shoved her in the direction of the library when she noticed that William had returned. He joined her in the library after the hostess's warning.

"I'll be glad to repeat a number I played this afternoon."

Ethel Tabor gawked at him and adjusted her hat again. "I'm sorry, young man, but no. I mean, I have other plans. Would you give me your autograph, please?" She produced her program from her bag.

He went to the desk. "Sure, if I can find a pen. You are . . . Mrs . . . ?"

"Just Ethel Tabor. T A B O R. Hhhmmm. I have a nephew who writes with his left hand. His daddy wanted to make him use his right one but his first grade teacher wouldn't hear of it. Clyde, my nephew, thought he was some kind of artist when he grew up but he ended up not worth anything at all." She paused as he finished. "My, my! Thank you! . . . with kind wishes. Well, you really are very nice." She opened her bag and slipped it inside it with a napkin. "I must say, you do quite well sitting up there with the orchestra all around you. I don't see how you keep up with the players. Or how the players keep up with you! What is that magic you do have?" She left quickly.

William breathed more easily. He sank into a chair. "God!" He was alone again in the library. He began sorting some music in a cardboard box. Malcolm Forrester was at the door when William looked up. "Hello" he called, "come in."

Malcolm was not hesitant to speak. "I'm glad you're still here." "I just want to say, to remind you of the master class for me on Tuesday morning." He paused. "For me and the Japanese girl." He waited while William filed several folders of music into proper place. He waited so long that William stopped and stared politely at this young student. "Sure," he agreed and stepped closer to Malcolm. "Care to sit for a while?"

As much as he desired this personal time with William, Malcolm did not know how to answer that. He had been swept away by the performance last night, and that was not the first time Malcolm had heard such a monumental piece of music. "I heard this afternoon," and he hesitated just how he was going to ask this, "that you are leaving . . . moving to San Francisco. You're actually . . . moving away?" He blinked his eyes and stared at the piano. He returned his vision toward William. "I just think . . ." William came nearer to him and looked strongly into the student's eyes. "Why, yes, I believe I will. In fact, my friend and I are leaving the next day. I believe I mentioned it earlier, maybe that's where you heard it. Right after the master class." Malcolm paused again. "May I have . . . your address?" That last question might have sounded too presumptuous, but it did not to Malcolm, not after that great lunch they shared.

William returned to the desk, opened the lap drawer and searched for a pen and paper. He smiled at him and then wrote down the Green Street location. "I'd be happy to hear from you sometime, Malcolm. Yes. Sure. That's Jerry's house address. I'll be there." Malcolm accepted it slowly, looking at it as he put it safely in his pocket. "Thank you." He nervously moved about and then turned to the door. "Mr. Kaplan . . ." he called, and then William interrupted, "Call me William, or Bill." And then Malcolm smiled, "Okay, William . . . Bill. I might try to see you Wednesday morning before you leave. Here at the condo . . . If that's all right." William remembered another moment just one year ago in Berkeley. "Sure, it's okay. Come by." The student smiled weakly and started for the door. He stopped. "I'll try to come by to say goodbye." He stepped out and closed the door.

Chapter Thirty-Six

"WELL, NOW, HERSCHEL IS happy," Julia declared as she stood in the archway separating the Taylors' living room from a hallway leading to their kitchen. "He doesn't know the house, mind you, but he can find the kitchen and make himself some coffee." He heard that remark from where he opened a cabinet door and spied the coffee can. "It's a long time before supper," he deduced, "and I don't like tea very much any more. Well, Sister," he continued, "I guess that tea party this afternoon was a success but I'm glad to be here." Sis was right there to assist him but it appeared he did not need any assistance. "Go on in and sit down," his daughter told him, "and I'll see to it that you get your caffeine." She was pleased to help. They hardly ever get to visit anymore. Her father was capable of doing several chores on the farm by himself. Even at his advanced age he was spry. She stood by the breakfast island between her kitchen and nook and watched him to make sure he would obey her. "Go on, Dad," she repeated and waited until he meandered to wait by Julia. "I'll start supper after we settle in." The phone was ringing and Dr. David answered it from the library.

Dr. and Mrs. David Taylor chatted with Herschel and Julia in the family room of their large stone house in South Denver, an old neighborhood full of affluent couples, families, with kids, dogs, cats, and two—and sometime three-car garages. Mary Louise drove their new Dodge Van to Sterling Saturday before the concert for a long weekend visit. The house was fairly new with plenty of upstairs bedrooms and bath rooms to accommodate visitors, designed much to accommodate the architect of many of the older homes.

"I'm a bit tired, Mary Louise," Julia whispered. 'This was a busy weekend for Herschel and I'm sure he's tired, also." The end of the weekend was like the end of the month, with April's rain entertaining a quiet evening. "I'm glad we could make it to Denver. I still can't undderstand how Billy keeps up with the players." She retained her pride for the pianist even though she did tell everyone that Billy is their son.

Sis heard her mother mention Bobby Martin merely that he was a good kitchen painter. Both her parents did not give this a second thought even though she did not approve of the nondescript house painter. She had heard her brother speaking against him when he voiced a disapproval this afternoon when they said their goodbyes. "Mom," she whispered as Herschel came into the room bearing his cup with a drawing of the Denver skyline on it. "Bill doesn't want you doing business anymore with Bobby." This remark from one who rarely sees Bobby Martin was mystifying to Mary Louise. "Darling," the quiet mother countered "he did a great job in my new yellow kitchen." To plan as they did for the doctor to take them back to Sterling was a treat. "Bobby told us he was glad to see that Angus got his food okay. while we came to Denver."

This was a special time for them, for David was off duty from the hospital. He had heard the remark which was now a local medical reference passed among his colleagues, that no one should get sick on the weekends because doctors stay at home. He had found this remark somewhere in a gift shop all printed neatly on a card and in a narrow black frame. Sis hung it on the wall in her kitchen.

This weekend had been even more special. William's repeat performance last night was a really nice occasion. David and Sis had third row center tickets. To the performing artist the lovely reception afterwards was not new to him, but the presence of the Ph. D. was doubly important. The greeting to William, the plaudits from many people David and Sis hardly knew, and the formal tea that afternoon were splendid. Herschel was not able to answer all the questions so many people asked. Often he only smiled and Julia provided all the family history.

While Herschel sat quietly in a chair by the window glancing through a magazine and sipping his coffee, Across the years, Julia was never certain if her husband enjoyed the delicate nuances of her life as much as she did with her own knowledge of a few composers. Herschel was the bread winner, that much she professed at the beginning of her life with him. He worked hard but according to the old adage, it was that he never played hard. He hardly ever stopped what he was doing until she had to plead with him to 'come in out of the rain.' For one seven-year episode of really hard work in the wheat fields, Herschel hired extra help. That was when William was often on tour or with summer school choir work at high school. It was at a time when Julia began to notice Herschel's reticence in his son's maturity. Sitting next to him, she reached over and gave a pat to his knee. "That was a good supper, Sis," she said, "I'm sure Herschel enjoyed it, too." It was late when Julia noticed how Herschel's magazine slipped off his lap as he began to nod. "It's time for us to go to bed," Julia announced as she rose from her comfortable position. "Which bedroom, Mary Louise?"

It was later when David put the cat and two dogs in the back yard under the protection of the new wire fence that surrounded the rear portion of their homestead. He verified the night light, put the car in the garage and turned off the front porch light. Sis looked in on the son and daughter, kissed them both, and closed the doors.

"David," Sis murmured with the tone in her voice that was a prelude to something important. The doctor could always know. "Yes?" he answered as he stepped out of his shower. "It better be a short whatever because I've got to drive to Sterling tomorrow." He then added, "Did you tell Julia that Bill and Dr Champion will be up to see them on Wednesday? They're flying to The City the next day."

Sis waited at first, not knowing exactly how to place her question. She waited until he had his pajamas ready to wear. Then he climbed in beside her. "I was just thinking. What do you think of Dr. Champion? Gerald B. Champion?" He could discern that she was still a curious wife. She had a pencil hovering over a pad on which she was ready to write his answer. After four seconds of silence, she looked at him. "Huh?" It was a fair question and she waited impatiently for his answer. From downstairs they heard the large clock on the mantle chime the late hour.

"He's a Ph. D. not an M.D." He looked at her with a silly grin. Then he realized by the look on her face that she was serious about a topic that she was going to mention. "You want to know what?" he put the question to her. They heard their two dogs barking at shadows in the back yard.

"Well," she began slowly, "This afternoon, Vivian was talking to me on a variety of subjects like she usually can do. And the mail business was really a mystery to her. You remember when Bill played last April, a year ago?" She recounted all the cities where he played his concert. They met in Berkeley at the end of the tour, Bill and this Gerald." David listened attentively as she continued. "And then mail started coming to Viv's address from Berkeley. Not to Mrs. T.'s condo where he lives. Or lived. Not just one thank you note like he usually gets. Usually those letters go directly to Hicks in New York and he has a girl, or someone, who answers for him. It's been going on for a year, it seems." David scratched his nose. "Vivian did tell Bill to ask this Jerry to use his own address, the condo, and I guess that's what this Champion did, after all."

"Is this leading up to some fantastic plot of yours?"

Sis was perturbed. "You remember once, a long time ago, I asked you about gay people?" Being around the younger crowd at church, she was accustomed to that word. She waited for a nod of his head or some affirmative sound. "That was about three or four years ago when the *Post* had that article about the condition."

He merely said while he relaxed under the covers, "I have a treatise downstairs in the library that will answer any and all of your . . . interests." He looked directly at her profile. "I'll get it for you tomorrow before breakfast." He leaned over and gave her a nice kiss on her cheek.

He saw her wiggle her lips and look at the ceiling. "Vivian thinks something is going on. She thinks this Dr. Champion is . . . peculiar. I just think that Viv has never known a thirty-one year old Ph.D. Vivian always gets tangled up with weird situations." She laughed, "all Viv's Ph.D.s have been fifty-five or sixty year-old white haired college instructors. She's always capable of jumping off the deep end. When I asked Bill if he had answered this guy's correspondence, he said Yes. Then, just yesterday afternoon before we all left for the concert, Bill announced to me just right out that he was moving to San Francisco. Just like that. Like they were leaving right after the concerto."

"Well." David decided to join in the recitation, "This . . . Jerry did tell me he has a brand new job that begins in another seven or eight days and he has to fly back . . . well, right after Bill does that master class at

D.U." The doctor continued by mentioning something right out of the blue. "I wish we could live in San Francisco. Denver is cold in January and February . . . sometimes. You want me to apply at a hospital there? I'm a good doctor." She growled at him. He compromised with "I'll show you that treatise in the morning. Remember, you asked me about left-handed people and I showed you a treatise on that." With a jovial laugh, he added, "Your own daughter is left-handed!" That was his bit of information for the evening. Then he stated surreptitiously, "Your dad told me he gets up at six thirty and puts on his coffee. Good night." He rolled over and successfully terminated the detective work.

The next morning, Sis woke slightly earlier than David. In her robe and slippers, she went to her kitchen and found her father sitting at the table with an empty cup to his right. "I'm used to making my own coffee but I guess I don't know your kitchen like you do." That was a bit of humor that his daughter did not realize he could project. She laughed. Once the full pot was percolating, she excused herself and made her way down the hall to the study. David was right behind her, lifting a large file from the second shelf to his right. The treatise he mentioned was in a stack. He pulled it and handed it to her. It was in his collection pertaining to Adolescence Psychology. She sat in his leather chair behind his desk as he started for his father-in-law. In an article from some magazine, she read. "*When one is gay, that person is part of a community, and it's not just gay bars full of sad young men or a television special on men holding hands walking down the street. Gay people are exactly that, a 'people.' When you come out you discover a mysterious close bond with others like you that is based on something much deeper than sex. What gays share is unrelated to geography, religion or ethnicity. What links them is their feelings. Can you remove what makes a person gay and maintain that unique sensibility that has played a disproportionate rule in the world's art, music and history?*" Someone—David?—slipped a piece of paper ripped from a magazine which noted a successful theatrical production endorsing the theory that modern medical science can predict if a fetus will be homosexual or not. In its margin was scribbled hurriedly the notation, 'would you abort your child if he will be gay?"

Julia passed the study door and said pleasantly, "Good morning, Mary Louise. I smell coffee."

Chapter Thirty-Seven

Late March, 1999

"IN THIS DAY AND time," Julia Kaplan remarked, "to go from Paris to New York is quite simple." She sat in the front porch swing that her husband made for her thirty years ago and directed her conversation to her son and his guest. It was mid-afternoon, just after a nice sandwich lunch complete with chocolate ice cream and chocolate cake. Dressed in her favorite summmer dress and wearing her only necklace, she made certrain that the good doctor of geology had plenty to eat. She had also noticed that her husband was far more talkitive than usual. She noted, silently, that he had focused his questions on this young man to the extent that she had to wait for a moment of silence before she could offer her own quetion or two . . .

Julia was content. She felt a warm surge of pride, accompanied as it was by several happy birds waiting from time to time in their large ooak trees. It was not her imagination. Herschel was not the awkward wheat farmer. Before William and Gerald arrived, he had selected a clean pair of pants long before Julia veriified any clothes. Waiting as she was for an opening in conversation, she looked directly at her husband. He was somewhat of a different Herschel with an obvious amount of self-esteem for their piano player. "Herschel and I," she began when she could, "have never been out of the United States and I think it would be great if I could see the Eifel Tower some day." She glanced at Herschel who was sitting opposite her in an old wooden chair. His clean short sleeved shirt had an ice cream stain on its front. She knew that he was patiently waiting for a time when he could return to his chores. Her attention was again centered on the two men who sat on the top steps just below her. "I am mighty pleased that Dr. Champion could come visit our fair city, and of course to see our humble home. I'm just sorry you have to get back to Denver tonight." Only in the past twenty years had she polished her social obligations by speaking in such a polite tone. In the back of her mind she placed the fact that her son was leaving Colorado. She felt another moment of sadness. She nudged the geologist with her right foot. "What do you think of our place?"

"Mrs. Kaplan," he began, "I've been a city boy all my life. In high school I was on the tennis team but it wasn't much of a team, with only four players." He glanced at William. "But we had fun. The closest I ever came to a cow was up state once when my brother and I went on a scout trip. We were to learn about cows and pigs and goats. I didn't pay much attention and I guessed Geoff wasn't much interested either. We flunked scouting." He looked around to Herschel and smiled and the farmer grinned at him in return. "But now I wish that I had had some country experience especially like what I see right here on your farm. Colorado is beautiful." The answer may have been a diplomatic one but it sufficed. "When I was five or six, my father explained to me that the bread we eat comes from wheat and that the wheat fields are far west of Monticello New York." Again he glanced quickly at Herschel Kaplan, then down at his hands.

Herschel felt pleased. He had been the source of all the hard work that went into his wheat farm, for it was still a good farm. A few men had, from time to time, come and gone to assist him in cultivation. He looked at William to discover that his son had, for a long while, been looking at *him*. Each time the son returned to this part of Colorado he recalled all the times when his father would argue with him. The farmer could never comprehend the young boy's pursuance of anything that was foreign to farming. With each spring there was so much to be done. Of course, for a short while, William milked three cows and he fed the guinea hens and brought in the eggs. Sis was there before she went off to the university and met David Taylor. That was not so long ago. The late April breezes from the main road swept through the front porch and Angus got up suddenly and joined them on the steps. The dog needed someone to pet him.

Their attention was drawn to an automobile coming along the main road from town. Vivian's Buick appeared. She slowed at the front gate and slowly made her way right up to where they were sitting, honking her horn loudly when she saw them. William and Jerry greeted her and Julia remained at the porch level. Vivian stepped out of her car, tugged at her slacks and waved at everyone. "I saw everyone I wanted to see and I'm ready to go back if you are." She leaned against the front left fender and swatted a fly. Julia invited her in for some coffee. "I've got a nice piece of chocolate cake saved just for you," she said. Then she turned to Herschel. "Let me put some more coffee on or can you do that, please." Herschel nodded. Before he entered the hall he paused and patted Jerry on the back. "I see you like coffee too," he whispered to the guest. Angus moved, stretched and walked away from them to ground level.

William was obviously hesitant in following the crowd. He stood up and spoke quietly to Jerry. "I got something to talk about with you. Let's go for a walk." To his father who was last to enter the front door, "I want to show Jerry the tractor and maybe some other things—my Rock collection. Go on in, will you, and we'll be back."

Silently they made their way down the path that led to the barn, past the old well with its new canopy and old bucket, ignoring a path they took when they first arrived. Angus again thought they were coming to be with him. They stopped at the old tractor so that William could peer back at the house to make certain everyone was inside it. They walked slowly to the barn door, opened it, stepped inside and smelled the odor of cattle and hay. Once inside the center aisle, William stopped and Jerry paused.

They braced the main door with a brick. "I want to keep an eye on the back porch," he whispered, "it's just a habit." He paused to glance at Jerry. "I just don't know when I'll ever see the farm again. It's a long ways to California."

"Jair," William began, folding his arms and leaning against a stall, "I'm glad you got to see the place. And Viv didn't mind a bit driving us today where I grew up, I guess you might say. It's a little out of my league. I've never been to your part of New York State where you grew up so I don't know what your farms look like." Jerry sensed a bit of nervousness in William and an uregency about this time alone, just the two of them. "But all this is fairly foreign to me now.". He looked toward the rear of the house and then directly at him. "Jair," William began again, "we're going to have to go back inside and eat some more. Mom would want it that way." He had difficulty choosing words. "I'm mighty happy about a lot of things. I got some clothes to take back to San Fran with us, some stuff I had here in the bedroom upstairs." He paused, looked back toward the house once again. "I'm really pleased about everything. I mean, about the way things have turned out. A year ago, I wouldn't have expected to start a correspondence, let alone meeting the one person who was to change everything for me." He looked directly at him. "And I mean everything." He waited and moved his position. "This is not easy for me to say. So bear with me." He stood away from a portion of the wooden wall and crossed to the large gate that separated the aisle from the hay-strewn roadway outside of it.

He tried to continue, "I've had a tough time of it. It hasn't all been peaches and cream." When Jerry tried to interrupt, William raised his hand. "No, wait a minute, let me finish. I just know that I'm glad I found you, that we met. I mean. It's like there I was, being a loner with only my music. A few people I liked, but not many. Vivian happens to be my favorite friend. I mean, before I met you. I'm not expecting you to understand, I guess, but I love you, Jerry." His mouth was dry and he took hold of the board that formed a gate. "I'm glad you want me in the house. With you. I'm glad for your job. I'm glad for a lot of things. I'm glad for . . ." but he did not finish when tears filled his eyes. "I just want you to know. I just want you to know that you are the best thing that's happened to me. I've got you and I've got my music. I just had to tell you, Jair! I just had . . ."

These minutes . . . seconds became more than crucial to the pianist. He had no idea how the geologist would accept this confession. He had been able to perceive much of what Jerry possessed in the way of personal intelligence. That was evident from the first breath they took at curb side after that concert one year ago. He was positive that Jerry could understand the turmoil of his conscience with what he had just heard. Jerry was there, still at his side, looking directly at him. He did not waver one bit. He did not register any degree of remorse. William began to tremble. He was anxious. He became fretful. He wanted Jerry to say something, anything.

"Billy," his mother called from the back porch, "come on, you two. Coffee's ready! You got to eat something before you go . . . back to Denver."

Silently they left the barn, closed the door, and made their way to the house with Angus wagging his tail. Vivian was at the back door with a cup of coffee at her lips. "Chocolate over chocolate," she laughed, "good grief, I'm glad we made this trip after all." She curtailed her joviality when she saw William wipe away his tears. Julia spooned the ice cream while Herschel poured the coffee. "California isn't so very far away," was all Vivian could say. They sat at the table and commented on the yellow kitchen. Angus barked at something he discovered in the back yard.

Herschel remained standing for a while and looked at Jerry as if he were surmising his stature, his bearing, his new friend. Then he sat down between the geologist and his son.

"I sure did like the concert Saturday night," Jerry said quietly. He moved so he could see William beyond Herschel. Then his eyes fell on Herschel's profile. "Mr. Kaplan, did you like the concert?" That was all Jerry could think to say. His question was a surprise to Julia. Her husband removed his work hat. "I had a difficult time adjusting to the hotel and I guess the reception." He turned so that he could speak directly to the geologist. "And the time when Mr. Young came up to me and introduced himself." Julia was hypnotized by what he was saying. She too remembered: "Mr. Kaplan," the conductor had said, "I want you to know that we all are proud of your son." Herschel responded, with Julia standing there, too. "Why, thank you, Mr. Young. Thank you very much!"

———

At Wednesday early afternoon, with Mrs. T on an errand, and her maid late in arriving, the telephone was ringing constantly, or so it seemed. Jerry was out of the condo on an errand to mail a card, with the mail drop which William often used just within a block. He finished packing but yesterday's master class was still inside his head. Thinking of the events of this past long weekend placed him in a strong and pleasant mood, one that could not escape his mind. The door opened and Jerry reappeared, this time with a visitor.

Malcolm Forrester was with him. William came out of his reverie but was expecting him. "Frankly, I'm glad to see you, again." He monitored Malcolm's expression before he added, "I think we covered the master class fairly well, with all the questions we had from the few others. Sit down. We won't be leaving for another hour, more or less, maybe longer. Don't mind Jair, he jumps around like that. You want some coffee?"

Malcolm was slightly nervous with an idea deep within his psyche that he should not be here, that his desire to say goodbye was interfering with a deeper reasoning of some sort. He sat on the sofa and looked all around him, the nice furniture, the décor, for he longed to possess such an artistic room for himself, some day. He got up and stepped in the library where the piano waited. He did not sit at the keyboard but merely struck a few keys to call back part of the polonaise he played yesterday. William reappeared with a cup of coffee in his hand, and together they returned to the main room. After one or two lengthy sips, William said that he felt like talking. "It's time for a break, anyway. I've said my goodbyes already." He eyed the young student. "Are you from Denver?"

"No. No, I'm from a little town west of Tulsa. You probably never heard of it." Then he smiled. "You mentioned that the Russian lady played the Ravel Left Hand. M. DuPres said yesterday that I may be ready for attempting it, myself. And not because I'm left-handed. That's why I was excited to hear what you thought of it." To William, Malcolm's appearance today was an altogether different one than he witnessed while eating lunch with the piano player that day. William sat and followed the trend of this student's thought progression. He was, actually, a bright and gifted pianist and at twenty-two years, on the verge of becoming a serious musician. How many times had he heard that himself from his own Miss Shriner? Malcolm had also asked about Chopin because the Frenchman endorsed the idea that he specialize in that composer.

It was his mention of the Ravel that prompted William to reach over the table to where a book of music was resting. He claimed it and handed it to Malcolm. It was the complete score for the concerto for Left Hand. "Here," William said casually, "it's for you. You'll need to have M. DuPres translate the explanations because I bought it in Paris and it's in French. It's yours. I'll just give it to you!"

Malcolm was stunned! He opened the cover page and in awe replied a soft "Unbelievable!" To that, William smiled, "Maybe this will be your first number to play when you are concertizing! Give it to me so I can sign it for you." Malcolm repeated his "Unbelievable." "There, now!" And he returned it.

Vivian Cole burst upon this chat with a flourish entrance and a bag of doughnuts. She was surprised but elated to see the student who performed so well yesterday. Malcolm asked, "I saw you there, did you like what you heard?" "Yes, oh, yes. By now I'm used to the classics." She looked into the library after throwing the bag on the sofa. "Where's the new doctor?"

"Try the kitchen, I think." So she did.

"Mr. Kaplan . . . uh . . . Wil," Malcolm paused, "I sure am glad you did what you did, about the master class, but especially about staying in Denver for the while. And I got to meet you. Quite a conincidence." To this, William's reply was, "I call such a moment like that a 'divine appointment.'"

Malcolm was not the least bit hesitant with what he thought. "You taught me a lot of things. The best was, you looked me straight in the eye and told me never to be . . . awkward or . . . hesitant about who I am." He chose his words slowly but well. I know I'm a piano player." That phrase caught William instantly. He asked where he had heard of that phrase but Malcolm did not hear the question. "Yeah, I just knew I was a pianist. I just knew it!" To William's request that he play a tune, Malcolm was chagrined. "Oh, no, I'm too wound up. Just to know you helped me. And giving me . . . ."

"Giving you what?"

"That I know you. You gave me confidence. You didn't exactly know that, I suppose. I was sort of doubtful about a lot of things." He waited, not knowing if William was to accept this from a twenty-two-year old student. "I wasn't . . . quite sure of myself. Well, I am now." He tossed the Ravel on the sofa next to him, stood up and went to the window. "I hope you don't think I'm too sentimental."

Without rising, he took a final sip of coffee and replied softly, "No. It's good to be sentimental. I'm that way all the time."

"It's like," Malcolm spoke as he returned to the sofa, "it's like I've known you for a long, long time." Malcolm stopped just as Jerry raced through on his way to a bedroom. Quietly, William rose and reached for the bag of doughnuts. He selected one and silently offered one to

Malcolm. "Go on," he said, "have one. You can thank Vivian." Malcolm grinned and did just that.

Vivian, the disciplined organizer, the woman about town, the sophisticated and brilliant genius, so she said, appeared with the invitation that it is time to leave for the airport. "We want to get there for goodbye drinks. I'm buying." It was not unlike Vivian to promote such a departure. Only Malcolm was surprised. "It's time to get on your horse, Willy, and ride out!" Jerry returned carrying his one piece of luggage and another carry-on bag. William made an announcement immediately. "Malcolm wants to come to the airport with us. Don't you, Malcolm?"

Again, the student was stunned. "Splendid!" was the answer from Vivian. "Okay, Malcolm, you can help with the luggage. "You all right?" It was Jerry's subtle question quietly to William as Vivian carefully made her exit through the condo's front door. "Never felt better."

On his way out, with two pieces of luggage, Malcolm said, "I just want to say . . ."

"You said it. Let's go!"

Chapter Thirty-Eight

April 1999

THEY STOOD TOGETHER ON the front porch, tired, but they looked out to the south to that part of the city. It had been somewhat of a wild time since Paris. Exhausted as they were from too much travel, across the continent, across an ocean, having been forced to behold a culture that was somewhat more foreign than they realized, from the sudden realization that their future was secured enough to congratulate themselves. They decided to sit on the top step, a place that they had already claimed as their own. For an eon they were silent, surrounded as they were by intangible togetherness, memories of a front porch in Monticello, younger, with a tennis racket in his hand, and one on the farm in Sterling, younger, with Angus looking at him with soulful eyes, with a brand new rock garden that Miss Shriner's brother gave him. By now both were accustomed to the winds off the Bay area, sweeping past the Ferry Building northward above the Embarcadero to rush down their street to Washington Square. If one of them would place his arm around the other, that simple gesture became more than the simple gesture; alone it would strengthen their joy. That is what each had in mind. So they sat there. This was home. This was their answers to all their questions. Reality was Green Street with Coit Tower in the background. Reality was also the noise of traffic near the church where Aunt Urs and Li went for the priest's blessings. Here was geology's future and William's new music.

Jerry once said, just two days ago that he wouldn't want it any other way. Here were their neighbors, the elderly gentleman walking by with his Jack Russell dog on a leash, the couple who once came over to hear

William play that night. Other people waved at them. Every morning William began his scales on the piano and Li began her new life with her two favorite men instead of the sweet lady who was no longer a Californian.

One afternoon in the first week of her new association, she knocked on the sliding doors at a time when William stopped playing to pencil in a practice reference. In a tender moment she begged indulgence with William for a sit-down conversation. Dressed in her prettiest red dress and slippers from Grant Street, she decided to come in Chinese attire even though she was, as she bluntly had told them, an American born in Sausalito of Taiwanese parents. In her kitchen she had a picture of them hanging on the wall next to the refrigerator. As elderly as they were, the parents managed to walk all the way from their small apartment on Vallejo Street, up one hill and down another, to visit their daughter and meet the nice man who plays the piano so well. They both were so sorry about the beautiful lady who decided to return to her homeland. But they could understand. Their own sparse rooms were full of their own memories of rolling hills on an island so far away from them.

"I've had this word with Mr. Gerald about two days ago when you both were unpacking. We went upstairs so not to disturb you and your music. Oh, before I forget, thank you for that little model of that tower. I don't know how to pronounce that French name." They were in the 'music room' as Jerry called it. Li smiled broadly when she looked at the instrument. "I want you to know that I think Mr. Gerald may be ill. He was so tired when he got home." This statement came as a complete shock, for he would never have been told unless someone would mention that to him. And that someone had to be the delicate Chinese-American of forty years. It was not the first time she had seen the strong concern in his eyes. "And that's another thing, Mr. William," and she grinned, proud of her heritage, "I'm well past forty. I may look like I'm thirty-nine, but I'm not." William was still seated on the piano stool. "You want to go into the front room?" It was always a comfortable location when she and Mrs. Ursula had to speak of domestic items, happy thoughts, even of drastic consequence.

Together, they made their way past the two doors that he closed separating the music room from the hall way. "Li," he whispered, "what do you mean?" He was at once poised on the edge of a leather chair but more so with a level curiosity. She sat opposite him on the ottoman. "I want to talk to you, please, before he comes home. His place of employment is just past the Pyramid Tower. He told me it is easy for him to come and go to work. Mrs. Ursula spoke to me two days before she flew to New York." William was still not used to her rambling when she wanted to say something specific. "She told me to mention this to you but not, especially, to Mr. Gerald. Only you and I are to realize what she thinks is serious situation." All this was aggravating him. He would never have suspected any word of illness of any kind. "What's wrong with him?" He wanted to know. He had to know.

Li nodded her head in affirmation. "Mrs. Ursula thinks that he has just worked too hard at Berkeley. She told me he looks pale and listless. I noticed this the moment you arrived from the airport. I want you to help me feed him good food and get him back to looking well again. That's all he needs, just my good food. I'm learning how to cook the Italian way." She laughed at this.

Apparently, Aunt Urs did not know what she was talking about in the first place or that this charming lady herself did not understand exactly what the aunt meant. Either way, it could be an alarming situation. "I feel now that I must do what I did, and that is, to tell you what Mrs. Ursula told me. Please. I hope you will help me watch over Mr. Gerald and that he is all right. Will you do that?" William instantly saw her sincerity in her Oriental background, her concern as reflected in her countenance. "I know he had been very busy and happy completing his degree at Berkeley. And you know what? He confided in me that he was so very pleased and happy to go to Colorado and meet all your friends. Yes, he told me that. He did tell me that he is pleased and happy that you are here with him. You are a nice companion, I think that is how he said it. I am so grateful that I am living here with you and Mr. Gerald. I shall be the good housekeeper that I was when Mrs. Ursula was here."

She stood up and joined her hands in front of her. "You are a good man, Mr. William." She suddenly changed the subject. "You play so well and the neighbors know that you will live here with Mr. Gerald. They asked me just yesterday if they could come over soon to hear more music. I said that I would ask." She grasped his arm and whispered confidentially. "Now, I must get to preparing dinner. "I'm glad you are here, Mr. William." And she left him standing, wondering, still not used to the delicate Chinese way of her being.

Two nights later, with more rain in May lightly spattering the sidewalk, William found time before dinner to pull Jerry onto the front porch on pretext of watching the water trail down the street. He wanted to talk, but he found that Jerry spoke first. The front door was closed and Li was in her kitchen. At this hour not many people walked down the wet street. The front porch setting was becoming their habitual location merely to sit and talk about France and the Arc Triomphe, about the French music shop where William bought a book for Dr. Young, even about the price of eggs in China. When Jerry would include that line in his casual conversation, Li would always remain mystified.

This time they stood together. "You are quite a guy, Billy!" He placed his hands on the railing and William stood to his right with the light from the lamp post not thirty feet away shining on both of them. "I've been thinking of what you told me in the barn at your home place. "And I have a lot to tell you, too. Since a year ago, you've been on my mind and I mean I've sometimes had a hard time of it trying to concentrate on what the good doctors were talking to me about." William tried to interrupt. "No. Wait a minute, let me talk. I was really surprised . . . no, astonished, when I got that first letter from you. No, I mean it. There I was, one half of my forty-five credit hours behind me and I thought I would have time to write a letter to someone I didn't know. Right out of the clear blue sky, I wrote you a silly fan letter—I guess it was a fan letter—and by God you answered. I guess I didn't know what to do, then. I didn't know you at all. You just appeared, you and your piano, and before I knew it, you answered and somehow I felt that the God, the Man Upstairs, was really a nice Guy to have you answer that silly stupid letter."

He had to interrupt. "It wasn't a silly stupid letter."

"Well, you know what I mean. Then one thing led to another. And you got to come to San Fran to get ready for that concert at Thanksgiving. Man, you really filled my life and I guess I never did tell you, properly, I mean. I don't know how all this happened, it just happened."

"Jair . . ."

"Let me talk! You had the barn and I have the front porch." He was using his matter-of-fact voice again so he stopped to choose his words. "I'm just not worthy of you, Billy. You are far too good for me and I don't know what in the hell to do about all this. I wanted you to come here with me and live here. I didn't know exactly how I was going to ask all of this of you. I . . . I just wanted you to be here with me. I was happy. I *am* happy. Dammit, I am. All the time on the plane I wanted to talk but I couldn't. I couldn't find words and certainly not with a lady sitting in the aisle seat next to us. I waited til we got here and then I had to concentrate on starting my new job. I want to be the best geologist there is." Jerry stopped and turned directly to face him with the street light full on his face. He took a deep breath. William saw him grit his teeth. "I'm not gay, Billy, I'm not *that* way." And immediately he added, "And I know you're . . . not . . . either. I met a guy in Boston that I thought I could talk to. He said he was a defrocked priest." Jerry stopped. William remained stolid. Jerry took a deep breath. "Well . . . ." was all he could mumble. Without interrupting him William softly agreed. "I know you're not, Jair. And so Jerry waited, as if he were pleased. He paused to see if this piano player were listening to him. "And then I came to U.C. and as sure as I am here, I met you. I guess things like that have a way of happening." William detected his hesitancy. "Dammit, Billy. I don't know a thing about music." He saw a smile light up Billy's face! "What are you grinning about?"

"I don't know one, not even one thing about geology that you know." A genuine chuckle made Jerry relax and he ended it with a great laugh. "I wish I had your genes. Like Vivian says, artistry is generic. I heard her say that at that Tea Thing." He stifled an urgent feeling to embrace his friend. "You got nothing to worry that nice handsome head about." He waited while a couple walked their dog on the sidewalk below them. "I'm happy, Billy, happy about a lot of things. I wanted to tell you when we walked the Bridge that time but I didn't. I guess I was scared."

"Scared of what?"

"I guess I don't know. I suppose I sort of knew that Aunt Urs would leave. I just knew she wanted to go home." He found his strong voice. He looked straight at William, took another deep breath and peered into his eyes. "You're the best pianist in the whole wide world, France, California, and Colorado included. That's what you are and I love you.

And I don't give a damn if all of Green Street hears it. He switched to his earnest voice. "Do you hear me, Billy?"

"That's saying a lot." William returned his bear hug and held it for a long time. Jerry laughed.

"Imagine that, one new geologist still wet behind his ears and one old piano player. Why — I'd never dream of such a thing. I'm shocked. Viv says I'm a freak. Am I a freak?" William started into the house. "Hey, where you going?"

"To open the wine I bought today. Come on. Let's eat."

Chapter Thirty-Nine

Late August 2001

WILLIAM WAS UPSTAIRS RUMMAGING through his lap drawer of an old desk. This piece of mahogany furniture had been in the house since the Griswolds moved into it . . . Apparently the original owners did not care for it. On it were an nineteen-century pen and ink bottle, an old upright oriental bell holder, and an electrified 1886 oil lamp. This old elegant desk was all that he could locate in which to place all of his correspondence, business and personal, from his agent to Mrs. Tomassi and his parents. Julia had been faithful to write of the change in the weather, the eventual break down of the truck and the recent death of Mrs. Martin. A least, she thought her obituary of this waitress was polite in calling her a married lady. Nothing was ever mentioned about her son, Bobby. Will sat on a chair that was not of the desk's generation but yet it looked nice. This letter collection, being evidence of sentiment, was altogether not necessary, he thought, but much of it was still valuable to him and to the writers. A touch of susceptibility to a variety of emotions was still important to him. As the collection enlarged over these past three years he was often amazed that he had learned to respect what his writers had said. He was not one to collect them but several were in a nice stack from Malcolm Forrester. Those earliest from Malcolm reminded him of his own scribbles to Jair in 1993. Will had become a writer of letters, himself, having begun quite some time ago when in Denver he received that first letter from Jerry. Dr. Champion was now downstairs listening to Li review the menu for their early Labor Day party. It had to be early for a variety of reasons, Li would be out of town on that Monday, Wil was rehearsing with the symphony, and Jair had to be in Sacramento in the field . . .

Wil had in his hand the most recent letter from Malcolm. He sat gazing at each envelope and was amused by how this pianist had done what he wanted to do and that was to write to each other. Before he placed it with those others, he put it down on the desk top, ready to answer it tomorrow, when he had more time to concentrate. He did notice, in this last letter, Malcolm mentioned his interest to visit soon. That was what he had learned to do, to concentrate. Malcolm had become a most reliable correspondent. His letters, most complimentary at first, soon formed a warm and welcome greeting. With news of the university, of his graduation with his notable senior recital, with his fervent willingness to explain all of his own intimate feelings, Malcolm had become a fascinating study in mortal existence. He was by far a serious twenty-five year old piano player. "Please forgive my sentimental jargon," was his final remark before his 'sincerely' but it was you who told me once that even you are sentimental and that it is okay to remain so. I promise I won't overdo that one word." From below, Jerry called up to him. "Will! Joe is here."

Joe Jones was the first to arrive, even though it was early. He was carrying a narrow bag. He said, as he entered, that it was such a fine day that he decided to walk up and around the Coit Tower before knocking on the front door. "It's been ages since I was in there that I forgot the great murals on the walls." Then he saw William. "Will, you look great. You still have those penetrating brown eyes. I found a violin I like." Joe Jones visited them often and told them he was jealous for them to have such a beautiful old house. "I still live in my little old antique of an apartment on Divisadero." After a greeting to Jerry, he returned to the pianist. "Will, I think you and Jerry were in it one Halloween. Do you remember?" He pulled from the bag a good sized bottle of wine. "Here. This is for us."

Arthur Preston brought Miss Bradley with him. He was very much the same and yes, the San Francisco Symphony was very much the same, too. A few new players, but that was to be expected. "Bertrand Wilson died last year, Will, while you were in Sydney, I guess you heard. Good get-together today! Nothing like a good Labor Day Party. Even it is still August. Let me see that piano you have." As they passed through the hall and into the music room, Preston mentioned, "Carter McKissick told me that he may be later than usual and to save a drink for him. And did you hear about the cable cars? No cars for a week while a section of Hyde Street is to be repaired. So I guess all the streets will be checked." While others came through the front door, he was delighted to see how Will decorated the music room. On the wall were several publicity shots in great frames of McKissick with the mayor of San Francisco. In another less conspicuous pose were Jerry and Will standing shoulder to shoulder on the Embarcadero with a nice view of the Oakland Bay Bridge in the background. "God, what a nice shot," he exclaimed loudly. "I'll have to give you one of me so you can place it side by side with McKissick."

Mr. and Mrs. Warren Lemmon couldn't find a parking place and had to walk three blocks to the house. He was not only the senior geologist at the office but he was retiring just before Christmas. It was a milestone for him and his wife who already had the pleasant habit of shaking hands with everyone. "It's all a part of the territory," she laughed, "I've been shaking hands since W.W. Two." Mrs. Lemmon was noted for wearing gorgeous hats, many of which were too outlandish in shape and color. "Not very many women wear hats anymore and I'm making up for lost time!"

Li Yang finally gave Will her last name and he wrote it down on the calendar in the kitchen. She came along later and wrote it in Chinese. Her proficiency on handling get-togethers was unique. With the presence of one kitchen helper who became a waiter of sorts, she bought the food, prepared it in a matter of two hours, and managed to remain calm and orderly as she had always done. The dining room table became a Chinese display of elegance, with candles and paper napkins she purchased herself at a gift shop in China Town. "You are a whiz," William whispered to her as she stood to admire her handiwork. "Thank you, Mister William, "you are a whiz, too!" For Jerry, she wore her red dress.

After dinner, with the guests in the main room or on the front porch, the telephone rang. Li answered it in the kitchen. With all the conversations and soft radio music, she could not hear well. It was long distance for Dr. Champion. She cupped her hand around the receiver. "One moment, please," she placed it on the counter by some plates, and went into the crowd to look for Mister Gerald. She found him standing by the front windows, talking to Mrs. Lemmon. "Excuse me, Mister Gerald," she smiled at the lady and noticed how Jerry responded. "It's for you. You want to take it in the kitchen? It's quiet there." She walked ahead of him. Jerry looked at Will as he entered the hallway. "Did you hear where the call is from?" But Li went into the pantry. Jerry placed his free hand over his ear. "Hello?"

The call was from Monticello New York, was from a man who did not know Jerry but was volunteering to pass on information. "Dr. Champion," the voice said, "you don't know me, but I live next door to your aunt. Aunt Ursula. Please accept my condolence. Your aunt died today." Jerry, stunned as he was, tried to listen. "She died at four this afternoon and we found your name and telephone number among her papers. We don't know who else to call. We're trying to reach Geoffrey in New York City. Do you know how to call him?" Jerry waited. "No. No, I don't. I . . . I've got to think this through. I'll fly home so if you can call me again, let me know when the funeral is. I . . . uh . . . thank you for letting me know. Mr . . . ?" "It's Grant. Dudley Grant. I live next door. Take my telephone number." And he gave it to him after Jerry reached for a pencil Li always had next to the telephone pad. "Please telephone me tomorrow and I'll have some more information for you. Call me, please. I'm sorry, Dr. Champion to tell you this. Good bye, sir."

He hung up. Jerry was standing by the refrigerator. He could not move. Li entered her kitchen and found him frozen in shock. She looked at him. "Mister Gerald, what is it?" She waited. "Mr. Gerald?" He told her the best way he could. He did not care to join the crowd. He cracked the door to the hall way but did not venture into the noise. Then he sat down at the table and tried to think. Li stood behind him and patted his shoulders and began to cry. The waiter entered. "Go get Mister William, please," Li whispered to her helper, "tell him to come here now."

In another hour, every guest was gone. Jerry sat on the ottoman and Will was opposite him in Aunt Urs's chair. They remained quiet as Li and the waiter cleared the remnants of the day. Will stood and lifted Jerry by the arm pits. "Come on," he said, "we're going to the front porch." There they sat down on the top step where they often escaped since the first time they rested together. They said nothing. Will put his arm around Jerry and between them their togetherness was all that they required. They sat there until the lamp light began to shine on them. They sat there until Jerry grabbed Will and returned his bear hug. They sat there until Li came out and offered them some coffee when the waiter departed. The front porch steps were their location for any such necessary togetherness as required. This was essential. No one else could understand it. They wept together.

Epilogue

Monday, September 10, 2001

WILLIAM HEARD THE TELEPHONE ringing as he raced up the front steps and opened the door. "Hello." He put the bag of groceries on the floor. Jerry was calling. "Hi, Bill! Surprise! I'm in Cambridge Mass. The funeral was last Saturday. I got to spend some time with Geoff. Yesterday we set out early and drove all the way. Geoff lives in Boston now. Oh, hey, I got to see the campus again. You okay? It's now five after six. I hope you're okay. I'll fly back tomorrow. I miss you. I love you, you crazy piano player! The flight is non-stop from Boston Logan but don't meet me since I'll use the shuttle bus. United flight 93, tomorrow. See you soon. Goodbye."

Two weeks passed and William had not practiced much since then. He ignored the TV with its insensitive repetition of the collapse of the towers. It was raining. He and Li were in the kitchen trying to fix something to eat. Someone knocked on the front door so he answered it. Standing there dripping wet was Malcolm Forester who softly said "Hi"!

William opened the door wide; tears welled in his eyes and he signaled silently for him to come inside. Malcolm set his suitcase in the hallway and grabbed his friend in a warm bear hug. William whispered, "Come in, you crazy piano player. Play me a tune."